WHO WE MIGHT'VE BEEN

THE BILLIE DIXON SERIES

If We Had No Winter
The Longer We Dwell
Who We Might've Been
Every Time We Fall

WHO WE MIGHT'VE BEEN

◆ ◆ ◆

A Billie Dixon Novel
Book Three

D. L. Pitchford

Straight on till Morningside Prints

First published in 2018 in the United States
by Straight on till Morningside Prints

Cover Design by Sarah Anderson of No Synonym Book Covers

ISBN   978 0 9987 9454 9

Straight on till Morningside Prints
11923 NE Sumner St., STE 709378
Portland, OR 97220

www.DLPitchford.com

For my husband,
whose secret-keeping skills
are as bad as mine

*It is never too late
to be who you might
have been.*

George Eliot

One

PLEASE DON'T HATE ME, PRUE'S TEXT SAYS. *I CAN'T DRIVE.*

After each failed date, she drives her silver Honda Pilot to my house so she can regale the most interesting parts of her evening, especially the point of its demise. Tonight, her date Graham insisted they check out some of the local color—he's new in town—and they went to a bar. Apparently, she's drunk.

Only when I reach the address do I realize why she asked me not to hate her.

Nestled between the other buildings, the bar is a narrow, two-story brick structure less than a block from the square. It's dirty and grungy, and bluegrass music spills from the open door. Pretty flags emblazoned with a red rose hang from the eaves, and below, in a gold serif font, the words 'Draft Horse' line the bricks.

That text was not enough of a warning.

The floor squeaks when I pause at the threshold to examine my new surroundings.

The long room is divided with tables on one side and the bar on the other. Beyond the bar, a door leads to what I assume is the kitchen, another to storage. Toward the back, there's an old-style jukebox and a few foosball tables, plus a sign for the restrooms. A narrow set of stairs leads to the top floor.

Most of the tables are empty, and a few people perch on barstools. But Prudence is nowhere to be seen.

"Oh my gosh, Billie, you're here!"

Some of the patrons, however, are familiar.

My eyes drift to the bar again, where Jimmy sits on a stool by the taps, his brown hair especially unruly from wearing his work hat all afternoon. But he's not the person who spoke. In fact, he barely looks up from his soda.

Beside him, Micaela's copper face lights up the moment she sees me, and she motions me closer. Her long golden-brown hair shimmers under the bar's pendant lights as she nudges a section over her shoulder.

Behind the taps, Xander moves to check on a customer at the other end of the bar. He doesn't spare a glance for me.

Micaela clutches my arm, and I cringe at the sudden contact. "Jimmy said you wouldn't make it, but I knew you'd come." When she giggles, her face flushes. "I'm so glad you're here. I need someone else to tell him how much of an idiot he is."

Jimmy sends me a weak smile and busies himself with cleaning his thick, black-rimmed glasses. "She's being nice. You know my writing abilities aren't that great."

I open my mouth, but Micaela beats me to the punch.

"I'm not 'being nice,' you idiot." She plucks up her cocktail and downs what little remains. "Your lyrics are great, Jim, and your voice isn't half bad. Billie, you convince him to start a band."

I lift an amber hand—

2

"I don't know what that entails." Jimmy shoves his glasses back on, pressing the rims into his freckled cheeks, and spins toward her, crossing a leg over his lap. "I play guitar. You need a drummer and a lead vocalist, maybe a keyboardist. I don't have connections."

"We'll make connections." Her thin fingers tighten into a fist atop the bar. "If you need a bass guitarist, you know I'm game. And yeah, a drummer would be a good idea."

He scoffs. "A lead vocalist, Micaela."

"You can sing. I've heard you sing." She tugs on my arm again. "Jim's got a good voice, right?"

I nod, but he doesn't look at me.

"My voice may not be 'half bad,' but it's really only appropriate for backup vocals. We'd need a lead vocalist."

"Let's get one!" She giggles again and finally releases me, but uncertain, I hover. "Have you told Billie about your latest song? It was so sweet and romantic. I wish somebody would write something so beautiful about me." Her line of sight gravitates toward Xander, who hunches over the bar and grins at a petite girl with feather earrings and a strapless dress.

He glances over but looks away the moment his gaze lands on me.

"Oh, come on." Jimmy pinches his eyes shut. "There has to be a really awesome guy out there waiting for you…"

Then, Xander slides over, a pint glass in hand. Shiny black bangs stick out from his backwards cap. "If you're trying to drop a hint, he won't get it." When he pulls the tap, thick frothy beer fills the tilted glass.

Micaela's wide eyes jolt between them. "What? No, I'm not. I mean, I'm not interested in Jimmy—no offense." Her ruby-red lips morph into a tight, apologetic smile, but he remains unfazed. "Besides, it's not like I'd have a chance, right?"

Jimmy flushes. "I don't know why you say that…"

She snorts. "Oh, please." She visibly relaxes as Xander carries the pint to its destination, then turns her attention to me. "Seriously, have you read his latest song? It's beautiful."

I shake my head.

Jimmy's completely red. "Come on. Billie's not interested in my cheesy lyrics. Can't we talk about something else?"

The knot in my stomach tightens.

But Micaela giggles. "Fine, fine. But whoever she is, she's very lucky."

I don't know where he got the idea I don't want to hear about his music because he primarily writes love songs. If anything, I'm deathly curious who they're about.

At first, I thought they were about Cynthia Allen, but true to his words, he moved on. He hasn't mentioned her name since May, and during the few times she's hung out with me and Prue, he says hi and moves on.

He's preoccupied with someone else, but I don't know who.

"Billie, sit." Micaela squeezes my shoulder and nods toward the open chair. "I'll buy you a drink."

"Oh, no—"

"Xander! Billie needs a drink." She twists, searching for him, but he's distracted by the girl with the feather earrings again. Micaela's pale when she turns back.

I step away. "Thanks for offering, but I'm not twenty-one yet."

"So?" She blinks several times, forcing her happy

demeanor to return. "You'll have a soda, right? Hang out with us."

I take another step. "I don't have time for a drink."

Her face falls. "I thought you came to hang out with us." She lets out a puff of anxious air, and her fingers toy with the rosary at her collar. She's never without it.

At her child-like, drunken pout, I have the urge to sit and talk and drink, but Jimmy didn't invite me like he told her. Because Jimmy knows better than to invite me to hang out with him and his new best friend at the bar where Xander spends every working hour hitting on scantily clad women.

"No, I'm sorry. I'm looking for someone."

Her lips curl up with excitement. "Do you have a date?"

Before I can answer, Xander returns, focused on me. "You want a 7 Up?"

"No, I came for Prue." My eyes dart around the room as if searching again, but she hasn't magically appeared while Micaela distracted me. "She said she was here."

Xander inclines his head toward the back. "Upstairs."

I send the group a quick thanks before heading toward the staircase. Micaela is the only one who reciprocates.

On the top level, I do a double-take. This is nothing like the ground floor.

Downstairs is full-on pub, completed by their Kentucky Derby theme—the roses, the bluegrass, pictures of stallions. But up here, everything is industrial and shiny. Instead of the rustic browns, the red is now paired with sleek blacks and grays. The barstools and booths are covered in a red velvet, and the counter is a trim stainless steel.

Prudence, dressed in the same bustier top and white

skinny jeans as when she left my house after class, leans against the bar, flushed and giggling. The guy next to her presses a hand to her bare shoulder.

I freeze.

You've got to be fucking kidding me.

He spots me first, a hint of surprise in his brown eyes, and pulls away. Like always, he hides his shock behind an obnoxious grin and his thick, ruddy-brown beard.

But Prue doesn't notice me until I tap her on the shoulder. She spins and throws her arms around me. "What took you so long? It's been hours!"

I roll my eyes. "It's been twenty minutes max."

She grips my shoulder. "I knew you'd come for me." Her once well-managed hair is unkempt and loose, and beneath the chestnut locks, her olive face is flushed. How much has she had to drink?

Despite myself, I smile. "What else would I do on a Friday night? Who's your friend?"

Prudence turns to him again. "This is Brent." She beams in my direction. "Not my date. Graham left ages ago, and thank fucking God. You should've heard him, Billie. I was late by like two minutes, and he kept joking about how I must've gotten lost. I told him my best friend's roommates work downstairs, but he kept saying I must have a terrible sense of direction."

I cringe. "Sounds like a keeper."

"Oliver Wood's got nothing on him." She tugs me to her side. "Brent, though, was nice enough to keep me company while I waited for you. That asshole—Graham—ordered me a Long Island. They're really strong."

On the bar, her free hand toys with a half-full Hurricane

glass. The liquid inside is a deep crimson.

"What are you drinking now, Prue?"

Her brow furrows as she lifts the glass. "I'm not sure, but it's delicious. Brent ordered it."

My nostrils flare.

"It's a zombie." His tone is matter-of-fact.

"Brent!" Prue tugs on me again. "Have you met my best friend?"

He flashes me his typical charm. It almost seems genuine. "How are you, Billie?"

I don't bother answering.

And Prudence is too drunk to pick up on the awkwardness. She turns to me with a quivering lower lip. "I'm sorry I ruined your alone time. I know how much you like nights when they're both working." She throws a short, "Her roommates are kind of jerks," to Brent before giving me her full attention. "And I'm sorry I'm drunk. I didn't mean to be. I swear, I only had the two drinks. Normally, my tolerance is a lot better than this."

"It's fine. I was watching a movie."

But she's already turning to Brent. "You should've met her roommate last year. Now, she was a piece of work…"

I shove my hand under my glasses and pinch the bridge of my nose. "Shit, Prue, come on."

Before she can say anything else, I hook my arm around her waist and help her down. She snatches her purse from the bar and sends him an emphatic wave as we struggle toward the stairs. Even with all our evenings at the campus gym, I can barely support her.

Of course, they don't have an elevator. Because a long, narrow staircase is exactly what drunk people need.

Today is not my lucky day.

"What's wrong?" Prue grumbles.

"Nothing's wrong. Don't worry about it."

She stumbles to a halt, not far from the stairs. "I may be drunk, but I know you. What's wrong?"

Wherever Brent is, Dahlia Finnick isn't far behind. I see her enough during our photography class, though I keep my distance. She is the last person I want to run into at a bar.

"We need to go." I reach for her again. "You've had too much to drink."

Prue scoffs. "No, I haven't. I told you. Only two."

"I believe you, but you don't know what was in the drink Brent Moulder got you. He's not someone you should talk to in a bar while you're drunk."

She tilts her head, her mouth and nose scrunched together. "What're you talking about, Billie?"

I run a hand through my auburn afro, untangling a few strands. "Give me your keys."

Prue lifts her purse and fumbles through the contents. "Yeah, yeah, I know. You're driving."

"That's why you called me."

She pauses to laugh. "How else would I get home? I'm not fucking walking around downtown in three-inch heels while I'm drunk—doesn't matter how small this town is."

I cast a skeptical glance toward Brent, sipping his beer. "What would you have done if I missed your text?"

"Assume you're dead." Finally, she yanks the keys free and tosses them to me. "Seriously, there are plenty of people who could drive me. You're just my number one choice."

I frown. "Please don't tell me you'd let Brent drive you somewhere."

Prue levels me with a fierce look. "How stupid do you think I am?"

"He's not a nice person—"

"Billie, I'd ask someone who works here. Jimmy and Xander may be assholes right now, but they're still reliable. Neither of them would put the moves on me while I'm drunk."

My hand clamps around the keys. "They're not assholes. They never did anything wrong."

Prue's face contorts into a stern glare. "Neither of them talks to you. We got home from study abroad, and Xander walked out of his bedroom with a skanky girl while you were unpacking."

"We broke up in March. He's allowed to sleep with someone in July. And I'm doing fine."

"It doesn't matter how 'fine' you're doing. That was an asshole move."

"He didn't know when I'd get back. And what would be the right way to go about that?" My voice is quiet over the sultry jazz. "Besides, that was four months ago. I'm over it."

She scoffs. "Well, assuming you're not lying—and you've yet to convince me—it doesn't change anything with Jimmy."

I bite my lip.

"You two never talked while we were in France. He's barely said a word to you since you got home. He's supposed to be your best friend."

I level my gaze with hers. "Prue, it's okay." I steady my voice and my breathing, and she calms to match me. "Jimmy and Xander—they're fine. You don't need to get all worked up about this on my behalf."

"Somebody should," she whispers. "You might be trying to be the better person here, but Xander didn't watch you cry yourself to sleep that night. Somebody should be mad."

"Come on." I tug on her hand, and she allows me to lead her toward the stairs. "Let's go to the house and finish my movie. You need to sober up."

Someone slams into my shoulder.

I stumble to a stop.

Dahlia Finnick's dark-brown eyes narrow in the low lights.

All I can do is stammer.

She sidesteps us and continues toward the bar, where Brent is waiting.

Two

AT THE BOTTOM OF THE STAIRS, PRUE YANKS HER HAND away from me. "That fucking hurts, Billie. Calm down."

My body shudders with a sigh. "Sorry."

I cast one final glance toward the upstairs. Dahlia looked at me like I am completely and utterly unimportant. And her little misstep? It wasn't followed by any sort of apology, and it was one hundred percent on purpose.

Surveying the downstairs doesn't bring me any comfort.

Jimmy and Micaela are sitting at the bar, talking and drinking. She's the only one with alcohol, of course, because Jimmy won't be twenty-one till August, but his grin says he's having fun now that his kitchen shift is over anyway. Behind the bar, Xander chats with them between serving customers.

There are more people here than earlier, but not many. On a Friday night, nine o'clock is early. Pretty sure Prue expected this date to include a meal she was not provided.

I lead her to an open spot and rest an elbow on the oak bar.

Xander joins us without pause. "Anything I can get you?" His cerulean eyes meet mine for a second before finding something—anything—else to focus on.

"Can I have some water? She needs to rehydrate, but we're leaving."

Hand clutching my arm, Prue rests her head on my shoulder. How much alcohol did she have?

"Bottled?"

"Do you have to-go cups? Tap's free, right?"

Without a word, he steps into a back room and returns with a foam cup and lid. "She okay?" He fills it with ice and water from the soda gun, covers it with the lid, and sets it and a paper-wrapped straw on the bar.

I tear open the straw. "What the hell is in a zombie?"

He casts a frown toward Prudence. "Rum, absinthe, and falernum syrup." The words are short and curt, but I'm more focused on the content than the uncomfortable context.

I scoff. "Absinthe. Awesome."

"Do you need help getting her to the car?" His mouth twists to the side, but I can't tell whether it's in irritation or concern.

Heels *click clack* across the hardwood floor nearby. A young woman, her tits spilling out of a plunging v-neck dress, leans against the bar beside me, and a flirtatious simper plays on her crimson lips.

"Cassie." Xander surveys her cleavage without shame. "I was wondering if you'd come in tonight."

She taps a red nail on the counter. "When are you off?"

He glances at the clock behind him and leans over the bar toward her. "A couple hours. What're your plans tonight?"

"I'm free if you are."

I stab the straw through the lid and hand the cup to Prue. "Where'd you park?"

Xander's too preoccupied with the sexy brunette to

notice our departure.

Near the exit, Jimmy sends me a wave, but beside him, Micaela watches the scene with a quivering lip.

Outside, Prue directs me toward her Pilot, parked on the next cross-street.

◆

Prue swallows the last of her second glass of water. Her glazed-over eyes study the screen as Thunder's fury bubbles under the surface. "Okay," she says, clutching the glass, "I know I'm sobering up, but what the ever-loving fuck is going on in this movie?"

I snort. "They had to rescue these women from getting married to a creepy old sorcerer, they just killed the bad guy, and now, they're trying to escape."

On the TV, Thunder's fury leads to catastrophic ends. The heroes barely escape before he explodes. I've seen *Big Trouble in Little China* a zillion times. It was the first film Xander, Jimmy, and I could agree on. We watched it several times freshman year—long before I realized it's one of my all-time favorite movies.

Now, "we" is me and Prue.

I lean over the cushion between us and take the glass from her hands. "You want any more?"

A sheepish smile tugs at her lips. "Do you want me to piss all over your couch?"

"We do have a bathroom."

She stretches to look over the couch toward the hallway leading to the kitchen and bathroom. "Yeah, but it's far away."

"You shouldn't let random guys buy you drinks anymore." I slide the glass onto the coffee table and pause the movie. "If you'd ordered for yourself, you wouldn't have gotten so drunk."

Prue runs a hand through her long brown hair and yawns. "Yeah, well, if Graham hadn't taken the liberty of ordering because I was two minutes late…"

I grimace. "Really?"

"Yeah, that was the first red flag."

"Why did you drink it?"

She scowls. "The bartender brought it over after I arrived, so it's not like he slipped anything in it. Besides, I will never let a man ruin my night."

In the time since we became friends—actual friends—Prue has shown herself to be one of the most strong-willed people I've met. I am continually impressed by her resolve.

"Snack?" I rise from the couch and offer her my hand. "And bathroom time for you."

Grudgingly, she accepts the gesture. We part ways at the bathroom.

When Prue stumbles into the kitchen, the popcorn has a few seconds left. She leans against the door frame and watches me with tired eyes.

"How you feeling?" I send her a smirk and pull the bag from the microwave before the timer goes off. "You should eat something."

"Yeah, I guess."

When I tear open the bag, steam billows out, and I lean back so it doesn't fog up my glasses. I dump the contents into a big plastic bowl and throw away the trash.

"I don't know why I do this, Billie."

I join her in the doorway and hold out the bowl. "Do what?"

"Go on dates with complete strangers." She pops a piece into her mouth.

"It's good to get out there. You're doing great."

Most of the time, Prue doesn't talk about Ruby, pretends their breakup at the end of freshman year didn't bother her, but I know it does. It would be hard not to be bothered by your girlfriend of six months telling you she can't handle your being bi—that it makes her too self-conscious, too worried about the competition.

She glowers, unimpressed. "Yeah, but it'd be nice if the guys who do online dating weren't uber creeps. The sex has been good, but you know, women make better lovers, so that's a given."

I snort.

"You know, you could get back out there too."

I link my arm with hers and lead her to the living room. "Prue, I'm not ready for a relationship yet, and I'm not interested in sleeping with someone to put myself out there. I want to get my life sorted out before I can bring someone else into it."

That was the main reason Xander and I broke up in the first place.

I settle onto the couch, and she plops down beside me. "And you know, until then, I have a healthy relationship with my dildo."

A long laugh bursts from her lips. "Trust me, you're not the only one. No other cock has managed to get me off in the last year."

I press play, but my phone lights up the moment I drop

15

the remote on the coffee table. This time, it's Imogene.

This fucking sucks, her text says.

Unease tugs at my stomach as I type up my response: *Everything okay? I can call if you want to talk.*

On the TV, Egg dumps a Bodai statue on Lightning's head.

Then, she texts: *No, it's fine. I'm going to bed.*

My stomach clenches. She's reaching out while pushing away, and that sounds eerily familiar.

Okay, I send her. *Have a good night.*

When I lay my phone down, Prue scoots closer and confiscates some popcorn. "What was that?"

I shake my head. "I don't know. Mo's going through some stuff, but she won't talk to me about it."

Prue's mouth curls into a toothy smile. "I'd say you two were like sisters, but you know, you are."

I roll my eyes. "Thanks for the reminder of how terrible I am with talking about my feelings."

"You're getting better anyway." She nudges me in the side and turns her attention to the TV.

Outside, a pickup truck pulls into the driveway.

Jimmy enters a moment later, tucking his keys into his pocket, and Micaela stumbles in behind him. She clutches the door frame to steady herself and flashes us a grin before struggling to close the door.

Jimmy pauses in the foyer. "Hey. You feeling better, Prudence?"

"Yeah, I'm fine."

He shrinks back at her curt tone. "We'll be in the kitchen."

Micaela latches onto his arm, and he leads the way as

she continues, I assume, their conversation from the car: "I'm just saying, we've been friends for like five months. You should tell me more about this girl you have a crush on. Don't keep everything to yourself…"

Her voice fades as they move farther away.

The movie is coming to its conclusion, and for the first time, Prue's attention is hooked to the TV.

"You can be nice to him, you know." I grab another handful of popcorn, but I struggle to find my appetite. "He doesn't—"

"When he's hurting you? No, thanks."

I force myself to eat a piece, then another. "It's okay, Prue."

"No, it isn't." She releases a long, sad sigh. "He barely talks to you, and he's supposed to be one of your closest friends. I thought you said he wouldn't choose between you and Xander."

"He's family. Even when we don't get along, he's like my brother. Siblings fight all the time."

Headlights flash across the walls and shift as the Camaro parks beside Jimmy's truck.

"Doesn't mean he isn't being a shitty friend," Prue says.

The irony makes me laugh. "It's not like I haven't been a shitty friend either."

A few seconds later, Xander comes inside, his leather jacket slung over one shoulder. He pauses by the door to hang up the jacket and runs a hand through his slicked-back hair. He doesn't bother to look our way before heading for the kitchen.

Prue bites her lip. "I know I was really drunk, but why were you freaking out at the bar? Xander or the alcohol?"

"You know that guy you were with?"

She nods.

"He's one of Dahlia Finnick's friends."

A grimace spreads across her face. "Fuck. She's who walked into you by the stairs, right?"

I scrunch up my nose. "I'm impressed you remember."

"I'll have you know, I've only blacked out once, and tonight was not that night." But while her words are confident and determined, her hand squeezes mine with tacit softness. "I'm sorry I was drunk."

"It's fine. You know I'm always here if you need me." By the time I reach for her, she's already retreated, and I slide my hands into my pockets. "It could've been four in the morning, and I would've come for you."

"I know." She tugs at the silver chain around her wrist. "But how much time do you spend around alcohol anymore? Jimmy and Xander don't keep it in the house. You never hang out with anyone who drinks regularly. I'm sorry I put you in that position."

My chest tightens. "Are you apologizing about the alcohol or running into Dahlia or about me having to pick you up at the bar where Xander and Jimmy work?"

"All of the above."

I snicker. "I see the guys on a regular basis. That's what happens when you live with someone."

Her fingers release the chain, and she relaxes. "Yeah, but you don't normally have to interact with them—or Micaela."

I frown. "She invited me to sit with them again."

Finally, Prue looks up. "Does she know you two dated? You'd think she'd pick up on the awkwardness between the object of her affections and his roommate."

"We didn't date."

Despite the heavy sorrow in her eyes, Prue chooses not to respond. "I think I'm sober enough to drive now."

My brow scrunches together. "I doubt that very much."

"One last glass of water before I go?" She nods toward the kitchen, where the soft voices of my roommates and Micaela emanate from. "Is it too much to ask for you to join me?"

"Of course not."

Jimmy, cheeks pink, rests against the counter with an open can of Coke. Micaela stands next to him, her hands clasped around a glass of water. On the opposite side of the kitchen, Xander rifles through the fridge.

Prue fills her glass with filtered water, and I hover in the doorway—as far away from everyone as possible.

Xander doesn't glance over.

"Okay, but you had this big thing for a girl over the summer," Micaela says into her glass. "It's the same girl, right?"

Jimmy fidgets with the hem of his Draft Horse shirt. "No comment." The red tee highlights his blush.

"Oh, come on!"

Prue downs her water, then pours herself more. I'm surprised she has room considering how much she drank tonight—water and otherwise.

Xander pulls back from the fridge with an apple and takes a bite as the door closes.

Micaela turns on him. "You know who it is, don't you, Xander?"

He shrugs. "That doesn't mean you're going to find out."

She takes another drink. "What're you doing now? Going to hang out with us?"

Her tone is hopeful—overly so—but Xander never lets her crush faze him. Despite his best efforts, the months he's ignored her feelings have had no effect on their existence.

"Nah, I've got plans."

Jimmy raises an eyebrow.

"Cassie asked if I could hang out." The apple crunches as he takes another bite, and a drop of juice slides down his chin as he chews. "I'm going over to her apartment for a bit."

Micaela's face contorts with disappointment, and I turn away when Prue joins me.

"Okay, I'm good," she whispers.

I need no further instruction before exiting the kitchen. We stop by the front door. "You sure you're sober enough to drive?"

"Probably." Her fingers toy with the knob, but she doesn't make a move to open the door. "You ready to go to bed?"

"I'm exhausted. Thought I might draw for a little while to relax."

She pulls me into a tight hug. "Okay. I'll text you tomorrow."

As I climb the stairs, their voices fade to nothingness, and I shut myself with my glass of water in my bedroom.

Without Prudence, the house is lonely and cold.

I flip open my laptop, log in, and play a song in my library. I crank the volume as Tool's "Schism" begins to play. I want to drown in the enthralling beat.

My favorite thing about this house is the window seat

in my bedroom.

Originally, this room was supposed to be Xander's because it has access to the roof over the porch. But before we moved in, he offered it to me. I like sitting in windows and drawing, and he insisted he wouldn't need the roof access—because quitting cigarettes would be "easy." Jimmy and I laughed at him then.

But this is Xander, so of course it was easy.

I curl up with the pillow and flip open a sketchbook.

Below, a car engine turns over. Xander's red Camaro backs out of the driveway and zooms down the street. He must be tired of waiting for his booty call.

The music switches to AC/DC's "Spellbound," and I press my pen to paper.

Three

"Alright, folks!" Rivera waltzes into the photo lab, notebook tucked under a thick arm. "We have five weeks till finals, and shit's getting real."

There's a chorus of subdued laughter, and I switch my phone to vibrate and pocket it.

Rivera stands in the middle of our circle of desks. "Unless you were sleeping, you remember our final is a partner project. Don't get your hopes up, folks. I'm the one assigning partners!"

Several students groan.

"You'll get your partners and the rubric today, but most of your work will be outside of class." He drops his notebook on the desk and withdraws a thin stack of paper. "You have to finish the current assignment, so don't get too excited about a new one."

He hands the stack to the nearest student, who takes a rubric and passes the rest on. I examine my copy while he reads off the assignments.

"Ogden and Clark. Alanis and Coopersmith."

The assignment seems straightforward. Like our previous projects, we'll use black and white film and our SLRs.

22

Contrast is essential for our compositions.

"Rooney and Davis."

Unlike our previous assignments, which have focused on cityscapes and an occasional found object, this project is a portrait. Thus the partner.

"Dixon and Finnick."

My chest constricts. I glance up to locate her.

Dahlia Finnick sits on the opposite side of the classroom, reclining in her chair. The separation was more my doing than hers. Once I discovered we shared the class, I knew I had to keep my distance. We haven't exchanged more than two sentences since we went our separate ways last May, and my life has been the better for it.

Her features are soft but distracted as she plays with her pen. She too looks my way, and at last, her eyes focus. Her hair, always loose and long, is up in a tight bun. The little makeup she wears is haphazard.

"It's a shame."

When I turn, Jay Ogden nudges me with an elbow. He uses the enlarger next to mine in the darkroom.

"What is?"

He rises from his seat with an aloof shrug. "I was hoping Rivera would assign us together."

"Oh."

On the other side of the classroom, Dahlia's intense gaze focuses on the pen twirling around her fingers. She is the last person I want to do this project with. I would've much preferred to spend hours alone with Jay than her.

"That would've been nice."

Jay's subsequent smile is wide. "I guess I have to work with Keith, though. See you." And he disappears across the

23

room to find his partner.

We exchange an occasional sentence while working in the darkroom, and he's always nice. But that's the most in-depth conversation we've had in the three months since the semester began.

"Let's do this."

This time, it's Dahlia.

Once in the darkroom, she heads for her enlarger, red from the safelight. Once again, her station is located on the opposite side of the room from mine.

I lean against the counter while she sets up, and in my pocket, my phone buzzes. I make sure no one has any photo paper out before withdrawing the device.

Imogene's face pops up on the screen. *Urgent,* the text says, and I roll my eyes. *When can you talk?*

I'm in class now, I send. *Tonight?*

"Can you get together in the studio this weekend?" Dahlia's curt tone draws my attention. "You must want to get this over with."

"Shouldn't be a problem. I work Saturday, but the gallery closes at five. Otherwise, my weekend's free."

"I'll put us on the schedule. Maybe Saturday night. No one else will want the spot. You have the same number, right?"

It's true. We're closing in on finals, so the photo lab is usually booked, but most students will be out drinking on Saturday night. Abstaining from alcohol has its perks.

"Yeah, that sounds good."

She returns to her transparent sheet of negatives for our current project. That must be my cue to leave.

But I can't stop watching her.

This is the first time I've really looked at Dahlia since our friendship fizzled out last spring. At the time, she was spiraling out of control. She doesn't seem any healthier now.

Her skin-and-bone body is ghostly pale. Her cheekbones, her collarbone, and the bones in her forearms are significantly visible. The low-cut tee reveals the smooth curve of her cleavage, but even her breasts are smaller than last I saw.

"What the fuck are you staring at?" She turns to me sharply, her face contorting with irritation.

I step back. "Nothing." I retreat toward my enlarger across the room. "I'll see you this weekend."

◆

"Okay." Prue stretches across my bed, holding her notebook above her. "Illumination."

I play with a loose thread from my sheets. "Most Gothic illuminated manuscripts were royal bibles and psalters from the middle of the Thirteenth Century, but during the latter end of the century, they started making prayer books with illumination for laypeople. God, Prue, why do I have to answer the questions?"

She snickers. "Because I learn better from playing teacher than student. And you have all this memorized." She pauses to frown at her notes. "And 'book of hours' is the term you were looking for."

"Yeah, okay. We should be working in the painting studio."

Prue shoots a glance in my direction, a smile on her red lips. "When you have your private studio, we can study while you paint. Until then, I'd rather be here where we can be comfortable."

Despite myself, I quiver in anticipation. "Oh, come on. I doubt I'll get it. I'm a junior, and there are ten available."

It would be an amazing opportunity. There are so many class studios in the art building, but the individual studios are reserved for students who apply so they have somewhere private to work. Most of those students are seniors working on their final project, but I want to spend this spring working on a number of personal painting projects. It doesn't exactly give me precedence, but I can dream.

Prue squeezes my knee. "Yeah, but you deserve it."

On the nightstand, my phone vibrates, and I stretch to reach it. Dahlia's name flashes across my screen. I didn't have the nerve to remove her from my contacts—our friendship meant too much to me. Apparently, that was a good thing.

I booked the photo lab for 10 Saturday night. Dress nice, the text says.

I stare at that message until the phone turns black.

When I look up, Prue sets her notebook down and pushes up on her elbows. "You okay?"

"I'm alright."

"What's the text?"

I slide the phone onto my nightstand. Where am I supposed to begin? "I should've said something as soon as I saw you..."

Prue waits, concern etched on her face.

"Dahlia and I are working on a project together." My gaze shifts to the open art history book on the bed between us. "We didn't get a choice. After running into her this weekend, I'm nervous. She gets under my skin."

"You're worried you'll get caught up in her again?"

I force myself to meet Prue's rich brown eyes. "Yeah, I am. I know she made everything worse during one of the most trying times of my life, but I have a soft spot for her."

She quirks her head. "It's okay to care about her. You two were close. Just be careful."

"Right. Careful."

I'm not sure how well I can manage careful. Not when Dahlia's involved.

Prue's brow creases with uncertainty, and she searches the textbook. "You know, I always thought she…" She hesitates, and the creases in her forehead tighten.

"Thought she what?"

On the nightstand, my phone lights up again.

This time, it's a phone call.

It must be Imogene. But she never calls from the house phone. She has a cell.

"Yeah?"

"Hi, Billie."

It's Mom.

Things have been calm and fine, but we've barely spoken since her wedding. This must be important.

"What's going on, Mom?" I shift, trying to relax, but I'm tense.

"I have an announcement. Your sister insists I should've told you sooner, but we wanted to be sure there weren't any complications before broadcasting it everywhere." She pauses a beat. "I am twenty-three weeks pregnant. The baby is healthy, and the pregnancy so far has been easy—"

"Wait, what?"

I cannot wrap my head around this.

She's three months away from her fortieth birthday, and

they've been married for seven months.

"You're going to have a younger sibling."

If—when—this child is born, it will be twenty-one years younger than me. That isn't remotely sibling-like.

But Mom continues: "We've switched my lithium to smaller doses, and they're checking it three times a week now to make sure there aren't any adverse effects. So far, everything is going well."

"Okay." My voice is weak.

But I don't know what to say or think.

I never imagined she would have another child.

Or that she would keep it from me for more than half the pregnancy.

"Are you alright, Billie?"

My phone beeps. A text or something.

I clear my throat. "Uh, yeah. Congratulations." I doubt my voice is convincing. I'm still in shock.

"I imagine you're studying or something." She releases a little sigh. "I'll let you get back to it."

"Okay. Talk to you later."

When we hang up, I check my phone. That beep was my alarm, not a text.

"You okay?" Prue asks.

I slip off the bed. "I have to take my pill. You want a bottle of water or something?" I'm not capable of reassuring her yet.

No amount of smiling could hide her worry. "Water would be great. And then, we'll finish this study session, Ms. Dixon."

I withdraw the bottle from my top drawer and tuck a blue pill under my tongue. I really should be better about keeping a drink in my room for these moments, but I slip through the door—and hope no one is downstairs.

I don't get my wish.

In the kitchen, Jimmy and Micaela take turns eating Doritos from the bag. Micaela grins the second she notices me. "Hi, Billie!"

Last time I brought glasses up to my room, I had to wash an impromptu load of laundry because Prue spilled all over my bed. So I retrieve two water bottles from the fridge and flash Micaela a smile.

As I open the first bottle, the front door opens and closes in the distance.

I hold my breath.

Luckily, the footsteps recede up the stairs. I cannot handle interacting with Xander right now.

"Do you have plans tonight?" Micaela leans against the counter. "We're going to practice in his room. I think I might have convinced Jimmy to search for bandmates. You wanna be our first victim?"

I gulp down more water and twist the lid on. "No, thanks. I'm studying for art history with Prudence."

"Oh." Disappointment laces her voice, but she keeps her grin in place. "Well, if you need a break, stop by his room and listen to a song or two."

Beside her, Jimmy uncomfortably stuffs his face with more chips.

The footsteps are back. They're too heavy to be Prue's.

"Cool." I grab the second bottle off the counter and step toward the stairs. I need to get the fuck out of here. "Gothic architecture's calling my name. Later."

I slip past them, but Xander turns the corner. We barely avoid a collision.

For a moment, all he does is stare.

Less than fifteen minutes after his last class of the day, he's dressed in his black slacks and red Draft Horse tee. He must have work right away.

"Do you have time to listen to a song, Xander?" Micaela's voice is barely louder than the blood pounding through my ears.

I blink and step aside.

"Nah." He slips past me and rifles through the freezer. "I work in ten. I need to head out now." He tears open a Go-Gurt from the door.

I press against the wall outside the kitchen doorway. To my right, the stairs lead up to the bedrooms, but my legs are shaking from the close encounter. Even living with him, I'm not used to him paying attention to me. We don't look at each other. We don't talk.

"Oh, that sucks," Micaela says.

Jimmy releases a short chuckle. "When are you done tonight?"

"Working till close. See you later."

Xander heads toward the front door—in the opposite direction. Thankfully, he doesn't notice me. The door shuts quietly behind him.

In the kitchen, Micaela clucks her tongue. "He works a lot."

Jimmy sighs. "Seriously, Micaela, if you're interested, you can ask him out."

"No, no." She titters, and her voice trembles. "I mean, I am interested, but he already knows. He wouldn't wait for me to make the first move if he reciprocated."

"Well, he's…"

"Just interested in sex?"

"Yeah."

"That, um, exchange with Billie was awkward."

Jimmy inhales sharply. "You know, they're in a weird place right now."

"They're both really closed off. Is that why they broke up?"

"Something like that…"

I swallow the saliva pooling in my throat and force my legs up the stairs.

Prue accepts the unopened bottle with a quiet, "Thanks," and I take the spot beside her with my own drink. "Okay, we need to go over Jean Pucelle." After a quick drink, she's ready to study more.

I groan. "Can't we take a break? We've been doing this for the last three hours. I'm tired of Gothic history."

She nudges away her notes, her face softening. "What was that conversation with your mom about?"

I frown and take a drink. "I'm going to be a big sister."

Prue cocks an eyebrow. "Aren't you already a big sister?"

"Again?"

She stifles a laugh. "So…is your mom pregnant?"

I nod.

"That's crazy. You'd be more like an aunt than a sister."

"Yeah, I will." I glance at the book. "I don't know what to say about it. I mean, I'm…"

"In shock?"

I shrug.

31

"We can talk about something else if you want."

I shift, and my focus gravitates toward the door. As much as my mother's latest news overwhelms and shocks me, I can't shake the discomfort from downstairs.

"I don't know why Micaela is so nice to me."

The words slip out before I can prevent them. It's the first thing that came to mind, and well, there it is.

Prue assesses me with narrow eyes. "You mean when she has a crush on your ex? Does she know you dated?"

"We didn't date, but yes." I run a hand through my auburn curls, tugging at the strands. "Things are so awkward, but she wants to be friends. I don't understand. I would've expected her to be more antagonistic toward me under the circumstances."

"You're not the one sleeping with him."

I shake my head. "Even if I were, she would…handle it with poise. I was so jealous last year, and he wasn't sleeping with anyone. I don't know how she does it."

"Don't be hard on yourself, Billie. You're doing great now."

"At moving on and not being jealous?" I scoff. "I've slept with one person and gone on zero dates in the past seven months. I know that shouldn't be a measurement of how I'm handling things—it's not like I dated much before him— but I'm not doing great."

She blinks forcefully. "Well, you're doing better than me. I've gone on a million dates, and I'm not any closer to a relationship."

"At least you're having sex."

"You slept with Matheo over the summer."

My eyes flutter shut. "That was a whim, Prue. Which is

why it hasn't been repeated."

"Whim or not, you slept with a sexy French guy in Paris. I didn't get laid in Paris."

I can't help laughing. Prue has a tendency to idealize the encounter because she didn't experience it.

In reality, it was a one-night stand with a guy who spoke broken English. Let's be real, my French is shit compared to a native speaker. We couldn't communicate. He was cute, but the sex was mediocre at best.

"I'm not saying it bothers me. It's awkward, and I don't think Micaela realizes how awkward it is."

Prue bridges the distance to pat my thigh. "It's okay to not be over your ex. You don't have to be okay with him sleeping with someone else or with Micaela having a crush on him."

I lean against the headboard and sift through my notes over Jean Pucelle's *Hours of Jeanne d'Evreux*. "What we had was great while it lasted, but it was never going to last. We're too incompatible. Really, Prue, I'm not hung up on Xander."

I flip to the next page, and she doesn't say a word.

A beat passes.

Then another.

"Billie, you still have his shirt. His favorite shirt."

"We need to get back to work..."

Four

ELISE GLANCES THROUGH THE FRAMED PAINTINGS WITH A frown on her tawny face. "The client brought in fifteen, but he didn't specify how he wanted them hung." She grips the folder with the client's information to her chest and runs a hand through her coarse umber hair.

"Should I call him and ask?" I shift my gaze to the office phone. "Maybe he forgot some paperwork."

My least favorite part of this job is answering and making phone calls, but they don't happen often. In fact, interacting with anyone other than the gallery visitors themselves is rare, though that's stressful in its own way.

But Elise shakes her head. "I'll take care of it."

She tightens her grip around the folder, and I lean forward to scrutinize the paintings.

The frames are all the same style—sleek black, flat, not taking anything away from the content. The paintings themselves are abstract—all bright colors, thick oil paint spread across the canvas like Jackson Pollock. They're beautiful in a strange way. Fascinating more than anything else.

In the pocket of my black slacks, my phone buzzes.

Elise is pretty lax about phone usage as long as nobody's

inside the gallery—and let's face it, there's rarely anyone in the gallery except during special functions—so I pull it out to see who's calling.

Imogene. We haven't spoken since Mom dropped the bomb.

I glance around the gallery before holding up the phone. "Elise?"

Her tired eyes turn to me, then she nods. "Take your break. I'm going to step into the office to make these calls."

"Thanks."

In the breakroom, I relax on a chair, resting my head against the wall. The gallery is in the middle of downtown, so the space is tight. Even in this room, I can hear anything in the main gallery, but this is as close to private as it gets.

"Hey, Mo. How's it going?"

She launches into a speech without a glimpse of salutations. Her words come out garbled, rambling, difficult to understand. "I'm sorry, I should've told you sooner, but Mom wanted to wait until they were sure—"

"No, no, it's fine. You didn't do anything wrong."

The last thing I need is for Mo to blame herself. Our mother's secret-keeping has nothing to do with her. Mom and Rob chose to hide the pregnancy, even from me, and that was their decision.

Imogene pauses, and her voice is steadier. "She's had me keep it secret for months, and I should've told you."

"Really, it's okay."

She takes another shaky breath. "I'm sorry, Billie. You know how Mom gets. The baby's super healthy, and her pregnancy's going well, but they're concerned about heart defects because of the lithium."

35

It takes a moment to register what she's saying.

"She mentioned they switched up the doses. It could cause birth defects?"

"The baby could be stillborn." She releases a long sigh. "But they want to do what's best for Mom too."

"Mo, are you upset about this?"

She hesitates. "I don't know."

I wish I could be there with her. Unfortunately, unless she makes a trip out here, I won't see her until May, when we celebrate her high school graduation.

"I'm surprised you're not."

My eyes wander the closet-sized breakroom. There isn't much here but the table and chairs, a fridge, and a small counter with a sink. Nothing to look at. "I mean, I wish she told me sooner, and the pregnancy bit's weird, but I'm not surprised she kept it from me."

She doesn't say anything.

"Look, I know you want us to be close, but we won't magically have a great mother-daughter relationship because we talked. Doesn't work that way."

Imogene harrumphs. "I know."

"Seriously, why is this bothering you?"

For a minute, she doesn't speak. "I guess I was hoping she'd wait to move on with her life until after I graduate. They're not moving to California till summer, but the baby's due two weeks after your birthday, Billie."

"Wow."

I hadn't done the math yet.

She huffs. "How's everything there? How's Jimmy?"

"Things are alright. He's alright."

The anxious trill in her voice sends a jolt through my

body. Shouldn't she have that information from the horse's mouth? She'd get better info from him than me. We don't talk.

"He still likes his job?"

"He likes it fine."

Jimmy applied at Draft Horse after we first moved in, and he was hired on the spot. Not only does management at the bar love Xander, but his recommendations are trusted implicitly.

His first day of work was the day I left on my study abroad with Prue.

Everything was different when I got back.

Through the open door, the bell signaling the front door has opened chimes. Elise is probably in her office and shouldn't be bothered.

"I need to get back to work, Mo."

"Right."

She hangs up without a goodbye, and I shove the phone back into my pocket. I don't have time to sort out how I feel.

The main gallery looks empty.

Closer inspection reveals a young woman with long honey-brown hair staring at the focal piece of this month's featured artist. She's tall but thin—the only curve is her ass, and it isn't much—but there's something oddly attractive about her.

She turns as my footsteps approach, and my chest twists with discomfort.

What the hell is Dahlia doing in my gallery?

I force my legs to keep moving until I reach her. "Have you been here before?"

Dahlia tilts her head, her teeth tugging at the thin bottom lip. "I didn't know you worked here."

"For the last five months."

She studies me a moment, pausing on my sheer button-up shirt. "You look good in professional garb." She turns back to the painting. "Who's Alejandro Garcia?"

I tug at the neckline to make sure no buttons have come undone. "He's our featured artist this month. Born in 1979 in Arizona, Garcia moved to the area as an eight-year—"

Dahlia turns back sharply. "I don't care about that."

"Then why are you here, Dahlia?"

She shrugs. "I wasn't going to come in because I thought it'd be boring, but here you are."

"Yes, I work here."

Her thin lips curl into a smirk. "What do you do around here? Are you qualified to talk to me about the artwork? Or are you just here to look pretty?"

My muscles are so tense my body trembles. "I know as much about the artwork as anyone else employed here. I may not be qualified to sell the art pieces, but I pull my weight. I'm a perfectly capable employee."

"Where's your boss?" Dahlia's lips curl with amusement. "They have no problem leaving me in your perfectly capable hands?"

I snort. "Dahlia, you can't afford one of these paintings. My boss wouldn't be interested in you."

"Then why are you talking to me?"

"I'm doing my job."

She grins, nodding toward the centerpiece. "Tell me about this painting."

I turn to the enormous oil painting. "Garcia painted

'Bridge over Tranquil Water' two years ago when he stayed in South Hero near Keeler Bay. It depicts—"

Dahlia's phone buzzes, and she takes a moment to read the text. My words falter as her face twists from smug and antagonistic to contemplative. Her jaw goes slack.

"Is everything alright, Dahlia?"

She turns off her phone with a scoff. "Like you care."

My stomach clenches.

Of course, I care. The ball of fury and self-destruction inside her is the same darkness that has followed me my whole life. And my mother. Probably Mo too. How could I not care?

"We may have stopped being friends, but I never stopped caring."

She slips the phone into her purse and returns her attention to me. She's beautiful when she smiles like that. "Tell me more about Garcia..." Her voice is soft, gentle—she hasn't used that tone with me in a long time.

I respond in kind.

◆

My dad's house is quiet when I slip inside. It's after dinnertime, and he's settled down to grade papers in the study to the left of the foyer. It's the only room with a light on.

He looks up from his stack of quizzes, joy written across his dark-brown face. "Mina, I didn't know you were coming over tonight." He's gotten a haircut in the last couple days, as his obsidian curls are short and tight and the sides fade into his beard.

"Surprise." I set my backpack on the floor beside the

39

open chair. "Can I stay the night, Dad?"

With a grin, he motions me to sit. "Of course. Will you do your homework with me?"

I sit and pull out my massive art history textbook. It's nearly seven hundred pages of information and artwork, but my class covers a small portion of the contents.

"I have a test tomorrow over Gothic art and architecture, and I need to go over the chapter again." I flip to the pertinent page near the end. "It's a reminder since I already studied all of this."

Dad chuckles as he returns to the top quiz. "How convenient you've been to the Notre-Dame."

I bring out my class notes and a mechanical pencil and jot down the vocab words and a time line of events as I peruse the chapter.

But despite being in the safety and comfort of my father's house, I can't focus.

Between Mom's pregnancy, how upset Imogene was, and Dahlia showing up at my work, I have no more spoons for the day. All I want is to curl up and fall asleep, but I have to study.

I tap my mechanical pencil against the page as I read and reread the introduction about Pope Urban II and the rise of cathedrals.

Dad lays his pen down. "Talk to me, Mina."

I stop.

"Something is bothering you. Why don't you explain it to me?"

A meager laugh escapes my lips. "I don't know where to begin."

He quirks a devious smile. "I find the beginning to be

an excellent starting point."

I snort. "Have you talked to Mo lately?"

"She called yesterday, but I was teaching my night class. Then, she missed my call today."

I probably shouldn't tell him—and I should've kept it from Prue—but I have to say something.

"Mom's pregnant. Due at the end of April, a couple weeks after my birthday."

He raises an umber eyebrow. "She must be halfway through. You found out this week?"

"Mom didn't want anyone to know in case of miscarriage or birth defects, you know, because of her medication."

"Of course." But he sounds skeptical. "You're upset you didn't know sooner?"

I give a one-shouldered shrug. "That's the thing... I think I'm supposed to be upset, to feel left out, but it doesn't bother me. It makes sense why she wouldn't want to tell anyone—there could be some serious side effects from her medication, and she needs to take it to function. And you know, this isn't the first time she's failed to keep me in the loop. It's expected by now. So I'm not mad at her, but maybe I should be."

For a moment, Dad's hazel eyes observe me, calculating.

But I shake my head. "Maybe it's because I'm not there to see everything. Mo's unsettled by it, and that surprised me. She was always so strong."

"She's a child, Mina." His voice is small but deliberate.

"She's eighteen. She's an adult now."

"An adult who, like you, never had the opportunity to be a child." He stretches to lay his hand over mine. "She spent her entire childhood taking care of her adult mother. Now,

41

your mother is stable, remarried, and about to have a baby. Can you imagine how displaced she must feel?"

I frown.

If it's anything like having your best friend meet a cooler girl who bonds with him over music while you're away for the summer—a girl who also has an enormous crush on your ex... Try as I might, I cannot help feeling they'll both replace me. So yeah, I know a little about displacement.

"You two talked a lot while I was gone for the summer."

"Yes. I spent every second I had with her." He clears his throat, and all reminiscence dissipates from his voice. "Aside from when Jimmy was teaching her to drive. He was a devoted companion."

I nudge a few auburn coils behind my ear. "I wish I'd been able to spend the whole summer with her. She was sick for the last ten days she was here. I barely got to see her." I twist my hand up to hold his. "Think we could convince her to spend next summer here too?"

Dad shifts his attention to the quizzes on his lap. "I suspect Imogene has other plans."

Five

THE ART BUILDING IS EMPTY SATURDAY NIGHT, BUT ON THE second floor, Dahlia leans against the panel where we swipe our IDs for studio access. She elected to wait for me.

"What took you so long?" She pushes away, and the door unlocks when she waves her ID over the panel.

"I didn't realize I was late."

Inside, the studio is a simple rectangular room with black walls, standing spotlights, and a two-person table with chairs in one corner.

"How are we doing this?" I drop my backpack on a chair. "I don't want this to take longer than necessary."

Dahlia assesses me in amusement and lays her bag on the table to reach her equipment. She hangs the SLR around her neck and removes the lens cap. "You've got your camera, right?"

I scoff. "Of course I brought my camera. I want to finish this tonight."

"I want to go first."

I pause in the middle of unzipping my backpack. "Modeling?"

Her sharp laughter echoes through the dark room. "No,

silly. I want to take your pictures. I told you to dress nice. What are you wearing?"

I set my camera on the table. "Clothes."

Dahlia turns toward the black backdrop to assess the area. "Nothing too dark, right? I need contrast. Preferably something tight."

Under my hoody, the shirt is a pale-blue fitted t-shirt. No patterns or designs. Not skin-tight, but not loose either.

She glances over as I tug my arm out of the sleeve. I shift uncomfortably under her gaze but yank the hoody over my head. It drops to the floor beside my backpack.

Dahlia undoes the toggles, then the zipper of her own coat. When she tosses it over the second chair, her pink shirt, complete with scoop neckline and three-quarter sleeves, is tight and thin enough to show her ribs.

She drags two spotlights toward the backdrop with an air of confidence I have never understood. She has a plan, but I have nothing to contribute.

I sort through the notifications on my phone. Nothing pertinent and only one text, a short one from Imogene: *Why are all men assholes?*

She's having boy trouble. Again.

I'll call you tonight, I text. *When I can.*

"You ready?"

I look up. "How are we doing this?"

Dahlia nods toward the opposite side of the room, lit up by spotlights. "I want you up against the wall."

I leave my phone next to the camera and slip past the spotlights. The wall is cold through my shirt, but I await further instructions.

Instead, she approaches.

She clucks her tongue. "Do I have to do everything?" Her petite hands press me flat against the wall, spread out my fingers over the cold surface, and she murmurs a quiet, "Glasses," before sliding them off my nose.

"I need those to see."

She lays a finger over my lips to shush me. "You'll get them when we're done with the shoot." She pushes my curls behind my head and tilts one cheek toward the wall. "Loosen your jaw. Mouth slightly open."

I comply. There's no faster way to get this over with.

"Good." Her voice is quiet as she runs a final hand over my shoulder. "Relax." She's blurry as soon as she's out of reach. Not that I can see anything once she retreats behind the spotlights.

A moment later, the camera clicks.

"Look at me, but don't move your head. Eyes wide, like you're surprised."

I locate the pink blur of her shirt. She's to my left, and I can barely see her without twisting my neck.

For a few minutes, the only sound is the camera shutter and Dahlia's quiet footsteps as she continually seeks a better angle.

"How are you, Billie?" She steps into the spotlight for a direct shot. "You and Xander still together?"

I frown—

"Don't move."

—and slacken my jaw, forcing my body to relax.

I don't know how she can ask the question. Dahlia may be an outsider, but she's probably taken more than a few glances to know Xander and I haven't been "together" for months.

"That's a shame," she says. "I was rooting for you two, you know."

I want to turn to her, to ask why she's lying so poorly. She made her opinion on the matter infinitely clear from the moment I took a sip of that bloody mary.

"Now that I think about it—" she pauses to take another shot "—I haven't seen the two of you in the same room for a long time. What happened?"

My lips clamp together, but that's all the response she needs.

Dahlia pulls her camera away. She's close enough I can distinguish her fuzzy features, but only just. "He seeing someone new? Or would you prefer not to talk about your ex?"

That must be my cue to speak.

"We were never technically dating."

Her derisive laughter reverberates off the walls. "As close as it gets, right? I can't imagine you in a real relationship. Let's switch up positions."

I'm sweating under the lights, but she sets the camera on the table and joins me.

At close range, her protruding brown eyes study me, but my gaze gravitates toward the smirk on her glistening lips.

"What position now?" My mouth is dry.

Dahlia doesn't hesitate before tugging at the neck of my tee. "You've got a great body. You should show more skin."

My jaw slackens. "What?"

"Oh well." Her hands slide down and clamp around my hips—I gasp—to shift my position, her mouth pulling to the side pensively. "You know…" Her cold fingers trail up my abdomen, dragging the shirt with them, until my

46

stomach is bare. "You'd look super cute in a crop-top."

I shiver under her touch. "I didn't bring extra clothes, and I don't own a crop-top."

She shrugs.

"What, you want me to take off my shirt?"

Dahlia snickers. "I mean, I'm not against it..." Her hands slide upward again.

I inhale sharply as the shirt grazes my nipples. "I'm not wearing a bra."

Her fingers skim the sides of my breasts. "It's me. We're alone."

"I don't want you to take pictures of me half naked for class." My voice is barely above a whisper.

"I wouldn't use the photos that show anything. You can trust me."

My eyelids fall shut, and I bite my lip.

I can't trust her. I know I can't trust her. But her fingers are warming up against my skin, and she lifts the shirt over my breasts. A soft fingerpad circles my erect nipple. I can't steady my breathing.

My eyes flash open. "You don't want to use them for our project?"

She shakes her head, a conspiratorial smirk on her wet lips.

"Then why?"

Dahlia steps closer, pressing against me, and I gasp as her hand engulfs my breast. "If you have to ask—"

"Knock, knock!"

She steps back, and I yank my shirt down. Light bursts into the studio from the newly-opened door. I can't see who it is, but I don't have to.

47

"Lia, I brought your food—oh!" He pauses, his silhouette in the bright doorway. "Hey, Billie."

I slump against the wall. "Hi, Brent."

Dahlia crosses her arms over her chest. "What the fuck are you doing here, Brent?"

I slip away from her to retrieve my glasses, and when I turn back, he's frowning.

"What're you talking about? You asked me to bring you some food."

But Dahlia is livid. "I did not ask you to bring me food. I'm not hungry."

Brent quirks his head. "Lia, you texted me two hours ago to bring you pie. What the hell are you overreacting about?"

"I said I'm not hungry."

I grab my phone and sit on one of the chairs, squeezing my legs together uncomfortably. My hard nipples protrude through the shirt. Thankfully, they can't see how wet my underwear is.

Dahlia scoffs. "Fine, we can take a break." She snatches the box from him and takes the open seat. Inside are two slices of cream pie.

I recline and flip through my phone, waiting. Mo hasn't responded to my last text, not even a confirmation.

"How you doing, Billie?"

Glaring, I turn off the screen. "I'm fine."

He offers me his typical grin from his spot against the wall behind Dahlia. "It's nice to see you again so soon."

"It is?"

"Of course! Aren't you twenty-one yet? You should come out with us. We go to Draft Horse all the time."

"Not till April." I'm too surprised to remind him I don't

drink. He probably doesn't remember.

"You've seen the bar." He doesn't acknowledge I spoke. "I mean, there are like four bars in St. Clare, but this one is the best. You'd have a lot of fun with us."

"Probably not."

"What a shame." Irritation laces his voice. "It's kind of lonely without Darius."

"What?"

Dahlia kicks him without turning around, and he rubs his shin with a deep frown. "That was unnecessary."

But she fiddles with the dials on her SLR as she chews, humming occasionally.

"Did we get enough photos?" I ask in a small voice.

Her lips twist to the side in concentration. "I know we booked this till midnight, but the studio's boring. We need a change of scenery. Explore around town?" She lifts her eyes to meet mine. "Or maybe we could do it somewhere more relaxing. You could come over to my apartment."

I swallow. "Is that necessary? This is a perfectly good place for portraits."

"I don't want good. I want perfect. This is our final, Billie. Don't you want an A?"

Of course I do, and she's well aware of that fact. But she's backing me into a corner, and I doubt being alone in her apartment is a good idea. Before Brent got here…

Well, I don't know what the hell that was.

Or what it was about to be.

"Somewhere around town," I concede.

She takes another bite, a smug smile on her lips.

"Are we done here?"

She shrugs. "I guess you can go."

49

Behind her, Brent's chortle echoes through the room. "Oh, come on, Billie. Don't go yet. You should hang out with us." He reaches inside his heavy coat and withdraws a couple dark bottles. "I brought some beer."

My mouth contorts into a scowl. "I don't drink."

He laughs again. "Don't be a killjoy. This is fun."

I scoff and rise from the chair to put my things away. The last thing I grab is my hoody.

In pure Dahlia fashion, she's unmoved by my irritation. "I'll text you so we can get together for another photo shoot."

"Sure." I'm already out the door.

◆

There are no cars in the driveway when I hook my bike up to a porch pillar, and the door's locked. I prefer when no one else is here.

I push the door shut behind me and maneuver through the dark house. The kitchen light is on, but it doesn't provide much visibility to the rest of the house.

Upstairs, I hang my backpack on my desk chair and collapse on my bed. I don't bother to turn on the light or shut my door, and the phone is still in my hand.

For once, the house is silent.

I love more than anything to listen to that silence. No laughter or musical instruments or people I desperately want to avoid but can't. No having to play nice even though I want to curl up into a ball and scream and cry forever. These quiet moments are the only times I enjoy this old house.

It's rather pretty in and of itself, but context matters.

No matter how much time has passed since we moved in, nothing about my living situation gets easier.

My fingers tighten around the phone, and I drag it to my face.

There's no Dahlia at the house either. No reason to be on edge or nervous or, well, aroused by whatever the hell that was.

The conversation with Imogene is up when I unlock it, and I press the 'Call' button before holding it to my ear.

It rings a few times before she answers.

"Hi, Billie."

"Hey." I slowly unzip my hoody, and the thick cotton falls to the sides. "How you doing?"

She grunts. "Could be worse."

"Did something happen with Damien?"

"Donovan."

I cringe. I wouldn't say I'm bad with names, but it's hard to be good with names when she goes through them so quickly.

"Right, Donovan. Is everything alright?"

Mo scoffs. "Everything's alright with him. He spent the last two months fucking two different girls. What does he have to complain about? If I dump him, it won't make any difference because he's still sleeping with her. Seriously, why the fuck are all men assholes?"

Now, I suppose, is the time I should tell her that's not true, that there are good men out there and she'll find one. But Mo's been through her fair share of guys, and I doubt many of them fit that descriptor. She wouldn't believe me.

And frankly, when the two men I considered some of the best specimens barely talk to me, I find it unbelievable too.

The stairwell light turns on. Keys jingle from the recesses of the hallway.

"I don't know, Mo." I keep my voice low, but with my door ajar, there's no way they'd miss it.

"I thought—" her pitch rises "—I thought he was nice… like the last one."

I don't remember who the last guy was. Kevin? Mark? Emilio?

"But apparently, 'nice' means insisting on bareback or not talking to you anymore after you have sex or screwing your best friend."

"I wouldn't call any of those guys nice, Mo."

Keys jingle, closer this time, and I lift up with my elbows as Xander, dressed in his black slacks and black Draft Horse tee, nudges his bedroom door open. Jimmy leans against the wall beside him and sends an anxious glance my way.

"No," she says.

I collapse as the guys step into Xander's room, leaving the door open. "You are going to break up with him, right?"

"I'm figuring out what to do. He doesn't know I know yet."

It's simple to me. If I had a boyfriend who cheated, I'd drop him without a second thought. But that's a lot easier said than done.

"Mo, you'll find someone better than Donovan, I promise. You won't be looking, and it'll hit you in the face."

"'In the face'?" Her voice crackles with uncertainty—I'm not the best person to talk to about this.

"So hard you'll feel stupid for not having noticed it sooner."

Six

WHEN I PEEK MY HEAD THROUGH HIS OFFICE DOOR, FELIX Quigley relaxes in his black swivel chair behind his Mac Pro, fiddling with the mouse. He crouches close to the screen, straight light-brown bangs falling in his eyes, one hand resting atop the glass desk.

The narrow office doesn't have much—a full-length shelf with art books, papers, and some knickknacks. Bright light streams through the window and reflect off the glass desk. Behind him, the white office has a splash of color: an enormous five-by-eight-foot self-portrait with a Fauvist color scheme.

When I rap my knuckles against the open door, Felix looks up, brightening when he sees me. "Billie, come in! To what do I owe the pleasure?"

I sit on the chair opposite him. "I just got out of class."

"You're in Painting II with Carole, right?"

"I am. It's my favorite class this semester."

Unfortunately, Prue got stuck in a different hour block, but we managed to get the same Painting III class next semester.

Felix's olive face transforms into a grin—his natural

facial expression. "I think you're trying to flatter me, Billie. Carole's going on sabbatical next semester, so I'm teaching Painting III. Have you signed up for it?"

I raise an eyebrow. "Isn't your schedule full enough?"

Laughter rumbles in his chest. "Yes, it is."

"Well, I am taking Painting III, but I came to talk to you about the individual studios."

"Did you fill out an application? Today's the last day."

We talked about this at the beginning of the semester. It was his suggestion when he heard about my ambitious designs for the school year.

After a quick rifle through my backpack, I pass the paper to him. It's a little worse for wear than when I put it in the bag. "Rivera and Carole signed off on it, which leaves everything to you."

He takes a moment to skim the front and back. "This looks great, Billie. You're the only junior who's filled out an application so far. No guarantee, but there's still room. Unless someone with more precedence hands me a form in the next—" he glances at the clock "—seven hours, you're all set."

Despite my best intentions, enthusiasm laces my voice. "That's awesome."

"Don't get your hopes up yet, Billie." He smiles too, but it's tight, a reminder.

And I'm trying not to.

But this—art and school—is all I have. Focusing on classes. Working at the gallery. Art makes everything else easier. And thank God. Nothing is easy right now.

"I imagine you'll sign up for one next year too?"

My nod is emphatic. "Absolutely."

"Excellent." This smile is less guarded, but his eyes dart to the computer monitor. "I need to get back to this, Billie. We'll discuss the studio in a couple days, alright?"

I check the time. "Yeah, I have a long study session ahead."

We say a quick goodbye, and I head out.

◆

I collapse on the bed next to Cynthia's hunched form and lay a wrist over my glasses. I didn't bother to shut the door on my way back from the bathroom.

At my desk, the swivel chair squeaks as Prue spins. "What took you so long? I need to complain more, and Cyn isn't any help."

I snort. "Sorry. I started my period yesterday, and I'm bloated and cramping, and it's disgusting." The cramping, thankfully, isn't bad.

Prue releases a sharp, high-pitched laugh. "Yeah, but it's a great excuse to get out of a shitty date."

This time, my laughter is full and loud and obnoxious. "Oh, God, are you going to recount another terrible date? I'm not sure I can handle another story." I rise up on my elbows, and we grin at each other.

"Well, I wasn't going to, but now that you mention it." She presses her fingertips together a la Montgomery Burns. "Short version?"

I nod.

"Two nights ago, met up with this guy at the Jittery Bug, and as we were saying goodbye—because, let's be honest, no chemistry—he told me he loved me." She shakes her head, eyes squeezed shut. "Now, he won't stop sending me dick pics." She snatches her phone from the desk. "Wanna see?"

"No."

Cynthia's voice is louder than mine.

But Prue pulls up the picture and spins the phone around to show us. Luckily, I'm far enough away I can't see any details, and she turns off the screen and lays her phone down.

I pinch the bridge of my nose. "I do not need to see some random guy's dick."

"Neither do I, but that doesn't stop assholes from sending them. I told him his dick was tiny and blocked his number." She reclines in the chair. "I don't understand why men think we want to see their dicks all the time. They must not realize penises are weird."

I collapse on the mattress and lay my hand over my abdomen in an attempt to quell the ache as a new wave of pain rears its ugly head. My hot palm is calming, but not enough. I'm waiting for the acetaminophen to kick in.

"You didn't used to have painful cramps," Prue says.

I roll my eyes. "I also used to weigh a hundred pounds. I had a period like four times a year. Which is definitely something I miss."

"Have you tried the pill?" Cynthia doesn't look up from her textbook, and her shoulder-length blond waves block her face. "I use it to regulate my period."

"It can help your cramps too, and bonus, no babies!" Prue pauses, then adds, "Or can you not take that while on antidepressants?"

My palm presses harder against my abdomen as the pain ebbs. "It's complicated. I've tried a few different pills, and

I just switched to one of those ring thingies that you shove up there." That was an awkward experience. Though no more than a pelvic exam or an ultrasound. "Mostly, the antidepressants make it hard to find a complementary one. Also, the birth control is less effective."

Prue inhales sharply. "I wouldn't risk that."

"Yeah, well, I wouldn't have sex without a condom unless I trusted him implicitly, so that negates any potential risk."

"So you won't go bareback in the heat of the moment?" She waggles her eyebrows suggestively, a smirk tugging at her lips.

I force down the laughter as I sit up. "What moment do you think I'm going to have? I can't think of any man I want to sleep with right now, and even if I did, the odds I would trust him not to lie about STDs aren't high."

Prue twists a strand of brown hair around her finger. "Fair enough. Wouldn't it be weird if you got pregnant at the same time as your mom?"

My nose scrunches with distaste. "It is way too early to consider having children."

At my desk, Prue pushes off with her foot, and the chair spins round. "I don't know…" Her hands grip the armrests. "I loved growing up with a huge family, and I want that too. Four kids. Maybe more."

I cringe. "That sounds awful."

Beside me, Cynthia flips to the next page. "I hate children."

Prue grins. "Well, we know who hates all of her little brothers and sisters."

Cynthia shrugs. "I don't hate them. They're practically adults now."

A long bout of laughter bursts from Prue's lips. "'Now' being the operative word."

But per usual, Cynthia is unfazed. "I have no interest in having children or sex. If I happened to find someone compatible, they'd have to understand that."

Prue's laughter fades to a smile. "Good luck with that. Most men don't understand the meaning of the word 'no.'" She turns her attention to me. "And this is why women make better lovers."

All I can think about is Dahlia in the photo lab that night, her hands on my breasts. And how much I liked it.

I clear my throat. "I wish you all the best with your female lovers, Prue."

But she frowns. "What about you, Billie?"

"What about me?" I shift on the bed and tap my fingers against my knee. "I might be okay with one kid, but twenty years old isn't a good time to make that decision."

Prue's furrowed brow deepens. "No, I meant...female lovers?"

I bite my lip. "Prue, if you're going to flirt with me, that'll put a pretty big damper on our friendship."

She snorts. "You're not my type. It's just, last year, I always got the impression you and Dahlia..."

I freeze.

Cynthia lifts her head. For once, the conversation has piqued her interest.

"No, we never... I would've told you if something like that happened." I cannot calm my pounding heart. How does she know? How could she possibly know?

Prue wrinkles her nose. "I know. I meant, I got the impression Dahlia had a thing for you."

"Oh."

I've started to think the same thing.

I've also started to think I rather like the idea.

Dahlia has always been special—at least to me—and she's beautiful despite her unhealthy habits. I don't know why the thought never occurred before.

What would've happened if Brent didn't interrupt? Does she want me?

Prue shifts uncertainly. "I mean, that's the only logical reason she obsessed over your relationship with Xander."

From this angle, all I see of his closed bedroom door is the hinges.

"She wasn't…she wasn't obsessed."

"Do you remember when we went shopping together? We were talking about the bet—" Cynthia chuckles, but Prue doesn't pause "—and Dahlia was so pissed off you were exercising with Xander. That you'd slept with Xander. Hell, that the rest of us were rooting for you two."

I bite my lip. "That can't be right. She was lonely."

"You know her far better than I do. But you know, as an outside observer…"

I rise from the bed, jittery with unease, before Prue finishes the sentence. "I'm going to grab a drink. Maybe a snack. You two want anything?"

The voices are loud, even before I reach the ground floor.

In the kitchen, Jimmy and Micaela are poring over one of Jimmy's worn notebooks and quietly debating a phrase in his latest ballad. On the other side, Xander spreads peanut butter over a slice of bread. And between them is my destination.

"Hey, Billie." Micaela's upbeat voice echoes through the room. "Sounds like you're having fun up there."

I pile three cans of soda between my arm and chest and close the fridge. "We're goofing off." Careful to give Xander a wide berth, I snag a bag of pita chips from the cupboard, but Micaela watches as I slip past everyone to make my escape. "See you later."

"So what're the plans for your birthday?"

I stop, one foot over the threshold, and turn around. "Huh?"

Micaela laughs. "Sorry, I was talking to Xander. His birthday's right at the end of the month, you know?"

"Oh."

"It's his twenty-first." Her gaze shifts between the two guys, who give her their full attention. "I figured you'd want to do something special, right?"

Body tense, Xander twists the lid on the honey jar and slides everything into the cabinet. "I mean, I'd prefer to let it slip into oblivion like every other year, but Jim's been planning something for the past eighteen months."

I hover in the doorway. I don't know why I haven't moved yet. This conversation has nothing to do with me. But I'm compelled.

"It's in the works," Jimmy confirms when Micaela turns to him expectantly.

"Is there anything I can do to help? Whatever you need."

Jimmy's brow furrows. "I appreciate that, but you know, everything's taken care of. This has been planned for a while." His eyes wander, drifting to the floor before returning to her with renewed focus. "And I already have an assistant."

Micaela's face falls. "Who?"

He turns my way. "Billie, of course."

That makes no sense.

The knife in Xander's hand clatters into the stainless steel sink. I'm not the only one previously unaware of this development.

"She's the only person in the world who cares as much about Xander as I do."

My chest tightens.

Micaela shifts to me, her pink lips tight enough they're white. "Are you sure there's nothing I can do to help?"

I force a smile. "Don't worry about a thing. We've got it all covered."

This time, she pouts.

Over her shoulder, Jimmy's eyes exude gratitude.

"I'll be upstairs if you need anything," I add before escaping.

Seven

Rivera underlines the top sentence with a thick line as I sit down. "Remember, folks—this is your last day to work on the assignment. It's due at the end of class." He beams at the class before adding a final line under his heading. "The rest of this class will focus on your portrait assignment, so I hope you get along with your partner. Get to work!"

He nods toward the darkroom.

Inside, Jay is set up at his enlarger when I reach mine, and once everyone is at their station, Rivera switches off the fluorescents. My eyes take a moment to adjust to the safelights.

"Hey, Billie." Jay grins between flipping through his negatives. "Got any big plans this weekend?"

I pull out my stack of photo paper. "Homework and shopping."

"Sounds exciting. Gotta love groceries."

Unsure how to respond, I turn on the enlarger light to get a better view of my negatives. Of the five photos necessary for this project, four are ready to hand in. I need to develop the final picture. But I don't remember which strip my favorite was on.

"Could you rearrange your homework and grocery shopping to free up an hour?"

I slip off my glasses and look through the—

Wait. What did he say?

I straighten up, but he's far enough away he's blurry, and I tug my glasses on. "What?"

Jay gives a noncommittal shrug, cheeks pink. "I hoped Rivera would partner us together because I wanted a reason to talk to you more. But since the stars won't align in my favor, I guess I have to do it myself."

"Oh."

"Do you think you could make time this weekend?"

I freeze.

It's not that Jay's unattractive. He's at least six-foot with straight blond hair, usually molded into a fauxhawk, and striking green eyes. Prue and I have run into him at the campus gym—she's commented on his abs and crooked smile multiple times.

But the thought never crossed my mind.

"Is the idea that awful?"

I clear my throat. "Of course not. I didn't realize you were interested."

He laughs. "So what do you say, Billie?"

"I have a project due on Monday that I haven't started. I'll be painting the whole weekend."

"Oh, no, it's fine." He returns to his enlarger.

At the center of the room, Dahlia drops a sheet of photo paper into the developer, a frown on her face. We haven't talked since Saturday night. I don't know what to say to her.

"But my friend's birthday party is next Saturday." He turns to me with a grin, and I add, "It'll be a lot of drinking 'cause it's his twenty-first—we're making a big thing of it—but you can come if you want."

"I'd love to."

I jot my number on the open page of my notebook and hand him the torn-off corner. "Text me."

He responds, but in the distance, Dahlia's lips twist into a sneer.

I can't take my eyes off her.

After a moment, she spots me, and her face softens.

I glance at Jay. "I'll be back."

Without waiting for a response, I join her by the developer. Dahlia looks away. "Can I help you, Billie?"

"We should get together again for the project, right?"

"We are running out of time." Her words are noncommittal at best.

"Any suggestion on locations?"

Aside from her apartment…

"I have a few places I'd like to try. Do you know that old bridge off West Avenue? The trestle bridge?" She gives me half a second to answer. "It's out of commission. It'd be pretty with the wind blowing in your hair."

I swallow. "Okay, sure."

"And there's the Catholic church off Main or Montefalco Chapel. There's something beautiful about creepy old churches, but I'm worried it'd be too distracting as a background, that it would take away from the focal point—you."

"Let me know when and where."

"How does Saturday look?" Her voice is mechanical, forced.

"Could be better, but I'll need a break from painting. Even if it's to do more homework."

Dahlia doesn't crack a smile. "Then let's plan for Saturday at, I don't know, two? I can pick you up or we can meet there at the bridge."

"That sounds great."

"Do you have a car yet?"

I shake my head. "Just my bike."

She huffs. "I'll pick you up. Where do you live?"

I release an anxious chuckle. "On Sandalwood. It's a ten-minute drive from campus."

Dahlia's gaze seeks out something behind me. "I'm not the only person you're giving your address to, am I?"

Behind me, Jay fiddles with the dials of his enlarger.

"You're going on a date with him."

I shuffle my feet. "You heard that?"

"I guessed from the way he looks at you. You shouldn't date him. You should…"

I turn back, uncertain. "I should what?"

Her intense brown eyes send a shiver through my body. I bite my lip. What would've happened if Brent hadn't walked in? Would she have kissed me? Do I want her to kiss me?

Dahlia scoffs and turns away. "Do whatever you want. I need to finish this project."

I step backward, swallowing down my discomfort at her sharp tone.

◆

Elise lounges in her office chair and runs a hand through her dark-brown locks. "What do you think, Billie?"

I study the two top sheets.

Both Frederick Noble and Chantelle Moreau are respected artists in St. Clare's little art community. Their art sells well. They're equally accomplished and respected individuals. They both fit the Payne Street Art Gallery's brand. And they both want to debut a new series during the March First Friday Gallery Hop.

We do not have space for both of them.

With a tight frown, I flip through the pages. "How many pieces are in each series?" The information should be here somewhere.

Elise sits forward and holds out her hand, and I hand her Chantelle Moreau's file. She skims the words, searching. "Twenty-piece set."

Finally, I locate the information in Noble's file and point it out. "Twenty-six pieces. That means more potential sales."

The tight scowl on her lips isn't convinced. "Most of Moreau's pieces are larger. They sell for higher." Her eyes narrow as she pulls the file closer for proper scrutiny. "'With potential for more.' Not that that gives me much to work with." She looks up again. "What do you think?"

"We can't bank on her having more than twenty pieces for us. What's more likely to sell? Twenty-six smaller pieces or twenty larger pieces?"

"If every piece sold, Moreau would be the more profitable choice, but that never happens." Elise's jaw tightens. "I'm going with Frederick Noble on this one. His pieces sell better during First Fridays because of the more equitable price."

As I depart, I drop Noble's file on her desk. "Should I start the paperwork? Or do you want Amelia to do that?"

A vein in her forehead twitches, and I inwardly cringe.

Amelia is a year older than me, but she's hardly a model employee. Technically, her job is a higher position than mine—I'm the lowest of the low—and she handles the paperwork. But she has a tendency to let important tasks fall to the wayside. Greg, the owner and Elise's sole superior, has flipped his shit on more than one occasion due to this behavior.

"You handle it this time. Amelia's busy." She switches to the next file on her desk. "Now, I need to decide which ten applicants to accept for the Emerging Artists exhibit in April. We've had over thirty submissions."

I pause, my hand on the door frame.

She's already immersed in the paperwork, but I have to ask. I sorted through those applications, read every file, examined every portfolio, and I know—I know—my artwork is more technically accurate than the majority of the so-called emerging artists who have applied for the show.

"Elise?"

She lifts her head. "What can I do for you, Billie?"

I muster up any remnants of courage. "Would it be presumptuous to fill out an application?" When she makes no response, I add, "For the Emerging Artists exhibit."

Mouth forced into a tight circle, Elise assesses me from her swivel chair. "How old are you, Billie?"

"Twenty."

"Have any of your pieces been on display?"

My face falls. The hallways of Bradford's Kelley Center for Fine Arts during class critiques definitely don't count.

She shakes her head. "Come here."

I shuffle across her office to stop at her desk again, but

I don't sit.

"Billie, you are a hard worker, and I appreciate what you do here." She clasps her hands atop the desk—she's all business now. "But you're a student and not at all qualified for a show here. I'm not trying to be mean, but you need to understand the reality of the situation."

She lifts a few files into the air to show me the thick folders. "These artists have been working and practicing and perfecting their skills for years. They've attended art schools. They've shown their pieces in salons, boutiques, bank lobbies, coffee shops, furniture showrooms—anywhere they could. They've participated in the First Friday Gallery Hop. They've submitted to shows, won awards. They've communicated and networked. They've gotten involved. They're not looking for a handout."

"I'm not either."

"Maybe not, but if I were to consider putting your artwork—no matter how good it is—into the Emerging Artists exhibit, that's what it would be." Elise flashes me a smile—the one she reserves for closing the deal. "You have to work your way up the ladder like everyone else. Do you understand?"

"Right." I step toward the door again. "I'll write up that paperwork now."

Eight

JIMMY POKES AN AEROSOL CAN OF SILLY STRING. "JESUS, how many different colors does this come in?" He leans close, following the long line of options, then the row below to examine the generic brand.

I turn to a nearby display of wrapping paper and gift bags, organized by the colors of the rainbow. "What are we getting? I thought you had a plan."

He clears his throat. "I do. Well, I did." He stuffs his hand in his messy brown hair, a sure sign he's getting frazzled. "Okay, not as much of a plan as I let on." He offers me a sheepish smile.

I take a couple steps toward a display of colored plates, cups, and flatware. "What do we need? Is there a theme?"

He tugs a crumpled paper from his pocket. "I have a list. I'm second-guessing myself." His exhalation tousles the paper. "I'm not the ideal party planner, and you know, this is for Xander. He has high expectations."

"Don't be paranoid." I try to reassure him, but I'm not sure I'm qualified to do that anymore. "You're his best friend. He'll love whatever you put together."

He turns to me with a grin. "Thanks for doing this, Billie,

69

and thanks for before. I appreciate you covering my ass."

"What the hell was that?"

Jimmy spends a few minutes scrutinizing the Silly String before taking two cans that glow in the dark. "Okay, please don't think I'm stupid or petty. I like Micaela, but I liked her a lot more when she was this cool girl in my Jazz History summer class. Before she got this huge crush on him. I mean, I enjoy hanging out with her, but she wants to talk about him all the time, and honestly, I find the idea of them dating kind of gross."

I cock an eyebrow. "Really? They seem…like they'd be a good couple. She doesn't strike me as someone who loses herself in a relationship."

His mouth tightens into a thin line, and for a moment, all he does is stare at his notes. "Maybe they could be good together, but you know Xander." His words are quiet, careful. "He doesn't know how to open up."

I return my attention to the plastic cups. By the black and white options, there's a set that glows in the dark. "Why don't you point the finger? It's no secret why he doesn't want to open up and start a new relationship. Is glow-in-the-dark part of the theme?"

"Yes." He turns on me. "Grab them."

"How many?"

"We'll have fifty people in and out of the house." He quirks his mouth to the side in concentration. "Or more. I don't know how many people aside from Kylie and Tiff will come from the bar. It could be a lot."

I reach for some plates, but he lays a hand on my arm.

"Just the cups. We won't have many snacks."

I grab two bags of glow-in-the-dark plastic cups, one-hundred-count each. "What else do we need?"

Eyes narrowed to slits, Jimmy reads his notes. "Tablecloths, straws, streamers, balloons, glow sticks. Maybe some confetti, but I don't want to clean that up… Everything needs to be white or glow-in-the-dark. Oh, and a fog machine or a strobe light."

It takes more effort than I have to hold in a laugh. "Why not both?"

He snatches a bag of neon-colored straws from the bottom shelf. "That might break my budget, but if I can afford it, yes."

"What about the blacklights to match this?"

"Already bought and paid for. They're cheaper at Walmart." He nods around the aisle, and I follow him to the balloon section. The closest option is white. "I also have highlighters and a gate for the stairs—I don't want to go to bed only to find some drunk couple messing around." He snags two rolls of white streamers.

"Our bedrooms conveniently come equipped with locks, and we have the only keys."

"True."

His arms are full, and mine will be in a minute. I search for a basket and discover a stack at the end of the aisle.

When I return, he drops his haul inside the yellow carrier with a grateful sigh, and I turn to the display of plastic tablecloths. Yes, some glow in the dark.

"No offense, but you give yourself too much credit."

I freeze. "What do you mean?"

"Seriously, Billie, he grew up with parents who were never there, went to fifteen different schools by high school, and had a total of one friend before Bradford. You think

71

you're the reason he's closed off?" He chuckles as he grabs three tablecloths. "I mean, yeah, you didn't help, but he never lets anyone in. We've seen and learned the most, but it's the tip of the iceberg."

My grip tightens on the basket handles, and he drops the tablecloths inside.

"He sidesteps every question about his childhood or parents. He never talks about his feelings—and it's not because of the typical I'm-a-man-so-I-can't-have-feelings bullshit because you know he doesn't believe that. He refuses to be vulnerable, as if sheer force of will could prevent him from getting hurt."

I take a shaky breath.

If Xander really thinks that, I already proved him wrong. Without trying—in fact, with every intention of doing the opposite—I hurt him more than I thought possible.

Before that moment, I always saw him as the strong one. He was my rock. I relied on him to keep me stable and secure, and although I ended things to learn to rely on myself, a small part of me expected him to remain a beacon in my life.

I misjudged how difficult that must've been for him.

"He puts on this show, pretending he knows what he's doing, and you find yourself trusting him, even though he's as lost as you are." Jimmy lets his words hang in the air. "We're adults, but we're not as grown up as we think we are."

I run over the list in my head and stalk down the aisle, Jimmy trailing behind me.

Glow sticks. There's a box of 150, and I offer it to him.

"Yeah, that's great." His voice is quiet again, and his pink cheeks squish against his glasses at his sudden recognition.

"I'm sorry. We don't need to talk about this."

I move to the next aisle. "We should look at the fog machines, right? Where are they?"

"At the other end…"

We pass a couple aisles, but I pause. "Do you like her?"

Jimmy stumbles to a stop ahead of me. "What?"

"Does the reason you think Xander and Micaela would be 'gross' have anything to do with your feelings for her? You like her, don't you?"

His mouth contorts into a frown. "I don't deny I've considered it, but not seriously. I like someone else." He releases a short laugh. "I know I don't have a chance with her. We aren't really friends, and she has a boyfriend. But I'm not over her yet."

Anxiety tugs at my stomach. I want to ask who, but he won't tell me. I'm impressed he said this much.

Jimmy scratches the nape of his neck. "What about you? You'd be okay with them dating?"

I tilt my head, assessing his concerned face. "Why wouldn't I be?"

His forehead furrows in disbelief. "Because, Billie…"

But he can't bring himself to finish the sentence.

"Jimmy, it doesn't bother me. She legitimately cares about him, and he deserves that more than anyone. If they dated, I'd be happy for him."

"Don't you still…?"

I grimace. "There might be some…remnants. But I have a date for the party."

Jimmy's jaw drops open. "Really?"

My phone buzzes in my pocket.

"Why is that surprising?" I pull the phone out, but my

irritation distracts me. "I'm allowed to date people. I'm not going to pine after him forever."

Jimmy shakes his head. "No, no, of course. I just didn't realize you were dating. Once again, I'll be the only one without a girlfriend."

I roll my eyes. "I'm not dating a girl."

"You know what I meant."

The text is from Dahlia: *Can't do it today. We'll reschedule.*

I scoff. She was never reliable before. Why should she start now?

When I look up, Jimmy's closer to a themed aisle.

He sends me a toothy grin. The lane he enters is all pink and sparkly. "Please don't think I'm crazy..." He stops in front of a display of tiaras with faux diamonds and feather boas. "We have to."

"You can't be serious."

"One hundred percent." He reaches out to stroke a boa, then nudges a few pink and purple ones aside to find a white boa with flecks of silver. "This is Xander. He'll love it."

I search the shelves, amused, for something—

There.

A pink and white sash with the words "Birthday Bitch" in a loopy script.

I yank it off the hook and dangle it in front of Jimmy's nose, smirking. "This is perfect."

His eyes light up.

◆

Jimmy parks his truck in the driveway and shifts into neutral before turning off the engine, but I stare at the red car parked beside us.

"Xander's here." I shift for a better view of the Camaro. "He was supposed to go to work."

Jimmy shifts toward the back seat, where the bags of party supplies are waiting to hide in Jimmy's bedroom closet. "Okay, go in and make sure he's not paying attention."

A quiet scoff escapes my lips. "What? No, you distract him. I can carry everything."

"My room is locked."

I hold my hand out, palm up. "So give me the key."

But he simply raises his eyebrows. "Why is it a problem, Billie?"

"We can drive around the block." I let my hand fall. "Maybe he'll be gone then."

"I have to write an essay for my music theory class, Billie. I can't drive around all afternoon because you're too scared to be in the same room as Xander."

"I'm not scared to be in the same room as him."

Jimmy snorts. "Right. That's why you leave the second he walks into the room or why you never look at him or why you stopped trying to be friends less than a week after we moved in together."

I stare at the fence blocking access to our measly backyard.

The truth isn't as simple as Jimmy believes. I never look at him because the moment his eyes meet mine, he looks away. He doesn't want to look at me or talk to me—let alone be my friend.

It was obvious after the first day he'd rather be anywhere else. Every smile was forced—badly enough I could tell how fake they were—and every look was pained. I cried myself to sleep that night.

And the next few nights.

Then, I flew to Paris for two months.

Hesitantly, I unbuckle my seatbelt and exit the truck.

◆

Inside, Xander's at the stove, and I text Jimmy: *He's cooking. You should be good.*

Keep him there, is the response.

How the fuck am I supposed to do that?

When I enter the kitchen, he's adding the top layer to a quesadilla, a spatula in his right hand. He glances over at my arrival, and I open the fridge and bend low to examine the contents.

Surely, I don't have to say anything. I'm blocking the exit.

A phone rings.

I pull back enough to watch as Xander spins toward the source on the counter, then answers.

"Hey, Rhea, isn't this like a month early?"

In the distance, the front door opens, and Jimmy, I imagine, carries the bags up to his bedroom.

"He wants to talk about what?" His voice is suddenly sharp and unmistakable. "I thought I made it clear a year ago. I don't—"

I rifle through the fridge, searching for nothing in particular.

On the other side of the door, the cheese sizzles. Then, the acrid smell of smoke.

"Fine. Put him on. I'll take the call."

I straighten up to my full height and close the fridge

door as he scrambles to flip the quesadilla while holding the phone. There's a hint of dark brown at the edges.

"Sir." His voice, devoid of emotion, sends a chill down my spine.

All I can do is stare.

It's not a tone he uses often, but it's decidedly familiar. All the times we spoke after my mother's wedding, he used that tone consistently up until we moved into this house. Occasionally, it still creeps into his voice.

"Skip the pleasantries, Dad. Let's not pretend this is anything other than what it is." His head jerks to the side, flipping loose hair away. "It's not on the table. I can't look past the drawbacks."

I open the fridge again and grab a bottle of water.

His knuckles, wrapped around the spatula handle, are white. "No, I won't change my mind. It's been three years since you first brought it up, and I feel the same now as I did then."

I try to twist open the lid quietly, but I'm unsuccessful. The sharp sound is cacophonous.

"Nan gave it to me."

Xander, though, is too distracted to notice.

"I never said that." He scoffs. "I have so many responses to that, I don't know where to begin. It's not some big expensive thing, and you don't care about the sentimental value. Nan gave it to me."

The cold water is refreshing on my throat.

Jimmy's footsteps return to the stairs, and the front door opens and closes again.

I stretch my head out the doorway. No one's in the foyer. How is Jimmy not done?

Xander turns off the burner now that smoke rises from the quesadilla. "No, because if I do, it will be one hundred percent my decision. Your opinion doesn't mean a thing." He slides the food onto a cutting board and grabs the chopping knife. "I don't care if that means I don't get my inheritance. Keep your fucking money. There's nothing you have that I want."

He shouldn't have a knife while angry.

He freezes. "What do you mean? I didn't..." His grip on the knife tightens. "Fine, keep it."

I glance toward the door as Jimmy returns. That has to be all the bags. There's no way this requires three trips.

"There's no point arguing with you," Xander snaps. "I can't win—and don't give me that bullshit."

The other person on the line is loud enough their voice carries across the kitchen, but Xander cuts them off.

"No, I'm done. I'll talk to you in a month when Rhea puts me on your schedule again."

When he hangs up, he slams the phone against the counter. His body is shaking.

"You okay?" I venture to ask.

If possible, he stiffens more at my voice. "Don't worry about it."

I take another drink of my water, and he dumps his half-burnt quesadilla onto a plate, snatches his phone from the counter, and stalks toward the exit. I step aside so he can pass.

Hopefully, Jimmy has everything hidden now. There's no way I'll take on Xander when he's literally fuming—

His arm knocks into mine. The bottle drops to the floor. Water pools across the linoleum.

"Shit."

Xander continues as if nothing happened.

I scoff. "Where are you going?"

He comes to an abrupt stop. "You can handle cleaning up a little water by yourself, can't you?"

I grit my teeth. "What the hell is that supposed to mean? Of course I can handle it, but you knocked it out of my hand. The least you could do is apologize."

He turns with a deep glare. "You should hold on tighter."

"And you should pay closer attention to where you're walking."

"This is a tight kitchen."

"Not tight enough you can't pass me without spilling my drink."

Xander's eyes narrow. "Fine. It was my fault. Guess what? I don't fucking care."

I huff, but he doesn't give me the chance to speak.

"I'm not helping you clean it up. You are the last person I want to talk to right now."

Without another word, he turns on his heel and heads upstairs.

For a moment, I'm too stunned to move.

I know he'd typically prefer not to be alone with me, and that conversation with his father didn't go well...but I'm struck by his reaction to me. Even before we were friends, he was never that harsh.

I pluck a towel from a drawer to clean up the water. It's all I can do to fight down the nausea welling in my stomach.

Nine

This time, Felix Quigley's door is closed, but on the other side of the narrow glass panel, he's typing at his Mac and chatting on the office phone.

I sit on a chair in the waiting area. He should be done soon. These are his office hours.

While I wait, I flip through my phone apps. Anything to distract myself.

Everything else falls to the wayside when I pull up my messages.

Mo and I haven't talked for a couple days. She hasn't said what she decided to do about the situation with Donovan. Which makes it sound like she doesn't plan to break up with him. I can't imagine why she wouldn't dump him on the spot.

How's your afternoon? I text her, then wait.

Inside his office, Felix returns the phone to the receiver, but he doesn't open the door. Instead, he fiddles around on his computer more.

The phone vibrates in my grip.

Boring as fuck, her message reads. *Cannot wait for this semester to end. Although, then I'm stuck with Mom and Rob.*

80

That, I can sympathize with.

Another text: *Speaking of, Mom had her ultrasound. Couldn't see the goods, so sex is undetermined. But she'll have more ultrasounds because of the lithium.*

I should care. This is something I should care about. But I can't bring myself to be happy or sad or frustrated about Mom's pregnancy.

The door opens, and Felix's upbeat voice booms into the waiting area. "Billie! I didn't realize you were here. Come in."

I turn off my phone and follow him inside. "I didn't want to bug you too much."

He flashes me a grin and drops into his chair with exaggerated effort, and I sit across from him. "What can I do for you?"

I hesitate, my hand gripping the phone. "Actually, I wanted to ask you. I never got confirmation or anything—about the individual studio—so I'm not sure..."

His face falls. "Yes." All exuberance is gone. "I sent out the emails on Friday to notify the students who will have an individual studio next semester."

I recline in the chair. "I wasn't one of them."

It's not like I had much of a shot, but I can't say I'm not disappointed.

"No, Billie, I'm sorry." He rests his elbows on the desk, hands clasped together. "I know you had your heart set on this, but students working on their senior projects get precedence. I got several last-minute applications."

"It's fine." I'm still processing, but I force a smile. "I figured I wouldn't get it since I'm a junior, but you have to try, right?"

"Absolutely."

When I rise from my chair, ready to leave, Felix calls after me. "Billie, don't take this as discouragement—it's not. Apply next year. You'll have seniority, and you'll get your studio."

◆

"You want to stay the night?"

I withdraw some sweet potatoes from one of the kitchen island's bottom drawers while Dad rifles through the fridge. "I want a relaxing evening for once, Dad. No drama."

He retrieves a gallon bag with two boneless chicken breasts, soaking in marinade. "Are things too stressful at the house?"

"Not much more than normal."

He makes a short humming sound.

After a quick wash in the sink, the potatoes are ready to go. I pat them dry, stab each with a fork, and wrap them in aluminum foil.

"Tell me what's going on, Mina." He pours a few table-spoons of oil in the pan, heating up.

"I don't know what to say, Dad. Nothing is going how it's supposed to."

He pauses. "How are things supposed to go?"

I push the wrapped sweet potatoes into a group and lean against the island. There are plenty of other things I could do, but in this moment, I don't want to.

How should my life be going?

Dad worries a lot—more than he should—but he under-stands me.

"Better than this," I manage. "I think I screwed up. Switching majors was a mistake."

"What are you talking about Mina? You're a wonderful artist."

I slump over the counter. "I didn't get the studio next semester." I turn to him, but he's facing away. "I vaguely suggested submitting something to the Emerging Artists exhibit in April, and Elise went off on me about how unprofessional and inexperienced I am. Carole says my brush strokes are rigid and unrefined."

With a pair of tongs, he lays the chicken breast in the hot oil. It spits and sizzles. "It's barely been a year and a half since you switched majors, Mina. You're working hard." He glances over his shoulder. "These things will get easier."

"Is the oven up to temp?"

Dad covers the chicken with the lid before stepping aside. "It's been ready for ten minutes. We got distracted by the puzzle."

I toss the potatoes on the rack and pull away from the heat, and when I'm out of the way, he returns to the pan. "Everything I do is wrong. I'm fucking it all up."

"What about your photography class? You said you have that portrait project. You have a keen eye for people."

My body stiffens. "I'm not sure I have a keen eye for anything, especially people."

He sends me a reproachful look. "Why do you say that?"

I bite my lip. "My partner for that project—we were friends last year, and I don't…"

"The girl with the flower name?"

"Yeah." I take a bag of brown rice from the cupboard and a measuring cup. "I think she might—I think I might…" I

83

run a hand through my hair. "I don't even know."

"What are you saying, Mina?" he asks as I fill the cooker with rice and water. "Do you think you might become friends again? Would that be alright?"

I push down the lever to start the rice cooker. "She doesn't want to be friends, Dad. She wants—well, I don't know what she wants. Maybe me."

He flips the chicken and covers the pan again before turning to me. "What do you mean?"

My gaze drops to the floor.

"You think she has romantic feelings for you?"

"That's what Prue thinks. She's usually right about people."

"What about you? Do you have romantic feelings for her?" Dad lays a comforting hand on my shoulder. "No one would think less of you."

I shake my head. "It doesn't matter what my feelings are. Dahlia's never been in a good place, and I cannot let her drag me down with her. She's unhealthy…"

"But?"

A rueful smile pulls at my lips. "But I care about her a lot. In spite of everything, I care."

"What about Xander?"

My shrug is involuntary. "There's nothing to say about Xander. Jimmy's friend Micaela has a huge crush on him, but he'd rather have meaningless sex than a relationship. I don't want to think about how many girls he's slept with now. I'm fairly certain he hates me."

Dad squeezes my shoulder again. "I doubt he hates you."

"Jimmy cornered me into helping plan Xander's birthday party. It's this weekend. At our house."

"Will there be alcohol?"

I snort. "It's his twenty-first, Dad. Of course there'll be alcohol." I let a beat pass. "But I will have a date."

"Dahlia?"

"A guy in my photography class."

"How did she take that?" He casts a curious glance in my direction and releases me. "How did Xander?"

I swallow, uneasy. "He doesn't know, and she...wasn't pleased."

"You like this guy?"

"I don't know him, but I have to try."

Dad pulls me into a hug. "You're doing fine, Mina."

Ten

JAY ARRIVES PROMPTLY AT TEN, RIGHT BEHIND A GROUP from Xander's business classes. Decidedly earlier than any normal person. He admires my outfit without shame. "You look beautiful."

Prue said the same thing after she zipped up the fitted white dress—so tight it looks like underwear. I wasn't keen on the idea, but with the blacklights, I needed to wear white and she insisted. There are no blacklights in the foyer, but my dress glows, unlike the highlighter design Prue drew around my eyes and hairline. Three glow stick necklaces dangle around my neck.

"Thanks."

Jay displays a bottle of whiskey with a ribbon stuck to the label. He texted me earlier for my friend's favorite alcohol. That was an easy question to answer.

I accept the bottle, and he follows me through the living room to the kitchen.

We replaced all the bulbs with blacklights and brought out a few lamps to add to the effect. White streamers, lit up blue-violet, hang from the ceiling and walls in arches and swirls. Most of the intricate designs were created and orchestrated by Prudence. Two dozen balloons bounce around the room.

The decorations are simple. We taped white sheets of printer paper along the walls, even the bathroom. White blankets lay across the couch. A glow-in-the-dark tablecloth is taped around the coffee table. A strobe light flashes from the entertainment stand next to the TV.

Jimmy did manage a fog machine too, which he set up on the stairs behind the gate. We could barely figure out how to put the gate up and take it down while sober, so drunken party-goers can't master it.

"This is intense." Jay examines the room with an appreciative gaze. "They went all out."

I frown. "Yeah, we did."

"Where's the birthday boy?" In the blacklight, his white t-shirt reflects well, but otherwise, he's wearing jeans and sneakers.

In the kitchen, I set the whiskey on the card table with cups, jungle juice glowing blue, and other assorted alcohols. "Not here yet. Like I said, you're early."

I have no idea when Xander will arrive, but it should be any time. Kylie, Draft Horse's general manager, insisted he have his birthday off. I have no idea where he went to kill time.

"You want anything?" Jay pours himself a cup of the jungle juice and takes a long drink. A tiny moan of delight escapes his mouth. "Have you tried this?"

Before I can protest, he fills a second cup.

"I don't want any," I say when he offers it to me. "Thanks, though."

His brow creases. "Really? Because—"

"I'd love some!" Prue brushes against my arm as she takes the drink. "You want some Mountain Dew, Billie?"

Grateful, I accept her half-full cup, lipstick smeared on the rim.

"I don't think we've met." She extends her hand to Jay, a playful twinkle in her eyes. "Prudence, and you are?"

He fumbles with his drink to shake her hand. "Jay Ogden. Billie and I are in Photo I together. You're familiar."

I take a drink of the soda. "Yeah, we've run into you at the gym."

"That's it." He flashes his crooked smile. "Good to meet you, Prudence."

She grins, then turns her attention to me. "Any idea when Xander will be here? Micaela was asking, and I lost track of Jimmy twenty minutes ago."

"He'd know better than me. Where'd he go?"

"If I knew, I wouldn't be asking you." She twirls the cup between her fingers and takes a tentative sip.

"*Billie!*"

We spin round to find Jimmy approaching, flushed. He hooks his arms around our shoulders, and I cringe at the sudden pressure.

"Billie, where's this date?"

My brown furrows. "How are you drunk already?"

Jimmy giggles. "I think I made the jungle juice too strong. I've had one cup."

"Well, he's standing right in front of you. This is Jay."

When Jay offers his hand, Jimmy shakes it thoroughly. "Jimmy Powell. Good to meet you."

"This is a nice house," Jay says. "Thanks for letting me come."

Jimmy squeezes my shoulders with a snort. "I couldn't prevent her from bringing a date to her own house if I wanted to." He releases me, twisting around and straining to see the rest of the room. "Xander should've been here twenty minutes ago."

I pull out my phone. It's five till eleven. Where is he?

Prue too examines her phone. "Cynthia's bailing." Her lips flatten into a thin line as she slips it into her pocket. "Now who am I supposed to hang out with?"

"You can hang out with me." Jimmy pokes her, but her body tenses at the contact. "But I need to find the birthday boy. He should be here."

"Hey, guys!"

We turn toward the entrance.

David, dressed in a striped shirt and white skinny jeans, saunters into the room. He claps Jimmy on the shoulder and gives me a quick hug. "Haven't seen you in ages, Billie."

"Hey." It's been months, but I return the embrace—it's nice to find someone genuinely happy to see me. "You seen Xander? Jimmy lost him."

"I did not!"

Prue rolls her eyes. "You're the one he'd contact."

David chuckles. "No sign out there, but you need to turn up the music so people can dance."

Jimmy cringes. "Okay, but we're listening to hours of Foreigner, Rush, and AC/DC. I don't think anyone wants to dance to that. But that's what Xander wants—if he shows up."

David snorts. "Not the best party music."

"You could start singing," Prue adds. "You've got a great voice."

David doesn't get embarrassed often, but his obsidian cheeks flush with pleasure. "If you're hearing rumors from Jimmy, he's biased."

A snort escapes before I can prevent it. Jimmy's had a bit of a crush on him since their vocals class last year.

But Jimmy steps out to call Xander without a reaction.

A hand presses to my shoulder, and when I turn, Jay's lips curl into a smile.

I step closer. "Sorry. People are...distracting. You wanna go somewhere and talk? Jimmy will sort out Xander."

"It's fine." His shoulder brushes mine. "What's the plan for tonight? Any party games? Or just dancing?"

"The main plan is for people to get trashed—well, for Xander to get trashed."

"How about a tour of the house?"

I swallow down the rest of the Mountain Dew and drop the cup in the trash can. "Sure, let's do a tour."

Jay follows me without question.

"It's not much." I gesture around the room as we walk. "This is the kitchen, obviously. Drinks, sink, fridge, whatever. Pretty straightforward."

In the living room, I point out the TV, couch, and a bookshelf, but he saw this room earlier.

We move on.

"This is the dining room—or supposed to be." The room is lit up by a chandelier of half a dozen blacklights. "We don't use it often." The table, like the coffee table in the living room, has a glow-in-the-dark tablecloth taped on.

"I was surprised when your friend said something." He pauses. "You live here?"

"Yeah." I move into the next room. "This is the foyer,

which you saw when you came in." I pause by the door. "There isn't much else."

Jay stops. "What about upstairs? You live here, so you have a bedroom, right?"

I turn to the stairs and pause at the bottom, and he joins me.

"It's blocked off."

"Yep."

The gate is on the third step, and even sober, I don't want to deal with the locking mechanism. Jimmy didn't want to lock the doors—he didn't want to lose his keys while drunk. I admit, I felt similarly. This dress has no pockets; my phone is shoved inside the bodice under my arm. It's uncomfortable.

On the other side of the gate, the fog machine is perched on a step, plugged in via an extension cord from the upstairs hallway. The fog is cold and moist against my bare legs.

"You have your own bedroom, right?"

I cock an eyebrow. "What?"

"You live with two guys."

"Yeah, so?"

Jay hesitates. "You're not…I dunno, sharing?"

My jaw tightens as I process. "They're my friends, I pay for my own room, and I'm not sleeping with either of them."

Jay finishes his jungle juice and sets the cup on the bottom step. "That's good to know." He steps closer, lays his hand on my shoulder, and presses his lips to mine.

The kiss is brief, but his hand lingers.

It takes a minute to adjust. Not because he surprised me—that kiss was utterly predictable—but because I don't know whether I want to kiss him. He's perfectly nice, though eager to jump into bed, but any awkwardness has stemmed from the fact that we don't know each other.

"Was that wrong?" He withdraws his hand. "I'm sorry."

"No, not wrong."

"I like you, Billie." His face morphs into his crooked smile.

"You don't know me."

He shrugs. "Then I want to get to know you. Would you mind if I kissed you again?"

"No."

This time, he wraps an arm around my waist and tugs me toward him. I stumble as his mouth meets mine. My back hits the wall, and he moves closer, supporting himself with a hand by my head.

I struggle to steady myself, and he pushes me harder against the wall.

And I let him.

Which is all I can say for my actions.

He isn't doing anything wrong. The kiss is decent, and if it were someone else, maybe I'd feel something. Hopefully something resembling arousal.

But he's not someone else, and I feel nothing.

He asked if I minded another kiss. My answer was accurate. I don't. But do I want him to kiss me? My answer is the same: No, I don't.

Jay moves his lips down my neck, nipping at the flesh, and his hand trails up to massage my breast. "You know," he whispers in my ear when I gasp at the pressure, "I'd love to see your bedroom."

He trails kisses along my collarbone, and I sigh at the touch.

Nearby, something crashes.

"*Shit!*"

That's a new voice.

"You're so fucking drunk. I know you're supposed to do twenty-one shots tonight, but you shouldn't be halfway there before the party."

My eyes flash open.

An East Asian woman supporting each arm, Xander stands on unsteady feet in the foyer, his leather jacket glimmering in the strobe light flashes. He stares at me.

I nudge Jay away.

"Something wrong?"

Xander stumbles, and the older Asian woman catches him before he falls. "Jesus, Xander, I didn't think you had that much. Where's the kitchen?"

The younger girl, her black hair in a tight bun, trails after them.

I take Jay's hand, nodding toward the kitchen. "The birthday boy's here."

But the front door opens again.

The woman who walks in barely glances up from her phone as she stalks toward the living room. I think he said her name is Cassie. And her white dress? It covers her as well as anything Jessica Rabbit wears.

The kitchen is a mess, but my focus is on Xander, sitting on a chair, his leather jacket slung over the back. Jimmy hovers over him, a second cup of jungle juice in his hand. Behind the chair, Cassie leans against the wall, still looking through her phone. The older Asian woman, in her late twenties or early thirties, forces a glass of water into Xander's fist.

93

"Sorry, Jim," she says, "he said he'd pick us up, but he got there four hours early and started drinking."

"It's fine, it's fine." Jimmy takes a sip. "I'm not surprised. He hates his birthday."

I step farther into the room, leaving Jay behind. "How much did he drink?"

Xander looks up, but his stern gaze shifts to Jimmy. "Seriously, dude, I'm not that drunk. I have fifteen shots to go."

He says it with complete seriousness. As if doing twenty-one shots is completely logical and, you know, not incredibly dangerous.

Someone shoves through—Micaela, wringing her hands. She pauses a foot ahead of me when she spots Cassie.

Jimmy crouches, his glasses sliding down his pointed nose. "You sure?"

But the older Asian purses her lips. "Then why did you fall over the second we're inside the door? You were acting pretty fucking drunk."

Xander scoffs. "Shut up, Kylie, I'm fine."

Ah, the GM.

"You shouldn't tell your boss to shut up." But she snickers. "You might lose your job."

He smirks. "Like you could survive without me. I train all your bartenders and make more tips than you."

"Because you flirt shamelessly with all the female patrons." She ruffles his hair. "But yeah, you're my star employee. Please don't kill yourself tonight."

And if that's Kylie, the younger girl is her little sister Tiff, who works as a waitress at the bar. She pours herself a cup of jungle juice despite Kylie's glare and stands beside Jimmy.

Behind Xander, Cassie puts her phone away and leans toward him. "No one as shamelessly as me, I hope." And she giggles when he turns and whispers in her ear.

"I guess the excitement's over." I turn to find Jay. "For now."

"Yeah, I guess."

Micaela pushes past me to leave, tears pricking the corners of her eyes.

Jay offers me his hand. "Want to finish that tour?" He gives me time to answer, but I hesitate. "Or we can grab another drink or something?"

We grabbed another drink.

Well, he got more jungle juice, and I got water. And twenty minutes later, we chat aimlessly in the living room.

He says something, but I'm not listening.

I'm too busy watching the drunken idiot at the center of the room.

The music is louder now, shaking the windows, but David was right—Xander's love for classic rock is not conducive to dancing. That's perfectly fine with me. I have no interest in dancing and would prefer Jay not ask, but a few disappointed people slump along the wall.

In the middle of the living room, wearing his glowing birthday sash, tiara, and fluffy boa, Xander has had eighteen shots. And he's not fucking stopping.

By now, he's too drunk to care about the consequences of his alcohol consumption. Especially with his hand clutching Cassie's ass over her dress.

"He's never been this drunk before."

"Huh?" Jay's brow furrows in confusion.

"Xander," I clarify. "Xander has never been this drunk before."

He slips his hand into mine. "You're worried about your friend. He'll be alright."

"Billie?"

A flushed Jimmy approaches with a deep frown. "Have you seen David? He went to grab another beer and never came back. I can't find him anywhere."

I glance around, but even drunk Jimmy isn't totally unobservant. "No, I haven't, sorry. I lost track of everyone."

A delicate hand claps on his shoulder, and he jumps. "Jim, when are we going to change this shit music? There's only so many times I can listen to 'Hot-Blooded.'"

I snort as Kylie sidles around him. "Good luck getting that past Xander."

She turns to me with a grin. "Considering he just drank shot number twenty, I don't think he'll notice."

But Jimmy shakes his head. "I don't care how drunk he is. He'll notice."

I'd wager he's right. Simply because Xander somehow manages to appear sober no matter how drunk he is. But he's never drunk this much so quickly before.

"I can't keep track of how many times he's tried to 'educate' me on music. At least we agree on Metallica." The happy memories tug at my lips.

Jimmy snorts, but his eyes reveal the raw discomfort.

Unspoken, but he's right again. The playful arguments Xander and I had over music and anime and freaking *Gilmore Girls* are no more. Reminiscing over the past only makes the present more difficult.

I bite my lip. "Where'd Micaela go? I haven't seen her

in a while."

"I think she left." Jimmy scans the dark living room, and his body stiffens. "Billie, did you invite them?"

"Who?"

I follow his line of sight to where Dahlia, wearing a white sundress and neon orange pumps, prances through the room. Trailing behind her, Brent already has a glow stick necklace and a cup of jungle juice.

"I didn't tell her we were having a party. She didn't hear anything from me."

A hand spins Jimmy around, and the space between him and Kylie reveals her little sister, Tiff. "Come dance with me." She yanks him toward the middle of the room.

He splutters under her grip. "I can't dance."

But he lets her lead him to the open space and wrap her arms around his neck.

Kylie scoffs. "She has a huge crush on him. I told her to leave him alone since he's hung up on another girl, but she won't listen to her big sister."

I nod.

Beside me, Jay says, "Hey, my little sister won't listen to me either."

Kylie locks onto me. "I don't think we've been introduced." She holds out her hand. "Kylie Guerrero, general manager at Draft Horse."

"I know. My roommates both work for you. It'd be weird not to know who you are." We shake. "I'm Billie Dixon."

Her face perks up—is that a good thing? "Oh, so you live with them? I don't recognize the name."

I pull away.

That's utterly predictable. I can't imagine Jimmy and

Xander discuss me while working. But there's a pang in my chest.

Kylie steps closer to the wall and lowers her voice to a whisper. "You must know him well, so I want to ask…"

"What?"

"You don't think he and Cassie are actually going anywhere, do you?" She flashes me a wide-eyed look, a grimace on her face. "Because I can't stand her."

I shake my head. "I have no idea. I just want him to be happy."

Kylie scowls—she was hoping for a stronger response. "Don't quote me on this please, but I wish he were with his ex. He was so happy last spring, and now, he's constantly angry. He's not over her yet."

"No." My voice is firmer than it should be. "Of course he's over her. He wouldn't be with Cassie if he weren't over her."

She tilts her head and stares.

On my other side, Jay releases a quiet laugh. "He really is one of your best friends."

"Of course he is."

But Kylie's lips flatten into a tight line.

Then, Dahlia, a cup of jungle juice in hand, squeezes between me and Jay. Her body presses against my arm. Behind her, Jay stumbles backward, but I have no time for him. "Billie, why are you hiding here?" She giggles and squeezes my bare shoulder.

She's had a drink or two or three.

Against the opposite wall, Brent wraps his hand around the waist of a random blonde. On the makeshift dance floor, Jimmy and Tiff are the only couple dancing, her head on his shoulder. And Xander is busy slipping his hand down Cassie's dress.

"We should dance," Dahlia says, drawing my attention again. "I want to dance with you."

"I don't."

Her grip tightens on my shoulder, and she steps closer, her eyes boring into mine. "I want to dance with you. You look cute in this dress."

"I'm going to get another drink," Jay says before disappearing into the kitchen.

My gaze follows him but stops as he passes the dancing couple. Her hands are entangled in his hair, his hands are on her waist, and their lips are sealed together. Jimmy is making out with a girl.

Dahlia scoffs. "Pay attention to me, Billie."

I've never seen him kiss someone. I couldn't picture him kissing someone. But there they are, right in full view of everyone—including her older sister, his boss.

Dahlia's thin fingers grip my jaw and draw me to her.

She's closer than before. Closer than I realized. And she stares. "Pay attention to me."

This time, her voice is soft, and I strain to hear her over the pounding music. She licks her lips. I am mesmerized.

But the moment she moves in, I press a hand to her shoulder, and she backs away.

My eyes search the room. Any reason not to look at her.

Jimmy and Tiff are dancing again, but his face is red. Jay hasn't returned from the kitchen. I don't know the last time I saw Prudence.

And Xander's missing.

Eleven

Hunched over the kitchen sink, one hand in his thick black hair, the other gripping the counter with white knuckles, Xander doesn't notice when I lean beside him. He's too busy hurling up his guts in the stainless steel basin. The tiara is long gone, but the sash and boa wrap haphazardly around his torso.

I run a hand up and down his spine. "Why in the world did you think this was a good idea?"

He pauses, heaving. Then, more comes out.

"Twenty-one shots is beyond stupid."

He grunts, though I doubt he understands. He slumps against me.

"Ready for bed?"

Another grunt.

I turn on the faucet and let the disposal run to clear the sink. Xander cringes at the whirring noise, burying his face in my afro, and I wrap an arm around him.

When the sink is clean, I direct him toward the stairs.

Someone clears their throat behind us.

I stop when I see her. "Dahlia…"

Her white sundress is held up by flimsy spaghetti straps,

and the skirt ruffles from the fog machine's damp breeze. The blacklights silhouette the curve of her waist, her hips, her slender legs.

"Can I help you with something?"

She lifts an eyebrow. "You're the one who needs help, Billie." Without another word, she tosses Xander's arm around her shoulder.

Upstairs, Xander's room is dark, but I hesitate to turn on the light. Unfortunately, I don't have a choice. In the months we've lived together, I haven't once been inside his bedroom.

The light is blinding, and he clings to me, burying his face in the crook of my neck. "Turn it off."

I'm impressed he can manage a full sentence. Throwing up must have been helpful.

"In a minute. We need to get you out of these sweaty clothes."

He needs help to sit—and again to keep from falling flat on his ass—but when he's steady, he hooks his hands around the edge of the mattress and squints at me.

The room itself is minimally decorated. Xander has never kept more belongings than what he can fit in his car. Most of the furniture here was purchased from the local thrift store, but the bed is different. When Charlie and Thea heard he was going to buy a frame and mattress via Craigslist, they added an extra to the truck of Jimmy's things. No matter how much he wanted to decline, Xander couldn't tell Thea Powell no.

I unwrap his boa first, then the sash, both of which require more coordination than he has.

Dahlia lays a hand to my shoulder. "I'll get some water."

101

Once she heads downstairs, I drop to my knees to yank off his shoes.

He struggles to focus on me. "I didn't think you'd come."

I pause, but his eyes are bleary.

"Tonight. To the party."

There's a line of sweat along his brow, and his grip tightens on the mattress. Somehow, his sentences, though mostly fragments, make sense.

"It's your birthday, idiot."

"Yeah, but…"

He doesn't have to finish the sentence. I can fill it with a thousand reasons I could've refused to attend tonight. But we don't talk. We aren't friends. He doesn't want me here. Hell, most of the time, he can't look at me.

I rise and step closer so he can focus on me. "Xander, I don't care what's going on between us or how long it's been since we've talked. This is your birthday party. I wouldn't miss it for anything."

It takes a moment for his blank face to morph into a reserved smile. "I'm glad you're here."

My face flushes at the unsolicited affection.

Warm arms wrap around my waist, and he lays his forehead on my ribs. "Dixon, I miss you." His hot breath permeates the white dress, tickling my skin.

Uncertain, I rest my hands on his shoulders.

"You smell funny. You wearing perfume?" He nuzzles, his hint of scruff digging through the fabric. Beneath my hands, he relaxes, the full weight of him melting around my body, his heat spreading. "I like you better when you smell like paint. Or that stuff you spray on your drawings."

I'm on fire at every contact point.

Laughter rumbles in his chest, shooting vibrations through my abdomen and below. "You don't notice the charcoal all over your face. That's when you're prettiest."

"Xander…"

"You're always pretty. Did you know that?" Then, his weight shifts—he almost supports himself—and one hand glides up my side, traces the curve of my breast, down to my hip. Goosebumps follow the movement, and an ache of desire surges through me. "You're absolutely gorgeous."

I close my eyes. "You're drunk."

"Do you have any idea how sexy this dress is?"

"You're drunk." My words are louder this time, and I pry his hands off.

He latches onto the mattress and flips his tousled hair out of his face. "Yeah."

I stumble backward.

He's supposed to be over me. He isn't supposed to talk like that or touch me like that, and I'm definitely not supposed to be aroused by nothing more than his warm hands and husky voice. But the damage is already done.

"Very drunk." Xander's fingers pry at the top button of his dress shirt—it must be constricting—but the alcohol has stolen all his fine motor skills. Dark, dilated eyes draw me in, pleading, begging for me. "Dixon, can you help me?"

My throat's dry, and I swallow to wet it. This isn't what I signed up for when I brought him upstairs, but I close the distance and work at the button. Even sober, it's not an easy task. "How do you get these stupid things on in the first place?"

At last, the button comes undone.

His alcoholic breath rustles my hair, and I release his

103

shirt. He's closer than I thought.

This time, Xander doesn't let me escape.

He drags me on top of him, mouth to mouth, and slides backward. Beneath us, the sheets are crumpled and folded over so his hips jut up, and my knees land on either side of him, digging into the fabric. A cool breeze brushes my underwear—the skirt of the dress must've ridden up—but his warm hand soon covers the exposed area.

I cup his face and open up when he nibbles my lower lip. The kiss is sloppy, wet, and slow, but my chest tightens with pleasure. I've missed his lips, his tongue, his fingers—which tug aside my underwear and trace the edge of my core.

His mouth is warm with cinnamon and whiskey plus the harshness of vodka—and the acidic bite of vomit. It isn't the most welcoming flavor, but he's relentless. My fists bury in the sheets, clenching when he thumbs my clit, and I roll my hips to entice him closer. He complies without hesitation.

He sucks my lip between his teeth and draws another line along my entrance. The slow, subtle contact drags a gasp from my mouth. His thumb continues the careful tempo, and I tremble when two fingers sweep across me again, then plunge inside.

I tear away, gasping, eyes clamped shut, and buck against his hand.

In response, he twists to reach the spot that drives me insane with need, and his thumb circles my clit with surprising coordination. His lips trail a flurry of messy kisses across my cleavage, and I clutch his shoulder to stay aloft, nails digging through the dress shirt. The pain would be a mild irritation sober, but now, he doesn't even acknowledge it.

He paws at my chest, eager to yank down the top of the

dress, but the material is stiff and thick around my bust—
and he cannot figure out how to withdraw my breasts to
play with them.

Because he's drunk.

This cannot be happening.

Even as he sweeps across my hot spot again, I wrench
away from his grasp and collapse at the foot of the bed. How
could I let myself do that?

One look at Xander is enough of a reminder. He watches
me, concern etched on his face, failing to articulate. The
hand that was just fingering me rests on his chest. Even
drunk and out of it, he's sexy.

"Dixon…" He can't manage to sit up.

"I brought a date tonight."

His hand stretches toward me. "Don't sleep with him."

I cock my head. "Xander, that's none of your business."

"Please don't sleep with him."

My heart pounds through my ears—his impertinence
astounds me. "How many women have you slept with since
we broke up?"

The mattress squeaks as he shifts his weight. "Cassie
means nothing to me."

"That doesn't answer my question."

But he's too drunk to care about the hypocrisy—and too
gone to listen if I point it out.

I stand and fix my dress right before Dahlia waltzes into
the room, a large glass of water in hand. I can't be in this
room anymore. I can't be near him.

There's little comfort in the half-light of my bedroom, but
it's the only solitary place available without leaving the

house to the drunks.

I curl up in the fetal position, struggling to prevent the tears.

I'm not sure why I'm crying. I've made my peace with Xander flirting with girls and sleeping around. That was an inevitable reaction to our failed attempt at a relationship. It doesn't bother me.

But every time I stand up, something knocks me down. Xander and that kiss. Felix's hesitant rejection of my studio application. Elise berating me about the exhibit. Every time I try to make something better, I'm pushed back to where I started. Only worse.

Nothing has made an improvement. I am so tired of trying the same stupid things over and over again.

The door squeaks.

"Hey." Dahlia's small voice creeps into the room. The door closes behind her. "You alright?"

I grunt. There's no need to lie to her.

"I'm sorry I took so long. I had to fight a couple people to reach the cups. What did he do?"

She doesn't wait for me to respond before lying down behind me, her chest against my back. A tentative hand rubs up and down my side, and my skin is still alight with goosebumps.

I swallow. "He didn't say or do anything worth discussing. He's drunk."

"He upset you."

After a beat, I turn to face her. "Xander's always been good at upsetting me."

Again, her hand presses to my waist, but she isn't tentative this time. "He was never good enough for you. You are…" Her rich brown eyes travel down my body, then up again, and her fingers come to a stop at my hip. "I hate how much he hurts you."

I want to laugh.

Because a few months ago, Xander would've said the same thing about her. That she's not good enough for me. That all she does is hurt me.

"I hurt him too, you know."

"Yeah, but I don't care about him." The hand at my waist clenches into a fist around the stretchy fabric, and the skirt shifts up my leg. "I care about you."

I nudge a strand of hair from her face, and Dahlia leans into my touch, presses her lips to my palm.

"I missed you, Billie." Her hand tugs my dress, pulling me flush with her, and my body responds without instruction. When I roll my hips against her, a little whimper escapes her mouth. "I never wanted to stop being your friend."

"Could've fooled me."

"Yeah, that was the point." Her fingers scrape along my ribs, then down my spine, until it finally settles on my ass. "God, everything about you is beautiful and sexy and perfect."

My fingers tangle into her hair, and I yank her mouth to mine.

Her lips are thin, wet, and warm, and I moan as the hand on my ass squeezes without restraint. The vodka on her tongue is pungent—the jungle juice—but something about her mouth is so incredibly Dahlia. Her rhythm is calculated and meticulous, and she suffers no uncertainty.

Even in this, she is fierce, aggressive, and entrancing, and that's clear the moment she forces my mouth open and bites down on my lip.

At last, her fingers relax, but instead of releasing me, they slide beneath the hem of my dress and underwear to seize a handful of my bare ass. Another moan stumbles from my lips, and she takes that as encouragement. Her slender fingers languorously massage their way between my cheeks until she reaches my slick, aching entrance.

Her thumb finds my clit, and I break the kiss, gasping.

Dahlia doesn't miss a beat. Her mouth trails down to my neck, and under my dress, her fingers strum a steady but anxious rhythm. Teeth scrape against my collarbone, nip at the sensitive skin of my neck, and lips trace searing kisses over heaving breasts.

I wrap my arm around her as she dips a finger inside my entrance, and I tug at the neckline of her dress. Her small breast spills out of the top, her nipple hard and dark against her ghostly white skin, and I circle it with my thumb.

This time, when she slips inside, she delves deep enough to find the spot Xander was just—the sound I release is some cross between a moan and a gasp and louder than I intended...

My fingers grasp her breast, and she whimpers. "Billie, I want you. I want all of you. Now."

She retracts. I'm cold without her, but she doesn't give me a chance to miss her. One small movement, and I'm trapped against the bed, my wrists pinned above my head. Panting, she straddles me, rocking her hips against mine. I bite my lip, trying and failing to repress a moan.

Dahlia lays a fleeting kiss on my lips.

My need only increases as she slides down my body. Her

fingers shove the dress up, then tug my underwear down, and the scent of my arousal fills the room.

She hums her approval at my exposed wet core, and her tongue darts out to circle my clit. My subsequent gasp is sharp and loud and eager, and she moans in response. "God, I need to hear you come. You're absolutely gorgeous."

My body stiffens.

Xander said that fifteen minutes ago. Drunk and horny, sure, but it's not the first time he's used those exact words. The last time we slept together, in the Powells' pool shed at my mother's wedding, he looked at me like I was the most beautiful person alive and said, "You're absolutely gorgeous." I cannot hear those words in any voice but his.

Dahlia sucks my clit between her lips, but I press a hand to her shoulder.

"Stop. Stop." A steadying breath as she retreats. "This is moving way too fast."

She sits up, a deep furrow in her brow, and I tug my underwear and dress into place. "I don't understand." Her hands clench into fists. "I've waited for you to be over Xander for the last year. How in the world is this too fast?"

I push up into a sitting position. "I've never kissed a girl before."

"So? It's not like you don't understand the female anatomy." She scoffs. "You definitely understand how to turn me on. Not that there's been a shortage of times you've managed that."

"You've liked me for a year?"

She crashes her mouth to mine in a brief but abrasive kiss. "You're incredibly dense, you know?"

I bite my lip. "Dahlia, I need to be alone."

109

She shrugs with a little smirk and rises from the bed. "No problem. Let's get together tomorrow. For the photography project." She pauses to flatten her sundress.

"Okay," I answer in a small voice.

"I'll pick you up around eleven." She heads for the door but pauses, her hand on the knob. "Oh, and Billie?"

"Yeah?"

"I want you. I'm not going to wait anymore." She sends a smirk over her shoulder, then yanks open the door and disappears into the darkness.

I collapse on the bed.

What the fuck was that?

Twelve

My mother's voice is calm and quiet over the phone. "We had the twenty-week ultrasound, so I wanted to make sure you're up-to-date."

I dump more Solo cups in the black thirteen-gallon trash bag. "Aren't you twenty-three or twenty-four weeks?"

Mom clears her throat. "Technically, yes, but we had trouble scheduling an appointment with the technician because of my job."

I pause, my fingers wrapped around another stack of cups. I don't know what my mother's job is.

"I thought you should know, the baby is healthy, and as far as we know, it's a girl."

The top cup is still full of jungle juice. Jimmy was too drunk to clean up last night. I've spent the last hour picking up the mess, but I've barely made a dent.

I dump the jungle juice in the sink, then the cups into the trash. "What do you mean, 'as far as we know'? Mo said they couldn't tell."

"Oh." Something jostles the other line. "Well, yes, that's what I meant. The technician said it's most likely a girl, but we're not positive. I didn't realize you were talking to

Imogene about the baby."

"Yeah."

But my eyes gravitate toward the handle of vodka on the counter, a quarter full. I dumped the remnants of the jungle juice earlier. It stayed out all night in an open container. It made a convenient bathtub for a few fruit flies.

The vodka's different. It has a lid. It hasn't been contaminated. It's usable.

Would it be inconsiderate to dump it?

"Well," Mom says, her voice quivering, "if you have any questions you can always ask me. You don't have to get your information from your sister."

I cross the room and wrap my hand around the glass bottle. It's cool to the touch, and my fingers, rigid and stiff, untwist the cap. "Okay."

Imogene may call under the pretense of discussing the pregnancy, but it feels like more. There's something she desperately wants to tell me, but she keeps holding back.

Mom releases a sigh. "I suppose I'll let you go. You sound busy."

"Uh, yeah." I lay the cap on the counter and upend the handle over the sink. The last quarter of vodka splatters into the basin, and I hold my breath and rinse the bottle. "I'll talk to you later, Mom."

When she's gone, I lean against the counter and roll my shoulders.

The house is eerily silent for 10:30 on a Saturday, but it's not like I expected either of the guys to be up this early. They were trashed last night. Especially Xander.

Instead of continuing my cleanup, I pull the bread from the fridge and fill the toaster. I had a yogurt earlier, and as little as I want to eat, I'm hungry.

Plus, the guys should eat. They must be dehydrated.

When the toast pops, I spread butter across the slice, then the second—and add two more to the toaster as the stairs creak.

A mop of messy brown hair peeks around the corner. "What're you doing up so early?"

I offer him a slice of toast. "You should eat something."

Jimmy steps into the room and accepts the food without question. He scarfs it down, but his tired eyes study me. "You dressed up for some reason?" He cocks his head and finishes the slice.

The toast pops, and I butter it while deciding how to answer.

Dahlia's supposed to pick me up in less than thirty minutes, so I'm dressed for the photo shoot—a sleek, gray long-sleeve shirt with a rather low neckline and a pair of black skinny jeans. Minimalist clothing works better for photographs. But I will admit the outfit is more form-fitting than my usual attire.

When I turn around, I put on a tight smile. "I get to play model for my photography class."

"Why're you modeling?"

"Partner project. I take pictures of her, she takes pictures of me."

"A girl?" His brow wrinkles with confusion. "And I was about to ask if you have a crush on the guy. You look… particularly nice."

I flush. "I'm not dressed up for anybody."

Jimmy pushes past me to fill a glass with water. "Okay, but now I believe you less. You're blushing." He takes a long sip, considering me. "Who's your partner?"

A frown tugs at my lips. "Dahlia Finnick."

He gags and spends a minute coughing before he can respond. "Billie, you can't—"

"It's a project. Don't overreact." I scoff as I turn toward the counter. "You don't have a say in who my assigned partner is—or who I spend time with."

Jimmy remains silent.

I move on. "Who was the girl you danced with last night?"

"Huh?"

"That was Kylie's sister, right?" I glance over my shoulder. "You two were making out in the middle of the living room. Or do you not remember?"

His face flushes red. "I mean, kind of."

"Kylie said she likes you."

He gives a one-shouldered shrug. "Yeah, she does, but I haven't…I mean, I—"

"Like the girl who has a boyfriend."

"Yeah."

I have no appetite, but I force myself to finish my toast. "Okay, but if you don't have a chance with her, why not date the girl who likes you?"

There's an off look about him—he's probably still queasy from all the alcohol. "It seems disingenuous to date someone when I haven't sorted out my own feelings."

I snort. "Can you travel back in time and tell yourself that? Because last year would've been a hell of a lot better if you hadn't spent the entire time pressuring me to date Xander when I hadn't sorted out my feelings."

"Yeah…" Jimmy clears his throat. "Speaking of Xander,

have you heard anything from his room? He's alive, right?"

I scoff and grab the final slice of toast, cool to the touch now. "I'm about to check on the bastard."

◆

Xander's room is dark until I open the blackout curtains, and sunlight streams into the room.

On the bed, Xander is twisted in the sheet, his black hair a sweaty mess. His Deadpool boxers don't cover much from his tossing and turning. He moans at the light and burrows under the pillow, but I don't give him the opportunity to hide.

I set the toast and ibuprofen next to the full water glass from last night and yank the sheets away. Not that they were covering much. "It's time to wake up. You need water and food and pain meds."

He grunts again but doesn't move.

I tug on his shoulder. "Come on, Xander. I don't have time for this. Get your ass in gear."

Finally, he shifts to face me and pops open an eye. "What time is it?" God, he looks and sounds awful.

"Going on eleven."

He buries his head deep in the pillow. "What the fuck, Dixon?" I strain to decipher his muffled words.

I tug him again. "You can sleep more afterward."

When he doesn't move, I sit on the edge and yank on his arm. Hesitantly, he allows me to drag him into a sitting position.

An arm snakes around my waist, and he rests his head on my shoulder. "Fuck. You smell good."

I pat his arm before offering him the water and pills. "Take these." Then, the toast.

He nibbles. "You're dressed all pretty…"

God, he's still drunk.

"Why're you all pretty?" He takes another tiny bite, but I can feel his eyes on me. His position provides a particularly good view of my cleavage. "Because God, I'm not lucky enough for you to dress like this for me."

I try to ignore the discomfort. "You may have the day off work and school, but some of us have obligations."

"That dress last night… You don't realize how hot you are—although, I admit, I'm biased." His exhalations tickle my skin. "You sure you don't have a date?"

I roll my eyes.

"You didn't go home with him, did you?"

"Who?"

"Your date last night."

"Jay?"

A pout tugs at his lips. "I don't know the asshole's name. I just know I don't want anyone to touch you."

I pat his shoulder awkwardly, and he settles against me again. "Sometimes, I want to be touched."

His chuckle reverberates through my collarbone. "God, I know you do. You're fucking sexy, you know that?" His arm tightens around my waist. "Living with you is hard, Dixon. All the fucking time hard." His finger traces a circle over my ribs. "And it doesn't help that I could literally write the playbook on how to make you come."

I inhale sharply. "How in the world are you this drunk?"

He gives a half-shrug. "I had around twenty-five drinks last night. I'd be surprised if I were sober." He hums an

116

unsteady rhythm. "Besides, when I'm drunk, I can hold you. I'd rather be drunk, trust me."

I scoff. "So, what, you'll keep drinking so you have no guilt about being attracted to me?"

He pulls back with a frown.

"And speaking as someone with an alcohol dependency, that's exactly the kind of person and situation I don't need in my life." I pry myself from his grip and climb off the bed. "If you want to drink, fine. But don't you dare expect me to thank my lucky stars when you drunkenly decide to grace me with your attention. It doesn't work that way."

He studies me a moment. "I didn't mean it like—"

"Yes, you did. Don't lie to make yourself feel better."

But all he does is stare. He's too drunk to think on his feet.

"Xander, you're the one who walked away. You don't get to tell me who I can or cannot sleep with—especially when you've slept with every female customer at the bar." I turn for the door. "Drink your water and go back to sleep."

The doorbell echoes through the house. Probably Dahlia.

"And you're the one who let me walk away." His quiet voice barely carries across the room. "You didn't stop me."

I lay a hand on the door frame, pausing at the threshold. "Go to sleep. When you wake up again, none of that will matter. You'll be sober. You can hate me again." I close the door behind me—before he can get out another word.

◆

There's a loud *thump* as we drive over the train tracks.

She turns onto a gravel patch on the side of the road and

parks the car. We haven't said a word during the trip.

A hundred feet from the road, the railroad curves into the distance, crossing a beautiful wooden trestle bridge. It's not very high, as it passes over a stream between the forested hills, but from this distance, the bridge is daunting.

Dahlia rifles through the back seat and pulls up with her SLR slung around her neck. "Let's do this."

The walk along the abandoned track is slow, and my hoody doesn't protect from the wind well. Dahlia, on the other hand, appears warm in her black wool coat. She still shivers.

I jog to catch up and match my pace with hers. "How are we doing this?"

She sends me a quick glance. "Will you be warm enough without the hoody? It's not photogenic."

"I'll be fine."

When we reach the bridge, Dahlia stops, lifting her camera to fiddle with the ISO and aperture. She removes the lens cap. "Let's get started, shall we?"

But I can't move.

I expected her to mention the kiss—the much-more-than-a-kiss kiss—the moment we got in her Honda Accord, but she didn't say a word. She hasn't been affectionate or flirtatious. And she hasn't mentioned anything from the party.

"How drunk were you last night?" I step closer, but she's adjusting the zoom. "Do you remember...?"

She pauses—a split second—then continues fiddling with the camera.

"Did you mean what you said?"

Dahlia shakes her head, but I'm not sure if it's to me or the camera. "Come on, Billie. Let's get you in position."

I trail behind her, and when she stops, I do too. "How do you want me?"

She catches my gaze. "Exposed. Lose the hoody."

"Right." My fingers, jittery from the cold, tug down the zipper, and I shrug the hoody off. "What's next, Dahlia?"

For a minute, all she does is study me, her gaze wandering up and down my body with a tight jaw. What in the world is she thinking?

"Dahlia?"

She meets my eyes. "Yeah?"

"Do you remember last night? Or were you too drunk?"

She lifts the camera to look through the viewfinder, but all I can do is stare. The camera clicks a few times. "We're doing a photo shoot, Billie, and it's cold out. This is hardly the time to talk about your impulsive behavior."

I blanch. "*My* impulsive behavior?"

She draws the camera away, a little smirk playing on her lips. "You kissed me, remember?"

Heat rises to my cheeks. "You do remember."

"Of course I do. I only had a couple drinks, and you— you're hard to forget." She lifts the camera again and presses down on the shutter with striking force. "I do like your impulsive behavior, though, and I wouldn't mind discussing it once we're somewhere warmer."

I turn away, examining the expansive hilly vista, considering.

Somehow, even after knowing her for the past year, she confuses me. I don't trust her. I can't trust her. And I have no idea what to make of last night…

Well, aside from the fact that I kissed her.

That was my choice.

And I wasn't drunk.

The shutter clicks several times consecutively, and she shuffles around to get a better perspective.

"Dahlia?"

The clicks stop.

"Yeah?"

Another gust of wind blows across our position, ruffling through the barren trees and my afro. Below us, the stream is dry and rocky, and suddenly, this seems like a terrible idea.

I was all too sober during that make-out session and far more eager than I anticipated.

I didn't realize it last night. But that kiss was the logical conclusion to all the hours I spent with her last year. Every time she cuddled up to me at a party or movie night, our legs entangled intimately. Every compliment and not-so-subtle flirtation. Every touch and smile. I thought she was my best friend. That we had our own secret code.

Obviously, I deciphered her key incorrectly.

Because it took a year for me to realize. She did whatever she could to spend more time with me. She hated Xander because I had feelings for him. It took a year to realize she liked me as more than a friend.

And I might, on some level, reciprocate.

It was a good kiss. A really good kiss. And she definitely didn't lie about her tongue. She would've made me come with that alone.

But Dahlia is still Dahlia.

My depression hasn't reared its ugly head in a few months—not like it used to—and I have my therapy with Byrdie once a month. But spending time with Dahlia isn't a good idea.

I hate to admit Jimmy and Xander are right since we're hardly on speaking terms, but she's a bad influence. She always has been, and until she takes initiative with her mental health, she always will be.

"You alright, Billie?"

I turn back. "Yeah, I'm okay."

She tilts her head, then drops the SLR, letting it dangle around her neck, and approaches. "I got some nice shots. If you want to go somewhere warmer, I'd be okay with that." She lays her hand on my waist. "My apartment's nearby."

I swallow down my acquiescence. "Let's finish up the shoot here. I'm not too cold. And I'd like to get some of you here too."

"A couple, alright? I want to pose somewhere warmer."

"Whatever you want. I can work with anything."

She lifts the SLR again and locates me via the viewfinder. "Sounds like a plan."

Thirteen

"I HAVE TO ADMIT..." JAY SHIFTS ON THE CHAIR. "I DIDN'T expect to hear from you."

My fingers wrap around the mug, hot from the chai latte. "I didn't expect to be here either."

He raises a blond eyebrow. "Why are you? You ghosted me Saturday night, and you haven't spoken to me in class since."

"I couldn't talk to you like nothing happened after I disappeared at the party." I take a deep breath. "I had to help Xander to bed because he was wasted, and then, I was done partying."

Jay's face contorts into a frown. "So, what, you went to bed with him?"

My lips form a tight line. "No. I was tired, and I went to my own bed. I don't...I don't socialize often. People are stressful."

"Is that why you weren't having fun? Or were you not having fun with me?" He takes a drink of his iced coffee. "Seriously, Billie, it's not a big deal. I'm just trying to figure out why I'm here when you weren't into me."

The scent of the masala chai tickles my nose. "I'm...bad

at dating."

He chuckles. "Isn't everyone?"

This would be so much better if he didn't interrupt. "I have a tendency to self-sabotage my relationships, so the date wouldn't have gone well under any circumstances."

He opens his mouth, but I don't let him speak.

"I was diagnosed with persistent depressive disorder seven months ago. I'm on medication now, in addition to a consistent exercise and yoga routine and therapy. I am prone to alcohol abuse, but I haven't had a drink in nine months. And I'm insecure and have trouble trusting people."

For a moment, Jay stares, brown eyes blinking as he takes it in.

I lift my mug with quivering hands and gulp down half my latte.

I've never said all those words at once before. I've known it—and so do those closest to me—for a while, but saying it together like that makes it all the more real.

Because why in the world would someone want to date that? I don't want to date that.

Jay runs a hand through his blond hair, and his lips quirk in an uncomfortable smile. "I'm sorry I tried to give you a drink. If I'd known, I wouldn't have bugged you about it."

My cheeks scrunch against my glasses. "It's fine...though I appreciate the apology."

He clears his throat. "I'm impressed by your honesty. Most people wouldn't be so forward. That's really brave."

"It's no less than you deserve. No less than anyone deserves."

"Yeah, but that kind of honesty is rare."

I shrug.

Jay takes a slow drink from his mug. "That still leaves me to wonder why I'm here. Don't get me wrong. It's nice to know why you ran off, but why did you decide to tell me all of this?"

I was hoping he wouldn't ask. This discussion point wasn't top on my priority list. Because he's right: I wasn't into him.

I tried to give the date a chance, including the first of three make-out sessions that night. All of those were a disaster in their own way. Jay's disaster? No interest, no passion, no arousal.

But what are my other options?

Xander, who only allows himself to feel things when he's drunk enough he doesn't have to hold himself accountable.

Or Dahlia, who's ten times more unstable than I ever was—and more importantly, who proclaims she won't wait for me anymore.

When Xander said that, it was an ultimatum: Commit now or I'm done.

But Dahlia's ultimatum doesn't have a second option. Commit.

"Billie?"

More than anything, I need to send a clear message. If not to either of them, to myself.

Because if I don't set boundaries, Dahlia will not stop, and past performance indicates I won't be able to resist her. Plus, I don't see Xander quitting alcohol any time soon. He works in a bar for God's sake.

And nothing sets a firmer boundary than getting a boyfriend.

"Look, I know I can't expect anything after that disaster,

but I'd like a second chance."

"So this is a second date?"

My mouth quirks to the side. "Could it be?"

◆

When Prue opens the front door, she's grinning and carrying a pizza box. "I don't care that you don't like pineapple." She leads the way to the dining room. "You can pick it off."

I release a laugh and follow.

She tears the box open, and steam billows off the extra-large pie. "You like everything else, right?"

I study the pizza as I slide into the seat beside her. Bell pepper, mushroom, onion, tomato, and of course, pineapple. "Sometimes, I hate that you're a vegetarian." I snatch a slice and pick off the offending fruit.

Prue rolls her eyes. "Okay, fine, next time, we can do half pineapple and half pepperoni. Would that make you happy?"

I nibble at the pizza. She knows the answer.

She retreats into the kitchen to grab plates, but I'm nearly done with mine when she returns. "I wish we had painting together this semester." She drops into her chair and takes a slice. "I mean, as much as I love having art history with you, we can't talk, and with back-to-back classes…"

"I'm sorry we haven't gotten together since Saturday. I spent all Sunday dealing with hungover people."

She cringes. "Bet that was fun."

"Oh boy, you have no idea."

Her eyebrow arches up inquisitively, and she takes a bite. I haven't told anyone about it because telling people means it really happened, but this is Prue. We talk about everything. "I had to put Xander to bed that night because he was, you know, completely trashed, and he...well, he kissed me."

The partial slice falls from her hand. "Are you fucking kidding me?"

"I wish I was."

"Where the hell does he—?"

"He was still drunk that morning, and he was outright hitting on me." I allow a tense breath and lay my crust on the plate. I lost my appetite. "I've been avoiding him since."

"Of course you have. What a complete asshole move."

"Prue, I doubt he remembers. Maybe that morning, but not the night before."

She huffs. "That doesn't excuse anything, and you know that, Billie."

I cringe at the reminder. I definitely know that from personal experience. I'm sure there are plenty of horrible things I said and did during the times I couldn't stop myself, and whether I remember them or not does not forgive or excuse my actions.

"Where is he? Because I—"

I lay my hand on her forearm. "Prue, I want to drop it. I'm not excusing it, but I'm not totally innocent either. I got carried away for a minute, and I was sober. For now, I want to pretend it didn't happen. This house can't handle more tension."

She clenches her jaw. "I get that, but you're wrong."

A wide smile spreads across my cheeks. "And I love that you tell me that."

"He needs to be held accountable for his actions."

"Well, I did give him an earful, but again, he was drunk. Probably useless." I turn my attention back to the crust on my plate and force myself to take another bite.

Prudence too picks up her pizza, but her scowl says she's moving on under duress. "How hung over was Jimmy?"

"Not bad." I finish the crust and awkwardly grab the smallest slice in the box. I doubt it will fit, but you know, food is important. "But um, the real kicker was having to deal with Dahlia for our photo project that afternoon. She was hung over too."

Prue frowns. "I don't like—"

"I don't either. But uh, you were right."

She cocks her head as the front door opens and closes. "What do you mean?"

Footsteps approach.

I bite my lip but force the words out quickly. "She has feelings for me."

Prue's jaw drops.

But my eyes follow Xander, dressed in Draft Horse garb, as he passes. Cassie, the girl from the bar, trails behind him, attached to her phone.

"Wait, Billie." Prue whispers, but it's too loud. "Did she say something? Or do something?"

I shake my head once. Firm. "Later."

Her brow furrows. "Yeah, okay."

"What about you? What have you done the past week?"

She shrugs to shake off her discomfort. "Trying to hang out with Cynthia. She's been too busy studying. I'm not sure she wants to be my friend anymore."

I grimace. "She's the most ambitious person I know."

"And that's saying something."

"I'm not that ambitious anymore." I heave a sigh. "That'd require me to have goals. Right now, I'm…floundering."

"You'll pull through." Few people can successfully reassure me, but Prue's kind words leave a comfortable tranquility in my chest. "You always do."

Xander and Cassie's hushed voices emanate from the kitchen.

Then, heavy footsteps on the stairs.

"How's the dating front?" I stuff the pizza in my mouth.

She gives a half-shrug. "No worse than normal. I haven't had a date with potential in two years, so basically, I'm going to spend the next sixty years alone."

I roll my eyes. "If you're not careful, you'll get as paranoid and ridiculous as Jimmy."

She snorts.

"You know, for the longest time after Cynthia rejected him, he insisted he was going to die a virgin."

"You spreading rumors about me?"

I turn to find Jimmy in the doorway. "True ones."

Those footsteps were coming down, not going up. Glad I didn't think it safe to bring up Dahlia.

Micaela peeks her head into the dining room. "Hi, Billie, Prudence." Her voice is quieter than normal, and her eyes flit nervously toward the kitchen, where Xander and Cassie are talking.

"Hey." I smile to reassure her.

Because no matter how stupid and inappropriate his drunken behavior was, my stomach dropped at the sight of Cassie. I'm sure Micaela's did too.

Then, David pops up behind her. "Hey, ladies, I'm heading out." He glosses over me to focus on Prue. "If I'd known you'd be here, I might've cleared my schedule."

Beside me, Prue snorts. "What were you guys doing?"

Jimmy quirks his head. "You didn't hear the music? Dave's singing with us now."

"Oh." I always forget he's a Music major too.

"Anyway…" David nods toward the front door, out of view. "I'll see everybody later."

Micaela turns to Jimmy. "I'm gonna go too. I've got that project to work on."

"Right."

When they're gone, Prue shifts in her seat, and Jimmy leans against the door frame. The quiet is awkward.

"Why'd David look at you like that?" I shoot Prue a pointed look.

Her mouth twists into a scowl, but her poking is good-natured. "Sometimes, I wish you were still unobservant. We spent a good while talking at Xander's party."

Jimmy lifts an eyebrow.

An irritated groan escapes her lips. "Fine, we made out. It's nothing. A walk down memory lane."

I open my mouth but struggle with the words. "'Memory lane'?"

Prue sends me a conspiratorial smirk. "He might have been my rebound sex after Ruby."

"He was our RA."

"That's why I never told you. Had to be a secret."

Jimmy glances toward the front door. "He's not our RA now. And he sounded interested."

"Well, I'm not. He's going to graduate in, what, five or six months? I don't want to get emotionally invested in something for him to leave, and I'm not in the market for a fuck buddy." She grabs another slice of pizza. "What about you, Jimmy? You still think you'll die a virgin?"

He stumbles over the threshold, his voice quivering. "If it makes a difference, I have a date tonight."

I scoff. "With who?"

Then, I remember.

"Are you dating her now? Your boss's little sister?"

He flushes. "She has a name, and yes, she's Kylie's sister."

Prue presses her lips in a thin line. "How little?"

Xander comes up beside him, Cassie behind him, occupied by her phone. "Tiff's eighteen, don't panic." His eyes seek me out but immediately shift away. "Graduating high school this May."

I eat my final bite of pizza and tilt the chair backward. "That's pretty young, isn't it?"

Xander elbows Jimmy in the ribs, a tiny smirk on his lips. "He prefers younger women."

Jimmy's face is on fire.

"Wait." I hold up a hand. "He's one of the youngest people in our year. Cynthia's birthday is, what, in December?"

Prue nods.

"She's eight months older than him."

Xander shrugs. "Doesn't disprove anything I said. I have to change."

I open my mouth, but Prue jabs me with a finger. "What?"

"Speaking of dates—" her voice is clear and loud enough Xander stops "—please correct me if I'm wrong, but…"

"What?"

She holds me firm and steady with a meaningful look.

"Two days ago, did I spot you leaving the Jittery Bug with your smoking hot date from Xander's party? Jay, right?"

Despite myself, heat rises to my cheeks. "I was about to tell you."

In my periphery, Xander is frozen.

"Since we didn't get a chance to talk Saturday night, we got together again."

"He kissed you," Prue says, as if arguing.

"Yep." It was on the cheek, but technically, she's right. "Let's go."

My head jolts over. Xander, not having showered or changed, moves toward the front door, tugging on Cassie's arm.

She yanks away with a scowl. "New clothes."

"I don't need clothes at your apartment. Or have you forgotten that?"

She follows him. "You have to shower first."

"Whatever."

They're gone from view, and a moment later, the front door shuts behind them.

Jimmy's face falls as his gaze settles on me. "You like him?"

For a second, I can't answer. "I think I could."

"Billie, what about—?"

I purse my lips. "What about you? Last we talked, the girl you like has a boyfriend. Why are you going on a date with Tiff when you have feelings for someone else?"

That shuts him up.

I push a strand of corkscrew curls behind my ear. "Maybe—just maybe—this will lead to something good."

Fourteen

DAHLIA PARKS HER CAR IN FRONT OF AN OLD APARTMENT building off King Street. It's a couple blocks from campus—decidedly closer than my house—but the paint is peeling and the windows are single pane.

She nods for me to follow, and I trail behind her as she climbs a steep, squeaking staircase to the topmost floor. "It's small," she says as she slips the key into the lock, "but I have a studio set up. It's a little more inviting than the campus one."

The door pushes open, and I follow her inside.

When she flips on the light, I examine the small room. Because that's all it is. It's a studio apartment, so the living space and bedroom are the same area. There's a tiny attached kitchen, where the counters are mostly covered with empty alcohol bottles, and around the corner, a bathroom and a floor-to-ceiling closet.

She has a full-sized bed in one corner and a desk beside it, and like she said, one corner is devoted to a studio, complete with backdrop, spotlights, and a few accessories.

I lay my bag on the desk and withdraw my camera. I drape the strap around my neck, remove the lens cap, and adjust the aperture. It's dim in here, but with the spotlights, that shouldn't be a problem. As a final thought, I leave my hoody on her chair and turn toward the backdrop.

Dahlia has the lights on now but left their adjustment to me, and those lights direct my attention to where Dahlia is unzipping her jeans.

"What are you doing?"

"I don't want to wear jeans under the hot lights."

"I'm not taking photos of you in your underwear for class."

Dahlia shrugs. "I have no problem with it."

"That's not…" I rub my temple. "Pajama pants or something? Shorts?"

Her jeans drop to the floor with little effort—that's how skinny she is—and her underwear is black and lacy and see-through. I cannot look away as she pads to the closet. Especially when she bends over to sift through her dresser.

She pulls on a pair of blue mini-shorts that swish and sway like a skirt and shuts the closet again. "There. Satisfied?"

"Let's do this."

But instead of settling under the spotlights, she approaches. "What do you want to do, Billie? You're in charge here."

I swallow the lump in my throat. "Take the photos." My voice is tiny and weak, even to my ears.

She sashays toward the backdrop. "When we're done with the photos for class, maybe you'll want to take a few for yourself."

She kicks her jeans out of the frame and plops down in the corner, legs spread, palms on her knees. This is not remotely appropriate for classes.

But she nods me closer, and I force myself to walk.

With her feet pressed to the wall, back arched so her chest sticks out, head twisted to watch me, Dahlia is stunning. She's always been beautiful, but she's never been so openly provocative. She hasn't chosen a position that isn't overtly sexual in the past hour. I'm exhausted from trying to convince her to be less risque.

Her exact words were: "If you want me in a different position, put your hands on me." She does not know how to switch off.

I check the number of photos left. One. Which means this is almost over. I move to the other side, adjust the focus, and take the final picture.

As I wind up the film, she crawls to a sitting position, her long honey-brown hair cascading down her shoulder. "What now, Billie?"

"Typically, the next move is to develop the film, but you know that."

Dahlia rises from the floor, but I take the camera to her desk and pile everything in my bag. I pull the strap off my neck, and as I slip the camera inside its bag, hands wrap around my waist.

I jump.

Dahlia giggles in my ear. "Don't be so paranoid." Her lips brush my neck, sending a shiver down my spine. "I'm not going to hurt you."

"We're here for homework," I remind her, zipping the camera bag shut.

"Not anymore." Her fingers, slow but steady, close

around the waist of my jeans, and she pries the button undone. I stiffen, but she doesn't hesitate. She slides the zipper down, and a hand slips under my panties. "Now, I get to play with you." Her teeth nip at my neck, and a finger extends to my clit.

"Dahlia…" But my voice has abandoned me. "We cannot do this."

With her flush against me, her laughters shakes my body. "What in the world is stopping us? Homework's done for now, and you don't have to be anywhere for the rest of the night." Her free hand snakes up my shirt to knead my breast, and she hums with pleasure at my lack of bra.

"I'm meeting my dad for tea." Despite myself, I lean against her shoulder, eyes fluttering shut, giving in to the sweet sensation of her finger circling my clit and her mouth sucking at my throat.

She tugs, and I allow her to lay me on the bed. "That's cute."

For a moment, Dahlia hovers over me, roving my body with trembling hands, and I whimper at the loss of her, drawing a smirk onto her enticing mouth. Her lips find the bare skin at the hem of my underwear, and at last, she yanks on the jeans, tearing them down my legs. The underwear comes off next.

Her fingers trace back up my legs, past my hips, to nudge the t-shirt over my breasts, and she climbs atop my waist, straddling me, to suck a nipple into her mouth.

I am, for all intents and purposes, naked.

"Dahlia…you need to stop." I struggle to gather my thoughts. "We cannot do this."

A hand, cold and clammy, rests on my hip as she swirls

her tongue around my nipple, but her eyes locate mine. "We can do whatever we want," is her simple rebuttal before continuing her play.

Alien Ant Farm's rendition of "Smooth Criminal" bursts to life.

I try to sit up.

Dahlia shoots me a warning look. "You don't have to answer that."

I quiver under her touch, but nudge her away. "Who is it?"

With a scowl, she snatches the device from her desk. "Your sister." She shows me the name but holds the phone to her chest when I reach out. "No, we're busy."

But I stretch out to take it—not that she prevents me—and swipe my thumb across the screen. "Mo? How's everything going?"

Imogene releases a sigh of relief. "Thank God I caught you."

"You okay?"

"Yeah, Mom wanted me to tell you about the ultrasound results."

Dahlia collapses beside me, and her fingers slide up and down my side, counting each rib.

"Wait." I shove her hand away. "I thought she already had an ultrasound."

"That was a month ago," Mo says, as if it's obvious. "And you know, the lithium. But they were able to see the sex this time."

"Oh?"

With meticulous care, Dahlia pushes aside my arm, and I bite my lip as she starts in on my second breast.

"It's a boy," Imogene says.

I guess I'm supposed to be excited about this—that's normal, right?—but I feel as excited as Mo sounds. As long as we're ruling out the excitement between my legs.

"Cool," I barely get out.

Dahlia lays her palm over my entrance, and a finger delves inside, but I push her away. This time, I don't give her the chance to try again.

I slip off the mattress and yank my t-shirt over my breasts. "How're you doing, Mo?"

A long groan crackles the line as I tug my clothes on, first the underwear, then the jeans. "I'm so ready to get out of this fucking town." Imogene's voice cuts through the tension. "There are 160 days till graduation, and it's too long."

I smooth out my clothes and search for a reflection. I don't want to leave looking like a booty call. "Why don't you come here for Christmas?" I say into the phone. "Stay with Dad again. Or you can stay with me. We'd love for you to visit."

"I wish I could. But Mom is making a big deal out of Christmas since it's the last year in this house and right before I go off to college." She scoffs. "Plus, she's pregnant. If I piss her off, Rob has to take the brunt of her overreaction."

I slip my feet into my shoes. "That sucks."

"Any chance I could convince you to visit me instead?"

"I'm spending Christmas with Dad."

Over the phone, Imogene groans. "You're a jerk. We could've suffered together."

When I turn around, Dahlia is curled up on the bed in a huff. She crosses her arms over her chest and juts out her

137

lower lip.

I tell Imogene, "Well, you can hang out with Jimmy. He can tell you all about his new girlfriend." I unleash a brief laugh, but Mo doesn't find it funny.

"Jimmy has a girlfriend?" She coughs. "How did he manage that?"

Dahlia won't look at me.

"Okay, technically, she's not his girlfriend. They've gone on two dates. Her older sister is their manager at Draft Horse."

"Oh." Something thumps on the other line. "I'm sorry, Billie, I should go."

I frown. "Yeah, alright. Talk to you soon."

"Christmas, at the latest. Good luck with your finals."

My grip tightens around the phone. "Thanks, Mo."

But she doesn't respond. She's gone.

And I'm stuck alone with Dahlia again.

Once the phone's away, I tug on my hoody. It's long past time for me to go.

Now that the room is silent, Dahlia shifts and catches my gaze again. "Why are you dressed? You're not supposed to leave."

I zip up my bag and sling it over my shoulder. "No. I'm not supposed to stay."

"Why not?"

"We cannot keep doing this. I'm seeing someone now."

Her eyes narrow. "Who?"

"Jay." Determination laces my voice. "The same guy I took to Xander's birthday party. We went on our third date last night, and it's going well."

Dahlia collapses on the mattress, her mouth set in a firm

line. "Fine. Leave. I don't want you here."

I force a smile, though she's expressly avoiding me. "I'll see you in class next week."

◆

"Sorry." I lay my lanyard next to the giant Dalmatian puzzle and take my regular seat. "My photo shoot took longer than I thought."

Dad slips a piece into place. "No worries, Mina. Have some tea."

No steam pools from the spout.

I pour myself a cup and sip the lukewarm tea. "I know, but I said I'd be here sooner. And like always, Dahlia is skilled at distracting me."

He cocks an eyebrow but doesn't say anything.

I pull out a handful of puzzle pieces and sort through the colors. We just had to choose one of his hardest puzzles. "She…well, I'm fairly certain it's accurate to say she likes me, and she is determined to, I don't know, win me." I roll my eyes, but I can't think of a better word.

"And you're not interested?"

"I can't be interested in her, Dad." I try to locate the background pieces first—anything that isn't black and white. "She's unstable at best."

"The same could be said for you." He sends me a challenging wink. "I'm certainly not saying you should pursue a relationship, but to dismiss her because of mental health concerns when you've been through something similar seems hypocritical."

I hook together my first two pieces. "I know, but that's

the reason we became such good friends. I identified with her, and I looked past her problems because I felt that connection with her. That was the wrong decision."

"I understand. But I also know how much you long for companionship."

For the past several months, I've had one friend. That isn't out of the ordinary for me, but when I've spent the past two years developing relationships, it's a shot to the chest. Prue is a great friend—loyal, kind, supportive, and she pushes me outside my comfort zone—but she isn't a replacement for the things and people I've lost.

We live in the same house, but all I see of Xander and Jimmy's lives is on the periphery. Our communication is minimal. Our smiles are half-hearted.

More than any time in the past, I am an observer, not an active participant. Not because I don't want to be, but because I no longer have the privilege to participate.

"I do, Dad, but that doesn't mean I should throw myself recklessly at someone who wants me for her own benefit. I wouldn't get much love or companionship out of that."

"So you're throwing yourself into your schoolwork again?"

"Yes, but..."

I'm not sure I'm ready to mention this to him—makes it seem more serious than it is—but if there's anything I've learned in the past two years, it's that Dad can tell when I'm lying.

"I've actually been on a few dates with a guy the past week."

He tilts his head curiously. "The young man you took to Xander's birthday party?"

I nod.

"I thought it didn't go well."

"It didn't, but you know, the second one was better... and the third. We're going to the Gallery Hop on Friday night." I connect another piece to the outside edge. "You know, if I could have a nice simple relationship for once— no drama, no jealousy, no pressure for commitment before I'm ready—that would be comforting."

Dad hooks in an eight-piece section. "That sounds lovely, Mina, but I'm fairly certain you'd get bored."

I let out a quiet laugh. "I won't know if I keep getting caught up in people like Dahlia or Xander."

He hums. "That might be true."

"But?"

He connects another edge piece. "Is dating someone you're not interested in a good idea for your mental health?"

I frown.

Of course not. And I'm sure Byrdie will have some choice words on the matter when we have our next session, but I don't see another option.

"I have to do something. Dahlia made her intentions clear. I'm not sure I can tell her no."

"Perhaps you should focus on your resolve rather than misdirection. If she's as determined as you say, having a boyfriend won't stop her."

I cringe. "The thought has crossed my mind."

Fifteen

DAHLIA GROANS AS SHE DRAWS THE PAPER OUT OF THE FIXER. "This is the third time I've developed this one photo today. I still need more dodging on your face." With the tongs, she dumps the paper in the trash, not bothering to rinse it.

I offer her a sympathetic smile as I pull my photo from the first rinse and drop it in the archival rinse.

She returns to her enlarger to try again, and I take my contact sheet. In the dark, it's too difficult to examine the tiny images.

Outside the darkroom, my eyes flit across the contact sheet.

It took significant effort to get a set of photos that weren't too risque, but I managed.

I lift my glasses onto the top of my head and study the sheet at close range.

There were a couple shots I liked, and—yes, there it is. One of her lying on the track, her hair sprawled out like a halo and a tiny smirk playing on her lips. She is beautiful.

I note the image's location and return to the darkroom.

It takes a moment to find the right negative and set everything up, and right before I expose the test strip, Jay returns to his enlarger. He didn't text or call me all weekend. I thought things were going so well, but he doesn't offer any salutations.

I hold my blank paper over most of the strip and flip on the light.

Five seconds. Move the paper to reveal more.

Ten. Move it farther.

Fifteen. Again.

And every five seconds after that, until the entire strip is exposed. Then, wait a final ten seconds before turning off the light.

I slide the easel blades away. The test strip is ready to develop.

"Did you like me at all?"

I hold the strip by the edges and turn to Jay. "What?"

He leans against the counter, his hands clutching the edge. "Did you actually like me or were you messing with me for kicks?"

My jaw tightens as I process the accusation. "I don't know what you're talking about, Jay."

Everything was fine when he dropped me off Friday night. We visited my gallery and the Jittery Bug and three other places for the Gallery Hop and joked about how our class artwork is better than half the pieces on display. Where the hell is this coming from?

His head jolts in my direction. "Look, I know you like to manipulate guys into thinking you're in a relationship, then pull the rug out from under them. I have to say, you're incredibly cruel."

My stomach drops.

I don't know what to make of this development. Has Jay

143

talked to someone? Are there rumors about me? Or did he come to this conclusion on his own?

No matter the circumstances, my stomach contorts into a tight ball.

His words ring strikingly true.

It was never my intention to manipulate Xander, to make him think what we had was serious. I thought he knew how confused and scared I was. I thought he knew, despite that fear, my feelings were real.

But despite my best intentions, I did manipulate him.

I bite my lip and meet Jay's eyes. "If you think I was leading you on, I'm sorry, but we've only been on a couple dates. I don't know what sort of commitment you expected."

"Nothing." His mouth clamps shut. "I wanted you to know, I'm not like those other guys, and I won't put up with you playing me hot and cold. Depression isn't an excuse for leading people on like that."

For a moment, I stare. "You don't know what you're talking about."

"I don't think you—"

"No." The hand not holding the test strip clenches into a fist. "Saying hi and smiling at me all semester doesn't ingratiate me into liking you. I don't owe you anything. And I certainly don't want you to 'put up with' me. If my honesty isn't good enough for you, I have no interest in continuing this conversation."

He opens his mouth, but I turn away, ready to put this test strip in the developer.

I nudge the strip around in the chemicals with the tongs, watching the clock.

Dahlia comes up beside me with a paper of her own to

add to the mix, and I make room for her photo in the tub for the last two minutes of my time.

"What was that about?" she asks quietly.

Jay's working at his enlarger again. The entire room heard that heated discussion. Hopefully, the fans created enough white noise to muffle our words.

"A mistake." Ninety seconds left on the clock.

"What happened?"

I check to make sure no one else is nearby. "I'm not sure, but I don't foresee us going on any more dates. Not that I'm losing much."

A short burst of laughter bubbles from her mouth, and she nudges my shoulder. "Good for you."

Fifteen seconds left.

"What are you doing over winter break? Staying on campus?"

Dahlia hesitates. "Uh, yeah. It's going to be lonely this year."

I move the test strip to the stop bath and hand the tongs to Dahlia.

"What about you?" She accepts them. "You're staying with your dad again, right?"

"Technically, I'll be at my house for most of break, but yeah, Christmas with my dad. Not going back to Missouri this year."

"That must be nice."

Four seconds over, I switch the strip to the fixer. "I'll be at the house by myself. Jimmy's going to see his parents, and he always takes Xander."

She moves her photo to the stop bath. "Big house must be lonely without anyone else there."

145

The strip goes into the rinse last, and behind me, Dahlia moves hers to the tub I just vacated. "I guess."

"We should hang out."

I eye her curiously. I should say no, but she's right. The big house is lonely enough with them there—probably more so without them. I'm not looking forward to that.

I turn to her, crossing my arms over my chest. "On two conditions."

"Yeah?"

"One—" I lift a finger "—no alcohol of any kind."

She purses her lips but nods.

"And two, you keep your hands to yourself without my express permission."

Dahlia removes her photo from the fixer and drops it into the rinse with mine. "I can do that."

"Then we can hang out over winter break."

◆

I flash the couple one last smile as they exit through the floor-to-ceiling glass gallery doors. "Have a wonderful night."

No one else is here, so I slip to the breakroom and grab my bottle of water.

Entertaining guests who desire interaction no more than I do is exhausting. Unfortunately, that's an important part of the job.

In her office, Elise pores over yet another stack of paper-work. It's the number one thing that occupies her time. I offer her a small wave as I return to the gallery, but she closes the file and rises from her chair.

146

Okay. What's this?

We pause in front of her office door.

Her face is stern, worry lines creasing her forehead. "Billie, I've wanted to talk to you the last two weeks, but I didn't want to interrupt your preparation for finals."

I swallow, nervous. "And now that they're over?"

"We need to discuss your work ethic." The furrow in her brow deepens—she wants to have this conversation as much as I do.

"My work ethic?"

"Yes." She brushes a dark-brown strand behind her ear. She's using her business voice. "I fear your work has suffered since we talked about the Emerging Artists exhibit. I understand you must be disappointed, but you cannot allow your work to suffer purely because you didn't get what you wanted."

What can I say to that?

Of course I was disappointed, but I also want to be professional. I wouldn't let my work suffer because of disappointment.

Elise would never listen to what I have to say, though.

Instead, I say, "I'm sorry my work has suffered, Elise. How can I make it up to the gallery?"

"I need you to have more energy—" she pumps her fist in a mock demonstration "—when talking to prospective buyers and answering the phones, Billie, that's all."

She makes it sound easy to scrounge up the energy to communicate with people. For her, it might be, but that time spent associating with complete strangers is the most stressful part of my day. More stressful than Dahlia.

"Of course," I say, nodding. "I'll take care of it."

147

She returns to her office, but I follow.

"Elise, have you made a decision about my request for increased hours over the break? I have plenty of time, and I'd like to be of use to the gallery while I can."

Classes ended yesterday, and I can feel the tug at the edge of my brain. Without classes, without a rigorous schedule, without an open campus, without the professors and classmates and friends to occupy my time, I'm already sinking. It's in every limb, every thought, and every breath.

I need those extra hours.

Elise pauses, her hand on the door. "I'm sorry, Billie, but I can't approve an increase in hours." She shuts the door behind her without letting me respond.

Sixteen

I PAUSE AT THE BOTTOM OF THE STAIRS, PB&J IN HAND, AS Jimmy drags his suitcase down, fighting it on every step.

He sends me a sharp glare when he reaches the bottom. "It's rude to watch me struggle."

I can't help but snicker. "You were in my way."

He shrugs it off and heads to the foyer, where Xander waits, clutching his keys.

For a second, I hesitate but follow him for a final goodbye.

Jimmy double-checks his pockets, then the front pocket of the suitcase, and heaves a sigh of relief when he withdraws his passport. "Thank God," he mumbles.

By the door, Xander has his hand stuffed into his jacket pocket. "Come on, dude. We've got to go."

I lean against the wall. "Tell your parents hi for me."

"Of course. I'm sure they'll give me a package for you."

Xander stares at the door, irritation written across his face.

"When will you guys get back? You staying the whole break or waiting till after New Year's or what?"

"I think the return flight is a week before classes start

again. I have to double-check." Jimmy glances toward the door, then back. "But Xander will be home after he drops me off at the airport."

I freeze. "Huh?"

Xander opens the door and marches toward the car, leaving Jimmy behind.

"He's staying here for the break. He wanted the hours."

"Oh."

Xander's waiting for him, but Jimmy approaches me instead. "Will you be alright? It won't be too awkward, will it?"

I shake my head. "It'll be fine."

"You sure?" His forehead creases with that old worry. "I can stay—"

"Don't be ridiculous. Your parents are expecting you. And you want to see Mo, right?" I scoff. "You're not staying here in St. Clare because Xander and I don't get along. That never kept you from doing your own thing before."

"It was different before. You didn't get along. Now, you don't even talk."

"We had a whole conversation about alcohol dependency."

He sends me a skeptical look. "When was that?"

My eyes drift downward. "A few weeks ago."

It wasn't much of a conversation either, and it wasn't actually about the alcohol.

"My point exactly, Billie."

"It'll be fine. I'll be with my dad, and he'll be working. We'll uphold the status quo and all that."

He tries to muster some enthusiasm, but it doesn't reach his eyes. "You wanna know what I think?" His suddenly emphatic tone catches my attention.

I nod.

"Maybe it wouldn't be such a bad thing if you two did talk, you know? As much as you two don't—"

Xander sticks his head inside, jaw jutting out. "Seriously, get your ass in the fucking car. We need to go."

"Yeah." Jimmy smiles one last time, then grabs his suitcase and heads out.

Xander shuts the door behind them.

Through the living room window, they pile into the Camaro, the suitcase shoved into the trunk, and I finish my sandwich as they back out of the driveway and head east down Sandalwood.

There's a tense ball in my stomach as the dusty red Camaro disappears around the corner.

What was Jimmy about to say? Xander and I don't what?

But Xander's face when he practically dragged Jimmy out of here.

Does it matter what Jimmy was going to say? Talking to Xander wouldn't achieve anything when he's that irritated by my brief conversation with our roommate. Or by the fact that we're stuck alone together for over two weeks.

◆

As soon as I allow her entry, Dahlia sidles inside the house with complete confidence. "Did they leave?"

I shut the door behind her. "An hour ago. I'm watching a movie."

We settle on the couch. She sits close, but it's no closer than all the times we watched movies or drank together last year. She grins—a smug grin. She's going to push my demands to the limit, test my boundaries.

I make more room.

"What movie?"

"*Gremlins*."

"It's not Halloween, Billie."

But I laugh. "What are you talking about? This is one of my favorite Christmas movies."

Her lips press into a thin line. "Well, once you're done indulging your creepy inner child, let's get something to eat."

I scoff. "Oh, come on. If I remember correctly, Dahlia, you love horror movies."

She rolls her eyes. "Yeah, but this is a child's horror movie. It isn't scary."

"It doesn't have to be scary, it's a classic. And quite frankly, your taste in movies sucks."

Her face lights up with amusement. "So sorry to disappoint you."

On the screen, the striped gremlin dives into the swimming pool. This is where shit gets real.

I trail over her thin frame. "You're actually hungry?"

"What?"

"You said we should get food when this is over. What kind of food?"

She shrugs. "Whatever you want."

"You'd eat a couple slices of pizza?"

"Sure."

Although, I'd wager, she'd purge it later. She is thinner than I ever was.

She rests her head against the couch, but she taps at her

leg and messes around on her phone to make her point. She's bored. Her taste in movies definitely sucks, but I'm not giving in.

Once the movie reaches its climax, she grumbles. "Come on, Billie. There are a million more interesting things we could do. This is stupid."

I snicker. "Like what?"

Dahlia scoots closer, her body flush against my arm, and whispers in my ear. "I want you." Her hand caresses to my thigh.

But I nudge her away. "Hey, I told you to keep your hands to yourself."

"No, you said I need to keep my hands to myself unless you want me to touch you." She sends me a little smirk. "I'll have to make you want me too."

I force more space between us. "You can't make me do anything. Besides, this is almost over."

She harrumphs. "At least let me cuddle you." She sneaks her head under my arm, resting against my chest.

Headlights stream across the living room walls as a car turns into the driveway. That must be Xander getting home.

Hesitantly, I let my arm drop against the top of the couch. Stopping her would require prying her off. I don't want to deal with the consequences of her overreaction.

A key twists in the lock, and the front door nudges open.

I keep my attention trained on the movie screen, but all movement by the door stops once Xander's inside.

Then, he scoffs and disappears into the kitchen.

And I can relax again.

Beside me, Dahlia does not relax. "When does he leave

town?"

I was afraid she'd ask that. Can't exactly lie when we're supposed to hang out regularly over break. "He's not."

"What?"

"I just found out." I shake my head, but my movement is rigid. "I thought he was going home with Jimmy, but he needs the hours at work or something."

Dahlia huffs.

All I can do is focus on the movie. It's the finale, but I've missed the last ten minutes.

"You're tense," Dahlia whispers. "I could give you a rub-down."

My eyes clench shut. That's taking things too far. "No, thanks. I'm good."

She adjusted quickly.

When I open my eyes, a blue Bug parks in front of the house behind Dahlia's Honda. That's Micaela's car. Ugh.

Xander's nowhere in sight, the movie's on the credits, and I need a reason to remove myself from Dahlia's grasp.

When the doorbell rings, I slip from her embrace to answer it.

I give Micaela a smile. "Hey, how're you doing?"

"Great." She returns my gesture with a nervous excitement. "Are the guys here? I'm heading to Indiana, and I wanted to say a quick goodbye."

Suddenly, Xander's behind me. "I just dropped Jim off at the airport. His flight was thirty minutes ago." He still has his shoes on. "I figured he told you."

As soon as he speaks, Micaela's face lights up. She's forgotten me.

And he has no interest in talking to me.

So I back away. Dahlia's waiting for me.

But when I sit down, I can't stop watching. Micaela's feelings are obvious, and most of the time, Xander lets her mild flirtations slide right off. He hasn't been interested in anything remotely relationship-like, but his charming smile widens when she blushes.

"Hey." Dahlia pokes my side. "Do you want pizza? Or were you thinking of something else?"

"I don't know." I lost my appetite.

Micaela gives him a peck on the cheek before waving at me. "Have a great break!"

Xander watches her for a minute before shutting the door and heading for the kitchen.

I grab my phone from the coffee table. It's after seven— long past when I should've eaten. All I had with my pill at six was a bag of chips. And I need to eat. I cannot let myself stop eating.

I rise, pocketing my phone. "Yeah, let's get some food."

Seventeen

"Wow," I say, following her inside the studio. "This is great."

Dahlia flashes me a grin and flips four light switches on the nearest wall. "I was surprised by how huge they are."

The fluorescent lights flicker on above, illuminating the six single-person studios along the left side of the room. They're partitioned by half-walls, but over winter break, they're empty, aside from a narrow table in each.

Dahlia's studio, the one in the far corner and the most secluded, is the only one with more than the table. She drops her box on the table, and I set down the one she asked me to carry as well.

"What're you going to do with all this space?"

She opens the first box and sifts through the materials. "Well, I have my Pinnacle Workshop this semester, so I have a lot of plans."

"Can I help?"

"Sure." She nudges the box I carried closer before diving into her own. "I'm focusing on screen printing, so I need the space. I have my own materials and tools. I'm not using any Bradford material."

156

"At all?"

The first thing when I open it is a wooden paper cutter—no wonder this thing was so heavy.

"All the computer stuff I do on my Mac, and I have a printer at my apartment. But yeah, I'll have all my screens and ink and everything here."

In fact, the box she sorts through is mostly different screens.

I yank off my coat and return to the box. I lay the cutter behind the box and pull out the next items: a squeegee, two bottles of emulsion and sensitizer, and a box of 250-watt bulbs. "Whoa. You're serious."

"The first thing I need to do is build myself a drying box so I don't fuck up the screens." She pulls out a blank screen, then a second. "There's no room in the darkroom for me to use, and I don't have extra space to build my own, so I have to be extra careful that it's light-safe."

When my box is empty, I turn to her. "Don't you have to put the emulsion on in the dark? Where would you do that?"

Dahlia pulls out more blank screens one by one. "Most emulsion isn't as sensitive to light while wet. As long as I do it in low light, it's alright. Then, they go straight into the dark to protect them as much as possible."

"Oh, okay."

"It's a time-consuming process." She sighs. "I mean, it's intensive when you have a studio set up for it, but doing all of this without the fancy machines and material will be so much harder." She withdraws the final screen and pauses to inspect it.

"How long—?"

Before I can get the words out, her phone rings, and she snatches it off the table.

She doesn't answer right away, only stares, jaw slack.

"What?"

"Oh, my God."

"What?" I ask again.

Her face transforms, and I don't have to ask anymore. She has the same smile she wore each time her phone rang last winter break. A display of pure excitement, even affection—something she's normally hesitant to display publicly.

"Hello? Darius!"

I should give her some privacy.

"Hey," I whisper, catching her attention momentarily. "I'll go downstairs to the snack machines or something. Be right back."

She nods but turns away, eagerly listening to her brother's voice.

In the silent art building, most of the first floor lights are off. Beyond the thick concrete walls, rumbling thunder echoes, and the windows quiver. Is it supposed to rain?

I pass the snack machines to the front entrance and press against the glass for a better view. The clouds above are thick and gray, heavy with rain, and it's dark.

The thunder rumbles again—any lightning is out of sight—and I check the weather on my phone.

Awesome.

On the other end of the hall, the snack machines are lit up by a back light. I slip a few quarters into the slot but hesitate.

I have no appetite. I said that as an excuse to give her space. But a quick check of my phone tells me I haven't eaten in four hours. I cannot stop eating.

With a deep breath, I punch in the code for some sour cream and onion chips, but when they fall to the receptacle, the lights flicker.

That's not a good sign.

I snatch the chips and scurry toward the stairs.

A flash of lightning bursts through the windows. Less than a second later, a crash of thunder.

Halfway up the stairs, the lights go out.

Shit.

Seriously, shit.

On the top floor, the studio is dark. "Dahlia? You there?"

Her voice reverberates off the walls, and I stumble toward her, my hand tracing the wall. She's still on the phone.

"Dahlia?"

She draws the phone away enough it lights up her face. "Gimme a minute."

I shake my head. "The power's out. We need to leave."

But she returns to her phone. "I'm sorry, Dar, but I gotta go. Call me next time you can."

◆

Outside, it's pouring. We're soaked from running to the car, and the rain pelts against the windshield as she heads off campus. Visibility is awful.

It doesn't let up by the time we reach my house.

I tug my jacket closer, my hand on the door handle. "Thanks for the ride. We'll get together later. Drive safe."

But Dahlia stoops into the back seat. "I have an umbrella." She offers me the handle.

159

I hold up a hand. "You'll need that when you get to your apartment. I'm not taking it."

"I'll walk you to your door. Relax."

Without waiting for a response, she pushes open her door and rushes around the car. I stumble out under the umbrella. This is surprisingly kind of her.

"Come on." Water streams down her face, and she leads me to the house by the hand. "Let's get you warm and dry."

The front door is locked, but I pull out my keys and finally relax once I gain entry. Inside, it's dark and vacant, but it's warm.

"Thanks for the umbrella."

She offers me a parting wave. "Later."

I close the door as she runs down the stairs, slip off my shoes, and grab a kitchen towel for my hair. Time to do a load of laundry, I guess.

The doorbell rings.

I rush back, patting my dripping hair.

On the other side of the door, nervousness tugs at Dahlia's thin lips. "How mad would you be if I told you I accidentally locked my keys in my car?"

I peek out but can't see anything from this angle. "Is the car running?"

"Thankfully, no, but my headlights are on. My car'll be dead by the time someone can come unlock it. I called a locksmith, but they won't be here for hours. This dumb weather."

I open the door the rest of the way. "Come in."

"Thank you." She grins when the door closes behind her.

"You can stay the night if you need to. I don't think the storm's going to let up." I point toward my wet Converse.

"Take off your shoes. All the big towels are upstairs."

Moments later, Dahlia examines my bedroom as she runs the towel over her wet body.

"I have some pajamas you can wear." I pull a couple sets from the top drawer of my dresser. I need to change too.

When I turn around, Dahlia's shirt is on the floor, and her jeans are next. She's wearing a pair of lacy red underwear, along with a bra to match. Then, she undoes the clasp. "It's amazing how much water soaks through your clothes when it's pouring that hard." She chortles, the bra now on the pile of wet clothing.

I clutch the edge of the dresser as her fingers slide under the hem of her underwear. They're added to the pile as well.

She accepts one of the towels from the hall closet and runs it through her hair. I cannot stop staring at her bare ass. When she bends over, her ass isn't the only thing I can see.

Oh my God.

Dahlia is naked in my bedroom. Why is Dahlia naked in my bedroom?

This is not a good idea.

She flips her hair up, the towel resting her shoulders, and turns, arm outstretched. "Peejays?" The towel doesn't cover anything.

Carefully, I extend the extra pair.

She cocks an eyebrow as she accepts them. "You're a little pale, Billie. You alright?"

I tear my eyes away and clear my throat. "Yeah, I'm gonna put all this wet clothing in the washer."

I pile her clothes inside my mostly empty hamper as she tugs on the pajama shorts, then dumps her wet towel inside. Her long hair, dark brown from the rain, barely covers her breasts. I lay my towel on top of the hamper and grab clean pajamas before heading downstairs.

◆

In the laundry room, tucked away under the stairs, I dump the contents of the basket in the washer, pour in some detergent, and start the machine. But I'm soaking wet.

For a moment, I lean against the top-loader as it fills with water and pat my hair with the towel.

This is not how the night was supposed to go. We were supposed to set up her studio, eat a late dinner, and go our separate ways. She certainly wasn't supposed to stay the night at my house.

She wasn't supposed to get naked in front of me.

And I wasn't supposed to stare at her naked body—or be turned on by it. She is so skinny. Her breasts are tiny. Her ribs, her hips, her everything is skin and bones. But the attraction is there.

I get hot thinking about our make-out session at Xander's party. If I hadn't come to my senses, she wouldn't have stopped. She would've made me come.

An uncomfortably large part of me wishes she had.

To be fair, I was already turned on.

I don't want to imagine how angry she'd be if she knew Xander had kissed me and touched me not ten minutes prior. That he was a large part of the reason I was aroused.

I heave a sigh.

The water inches toward the rim of the washing machine tub, but I need to put my wet clothes in. Thank God I had enough foresight to bring pajamas with me.

I run the towel over my body, then lay it atop the dryer and strip off my clothes. The hoody soaked through to my shirt, but my underwear is dry. I wouldn't be surprised if Dahlia's were too.

A cough sounds behind me.

I snatch the towel off the dryer and spin around, covering my bare skin.

Xander, dressed in soaking wet work clothes, stands in the doorway. "That's not what I expected to find in the laundry room."

Heat rises to my cheeks. "I thought it'd be safer to change down here."

A beat passes during which he only stares, his eyes following the curves of my half-naked body, a puddle forming underfoot. He wets his lips before managing to speak. "Why's that?"

"Well, I didn't expect you home yet."

"Or consider I might have the same idea when I got here?" He pushes away from the door frame and tears off his black work shirt. "This storm's crazy."

I nod, mute.

I've seen glimpses of his tattoo before. I was in France this summer when he got it, but we live together. Although he makes an effort to remain covered, it's nearly impossible not to see him shirtless. But I don't normally get to ogle him. I've never seen the tattoo in so much detail.

A Chinese dragon twists around the left side of his ribs and chest and to his back. The style is immediately recognizable.

"Did you seriously get a *Fairy Tail* character tattooed on your chest?"

163

He snickers—then unbuckles his belt. "Igneel's a badass."

"I'm not disagreeing, but that seems…"

He shakes his slacks down and slips his socks off with them. He looks at me as though unimpressed by my current scantily clad state, yet a hint of an erection tents his boxers.

"I don't know." Can he hear me over the hum of the washer? "Extreme?"

Xander laughs, but he surprises me when he turns toward the door. "Let me know when yours is in the dryer, and I'll start my load."

"Xander…"

He throws a glance over his shoulder. "Yeah?"

I step forward, and the towel brushes my bare legs. "My load's small if you want to put your clothes in too. It wouldn't be a problem. I just started it."

After a beat, he silently turns and plucks his wet clothing off the concrete floor.

When he approaches, I can't breathe.

He pauses beside me, his arm grazing mine as he adds his soaking work clothes to the open washer. "Thanks." His eyes travel along my side, taking in the expanse of exposed flesh.

I shift so the towel blocks his view. "Uh, no problem."

He gives my barely covered body a final once-over and heads for the door again. "I'm gonna take a shower."

"Okay," I say in a small voice.

When the stairs creak above, I shove the towel into the washer, close the lid, and get dressed.

Goddammit. He wasn't the only one looking.

And Dahlia is upstairs in my bedroom.

Eighteen

A SMILE LIGHTS UP DAHLIA'S FACE WHEN I OPEN THE DOOR, and she sets her phone on my nightstand. There's space for me on the bed. Beside her.

I clear my throat. "You made yourself at home."

She offers me a grin. "Yeah, well, how long does it take to start a load of laundry?"

The pounding rain and crashes of thunder cover the sound of the shower running. She doesn't realize Xander's here. The shower shuts off promptly, and I close the door. She doesn't need to know he's here either.

"Sorry." I approach slowly, trying to quell my anxious stomach. "You know, there's a perfectly comfortable couch downstairs."

Sharing a bed is inviting trouble.

But Dahlia pats the mattress. "I want to sleep with you."

I swallow audibly.

When I slip under the blankets and cover myself, desperate to relax, Dahlia twists toward me. A smirk plays on her lips. "What will we talk about? You won't fall asleep for hours, so we should pass the time."

"I actually sleep better than before."

To be fair, that requires yoga and masturbation. Not an ideal bedtime ritual, but it's better than a bottle of wine.

Her narrow eyebrow arches up. "Is that so?"

"Most of the time."

But I can't masturbate with her in my bed.

She presses a hand to my shoulder. "Billie, relax. You don't need to be nervous."

I avert my eyes. Having Dahlia in my bed gives me a million reasons to be nervous.

Then, she withdraws. "I said I'd keep my hands to myself, and I will. Until you change your mind."

I stretch my shoulders to loosen up. "What do you want to talk about?"

She shifts onto her back, shoulder to shoulder with me. "You decide."

"How?" A scoff tries to slip out, but I prevent it. "Dahlia, we haven't been friends for months. I'm in a different place now. I don't drink, I don't party, I don't smoke hookah, I don't spend hours loathing my mother. What are we supposed to talk about?"

When she speaks again, her voice is hushed. "You're not going to ask about Darius?"

I turn to her. "Huh?"

"The phone call at the studio. It was Darius." She stares at the ceiling, her voice thick with emotion. "You don't want to know what's going on?"

Of course I want to know. I just never expected her to offer an answer.

"You've never been particularly forthcoming in the past." I give a light shrug. "I figured, if you want to tell me, you will."

"On the final day Darius was home for Christmas break last year, the woman who calls herself our mother discovered we're communicating. I don't think she realized I attended Bradford, because she let him come back that semester. He pretended everything was fine, even though it wasn't."

That's why she was so distant after I went to Springfield. I thought she was mad at me.

Dahlia's voice trembles. "Over the summer, she learned we were going to the same school, and she pulled him out of Bradford. That's why he isn't here. He's enrolled in a local community college, and he sneaks phone calls to me."

My brow furrows. "How can she stop him? He's twenty-two."

"That doesn't mean she can't control him. He'll never get out from under her thumb. He lets her do these things over and over again."

"I'm sorry."

Her eyes glisten with unshed tears. Dahlia doesn't get emotional often, but her twin brother is one of the few things she truly cares about.

To my surprise, she buries her face in my chest. "And Brent doesn't help anything. He acts like it's no biggie and I'm being overly emotional. God, he's such an asshole sometimes."

Part of me wants to laugh. I could've told her that ages ago.

Instead, I rub her back to calm her. "Sometimes, I don't know why you're friends with him."

She chuckles, and her hot breath permeates my t-shirt. "Because he's all I have."

"That's not true."

When Dahlia blinks, a tear slides down her cheek. "What do you mean?"

My fingers trail along the side of her face, and I thumb away the tear. "You have me."

It takes no effort to bridge the gap and press my mouth to hers, and her response is immediate. She wraps tighter around me, clinging in desperation, and I nip her bottom lip, soft and slow. She opens without hesitation and squirms at the encouragement.

For once, she lets me take the lead.

And I do.

She's cold—a hint of dampness remaining from the storm—but her stomach is taut and smooth. I trace the nubs of her spine until her shirt bunches under her arms, and although she returns my kiss, that's all she does. Even as I tear the shirt over her head, she makes no move to touch me.

Her breasts are small, but the nipples are thick and firm, and she mewls and pants when I tease them. Her sounds, soft and sensual, send an encouraging jolt of desire to my core, and I buck against her for some much-anticipated friction.

But although she releases a long moan, her hands stay firmly in place.

I pull back. "Dahlia…"

Her wide brown eyes flutter open. "What?"

"Aren't you going to touch me?"

She quirks a smile. "I'm keeping my hands to myself."

I suck her bottom lip into my mouth and nibble. "Don't."

When I pull her into another kiss, her hands, at last, make contact. She drags me on top to straddle her, our lips barely keeping together, and her slender fingers slip down my pajama bottoms to grope my ass. I roll my hips against hers, and she gasps into my mouth.

How much pleasure that simple sound arouses surprises me, but I don't know why.

I admit, despite her month-long blatant pursuit, I never expected this moment to occur. Her want for me has always been present, but only now do I realize, my want for her has been too. There is no specific action or moment when the attraction began. It feels as if it has always been here.

Now, there's no turning back.

She removes my shirt and plays with my breasts for a long time, leaving me with little to do but moan under her attention. But removing my pajama shorts is a struggle. Not that Dahlia lets that stop her.

A hand slides between us to reach my entrance, and she dips inside, gathering my wetness on her fingertip, and circles my clit. I latch onto the headboard, gasping, rocking my hips against her poised fingers, and she moans with pleasure at my reaction and increases the pressure.

I don't know how she manages, but she yanks my shorts and underwear the rest of the way off and tugs my hips closer, dragging me up against the headboard. I lay my forehead on the cold wall for support and whimper as her fingers pull away. Relief pools in my abdomen when her tongue replaces them.

Tears prick my eyes as she sucks my clit between her lips, and I moan her name, my breasts smashed against the wall. Her fingers, digging into my ass, keep me in place, but all I can focus on is her lips and tongue and the steady, scorching ache as my arousal builds, as she ravages me.

169

A sharp gasp, followed by a hoarse sob, escapes my mouth as two fingers slide with ease inside my slick entrance. When she locates my hot spot, my moans are louder than I expected. Louder than the thunder. Pleasure surges through me, and I cannot contain myself. I don't want to.

Dahlia does not relent after I come. Her fingers continue their massage, her tongue its mesmerizing circles around my clit, until I'm needy again.

My hands clamp onto the headboard so hard the wood digs into my palms. I release a shuddering moan as she shifts, and I barely stabilize myself when she yanks me closer, no longer gentle. She is merciless and determined, and she does not free me until I come again.

Afterward, I collapse beside her, and Dahlia studies me with a proud smirk on her swollen lips. I shove my curls out of my face, waiting for my heart's unsteady beat to calm.

The rain pelts against the window, and a long rumble of thunder shakes the house. That's nearly as loud as I was.

Fuck.

We're not alone.

I stumble off the bed to retrieve my clothes.

Dahlia pushes up, mouth falling open. "What are you doing?"

I tug my pajama bottoms up and clear my throat. "I, uh, need to check the laundry."

She sends me a skeptical glance but doesn't argue.

◆

The house is dark, but I don't bother turning on the lights. I know where everything is without hesitation. In the dark,

I can pretend that was some strange fantasy and Dahlia isn't partially naked in my bedroom, waiting for my return—waiting for her turn.

Inside the laundry room, the dryer's running. Xander must've switched it over.

Limbs shaking, I wander into the kitchen for some water. I need to replenish. I fill a glass and take a sip.

"So that's who the car in the driveway belongs to."

I jump, nearly spilling.

When I look closely, Xander is standing in the far corner, near the pantry. The can in his hand glistens with condensation.

"What?"

"I didn't recognize it right away. I was busy getting out of the rain. I get it now." He slurps at his drink. "Since when are you fucking Dahlia Finnick?"

For the life of me, I have no explanation.

He scoffs. "You have nothing to say to that?"

"She accidentally locked her keys in her car."

Xander barks with laughter. "Yeah, I'm sure it was an accident. She hasn't been trying to bed you for over a year."

"That's none of your business."

He slams the can on the counter and steps closer. "She's using you. Like she always used you. How are you so fucking blind?"

My lips contort into a snarl. "I'm not blind."

"Oh, so she's bad for you and you know it, but you go back to her? Why are you taking care of her? She's an adult. You can't save her."

I furrow my brow. "Are you accusing me of the same thing you wanted to do for me? I never asked you to take care of me, and I'm not trying to save her."

Xander releases a derisive snort. "What do you want?"

"I want her to save herself."

He rolls his eyes. "You have far too much faith in Dahlia Finnick. This is going to blow up in your fucking face."

"Maybe." I shrug. "But like I said, that's none of your business."

"Are you—?"

"No." My hand clamps around the glass, squeezing too tight. "We're done. We have been done for nine months. My love life is no longer your business, so keep your fucking nose out of it." I fill the glass one last time and turn toward the hallway. "Thanks for putting the clothes in the dryer. I'm going to bed."

Where Dahlia is waiting for me.

Nineteen

DAHLIA LEFT EARLY THIS MORNING. NO WORD ABOUT THE fact that, theoretically, her keys were locked in her car.

I'm sure, if I'd asked, she would've had an answer. Maybe she called a locksmith. Maybe she knows how to jimmy a lock. Most likely, her keys were never locked inside in the first place.

But it's officially eight in the morning. Late enough I can call Prue without disturbing her "beauty sleep."

She answers on the third ring. "Fuck, Billie, what do you want?"

As it turns out, not late enough.

"I think I had sex last night."

She takes a deep breath, and when she speaks, she's calm. "What do you mean, you 'think'?"

"I don't know." I bury myself under the covers to quell the anxious ball in my stomach. "What counts as sex when neither party has a penis?"

"Oh."

"Yeah."

Prue clears her throat. "Things with Dahlia are moving fast."

"Yeah." I don't know how to move slowly. "I'm worried it's too fast. Especially since I have no experience here. I mean, if we dated, what does that entail?"

"No offense, Billie, but you're overthinking. If you need a dick to get off, use some toys."

Even over the phone, heat rises to my cheeks. "Oh, that's definitely not a problem, but I don't know what to do with her."

She snickers. "I know you've never played with someone else's female anatomy, but she knows what she likes, trust me. Ask her."

"I don't feel comfortable asking her."

"I figured you'd say that." Prue sighs. "Billie, if you can't talk to her, if you're uncomfortable, and if she's pressuring you, you shouldn't date her."

"I know that."

"Do you? Because you tend to get in over your head despite your best-made plans." She pauses, but when I don't respond, she adds, "Do you like her? Or are you just caught up in Dahlia being Dahlia again?"

A rueful smile sweeps across my face. "I think I've always liked her, Prue, but it was hard to notice when Xander was in the picture."

She tsk-tsks. "Billie, don't you understand? Xander's still in the picture. He may be fucking random girls and whatever else he does while single, but he's in the picture."

"We're roommates."

"Right."

I roll onto my side. "I should let you go, Prue. Thanks for talking to me."

"Anytime."

After we hang up, I lie on the bed, the phone clasped between both hands, and stare across the blurry room. I didn't bothered to put my glasses on after I couldn't fall back asleep.

I don't want to get up. I don't want to do anything.

◆

My six o'clock alarm blasts through the living room, and I blink a few times as I shift my attention between the television and the phone. I turn the alarm off but stare at the screen.

There are three texts from Dahlia I need to respond to, but that's not what catches my attention.

When did it hit six?

Outside, the sun has set, and the house is dark. I never bothered to turn on the lights. I hadn't noticed the time.

With a deep breath, I stretch to reach the remote. The screen freezes on Bradley's bloody face. I'm on episode sixty, and I started my *Brotherhood* rewatch a couple days ago. I haven't done much other than sitting on this couch—and texting Dahlia.

She's come over occasionally since the night of the storm, but I've only felt comfortable inviting her while Xander's at work. Then, I don't have to deal with his judgmental looks or her sudden clinginess the moment he's in the room.

Plus, I don't want to do anything sexual with him in the house.

I set my feet on the floor and lay my head in my hands as a yawn takes over. I shouldn't be this tired yet.

The front door opens, and Xander hangs his wool coat

175

on a hook. Underneath, he's wearing a red Draft Horse shirt.

We haven't talked since our argument four nights ago.

I want to look away—I know I should—but the energy it takes to move, to cast my gaze elsewhere, is more than I have. I'm exhausted.

When he spots me, he frowns. "Why's it so dark in here?"

I shrug.

He scoffs and stalks into the living room to flip on the overhead light.

The sudden brilliance overwhelms me, and I hunch over, covering my adjusting eyes.

"Have you gotten up since I went to work?"

I had to pee at one point, and I grabbed a snack at the same time, but that's all.

"Yeah, I didn't think so." He rolls his eyes and heads for the kitchen.

With campus closed for winter break, I have nothing to do. I have twenty hours of work each week, but that's not enough to occupy my time. I have no reason to go anywhere or do anything, and I don't know what to do with myself.

I struggle to my feet and wander toward the kitchen. I pass the dining room, which now has the light on, and into the kitchen, lit up as well.

Xander is putting together a sandwich, and I pause in the doorway as he slathers a layer of peanut butter on whole wheat bread. "Have you eaten today?"

"I had some popcorn." I lean against the frame—my unsteady legs can't support me for long. "I haven't done enough to get hungry."

His nostrils flair. "And you can't do anything if you don't eat."

176

"I'm fine, really."

"Says the person with chronic depression." He twists the lid on the peanut butter and slams the two slices together. He approaches me with the sandwich held out. "Eat."

I stare. "You made that for yourself."

He purses his lips. "I can make another. Eat."

I accept it slowly, and he waits till I take a bite. Only then does he return to the counter and start another sandwich.

"When did you go to sleep last night?"

"I don't know."

"Your light was on when I brushed my teeth." His words are disapproving.

"If you knew, why did you ask?"

He sends me a quick glare, and I take another bite to appease him. "When did you last shower?"

I swallow down the food. "I don't know. A couple days ago?"

"Have you been practicing your breathing exercises?" He stabs the bread while spreading the honey.

"Yeah."

"What about exercise? You still working out?"

I take a moment to eat more before I can speak. "The campus gym is closed, and I can't afford a membership off campus."

"So that's a no." He chucks the peanut butter and honey into the cabinet and tears into his own sandwich. After he swallows, he continues his interrogation: "You still keeping an art journal?"

My nod is small, but he inclines his head in acknowledgment.

"Has anything happened? Have you cut down your

177

therapy sessions or something? You're still seeing Byrdie, right?"

"We meet once a month now."

Xander's eyebrows draw together. "Do you need to see him more often?"

"I don't know."

"Has anything changed?"

Uncertain, I check my phone. It's fifteen after now, and I—

Shit.

"I have to take my medication."

He levels me with a serious gaze. "Where is it?"

I angle my head. "In the top drawer of my dresser. Why?"

He gulps down the remnants of his sandwich and marches to the stairs. He barely bothers to throw the words, "Because I'm going to watch you take it," over his shoulder before disappearing from view.

I finish my sandwich while he's gone, and when he returns, he has the orange pill bottle in hand. He fills a glass with filtered water and brings them to me.

As promised, he doesn't leave my side as I swallow the blue pill, relaxing until I offer him the glass.

"Drink it all," he commands.

He's staring so intently I don't know what else to do, so I raise it to my lips and drain the glass.

I hover in the doorway as he sets the empty glass by the sink, but he doesn't return. Instead, he faces the basin, hands gripping the edge of the counter.

I have to say something.

He flinches when I lean beside him.

I reach out a hand, but I can't make contact. "I'm not

magically better because I'm on meds now, you know. I have ups and downs. This is normal."

Xander casts me a momentary glance before turning back to the sink. "You need to be vigilant about taking your pills." For the first time, his voice is relaxed.

"This is the first time I've been late in two months."

He steps closer. "Don't make it a habit. You cannot lay around watching *FMA* all day just because there aren't classes."

My hand drops to the counter. "What am I supposed to do? No classes, my request for more hours was denied, and Prue's out of town. Dahlia is my only friend here, and she's not mentally sound."

His face contorts into a sneer at her name. "This is exactly what I meant—"

But I narrow my eyes, and he closes his mouth.

For a while, he stares into space, and when he returns to me, I look away.

"You've worked so hard."

"I know."

He steps closer again. "You can't let her mess everything up. You have to take better care of yourself, Dixon." His fingers caress my cheek, push my hair out of my face, and I'm entranced by his beautiful blue eyes.

All I can do is nod.

"That means you need to exercise. If you break the habit, it'll take a whole month to get back to working out regularly again."

"How am I supposed to do that?"

"I still run every morning." His voice is quiet, barely above a whisper. "Come with me while the gym's closed."

I force myself to look down. "You wouldn't mind?" At this distance, all I can think about is kissing him.

"I think I could manage." His fingers thread through my hair, and he tugs me into his arms. "It might be cold."

Here, in his arms, I'm warm, comfortable.

I bury my face in his shoulder and hold him tight, inhaling his scent. I wish this moment could last forever.

But it has to end.

"I can handle the cold."

"A little too well, Dixon." He rests his head against mine, relaxing, and I melt into his arms, relishing this heat, this connection. "Please don't scare me."

My neck muscles tense. "You were scared?" I whisper against his chest.

He doesn't say anything, but his fingers massage an anxious beat along my spine. It's nothing short of an admission.

I press closer. "I'm sorry. I never meant to scare you."

"Don't bother, Dixon. I'm always worried."

My lips twist into a grimace. "I told you, I can do this on my own."

"I know." His grip around me tightens. "You're incredibly strong, even when you don't have any faith in yourself. But that doesn't mean I stop worrying."

But in his arms, I'm not strong. My legs are unsteady and weak.

I lay my head on his chest again. I have to relish every second before we're back to reality.

Twenty

By the time Xander returns from one of his runs, I typically escape to the painting studio or work. Being in his vicinity when he's hot and sweaty and shirtless is generally a bad idea.

Today, I don't have much choice.

He tears off his shirt the moment we get home, per his normal routine, and heads for the kitchen. Breakfast is his next step, of course.

"You're faster than before." Xander sends me a sidelong glance as he whips a couple eggs in a bowl. The burner heats up, and his slice of whole wheat waits in the toaster.

I stoop to examine the fridge's contents. "So are you." My Greek yogurt's at the back, behind the half-empty bottle of orange juice, and the fridge jolts shut.

"That's what happens when you quit smoking." He pours the eggs into the skillet and rinses the bowl, then pushes down the lever on the toaster. "I was surprised by how quickly my stamina increased when I quit over the summer."

I tear off the foil lid but can't help staring. I definitely don't remember any need for his stamina to increase. Does he last longer?

I blink away the thought and grab a spoon. "Congrats, I guess."

My phone, sitting on the counter, vibrates. It's probably Dahlia. She's coming over this afternoon so I can see her before spending a week at my dad's.

When I turn round, Xander's beside me, reaching for the cupboard.

I nearly drop my yogurt.

He pulls back with a plate. "Little jumpy?"

I try to stay nonchalant, but my eyes won't focus on his face. "Yeah, sorry." My voice comes out as a whisper.

But he simply returns to the stove and nudges the scrambled eggs around the skillet, and I start to eat. The eggs hiss on the stove, but I force myself to study my yogurt.

It's natural to be attracted to him. That doesn't just go away.

An uneasiness clenches my stomach at the thought of Dahlia. She thinks I'm over him, and I am, but the attraction still exists. She doesn't know how easily Xander turns me on.

When the toast pops, Xander slides closer to butter it. The eggs sit on the plate, steaming, and he clears his throat.

Anxious, I meet his gaze. "Yeah?"

"I need a fork, Dixon."

Oh.

"Right." I step out of the way. "Thanks for letting me run with you. I appreciate the gesture."

He grabs a fork and his plate and heads for the dining room. "No problem."

I follow wordlessly.

At the dining table, he sets down his phone and stabs his

fork into the scrambled eggs, and I stand in the doorway, my yogurt half gone. I feel like we're supposed to keep talking, but for the life of me, I don't know what to say.

Xander averts his eyes. He doesn't know what to say either.

The table vibrates.

We don't have to talk. His phone's ringing.

He frowns at the number and answers the call with a deep furrow in his brow, his fork abandoned. "Yeah?"

I look away.

"What do you mean you're home for Christmas?" His voice is instantly alarmed. "You're never…"

A few more bites. The yogurt's gone.

He scoffs. "I see."

I scrape at the sides of the plastic cup. I admit, I want to be nosy.

"No, I see what you're doing. You want me there so you can convince me to—" he glances at me, then away "—well, that."

The container is empty now. I don't have any excuse to stay in the room.

"Dad already tried. It's not happening." He groans. "I'm not going back. I have work. And I don't want to see either of you. Have a good holiday." He slams the phone on the table and scarfs down the rest of his food without sending me so much as a glance.

My hand grips the yogurt cup, and I build up the courage to speak. "Who was that?"

He pauses before stuffing in the last bite. "The woman who gave birth to me," he says after swallowing.

"Oh." I grimace. As long as I've known him, he's never

been close with his parents, but the term is surprisingly unfeeling. "Your parents want you home for Christmas?"

"It's not nearly as pleasant as you make it sound. Besides, Christmas is like two days away." With a sharp glare, he rises to take his dishes to the kitchen.

I trail behind. "They don't normally make that kind of effort, do they?"

He snorts while rinsing his plate. "The only reason they're making an effort now is because they want something. They never call unless they want something."

"You never know." I drop my yogurt cup in the trash and plop the spoon on the counter with the other dirty dishes. "Maybe they—"

Xander shuts off the water and turns on me with fierce determination. "Do you want to run with me tomorrow?"

I'm caught aback, but the change in subject shouldn't be a shock. Xander keeps his cards close to his chest.

"Oh. I can't."

He looks away, mouth set in a tight frown. Is he disappointed?

"Xander, tomorrow's Christmas Eve. The gallery's closed till January. I'm heading to my dad's tonight to spend the week with him."

He wipes his hands with a towel. "Right. Of course you are."

I tilt my head, considering him. "What will you do for the holiday? You working?"

He shakes his head. "My last shift is eleven to five. The bar's closed for the next three days."

"So you'll be here the whole time?"

He drops the towel on the counter. "No different than

normal. I'm always alone for Christmas."

I step closer. "That's not true. You've spent the last two Christmases with Jimmy and his parents. Besides, 'normal' doesn't make it okay."

He shrugs and heads for the exit. "It doesn't matter, Dixon. It's just Christmas."

"No."

Xander spins round with wide eyes. "What?"

"It does matter. You shouldn't be alone for the holidays because it's normal." This is where I put my foot down. "Come with me to my dad's house."

His eyebrows shoot up to his dark bangs. "Is that...?"

In the distance, my phone chimes again. I never read her first text, but this takes precedence over Dahlia.

"You know you're always welcome." I'm determined now. "It doesn't matter if we haven't been friends. You shouldn't be alone for Christmas."

"Really, Dixon, it's not..." But he trails off uncertainly.

"What else would you be doing?"

"I don't know. Video games, exercise, nothing special."

"You don't have to be here alone to do that. Come with me."

For a moment, he stares, pensive, his jaw set firm. This isn't the best plan—or a good plan—but I cannot let him be alone for another Christmas.

He blinks. Forcefully. And then, he beams. "Okay."

◆

Dahlia, her honey-brown hair splayed across my pillow, reclines on the bed in nothing but a pair of sheer under-

185

wear while I pack. "What am I supposed to do while you're hanging out with your dad?" She flips to the next page in her magazine.

I dump some underwear and a bra into my backpack. "Hang out with Brent?"

No idea when she saw him last. She's spent as much time with me as I've allowed, but I haven't let her to spend every night in my bed like she wants.

Dahlia scrunches her nose. "Unlikely." She turns up the volume on her phone as her playlist transitions to a new song. More electronica.

I grab sweaters from my closet. "I don't know what to tell you. We can text and stuff, but the whole point of spending Christmas with my dad is to actually spend the holiday with him."

She rolls her eyes. "Billie, you're an atheist."

"So's my dad." I force the next few items inside. The bag's nearly full, but I only have a couple more items to pack. "That doesn't mean we can't use it as an excuse to spend time together. It can be a secular, family-oriented holiday too."

She drops the magazine onto the mattress. "You don't have to win every argument, you know." She saunters to me with a smirk and lays an open-mouthed kiss below my ear. "But I love watching you get all fired up."

I nudge her away. "You should get dressed. I have to go."

Her tongue trails saliva down my throat, and her voice is thick with desire. "Or we can go back to bed. You can go over in the morning. Not tonight." Her fingers tug at the neckline of my t-shirt. "You should be naked."

I press a quick kiss to her lips but make a point of pulling away. "I don't have to, you're right. But that's the plan.

Really, you need to leave."

Dahlia drags me into another kiss, and her hands grab my ass over the jeans.

A knock echoes through the room, and the door squeaks open.

I must not have closed it all the way after retrieving my toiletries.

"Hey, I'm ready to…" Xander pokes his head through the gap, hair damp from a post-work shower, but he stops, eyes bugging out, the moment he sees us. "Uh, sorry. Didn't realize you had company." And he immediately recoils.

"No, wait." I untangle myself from Dahlia's grip and zip up my bag. "I'm ready too. Dahlia was leaving." I send her a pointed look.

But Dahlia's face is blank as she stares at Xander, awkwardly hovering in the doorway and avoiding her nearly naked body.

He clears his throat. "I'll meet you downstairs." And he's gone before I can protest.

I slip on my Converse and toss my backpack over my shoulder, but Dahlia doesn't move. "Come on, Lia, I need to go."

"Is he going with you?"

Right. Forgot to mention that part.

On purpose.

She was supposed to leave before he got home from work, but she refused. And I admit, I got a little distracted by going down on her that I didn't notice the time.

"Yeah, he is."

"Why?"

The word comes out with such vehemence I am stunned

into silence.

When I don't speak, she turns away to retrieve her clothes. "Right," she grumbles as she pulls on her shirt, "no need to tell me your ex is going to spend Christmas with your family. No reason to keep me in the loop." She yanks her jeans over her tiny, sheer-covered ass. "The fact that we're sleeping together is completely meaningless."

"Dahlia…"

She steps into her flats and snatches her purse from my nightstand, but I latch onto her arm when she tries to pass.

"Dahlia, calm down. Xander and I are over, and you know that. Nothing's going to happen."

She releases a high-pitched scoff and tears away. "Don't try to humor me. This isn't a fucking overreaction."

I follow her downstairs, all the way to the front door, but she blazes right past Xander, now in his leather jacket. "Dahlia, wait!"

The door slams in my face before.

I strike my fist against the door. One glance out the window, and her car tears down the street. Dammit.

Xander clucks his tongue. "Well, that was…"

I grit my teeth. "Come on, let's go."

Twenty-One

THE KNOB DOESN'T TURN, AND I TUG OUT MY KEYS TO unlock it. Xander, backpack hanging from one shoulder, stands on the bottom step.

"Hey." I nod him closer and open the door. "Come on."

He trails behind me. The last time he was here, we were making out in the dining room when my dad wasn't looking. And when he was looking. Dad shook his hand and sent us away to take care of our urges.

I slip my shoes off, hang up my coat, and signal for him to do the same. "Dad, I'm here!"

Xander closes the door and waits. Despite my instructions, his signature leather jacket and Vans stay firmly in place. His grip on the backpack strap is unwavering.

"Dad?"

Footsteps echo through the house. He's coming from the kitchen. "Mina, I was about to…"

His words trail off the moment he sees Xander.

I step closer, imploring Dad to understand. "We can make up the couch, right?"

He clears his throat. "Of course. We have plenty of blankets."

Xander shakes his head. "You don't have to worry about me. I'll be fine."

I send him a sharp glare. "You said you'd stay with us. You need blankets."

His mouth tightens into an uncomfortable smile.

At last, Dad beams. "Feel free to lay your things in the living room. I'm sorry we don't have another bed."

Xander shrugs away the apology. "It went to a good cause."

When Xander, Jimmy, and I moved in together, Dad let me take one of his spare beds to the house. Not sure how I would've afforded one otherwise.

Dad nods toward the kitchen. "I'm doing some prep work for dinner tomorrow night. I'll make sure we have enough for three."

He disappears into the kitchen, and Xander wanders into the living room uncertainly.

There's a crackling fire in the hearth, plus Dad and I already decorated the tree. In addition to the two stockings on the mantle, Dad also moved out the photo from the second guest room—the one of the two of us—and another of me and Mo when we were little, before she straightened her hair.

Xander drops his backpack on the floor and studies the photos. His calloused fingers wrap around the wooden frame of the picture of me and Dad. "You were so young."

"That's what happens when you're twelve."

He snorts and wanders to the other photo. "I hardly recognize her. She looks totally different with an afro." He returns the frame to the mantle.

"Yeah, she's been straightening her hair for years. Most

people don't realize she's biracial."

He twists around to face me. "Dixon, this is a bad idea. I shouldn't be here."

I pad behind the couch, where the record albums are tucked away on a shelf, and slide my fingers over the spines. "The funny thing about that is, I understand that feeling far too well. I've felt out of place my entire life, and it took significant effort to get comfortable in this house." I cast a glance over my shoulder as I tug out Queen's *A Night at the Opera*.

Xander raises an eyebrow.

"But you're the one who manages to make yourself at home wherever you go, no matter the circumstances." With the record in place, I power on the machine and start the needle.

The song starts slow and quiet, but the tempo steadily increases, and Xander climbs onto the other side of the couch, his knees digging into the cushions so he can see.

Finally, Freddie Mercury belts out the opening lyrics of "Death on Two Legs."

"You know, this song is perfect for you, Dixon." His familiar words send goosebumps down my back.

I study the spinning record, and I swallow down the lump in my throat. "This is my favorite Queen song, you know."

"Had you heard it before two years ago?"

"I guess I should thank you for introducing me."

"Dixon, I—"

But when I turn to him, he can't finish the sentence. He can't look at me.

"I'm going to go help my dad in the kitchen. Why don't

you play a game or something? You brought your laptop, right?"

"Yeah." He backs off the couch. "Yeah, I did."

And I head for the kitchen.

◆

"The duck should be done in ten minutes. It has to rest, though." Dad pulls the meat thermometer out, closes the hot oven, and steps out of my way.

I pile the cooked bacon on a paper towel-lined plate. "Sounds good." When the meat's out, I add two tablespoons of butter.

Dad pauses beside me. "What's he doing out there? He's spent the last twenty-four hours on his computer."

Aside from the flurry of keystrokes and mouse clicks emanating from the living room, the house is quiet. Xander's used headphones for every game, which he plays with scientific precision.

"Are you going to tell me why he's here?"

I send Dad a glance, and he offers the bowl of chopped onion. "He was going to spend Christmas all by himself." I dump the onion in the pan and stir it with the wooden spatula.

"Which was his choice, Mina." He gives me the Brussels sprouts next, and I add them as well.

I pause to stare at the sizzling vegetables. "I know that."

"How did you convince him to come?"

A frown spreads across my face, and I continue stirring. "I told him to."

"You make it sound easy." Dad's tone is light,

192

weightless—skeptical.

It was easy. Much easier than I thought it would be. His resistance was half-hearted at best, and he caved the moment I refused to.

"He didn't want to be alone, but he'd never admit it. This is Xander, after all."

"Are the potatoes ready?"

I stab one with a fork. It slides off into the boiling water, and I step out of the way so Dad can drain the pot. He mashes the potatoes on a hot pad while I finish the Brussels sprouts.

A few minutes later, I pour the sprouts into a serving bowl and push the pan to the back burner. Dad, per usual, will clean all the dishes after we eat.

"Do you think I should've left him alone?"

Dad checks on the duck again, then pulls the roasting pan out. "Of course not," he says as he closes the oven. "But I'm uncertain what your motives are, Mina. Did you ask him here because he's your friend and you care about him? Or did you ask him here because you care about him?"

The emphasis on the second question renders me motionless. I don't know how to answer that—without lying.

Despite how distant we are, I never stopped considering Xander a friend—one of my best friends—and he has, on occasion, used the word in regards to me. But for obvious reasons, we haven't been good friends in the last nine months.

As much as I wish that were the reason I didn't want him to be alone for the holidays, I shouldn't lie to myself.

"I—"

But I don't want to say it out loud.

Dad meets my eyes with a knowing smile. "What does Dahlia think of him being here? You two are..." He tilts his head. "Well, what are you?"

I bite my lip. "How am I supposed to know?" I hover by the serving bowls. "She's insisted on multiple occasions that she doesn't date, she doesn't do labels, and she wants everything private. Are we in a relationship? Are we fucking around? Is what we're doing considered sex? How can I know?"

Dad pauses beside me. "You could ask her. I'm sure she has an opinion on whether you two are in a relationship."

"It's been a week since...well, since things got serious." I move to the cabinet to retrieve plates and silverware, but my hands are shaking. My sex life with Dahlia is not something I want to discuss with my dad. "But you're right, she was pissed when she found out I invited him. She hasn't talked to me since."

"You don't seem particularly bothered by it."

"I don't know how I should feel about it. If we're not dating, it doesn't matter." I shake my head. "Basically, she's pissed because she doesn't get to monopolize my time for a few days."

"And because you're spending our family holiday with your ex-boyfriend, Mina."

I glance toward the living room, nervous, but our conversation hasn't magically conjured him.

"Can you honestly tell me you don't harbor any feelings for him?"

"There's nothing between me and Xander."

The skeptical look on Dad's face reminds me that's not an answer to his question, but I'm not capable of providing one honestly.

In the distance, the laptop closes, and Xander appears in the doorway. "Am I in the way if I want some water?"

"Of course not," Dad says. "Get out the other glasses while you're at it."

Xander follows his directions without question, pulling out three tall glasses and filling each with water, and I carry the plates and silverware into the dining room. He follows me, sipping while I lay out the plates and utensils.

Dad and I always sit across from each other, but I hesitate with Xander's placement. It's odd to put him by me, but the idea of sitting him next to Dad is equally strange.

I hover, the plate and silverware in my hands, but Xander approaches and sets his glass next to my place setting. "Here's fine."

I hesitate again but lay the dishes on the table.

Twenty-Two

Upstairs, I tear off my clothes and toss the dirty laundry in the hamper.

Dinner could have been worse, but it was awkward like the first night. Uncomfortable conversation, strained glances, and an eerie silence while we chew.

I'm exhausted from the close quarters.

With Xander sleeping on the couch, this bedroom is the only place I can relax.

I tug on a shirt and pajama shorts from the dresser. I never pack much when I visit my dad. It happens so often I keep clothes here.

After a sigh, I force myself toward the door. Dad's cleaning up, and I promised I'd help.

Downstairs, I knock on the door frame to draw his attention. "How can I help?"

"Don't worry about it, Mina. It won't take long." Dad observes my outfit before returning to the roasting pan. "Besides, you look ready for bed."

I step closer. "Not until we clean this up. We used like a million dishes to cook a giant meal, Dad. I'm not letting you clean it up by yourself."

He nods toward the island, where the majority of the dirty dishes sit. "Bring them closer?"

After I complete the task and fill the counter by the double sink, I wait. "And now? You're doing all the work."

His mouth forms a tight smile. "Mina, are you going to kick me out of my own kitchen?"

A quick laugh escapes my lips. "If I have to." I press a hand to his shoulder. "Come on, Dad. You've been laboring away all day. Take a break. Let me do the dishes for once."

At last, he withdraws his umber arms from the soapy water. "You can machine wash all the plates, but the pans need hand-washed." He pats his hands and arms dry with a towel.

"I know." I nudge him toward the door, and he gives me one last hug before retreating. "Night, Dad."

I pull out my phone as his footsteps trail upstairs. Xander will play video games for a while, so I doubt he'll mind if I listen to some music.

The first song is Blue October's "I Hope You're Happy"—one of their few not-completely-depressing songs—and I dance to the beat as I scrub the pan, mumbling along with the lyrics. This has quickly become one of my favorites.

When the roasting pan is clean, I move on to the next pot, and the song switches to "Double Vision."

"Since when do you listen to Foreigner?"

I spin toward the door.

Xander, empty glass in one hand, sends a smirk in my direction. "Or have you lied to me the whole time I've known you?"

I return to the dishes. "I'll admit, classic rock isn't so bad."

197

He sets the glass on the island and approaches. "You want help drying?"

My brow furrows. "Towels are in the third drawer."

He retrieves a fresh hand towel and stands beside me to wipe down the pans on the drying rack. "I forgot how good a cook your dad is." He piles the clean dishes on the island—he doesn't know where anything goes. "Thanks for inviting me."

I shrug. "No problem."

"Do you—?"

The song fades out, but my phone shifts abruptly to Alien Ant Farm. My ringtone. I rush to dry my hands.

Imogene.

I answer immediately. "Hey, how's the party?"

Sniffling is her only response.

"Mo, what's wrong?" I slump against the island. All I can focus on is the tile floor. "Did something happen?"

"No," she finally says. "No, I just needed to talk to you."

"You sound upset."

She releases a shaky breath. "I miss you."

"I miss you too, Mo." I try to laugh. "See, you should've come here for Christmas. Screw Mom and her pregnancy brain. You should be with me and Dad."

She sniffles again. "Too late for that."

"Right..."

"I wish I had."

Xander finishes the last clean dish and waits beside me.

My hand tightens around the phone. "You with the Powells? Go hang out with Jimmy. Messing around with him always puts you in a good mood."

Imogene snorts. "I don't know what you're talking about.

Jimmy's boring."

I frown. Since when does she think that?

"Besides," she adds, "I left the party an hour ago."

My frown intensifies. "That's early."

"I couldn't be there anymore." She pauses, and her voice is eerily calm when she continues. "I'm glad I caught you before you went to bed."

"Yeah, no worries." But my stomach twists with unease. "I'm here any time you need me, Mo. Always."

"Goodnight, Billie." She hangs up before I can reciprocate.

For a moment, I stare at my phone's black screen. Imogene may be the more emotional one, but she doesn't cry often. She knows how to keep things under control.

Whatever she's upset about, it's serious.

"Everything okay?"

I send Xander a fleeting glance. "Not really."

"Did she say what happened?"

"Of course not."

"You're worried about her."

The phone is cold through the red t-shirt when I press it to my chest. "Mom and Rob are having a baby and moving over the summer. She's graduating high school this year. Her boyfriend cheated on her, and I think she might still be with him. She won't talk to me." I release a short laugh and face him. "And I'm officially the biggest hypocrite."

But Xander's too busy staring at my breasts to respond.

I roll my eyes but look down, in case I splashed myself with water and managed not to notice.

Oh, shit.

The shirt.

The Charmander shirt.

His favorite shirt.

I turn away, but it's a bit late to hide it.

How am I supposed to explain this?

Of course he knew I had it, but wearing it? He probably thought I boxed it away or threw it in the trash. I doubt he expected the truth: I've kept it at my dad's house since our "breakup."

Xander clears his throat. "You may be a hypocrite, but you probably understand why she doesn't want to talk about her problems."

Apparently, we're not going to discuss it.

"It's a lot easier to keep things to yourself. Once you say something out loud, you can't pretend it doesn't exist." I drop my phone on the island and return to the sink.

Xander doesn't move.

"Thanks, by the way," I throw over my shoulder, "for looking out for her and entertaining her over the summer. Dad was so happy to see her, but he had to teach summer classes and I was, you know, halfway across the world for most of her visit. Thank you."

"Don't worry about it. Jimmy did most of the entertaining. I didn't participate, trust me."

A muscle in my jaw quivers.

That makes it more confusing why she insisted Jimmy's "boring." In all the twelve years we've known Jimmy Powell, she has never considered him remotely uninteresting. She had the biggest crush on him when she was eight.

"I'm worried she's getting reckless." I run the cool water over the pot. "She was always the responsible one, but now, she has no one to take care of. I don't want her to get herself in trouble." I heave a sigh. "She hasn't exactly had the best role models."

Xander steps closer and takes the pot from my hands. "I don't know. If she spent some time around you now, she'd find you're a pretty good role model."

I dunk the last jelly roll pan under the water, trying to draw attention away from my flushed face. "Well, what about you?"

For a second, Xander doesn't say anything. "What about me?"

I don't have the audacity to meet his gaze. "We always talk about me and my problems. What about you? Why do your parents want you home so much?"

"I'm twenty-one now." The words come out with biting force. "Which means I get my inheritance if I meet the legal parameters set out in their will."

I tilt my head. "Don't you usually get an inheritance after your parents die?"

"It's called a 'living inheritance.'" He scoffs. "And West Palm Beach is not home."

I hand him the pan and grab a clump of silverware. "How much is it? The inheritance?"

Xander shrugs. "I think the gift tax exemption caps at fifteen thousand now, so double that because it's a split gift. Plus company shares."

The forks and knives slip from my grasp and clatter loudly into the sink. "What? Thirty thousand dollars and they just want to give it to you?"

"It sounds like a lot, but that's one year of tuition without my scholarships, and I already pay tuition myself."

"Part of that's loans, though, right? You could pay off

your student loans."

He scowls. "I'm not taking their money. Even if I was okay with their requirements, which I'm not, it's a bribe. Like every other gift they've sent."

"You don't know that. It's been a year and a half since you saw them. Maybe they're using it as a reason—"

"Don't talk like you know anything," Xander snaps. "They don't give a shit about me, and I will not cave."

My mouth clamps shut, and I turn back to the sink.

When he speaks, his voice has lost its edge. "I'm sorry, but this isn't something I want to discuss."

I pull the clump of silverware from the dirty water. Everything left can handle the dishwasher. "I know you don't want to hear it," I say, slipping the knives and forks into their caddy, "but if you keep all that anger inside, you're going to explode."

He shakes his head. "There's no point in discussing it."

I suppose I should feel honored. Xander doesn't talk about his family to anyone but Jimmy, and I doubt he shared this tidbit. I'm impressed he's willing to share with me of all people.

"Closure."

He turns to me sharply.

"That's the point. If I'd never gotten mad at my dad or fought with my mom, it would have taken a lot longer to resolve our problems—if ever. It was stupid and wrong and mean, but I wouldn't be spending this holiday with my dad if my emotional reactions hadn't forced me to act."

He considers me a moment, and when he speaks, his voice is small. "I'm not sure I'm ready for closure."

I rinse the stack of plates from the counter in the dirty

water and slide them into the washer. "Out of curiosity, what're the requirements?"

Xander's laughter is strangled. "I have to get married."

My mouth drops open. "At twenty-one? To who?"

"Their preference was Em. Our parents started planning before we graduated high school."

"They want you to marry your psycho ex-girlfriend who literally stabbed you?"

He snorts. "Well, when you put it like that, they sound crazy. The second requirement was more on point: I have to work at the company."

My brow knits together. "How are you supposed to do that and college?"

"Considering they intended for me to study business at Stanford, it would be easy. The San Francisco hotel is in San Mateo, which is a twenty-minute drive from campus."

"Oh."

An unhappy nausea whirls around my stomach. If he'd done that, I never would have met him.

I've spent the last nine months wondering what my life would be like without him. My conclusion? I don't want that to happen. My life would have taken a drastically different and destructive path if Xander Theroux hadn't chosen Bradford.

"Their final requirement was a little vague—'plans for a family.' Go figure."

I swallow down my uncertainty. "Wait, they expect you to be married and have a baby on the way at twenty-one? Isn't that ridiculously early?"

A smile tugs at the corner of his mouth. "Not at twenty-one. I was supposed to get married a couple years ago—or at least engaged. That was their plan. Can you imagine marrying and having a kid with your first boyfriend?"

I grimace. Parts of that are easier to imagine than others.

"Sorry, that was… I didn't think before—"

"No, it's okay. It's, uh—" heat rises to my cheeks "—not that far-fetched."

Beside me, Xander stiffens. "What?"

I hesitate.

Aside from my dad, the only person I've willingly told about my abortion is Byrdie.

"Do you remember, at the end of freshman year, I disappeared for a few days?"

Xander shifts uncomfortably. "You spent the weekend at your dad's house. You said you were studying for finals."

I release an anxious chuckle. "Well, that's true, but it's not the whole truth. I was recovering from an abortion."

His lips press into a firm line. "That bastard got you pregnant."

I busy myself with putting the last dishes in the washer. "The condom broke, but he didn't tell me. And since I only had a period every few months, I didn't realize until I was seven weeks along." I retrieve the detergent from below the sink and fill the open tab. The door closes with a click.

"I should've beaten him to a fucking pulp." Xander's knuckles, gripping the counter, are white. "I should've—"

"What would that have achieved?" I slide the box under the sink and stand beside him. "Nothing would have changed."

For a long moment, I wait for him to ask the questions. Was it painful? How much do I remember? Why did I do it? Do I think about the baby? Do I regret it? Am I ashamed?

I don't know how to answer those questions.

Instead, he takes a shaky breath. "Do you remember that party you were supposed to go to?"

My brow furrows at his sudden tangent. "He wanted me to meet his friends."

Xander's swallow is audible. One of his hands clenches into a fist. "He said your legs wouldn't be clamped together so tightly after a couple drinks." He lets out a brooding sigh. "And instead, I got you angry enough you didn't care."

When in the world did Zane say that?

I study his tense form, but per usual, Xander refuses to give anything away. "I don't understand why it bothers you so much. Why Zane bothers you. It was almost two years ago."

His mouth tightens. "What he did was unacceptable. He preyed on you because he could. Because it made him feel powerful." A frustrated puff of air escapes his nose. "And I failed to protect you."

I compress my fingers over his fist. "You did not fail me. The fact that he manipulated me does not in any way reflect upon you. You're not weak because he took advantage of me." For once, his skin is cold, but he warms under my touch. "You're one of the strongest, kindest people I know."

Beneath my hand, he stretches and extends, and his fingers entwine with mine. "I don't know how it doesn't bother you."

"It does." I offer him a comforting squeeze. "When I think about what happened, it does. But most of the time, I can be reminded without reliving the memories—and I have you to thank for that. You helped me find closure."

I never imagined Xander too needed closure.

"It was a long time ago," I add, "but I need to clarify. Yes, I was angry after our fight, and that was the final straw that led to Zane's…actions. But you aren't the reason he was able to take advantage of me. His behavior was entirely his own."

His fingers clench around mine, his body tense.

I squeeze back. "Besides, I was only angry because you managed to hurt my feelings. For the life of me, I didn't know why it bothered me so much. I couldn't figure out I was starting to like you." Under my breath, I chuckle.

I was far too caught up in my own problems to notice, and I had no idea the depth of my own emotions. Every feeling, every spark, was written off as pure physical attraction because I didn't know how to process the fact that I was falling for him. The amount of time it took him to settle in my affection surprises me, but that surprise is nothing to the deep-seated fear and panic that mounted when I realized. By then, I was too far in.

And now?

"You know I didn't mean it, right?" His thumb rubs across my knuckles. "I didn't sleep with you because I wanted to get laid. I wanted you. I always wanted you."

Now, I'm far too aware of my own feelings.

My breathing's shallow, shaky. "I wish I could say the same. I didn't like you much when we first had sex."

"I couldn't pretend not to like you after that. Not that I was good at it before we slept together. But that night you fell asleep while we were watching TV, after we hadn't talked for weeks—that was the moment I realized I loved you."

For a moment, we stand in silence, his hand, propped against the countertop, clutching mine.

My chest constricts.

He loved me.

A part of me always knew, but he never said it. And I wouldn't have believed him if he had.

I close my eyes.

He loved me.

Past tense.

It stings.

Why would he still care for me? He sleeps with every single woman who comes into the bar. And if his feelings remained, could we have a stable, healthy relationship now?

Besides, Dahlia's in the picture. I may not understand the extent of our relationship, but it's not fucking around. She wouldn't be so upset if it were.

Yet, his words—the past tense—still sting.

I blink away the tears and withdraw my hand. "It's past my bedtime. I should sleep."

As I reach the stairs, the dishwasher fills with water.

Twenty-Three

CLINKING AND CLANKING EMANATE FROM THE KITCHEN AS I pad down the stairs.

"Morning." Dad is putting away the clean dishes. "You want to help make breakfast? I thought we could have pancakes."

"Great idea, Dad. Have you made the batter yet?"

He shakes his head. "I was organizing first. I've got some yerba mate steeping. You want to start the batter?"

The ingredients and recipe card sit on the counter, and I reread the directions before getting to work. When the mate finishes steeping, Dad pours out a couple cups and passes me one, despite my flour-coated hands.

I pause to sip the hot tea, and Xander stumbles in with tousled hair and heavy eyes.

"Good morning, Xander." Dad motions him to sit at the island, where I'm putting together the batter.

Xander grunts out a response and accepts a cup of tea, and Dad returns to the sink. "What're you doing, Dixon?" Skeptical, Xander assesses me as I whisk the mixture.

"Aren't you hungry?"

He takes a drink. "A little."

"Well, I'm making pancakes."

"The griddle's ready when you are, Mina." Dad comes up beside me to check on the batter, and I shake out the whisk. "How do you like your eggs, Xander?"

"However you're cooking them."

"Over medium it is."

The griddle sizzles when I pour out three circles, and bubbles rise as they cook.

"How did you sleep?" Dad glances at Xander as he adds a tablespoon of butter to the frying pan. "I hope the couch was comfortable." He twists the pan around until the melting butter coats the pan, then grabs the carton of eggs. "One or two?"

"Two."

I flip the pancakes. They're a perfect golden brown.

"You're getting much better at this, Mina," Dad says in a quiet voice before returning to Xander. "You look tired."

I lean against the counter while the pancakes finish cooking.

Xander shrugs. "I didn't sleep well. The couch was fine, though."

Does his inability to sleep well have anything to do with how abruptly our conversation ended last night? Because I didn't sleep well either.

After hours of reliving that conversation, I passed out around three. I remember every smile, every sigh, every gesture—and I nearly made myself sick wondering what could have been.

"Hopefully, you have better luck tonight," Dad says.

My grip on the spatula tightens, and I push a few strands of kinked auburn hair out of my face. I need to focus on the task at hand, not my inability to maintain a healthy relationship.

The pancakes are dark when I peel them off, and I pour on the next three.

Dad lays two over-medium eggs on the same plate, and I carry it to where Xander sits at the island.

"There's butter and syrup." I nod toward the essentials, and when his tired eyes land on me, an easy smile spreads across his face.

My chest constricts, my cheeks flush with pleasure, and I beam before returning to the stove.

"Sit down," Dad says in a quiet voice when I pile the new pancakes on a fresh plate. He slides some eggs onto it as well and takes the pitcher of batter from my hand.

I take the other stool by Xander, and he slides the butter and syrup over when I join him. A third of his food's gone by the time I sit down, and I spread butter over each pancake and pour a liberal amount of maple syrup on my food, eggs and all.

I slice them as an attempt to postpone eating. After last night, I have no appetite. But eating is a good excuse not to look at him.

Because Xander's still staring.

I raise an eyebrow. "What's wrong?"

Amusement tugs at his lips. "You have batter in your hair." He slides his hand over a few strands, and thick batter gathers on his fingers. He wipes it on his napkin, chuckling quietly, and gives me a once-over before turning to his food.

"Thanks." The word barely escapes my lips.

For a moment, the only sound is the pancakes sizzling on the griddle and Xander's fork scraping the ceramic plate.

"Should I clean up the bit you managed to get on my shirt too?"

He's right. A daub of batter sits directly on the Pokémon's face, right over my breast.

"No, no." I grab a napkin, too flustered to look at him.

Xander chuckles—a long, full laugh I haven't heard in a long time—and moves on as I scrape at the shirt. "I didn't know you cooked."

"Dad's been showing me a few things."

Dad joins us with a plate of his own food and stretches across the island for the butter and syrup. "She cooked the Brussels sprouts and bread pudding last night."

"Like I said, he's showing me a few things." I swallow down my blush.

"What are your plans for New Year's Eve, Xander?" Dad asks. "Mina and I are going to watch the ball drop. You're welcome to join us."

Xander laughs. "Well, I work in a bar, and New Year's is a big night. I won't be done till three or four in the morning."

Dad nods. "How unfortunate."

"I won't have work on New Year's Day, though. We're closed again."

I turn back to my plate. "You'll be able to sleep in."

"What about you?"

Discomfort rushes through my body. "I don't know. I have to talk to Dahlia."

◆

Dad presses a kiss to my cheek as I take the kettle off the stove. "Don't stay up too late, Mina."

211

I return the embrace as much as I can while holding a container of piping-hot water. "See you in the morning."

He disappears from the kitchen before I finish pouring the water into the teapot. Nothing caffeinated tonight. It's past ten.

While it steeps, I lay my phone on the island and flip through my messages.

Dahlia hasn't called or texted me since I got here. Not that I'm surprised. She's probably hoping I'll limp back to her with an apology for keeping her out of the loop—and for inviting Xander in the first place.

"What's the smell?"

I glance over as Xander wanders into the room and grabs a glass from the cupboard. "Sweet orange and pomegranate."

"Smells good." He fills the glass with ice water and steps around me. "Have a good night." Last I saw, he had his laptop open to Steam in the living room.

"Do you want some?"

He turns, one foot over the threshold, to examine me with a tight frown. "Some tea?"

I shrug. "If you want."

"I'm not a big tea drinker."

With a chuckle, I pour myself a generous serving. "I feel out of place if I don't drink tea while I'm here. My dad converted me."

Xander smirks. "He's got you cooking too. You're a regular fifties housewife."

I snort. "Way to make it sound incestual."

"Didn't mean it like that."

"Besides, I'd be a terrible housewife." I tap a finger on the island, uncertain. "Should I get out another cup?"

Finally, Xander returns and sets his water on the island between us. "Sure. I've never had orange pomegranate tea before."

I pour him out a cup and slide the steaming drink toward him.

"Thanks."

At last, I sip the fragrant liquid. Hot but not scalding. "Why did you decide to major in Business?"

Xander turns to me with a challenging gaze. "Why did you decide to major in Fine Arts?"

I repress an amused smile. "Because I don't know who I am if I'm not drawing or painting or doing something creative. Now, don't avoid the question."

He releases a short bark of laughter. "That's what I like about you—you have a reason for everything. You make a plan, you implement, and if it doesn't go well, you reassess and try again."

"My plans don't work out that well. And learning how to adapt is something I've yet to accomplish." I take a drink. "But you've always been good at that. Adapting."

His mouth twists into a smirk. "I think you overestimate how purposeful I am. You know I bullshit my way through life, right?"

"But when you focus your resolve, you can do anything. That's powerful."

Finally, he takes his first drink. "Fruity."

"So why business?" I rest my elbows on the counter and study him. "Your father runs his hotel business, right? He built it from the ground up. And you've specifically said you have no interest in joining the company. So why major in the one thing that would help you follow in his footsteps?"

213

A faint pink tinges his cheeks. "Why did you want to follow in your dad's footsteps after the divorce? Why major in Math? Why cryptography?"

"Because even though I was mad at him, I loved my father more than anyone else in the world." It's my turn to smirk. "I don't think you hate him as much as you pretend to. Look who has the daddy issues now."

Xander snorts. "Don't get too cocky, Dixon."

But I jab his arm with a finger. "You, my friend, are a hypocrite. So, truth?"

"Why I'm majoring in Business?" He crouches over the island, his hands wrapped around the teacup. "It seemed like a good idea to play into my natural abilities. Running a business requires ambition, taking risks, and people skills. And just because I'd like to someday have my own business doesn't mean I want to own and operate a chain of ridiculously expensive luxury hotels."

"Yeah, but I imagine running a business also requires making a plan and sticking to it. That must be difficult for someone who bullshits his way through life."

"A partner who's analytical, good with computers, and can keep me on track with a solid plan would be an easy solution to that."

"As long as she can do more than clicking and double-clicking."

A soft laugh escapes his lips, but he studies the teacup. "She's definitely more qualified than that." He coughs, then takes a drink. "My imaginary partner."

My eyebrow arches up. "And what sort of business would you and this imaginary partner run?"

"I never got that far into planning."

"Sounds like you need that partner sooner rather than later."

"If I'm lucky."

I scoot closer and nudge him with my elbow. "If you taught me anything, it's that you can't rely on luck. You have to go after the things you want. You can't wait for them to come to you. And you can't give up."

He releases a rueful laugh. "I'm pretty sure I already gave up." Instead of letting me respond, he levels me with a determined gaze. "What about you, Dixon? Going to get your MFA?"

"That'd be awesome, but I don't want to rack up my student loans. I don't know where I'd apply. I know it's a year and a half away, but I like being here with my dad."

"You know what would be cool?" His cerulean eyes sparkle with excitement. "If you could get your drawings in a gallery. You could pay the bills if you sell them at exhibits. Your artwork is intricate and beautiful—people would love them."

I flush at the compliment.

Xander slurps down the remnants of his tea and lays the cup delicately in front of him. "You know, I didn't expect you to keep the shirt."

I close my eyes. "It's your favorite shirt. I wouldn't get rid of it. I know, I should've given it back."

But he simply says, "Keep it. I think you've got squatter's rights by now."

When my eyes flash open, he rinses his cup and sends me one final smile before saying goodnight.

215

Twenty-Four

I LEAN AGAINST THE DOOR FRAME.

In the living room, Xander slips his gaming laptop inside its case, then inside the backpack. All the accessories—headset, mouse, external cooling fan—have been packed away.

"You're leaving."

He glances back before returning to his task. "Kylie called. She's reopening the bar for an evening shift at five, and I said I'd help out. She got restless with nothing to do but her husband."

I snort. "Isn't her husband the owner?"

"Co-owner, but yeah." He shoves in the last of his things and turns to the blankets we pulled out for him. "They're both workaholics." He folds up and stacks the two blankets on the closest cushion before turning back to me.

It's inevitable, but these two nights are the best nights I've had in a long time. And when he leaves, all that goes out the window. We're back to what we were before: roommates who never talk or look at each other. That transition was hard enough the first time.

"So I'll see you at the house later? When will you be

back?" He dons his leather jacket, then backpack. His shoes are already on.

I shrug. "I'll be here for a few more days. I want to get in more father-daughter time over break."

"Good idea."

He approaches, ready to head for the door, but Dad comes out with some sandwiches on plates.

"Lunch?" Dad glances between us, and as I take the plate proffered toward me, he focuses on Xander. "Leaving so soon?"

Xander gives a half-hearted shrug. "I got called in to work. Sorry to leave in a rush."

"Let me put this in a bag for you."

Dad retreats into the kitchen, and Xander pauses awkwardly beside me. "Thanks for inviting me, Dixon. I'm glad I came with you. Even if you bullied me into it."

I lick my lips, but my mouth is dry. "I liked being able to talk to you."

He nudges me. "You know we live together, right? We can talk anytime."

But we won't.

These two days have been a nice reminder of what could have been—who we might've been to each other. But any remaining feelings he has for me are against his better judgment, against his will. And when we go home, I cannot live in this fantasy.

"Yeah."

Dad comes back with the sandwich in a baggy. "It was nice to see you, Xander."

Xander holds the food close to his chest and smiles. "Thank you for your hospitality, sir."

When he's gone, Dad wraps an arm around my shoulders. My hands are clamped around the plate of food. I haven't managed to eat anything yet.

"You look tired," he murmurs into my hair.

But I shake my head. The Camaro is long gone now, but the weight of it—the weight of Xander—hangs on my chest. "Dad, I'm so stupid."

"Nonsense."

I welcome his embrace. "I thought I was over him. I'm supposed to be over him. But it's been nine months, and these feelings won't go away." My eyes fall shut. "I hate emotions."

Dad chuckles. "Why in the world would you think that? When you care about someone that intensely, it doesn't go away so easily."

He directs me toward the dining room, and I stumble along with him.

"I wish it would." I set down the plate and collapse into my regular seat. "Our relationship—if you can call it that— was a horrible, unhealthy mess. He knows as well as I do reviving that would be a disaster."

Dad takes his seat across from me, where his plate of food waits. "You're not in the same place you were nine months ago, Mina. Things could be different."

I pick up my sandwich. "No, they can't, Dad. We've both moved on. I have a girlfriend."

Or I think I do.

"I thought you were uncertain."

Dahlia Finnick may be manipulative and vindictive. She may be anorexic and probably has worse depression than I do. She may be controlling. She may have some seriously deep-seated problems because of her mother. But we have a connection.

I understand her. I see her.

◆

Dad parks his Buick in the driveway behind Jimmy's pickup. The red Camaro has a light dusting of snow. Xander hasn't gone anywhere since last night. He must be inside.

"Thanks for driving me, Dad."

His lips curve into a smile. "Of course, Mina. I wouldn't let you walk in this cold."

I check my phone—I've held it in my hand the entire drive—but I haven't gotten a text.

Dahlia hasn't been receptive to my attempts to apologize. My last text was asking her to spend the night. I figured she'd appreciate that. She's always the one to suggest sleeping over.

I turn off the screen and slip the phone into my pocket. "I'll see you Friday night?"

"What do you want to make for dinner?" Dad pulls my backpack from the back seat. "We could do something special for New Year's. It'll be the two of us?"

"Right."

Xander certainly won't be there.

I open the door and slip the bag over my shoulder. "Stuffed mushrooms?"

"Do you want shrimp or lamb for the main course?"

"Surprise me." I give him one last wave before heading toward the house.

The front door is locked. Not that I'm surprised. If

Xander hasn't gone anywhere, why would the door be unlocked? It takes a moment to find my keys.

Inside, it's dark.

But not quiet.

The TV is blasting "Another One Bites the Dust" at high volume, and Xander is lounging on the couch, messing around on his phone. His boxers, covered in a Triforce pattern, don't hide the erection.

I bite my lip and stumble backward, shutting the front door with a *bang*.

"Shit, sorry." He scrambles to his feet. "I'll get dressed." He disappears upstairs without another word, and all I can do is stare after him.

Was he looking at porn or something?

I slip off my Converse and follow him upstairs.

When I unlock my bedroom door, the song downstairs is changing to Foreigner. Yet another of his favorite bands.

I drop my backpack on the bed.

Of course, our first encounter is the most awkward encounter ever. He's going to get dressed and go back to whatever he was doing or about to do, and I'm going to stay here in my room. And we're not going to talk anymore.

Again.

I toss my dirty clothes in the hamper and put everything else away. Normally, you visit your parents to do laundry, but that doesn't mean anything when the Powells surprised us with a washer and dryer.

When I pull my phone out, I haven't received any responses. I text her again anyway: *I'm home and I want to see you.*

Maybe that admission is enough for her to swallow her

pride. But I wouldn't be surprised if she made me beg.

"What're your plans for tonight?"

To my surprise, Xander stands in my doorway, dressed in jeans and an Iron Man tee. The erection is gone, but I doubt it'd be difficult to revive.

I blink the thought away—and focus on the important part of this: He stopped by my room just to chat. He wants to talk to me, to spend time with me. He doesn't regret our intimate conversations. Maybe—just maybe—he missed me the past few days.

I never expected that.

"Nothing special. The gallery opened today, but I'm not scheduled till tomorrow morning."

He shrugs. "I've worked thirty-five hours the last three days, so today's my day off. Thought I might watch a movie."

I blink a couple times. "That's three twelve-hour days."

"Yeah." He leans against the door frame, an amiable smile playing on his lips. "The rest of my shifts this week are short, though."

"No wonder you were lying around in your underwear. You must be exhausted."

Xander meets my eyes, and a flash of heat spreads through my body at his intense gaze. "I'm twenty-one—I think I can handle it. Besides, the money makes working a sixty-hour week worth it. Overtime pays well."

I lay my laptop on my dresser. "Are they short-staffed over break?"

"That's a lot of it. Thankfully, most of our customers aren't college students."

"Right."

"So you're back."

"Yeah, I am." My backpack is empty now, but I'm not sure I want to focus on him.

"You wanna run with me in the morning?"

This time, I do turn. "You're still willing to put up with me?"

He chuckles. "Yeah, I can manage."

I turn away—zip my backpack shut with my head down in an attempt to hide my delight. Because I'm not supposed to be happy about that.

I'm not supposed to be excited for tomorrow morning's run.

There isn't supposed to be a jolt of energy at the realization we're alone together for the next week.

And I'm definitely not supposed to be pleased he stopped by my room to talk.

On the nightstand, my phone buzzes.

Dahlia. Finally.

Too short notice tonight. But I might be able to swing by after you're done with work tomorrow.

"You wanna watch *Repo!* with me?"

I shoot him a smirk. "Don't tell Jimmy you're watching it without him. He'll freak."

Xander dons a wide grin. "But if I watch it without him, I don't have to listen to him singing the entire movie. Have you eaten?"

That's a fair point.

"Don't feel obligated, but I'm gonna make some food and put on the movie if you're interested."

I nod.

When he disappears, the phone has faded to black in my hands. I was too busy talking to him to answer her text.

I swallow, trying to focus my energy, and respond: *That would be awesome.*

I know I shouldn't, but there's no one else to talk to or spend time with. And it's easy to do gesture drawings of the scenes. Me and Xander sitting alone in the dark isn't the best idea, but it's *Repo! The Genetic Opera.*

It's just a movie.

Twenty-Five

IT TAKES A MOMENT TO HOOK THE WIRE TO THE FRAME, but these wires are sturdy and strong, and despite how tedious this is, they're the best way to display the artwork for January's Gallery Hop.

Beside me, Amelia gasps and nearly drops the painting. I pause to catch a glimpse of her. "What was that?"

She clutches her hand to her chest and bites her lip. "I pinched my finger."

I roll my eyes. There are more pressing matters than a pinched finger. "New Year's is First Friday this year. We have to get these up quickly—unless you want to come in and finish at the last minute."

Amelia shoots a glare through her blond hair. "You may not have plans for New Year's Eve, but not all of us are antisocial and weird. My boyfriend and I are going to do a barhop tomorrow night."

"You driving to Burlington or Montpelier?"

She shakes her head.

I inhale sharply. "A barhop in St. Clare. I don't know what to think."

"Five bars is plenty, trust me. I'm going to be trashed

after the first one." She snickers and returns to her work. "And then, Simon's going to take me home and fuck my brains out."

There's no Elise in sight, but this isn't appropriate office conversation.

Also, is the alleged Simon going to drink? Because that might ruin her plans for pre-consensual drunk sex on New Year's Eve.

"What about you?"

It takes standing on my tiptoes and an enormous amount of effort to hang the painting. The wire has to slip into the bottom hook of the wall hanger. It's a hell of a lot harder than you'd think.

When it's attached, I step back to judge the balance by eye. "What about me?" It's a tad crooked.

Amelia pauses beside me and assess the thirty-by-forty-inch canvas now displayed across the front wall. "You know, it amazes me the shit that gets into galleries."

I swallow.

"This looks like a three-year-old did it." She scoffs. "And yet if either of us wanted to display our art, we have to convince a salon or bank or something to put it up. It's ridiculous."

My eyes flit around the room again. The last thing I need is Elise overhearing a conversation and assuming I'm ungrateful.

Even if Amelia's words are true, that's not how it's done. Apparently.

"Oh, come on," I try in a quiet voice. "It's not that bad. A simple painting isn't necessarily a childish one."

She snorts and returns to her work. "You're way nicer

than I am, Billie."

Not nicer. Smart enough to keep my mouth shut.

Amelia's stringing the wire on the back of her first canvas. I reach for my fourth.

"So what are your plans for tomorrow night? No big bash with your friends?" She pauses to glower at me. "Are you seeing anyone?"

I shrug but try to focus.

"What, do you not have any friends or something?"

I bite my tongue, but there's no point in keeping quiet. I much prefer the shifts I work alone. There's tension with Elise, but it's better than Amelia not knowing how to take no for an answer.

"Most of my friends are out of town for the holiday," I say.

Prue's with her folks in Chicago. Jimmy went home to Springfield. And I'm stuck here with no one to talk to but Xander and Dahlia—the two people with whom I've had the rockiest relationships. Lucky me.

"So you don't have any plans?"

I try to repress the awkwardness from my smile, but it's impossible. "I'm having dinner with my dad, and we're going to do a puzzle."

Amelia snorts. "You're joking."

Not remotely.

I tie the final knot in the wire and struggle to my feet. "No, it'll be a relaxing night for me. Laid-back."

"No holiday sex?"

Despite myself, a deep blush spreads across my cheeks, but she can't see anything as I rise to hook the canvas onto the hanger.

Dahlia's mad, so I'm not predicting anything spectacular for New Year's. It took a considerable amount of grovelling to convince her to hang out after my shift today, and I have to admit, I'm nervous. I have no idea how this will go.

But I have to see her.

I miss her.

"Probably not," I say in a quiet voice.

I don't know where she stands on our relationship, but we're not screwing around. I've dealt with too much and been alone too long to be okay with just fucking.

Now, I need to make sure she feels the same.

◆

"Will you sit with me?"

Hesitantly, Dahlia joins me on the couch, her arms crossed over her chest. "Okay, you badgered me until I caved. I'm here." She examines my living room as if it's the first time she's been here.

Yes, she's here, but she's also late. I've been home from work for two hours.

I scoot close enough our legs brush, my bare knee against her jean-covered one, and pause the show. I'm near the end of my *Brotherhood* rewatch. It's nearly ten, but I've been wearing pajamas since my post-run shower.

"Why am I here?"

I tug her nearest arm free and clasp my fingers around hers. "I wanted to see you. I missed you."

Despite holding a stern pose, chin jutting out, Dahlia lets me hold her hand. "How could you miss me when you've spent all your time with Xander?"

I squeeze her. "It's not that hard."

She doesn't respond when I kiss the side of her mouth, but that doesn't stop her from enjoying the attention.

"You're special."

This time, when I kiss her, she turns to meet me, and what was meant to be a chaste kiss is anything but.

I'm not particularly in the mood, but I'm glad she came, so when she tugs me onto her lap, I oblige. She takes charge without hesitation, yanking my t-shirt high enough to grasp my breasts, and I gasp at the unprovoked pressure.

"I missed you too," she says between pants, and she shoves me down on the couch, knocking the air from my lungs. An eager smile tugs at her lips as she traces over my chest down to the waistband of my pajamas.

Lights flash across the walls. Xander's home from work.

This wouldn't have happened if she'd been on time, dammit.

Dahlia groans but lies between me and the back of the couch, every inch of her thin body touching mine. As I yank the blanket over us, her hand aimlessly massages my breast, and she kisses me again.

The front door opens and closes.

When Xander spots me, he raises an eyebrow and heads upstairs.

Somehow, he wasn't disappointed.

That makes no sense. He made his feelings about this relationship clear. As he sees it, Dahlia is a threat to my mental health, and that's probably true. Has he suddenly decided not to interfere?

Dahlia giggles once he's gone, and her hand sneaks under my waistband. "Am I crazy if I want you right here, right now? You're so sexy."

I inhale sharply as her finger ignores all previous precedence and dips inside my entrance. "A little bit," I manage. "We're not alone anymore."

And we barely kissed. I'm nowhere near arousal.

But she sweeps across my clit with a happy sigh. "He's upstairs, and you're covered by the blanket." She trails wet kisses down my neck and sucks at my collarbone.

"That's not the problem."

"What is?"

She strums my clit with scientific precision, occasionally delving into my heat to gather my growing wetness—and I can no longer focus. Three thin fingers claim my heat, and all that comes out is a gasping moan.

The stairs, on the other side of the wall, creak with use. Xander's coming back down.

Surely Dahlia hears it too, but maybe she's caught up in the moment.

Instead of stopping—or even pausing—she thrusts into me again, fingers curling upward, raking across my hot spot. I clutch the cushion to get control of myself, but she continues her assault, and I cannot hide the sob that racks my body.

The problem is definitely my inability to keep quiet.

Xander must be in the kitchen. Even as I muffle my moans with the pillows, there's no way he can't hear me.

"Stop, stop!"

She hooks her ankle around mine and traps me beneath her, keeping my legs firmly spread. "He needs to know you're mine." Her free hand yanks up my shirt, and her mouth captures the nearest nipple, scraping the soft tissue.

"Dahlia, wait, wait…" My words come out as a shrill cry, but my traitorous hips buck against her unyielding hand.

She crashes into me with a forceful accuracy that draws another moan from my lips. Her thumb sweeps around, then across my aching clit until I don't know how to speak or think or breathe.

All I touch and all I feel is Dahlia.

When my body regresses to mere panting, she slows and finally retracts. "You're beautiful. Completely and utterly beautiful." She releases a long, content sigh, resting her head above my breast. "I love you."

A high-pitched, tinny sound filters from another room as something hits the linoleum floor.

My eyes flash open.

Xander's still in the kitchen. He heard all of that.

I push up, letting Dahlia fall off, and yank my shirt down. "I cannot believe you," I snap, turning to her. "I specifically told you to stop. How could you do that?"

But Dahlia sports a proud grin. "Oh, come on, that was fun."

"Maybe if we weren't in the living room, and maybe if Xander weren't here."

She scoffs. "Who cares if Xander hears us? You didn't seem to mind too much."

I rise from the couch and back up till my calves hit the coffee table. "He didn't hear us—he heard me."

Dahlia follows me and slides her hands around to hold my ass. "I'm claiming my territory."

I step out of her grasp. "I'm your girlfriend, not your territory."

A soft smile sweeps across Dahlia's features, and she

closes the distance between us. For once, her kiss is gentle. Languorous. Delicate.

I tear away, reeling. "I need space. We can talk later."

"Sure." With a bounce in her step, Dahlia snatches her purse from the floor and heads for the front door.

When the door closes behind her, I collapse on the couch, all remaining energy depleted. I sit with my head in my hands, trying to calm my breathing.

Wait.

Did she say she loves me?

"Some girlfriend you've got."

I check to make sure my clothes are properly in place.

Behind me, Xander stands in the doorway from the dining room with a bowl and fork in his hands. "I mean, I'm not going to say I told you so, but..." Instead of finishing, he stuffs a large bite of Caesar salad in his mouth.

"If you say, 'I told you so,' I might punch you," I grumble, turning away.

"Dixon, why are you doing this to yourself? You know she's not stable." His fork scrapes against the bottom of the bowl. "She's bad for you."

"When we became friends last year, it wasn't because it was convenient. Sure, we lived together, but we bonded because...well, because she is me." I pause, uncertain, but force myself to finish the thought. "I don't know how else to explain it."

Xander scoffs. "You're not the same person. And if you were, why would that make a good relationship?"

"No, I mean, I connect with her." Anxious, I nip at the loose skin on my lip. "An unhealthy relationship with her mother, a dad who disappeared, and years of untreated mental illness? She's unhinged, sure, but that's who I might have been if it weren't for Byrdie and pills." I want to look, but I'm scared to see his face. "And you."

Silently, he moves around the couch to sit beside me. "But you're not like her," he says in a small voice, the salad bowl resting on one knee, his hand on the other. "You are ten times stronger and smarter and braver than she is, easily."

I bridge the distance and thread our fingers together. "Thank you for believing in me after all this time."

He squeezes my hand. "Please be careful."

Twenty-Six

"DIDN'T YOU FINISH WATCHING THIS?" PRUE SHOOTS AN unimpressed glare at the television, where a giant fluffy dog pounces on Edward Elric.

I shove a forkful of penne pasta into my mouth. "This is my favorite anime. I can rewatch it."

"So soon?"

"It's been three days. And this is episode four."

Prue steals my fork. "So do I get to interrogate you about Dahlia yet? Or do I have to sit through two more episodes of this?"

I take the fork back when she's done and send her a scowl. "I told you to get your own fork if you were hungry. I made plenty of food."

She relaxes against the couch. "Yeah, but it's more fun to steal it from you."

I stretch to reach the remote and pause the show as Shou Tucker provides the brothers access to his lab. "Fine, we can talk." I'm not sure I'm emotionally prepared to watch this episode again. "What do you want to know?"

Prue studies me, her eyebrows scrunched together in thought. "When we spoke on the phone, you were so nervous but you wanted to talk. Why don't you want to talk now?"

I offer her an anxious smile. "The novelty's worn off?"

"The truth, Billie."

"Dahlia told me she loves me."

Prue's mouth gapes. "She what?"

"Right after fingering me here on the couch while Xander was making food in the kitchen." My stomach clenches at the thought. "We had a big fight about it. We haven't spoken in a few days."

"You got mad because Xander overheard you two messing around?"

"No." I take a deep breath, trying to ignore the heat from my flushed cheeks. "That's part of it. But I told her to stop when he came downstairs, and she completely ignored me and kind of…went for it."

She grimaces. "Oh. That's awkward."

"She was using me to make a point." I set the bowl and fork on the coffee table beside the remote. I've suddenly lost my appetite. "She wanted him to listen."

Prue pulls her blanket over her chest, her mouth set in a frown. "She shouldn't have any reason to be jealous."

No words come.

When Prue and I talked last, that was true. Xander and I just had our argument about Dahlia—an argument I definitely won. But then, Christmas happened. That changed everything.

"Billie, should she be jealous?"

"I took Xander with me when I went to my dad's for Christmas. He was going to stay here, and I…didn't want him to be alone again." I hug my legs to my chest. "Nothing happened, but we talked a lot. About everything. It's so easy to talk to him."

"And Dahlia?"

"What do you mean?"

Prue shrugs. "Is she easy to talk to?"

I purse my lips. "You know she isn't." When she doesn't say anything, I continue: "I have to walk on eggshells so she doesn't overreact. It's a lot easier to open up to someone who opens up in return."

"Xander opens up to you?"

Before I can prevent myself, I'm beaming. "He does. He did. We talked about his family and his plans after graduation. I don't know if he shares that much with Jimmy."

"You still like him."

I grab the remote and press play again. "Don't be ridiculous. We're talking about Dahlia, remember?"

She snorts, loud. "Yeah, about how Dahlia is jealous because you still like Xander."

I shush her. "He's upstairs."

Prue glances toward the foyer. "Sorry."

A car stops along the sidewalk out front, and I push up for a better view outside the window. It's a small lime-green car, and when the passenger door opens, Jimmy's bushy hair pokes out. Excitement bubbles in my stomach as he retrieves his luggage from the back seat, and he gives the driver a final wave before approaching the house.

The green car disappears into the distance before he's halfway across the lawn.

I turn to Prue again. "Jimmy's home."

"Yippee." But her voice is flat.

The front door nudges open a moment later, and Jimmy

struggles to carry his bags inside. I rise from the couch to help. He's returning with far more than when he left.

"Thanks," he says as the door closes, but he freezes when I wrap my arms around him—we haven't been on hugging terms lately—but he softens and hugs me back. "It's good to see you too, Billie."

When we pull apart, all I can do is smile.

"You didn't get into too much trouble while I was gone, did you?"

"No trouble."

He follows me to the living room, where Prue is waiting. "Okay, I was joking, but something happened. Hey, Prudence."

"Hi, Jimmy."

I take my seat again, and he settles on the nearby chair, separate from us. "How was the trip? Did you tell your parents about Tiff?"

I'm surprised when he doesn't flush thinking about her. "The trip was good, and yeah, I mentioned her."

"And?"

"They were more excited than they should've been. I don't think it's going to go anywhere." He reclines on the armchair, but his body is tense. "You know, holidays with my parents are weird without you there."

I shrug. "You had Mo, right?"

He crosses one leg over the other but makes no move to speak.

"What?"

"Speaking of Imogene," he says, unable to look at me, "I got to meet Donovan. When did she get a serious boyfriend?"

My fingers grasp the blanket. "She is still dating him."

"I didn't catch his last name."

I groan. "Why is she still dating him? She called me over a month ago when she found out he was cheating on her."

"I didn't realize they were serious. She's never brought anyone to meet our parents before," he says in a quiet voice. "She looked good, though. And your mom." He wants to change the subject. "She's so pregnant. When's she due?"

"Right before my birthday." I seize the pasta again and stuff another forkful in my mouth. "Is she doing okay? Mentally, I mean."

Jimmy shifts his weight. "I didn't spend any time with her, but she seemed...exhausted."

Despite my irritation, I snort. "Yeah, pregnancy does that."

A short chuckle bubbles from his throat. "Right, because you know so much about being pregnant."

I shrug it off. "I've researched—and I am a woman."

"Okay, fine."

We fall into silence, and the only sound comes from the TV. Prue doesn't want to interrupt our conversation—or she hasn't forgiven Jimmy for "abandoning" me as a friend. I don't know.

On the screen, Mustang and Hawkeye walk down the enormous staircase to where Ed and Al are waiting in the rain.

"Shit. You're watching this episode?" Jimmy shakes his head. "I thought you finished this show."

My brow furrows.

"Xander mentioned it when we talked last."

"So?"

"It's his favorite anime—and manga."

"It's one of the best," I add.

"You know…" Jimmy bends forward, a smirk creeping onto his lips. "There's no way you'll convince me Mustang and Hawkeye have a platonic relationship."

I roll my eyes. "That would be super inappropriate in the military."

"Which explains why they hide it. Come on, the way she flips out when Lust says he's dead…"

I readjust my position, leaning forward instead of relaxing. "She's his bodyguard. It's her job to protect him."

"And you know, they use her to get to him. Bradley and the creepy doctor with the gold teeth. They know how important she is to him."

"They're colleagues. Friends."

"He calls her his queen."

"She is the most important chess piece in his plot and his staunchest supporter."

"Yeah, that's what I'm saying. They'd do anything for each other. They'd die for each other." He sends me a meaningful look. "They're in love."

I shift uncomfortably, and beside me, Prue struggles to hide a snicker.

"I think they're having sex."

I freeze. The way he says that is different—anxious, unnerved. He's not talking about Mustang and Hawkeye. "Who?"

"Imogene and her boyfriend."

I grimace at the penne. "I was afraid of that." Not that they weren't before, but I hoped she would put her foot down considering the circumstances.

Prue pushes up from the couch and mumbles, "I'm gonna snag a drink," before giving us some much-desired privacy.

Jimmy runs a hand through his messy hair. "He grabbed her butt at the New Year's party—right in front of me and my parents—and she shrugged it off like it was nothing."

I set the bowl down. "Your parents saw?"

He nods.

"'Grabbed' like how?"

"'Grabbed' like he had a handful of her ass under her dress." Jimmy shifts in the chair, his movement jerky and tense. "She slapped him away, but when my dad tried to have a talk with him, she said it was fine, and they left."

I clasp my hands and stare at the interlaced fingers. "So when you said she looked good, you were lying to make me feel better?"

"No. I don't know. Maybe." He gives me a moment, but when all he receives is silence, he continues. "I saw her once after that, and she barely said anything to me." He pauses. "I don't like him."

"Well, he sounds like a stand-up guy."

"He's an asshole." The word comes out with so much vehemence, I stare.

"That is her type," I say slowly. "Not that I've met many of them."

He shifts uneasily, jaw clenched.

And all I can do is stare.

In all the times Jimmy's gotten upset over a girl, he was moping. A big mess of woe-is-me mumbo-jumbo because his crush doesn't return his affection.

But that's not what this is.

239

He's angry, and he's worried. About Imogene, who he's known for thirteen years. He's protective. That could be brotherly affection—we're practically related—but it isn't. I know it isn't.

She had a huge crush on him when we were kids, but she moved on before starting high school. I never imagined Jimmy would have a thing for her.

"I hoped her staying here for the summer and spending quality time with Dad would help her, but I guess I overestimated things." My voice quivers. "You spent a lot of time with her, right? Did she see anyone? Dad said she never talked about any guys."

"We didn't talk about her dating habits, and she didn't introduce me to anyone." But the way Jimmy shifts uncomfortably says he knows more than he's telling. "Besides, she knew three people in this tiny town."

I snort. "This is Mo. Guys have flocked to her since she turned thirteen, whether she's looking or not."

The stairs creak.

Xander emerges a moment later, dressed in his work clothes. Draft Horse's insignia is bold and takes up the front of his black shirt. His eyes light up at the sight of Jimmy. "Hey, I thought I was picking you up tomorrow."

"My flight changed." Jimmy meets him halfway and wraps him in a hug.

Sometimes, they act like they're married.

Prue returns, a glass of water in her hand, and sits with me as they separate. "Have you told him yet?" She keeps her voice quiet, but it's not quiet enough.

"Told who what?" Jimmy asks.

My mouth gapes. Which thing am I supposed to tell

240

which guy?

But Xander's lips tighten. "Dixon has a girlfriend."

For a moment, Jimmy blinks. "What?"

I huff. "I doubt I can call Dahlia my girlfriend. We haven't talked in the last five days."

"For good reason." Xander's sharp words leave no room for argument.

Jimmy is still at a loss for words. "How is that possible? Are you a lesbian now?"

Prue rolls her eyes. "Please don't erase me. It's not an either-or situation."

And Xander elbows him in the side. "Don't take your sexuality cues from *Buffy the Vampire Slayer*."

Jimmy collapses onto the armchair again. "Sorry, I'm…"

"Shocked?" I offer.

Xander snorts. "Sheltered."

Jimmy licks his lips and meets my gaze. "Billie, are you sure this is a good idea? I mean, Dahlia Finnick is an alcoholic. She may not be diagnosed, but she's an alcoholic. You shouldn't be around that."

"She doesn't drink when we're together. She hasn't mentioned a single party. She makes an effort. She cares about me."

"Does she really?" His voice quivers, skeptical.

I want to answer affirmatively. To insist she does. But I'm not convinced she cares as much as she thinks she does. She said she loves me—unless I imagined it—but those words are meaningless if she treats me like an object.

"I hope so."

Twenty-Seven

BLOWN UP TO POSTER SIZE, THE PHOTOGRAPH OF
Montefalco Chapel—the campus church named after the
town's namesake, St. Clare of Montefalco—is crinkled and
pinned to the studio wall. In front of me, my forty-eight-
by-sixty-inch canvas is two layers deep, but something is off.
I don't know how to fix it.

For Painting III, Felix let us choose a five-piece semester
project, and when I struggled to find an intriguing subject
matter, I snapped a few cityscapes around town. The
weather's too cold to paint outside, but at the end of the
semester, it will be better.

Maybe then, I'll figure out what the fuck is wrong with
this painting.

I drop my paintbrush on the supply cart and sit down
to examine the canvas.

Is it the color palette? The line work? The contrast?

Nothing stands out.

I snatch up my brush and use it to measure and compare
the lines.

"Redrawing the lines? You haven't finished the second
layer." Felix hovers a few feet behind me.

I twirl the brush between my fingers. "Something isn't working." Maybe he can help.

He lays a hand on the back of my chair and examines the painting and photograph together. "What bothers you?"

"I don't know. Everything."

His lips curl up in thought. "It looks perfect, Billie."

The words are blasé—enough so a deep frown spreads across my face.

"No, it doesn't."

Felix steps around the chair, his typical grin in place. "From a skill standpoint, your line work is fantastic. You've been perfecting it for a long time. Technical skill is important, but if you're struggling to find something wrong with the painting, it's this: Yes, there is merit to realism, as with all artistic movements, but if you want to make your art exactly like your subject, invest in a high-quality DSLR."

I open my mouth to protest.

But his face is serious. "I saw your painting studies in France, Billie. Beautiful studies of Laval and Vuillard and Giacometti. But you haven't transferred any of that experience to your original work." His tone warms as he adds, "You're a much better artist when you're not being a perfectionist."

He's right, of course. It's his job to be right.

"Why did you decide on cityscapes?"

"It seemed logical."

"Well, there's your first problem." He steps closer. "Every action—especially your choice of subject matter, composition, and color palette—must be intentional. You can finish this painting, but I suggest a brand-new project if you feel this strongly. We're early enough in the semester—and you work fast when you get going. You won't have any problem finishing on time."

He squeezes my shoulder before moving to the next student, and I stare at the painting again.

When class ends, Prue approaches from two easels over. "You ready?"

I put away the last of my paints and don my hoody and lanyard. "Yeah."

Her SUV is parked below, the silver shimmering in the sunlight. P!nk bursts to life when she starts the engine. I turn down the volume, and she sends me an apologetic smile.

Once we're out on the road, heading home, I stare out the window. "I don't know what I'm supposed to do."

"About what?"

She pauses at a stop sign, her blinker flashing in time with my heartbeat, and turns onto the bigger street after two cars pass.

"Felix says I'm overthinking."

"Your cityscapes?"

"He says I should focus on photography if I want my art to look perfect. I suck at painting."

She hums. "Maybe you'd do better with a different subject. What's your favorite thing to draw?"

I pause, considering.

Of all my drawings during the last few years, the ones I love the most are the ones that evoke emotion. Jimmy's nervous face. Dahlia during one of our drawing class sessions. Xander screaming at his video games.

"People."

Prue glances my way as she turns onto King Street. "You should paint portraits."

◆

Someone is giggling in the kitchen when we arrive.

One of my favorite things about winter break was that I didn't have to see Micaela. I'm glad Jimmy has another friend, but I could live without the longing looks she sends in Xander's direction.

Prue follows me to the source. I need food, and Prue's always up for a bag of chips. Always.

In the kitchen, Jimmy and Micaela lean against the counter, elbow to elbow, while Xander pours out a few drinks. He twirls the bottle between his fingers, but I roll my eyes at the bartender trick as I pass.

"Hi, Billie." A bright smile spreads across Micaela's face. "You wanna join us? No alcohol. The spoilsport made me put my tequila back in the car."

"It's grapefruit, rosemary, and seltzer," Xander throws over his shoulder.

Jimmy shifts so he and Micaela are no longer touching. "And Dave'll be over in fifteen so we can practice."

Xander pours out a third drink, then stoops to light up his phone, sitting on the counter.

My own device says it's a couple minutes till six. Xander's making sure I take my pill on time.

Before I can put it away, the screen lights up. A call from Imogene.

I answer immediately.

"Want the latest?" she asks without so much as a greeting.

245

I relax against the nearest counter, and Prue tears into a bag of Fritos. "About the pregnancy?"

"She's like seven months pregnant now. She's starting to waddle." But Mo's information is as detailed as her tone is interested by the topic.

"What about you, Mo? How are you doing?"

Across from me, Jimmy's eyes are glued to Xander's drink-mixing skills.

Imogene's sigh crackles the line. "I got accepted to the University of Virginia. And a few other places. But that's the one I'm leaning toward most."

"You don't sound excited. Don't you want to—?"

She scoffs. "Billie, I'm getting an English degree, and I'll figure something out after that. I don't have to know what I want to do with my life yet."

"Yeah, but an English degree?"

She scoffs. "I learned everything I can't do with an English degree from *Avenue Q*, thanks. Besides, writing is what I'm good at."

My fingers cramp around the phone. "I know. I just want you to be happy."

"I'll figure it out."

I don't want you to turn into me.

Across the room, Xander finishes up the drinks with a sprig of rosemary. Micaela chats with the guys, but Jimmy is pointedly looking away from me.

"Mo, do you want to say hi to Jimmy and Xander?"

Jimmy turns with parted lips and shakes his head vigorously.

Xander, on the other hand, drops everything and grabs the phone before she can answer the question. "Hey, how you holding up?"

I watch curiously.

Prue nudges me. "I'm ready to go upstairs when you are. Once you get your phone back."

I nod.

Xander chuckles. "UVA, huh? Yes, I have excellent hearing." He pauses for her response. "You sure you wouldn't rather be dancing? Because you're a damn good dancer, Mo. I'm sure Jim and everybody else would agree."

Since when does he call her "Mo"? Have I missed something?

He groans. "Alright, fine. But you've got my number. Call me if you need to talk, okay?"

I bite my lip. Now, my whole family adores him. Because somehow, he and Mo are friends.

When Xander hands me the phone, our fingers brush during the pass, and we beam as I press the phone to my cheek.

Imogene and I exchange a few parting words—she has to have a family dinner—and I return to the fridge, despite Prue's impatient glare. "Some of us need more sustenance than a bag of Fritos," I tell her.

Inside, I grab two sodas, my Greek yogurt, and some cheese sticks.

Behind me, Xander snorts. He starts passing out the drinks. "You need healthy carbs, not that shit."

I send him a quick glare as my phone vibrates in my hand. "How much straight sugar is in that drink you made?"

He sniggers but doesn't answer, and I grin.

I don't know what I expected after classes started again, but us remaining friends wasn't it. With the way things ended, I thought we could never be friends again. I thought I'd never have to struggle with "only friends."

When Xander breaks eye contact, he hands a glass to Jimmy, who studies the concoction appreciatively after a sip, and the second to Micaela.

A soft smile spreads across her lips when their fingers touch. "Thanks, Xander."

He bends closer and whispers something in her ear. Something that brings a blush to her cheeks.

I feel sick.

The text is from Dahlia. We've barely spoken since I last saw her, and we don't have class together this semester.

I want to see you, is all it says.

I text back: *Okay.*

Twenty-Eight

"You don't have much space." Dahlia reclines on the makeshift stage, preening under the spotlights, supported by a pillow and blanket. While she stays planted, her eyes wander the studio.

I sweep a line of violet—the color of her blouse—across the painting.

The first step was to go over my initial cityscape with a layer of gesso and ultramarine to render the canvas usable again, then setting up the stage. I did that during a class session because I doubt I'll paint any portraits during class.

"Thanks for agreeing to do this." I lay down another violet line.

"Like I'd pass up an opportunity for you to paint me like one of your French girls."

I roll my eyes.

It takes less than ten minutes to redraw the lines. Then, I mix colors again. A painting doesn't really get interesting until the third or fourth layer.

"I have to admit," I add as I mix a dark chromatic gray, "I'm kind of nervous. I'm glad you're my first."

She tilts her head, ignoring the fact that she needs to stay still. "First girlfriend?"

I frown. "Is that what we are?"

"You said it first."

"Dahlia, we haven't talked in two weeks." I scrape the paint into a single daub and rinse the brush. I have to mix a few more colors.

"That was your decision, Billie, not mine. I gave you space."

A shiver runs down my spine. "You forced my hand."

On the glass palette, I now have a rich brown, golden brown, and a blend of cobalt and dioxizine purple in various shades. I mix one last pink and move back to the canvas.

"Besides," I add when she remains silent, "I meant I'm glad you're my first model. I have to do five of these portraits."

Dahlia settles into position, but her stern look says she's thinking. Seriously thinking.

The first two layers go down with house painting brushes—they're big enough to lay down a lot of paint at once, and you only need a general image at first. Once everything's in the right place, regular brushes add the details. I'm not yet to Dahlia's details.

"So are we going to talk about what happened?" she finally asks. "Or are you going to fester?"

My hand, sweeping along her leg, quivers. The line juts to one side before I retract.

"You have something to say. Why are you holding back?"

I purse my lips. "Dahlia, we talked about this after it happened. I'd repeat myself."

She rises to her feet and approaches. The stage isn't far away—like she said, not much room—and she reaches me in a few steps. "Do you want me to apologize for making you uncomfortable?" She pries the brush from my fingers.

"It's not that simple."

The brush clatters onto my supply cart.

"What can I do to make it up to you?" Her arms wrap around my waist, but I hold my hands away. Her lips press to my collarbone. "I'll do whatever I can to make you happy." And her tongue sweeps along my collar.

I squeeze her shoulder. "I think we have different definitions of 'happy.'"

She withdraws, giggling. "Bringing you pleasure doesn't make you happy?"

"No, sex doesn't make me happy. I've tried that. It didn't work."

All it did was ruin one of my most important friendships. Not that Xander minded how much sex we had. Not at all. But to say our sex was based on mutual affection instead of providing myself with a new outlet for my depression and anxieties would be a lie. Affection was part of it, but Xander was more invested than me.

Dahlia's lips trail up to my jawline. Her teeth tug on my earlobe. "Well, you haven't tried it with me."

"No."

She smiles, unmoved by my firm tone.

"Sex doesn't make up for your selfish behavior. If I tell you to stop, you need to stop. That's what consent means."

Dahlia lays her head on my shoulder. "Anything you say, pookie."

I nudge her off. "If you can't respect me, we need to end this here and now. I will not be an object for you to play with. You don't get to use my body to make a point."

251

When her forehead rests against me, I close my eyes and hold her.

"I'm sorry, Billie." Her words tickle my damp lips. "I got wrapped up in my own jealousy. I wasn't thinking straight. The last thing I want to do is hurt you."

When she kisses me again, I let her. Like so few other times, she is soft and slow. She doesn't push, doesn't nudge, doesn't badger. And as she breaks away, she holds me tight against her frail body—as if holding me will keep me from letting her go.

"You promise nothing will happen with Xander?" She releases a nervous titter. "I'm paranoid, but I don't want to lose you."

I wrap an arm around her waist and peck her temple. "Xander and I are over. You don't have to worry."

She breathes a sigh of relief, and I pull her into another kiss. She reciprocates without hesitation, her hands slipping under my shirt to touch bare skin, her mouth opening so our tongues tangle together.

But the moment her fingers grasp my breast, I break away.

"We're not doing that here."

Her eyes narrow for a moment, but she allows a puff of air and forces a smile into place. "Anything you say."

"We should get back to work." My palette has been open and unused for too long—the paint's drying out.

◆

"You know, I was excited when we first talked about having a sleepover." Prue shovels another spoonful of my strawberry yogurt into her mouth, her legs dangling over the edge of the counter. The gentle tap of her heels against the cupboards almost covers the sound of Jimmy and Micaela practicing upstairs.

I roll my eyes. "Until I mentioned inviting Dahlia? Do I get my food back?"

She glares, and instead, I retrieve a second Greek yogurt from the fridge. "Yes, until you invited Dahlia. What's the point of a girls' night if you invite your girlfriend?"

I recline beside her and tear off the aluminum foil. "Dahlia's a girl too. It'd be rude not to invite her."

"Yes, but the premise of a girls' night is having a night for girl friends—not girlfriends." She opens the drawer next to her leg and offers me a clean spoon.

"That's an oddly specific distinction."

Upstairs, the *twang* of guitars comes to an abrupt stop.

"I invited Cynthia too," Prue adds. "I might actually wrangle her away from her textbook this time."

"I don't know the last time I saw her."

Prue shrugs. "Neither do I, and I live with her. I don't know where I'll live when this school year is up. Cyn wants one of those fancy one-person apartments on the top floor of the Towers."

"Sounds like you need a new roommate." I scrape up the end of my yogurt and rinse out the cup.

"You don't happen to need somewhere to live after your lease is up, do you?"

When she hands me her empty yogurt cup, I rinse it too. "I have no idea what my housing situation will be in May." I turn off the water and drop the containers in the recycling bin. "If I didn't live with Jimmy and Xander, we probably wouldn't be friends anymore."

"Hey…" When Prue pulls me into a hug, her head rests against my bun. "I know you worry about that, and I don't help. But you know they care about you, even when they're being stupid."

My laughter's muffled by her arm.

But Prue releases me when Jimmy, Micaela, and David stumble into the room.

Micaela bounces over, her face alight. "Oh my God, did you hear that?"

I shake my head. "Hear what?"

"That song!" She yanks Jimmy closer by the arm. "He's brilliant."

Jimmy scratches his head. "It's nothing, Micaela. Stop making a big deal out of it." His face is bright red.

"No, no." She turns on him. "The next time we play that, we're recording it. Right, David?"

In the doorway, David shrugs, not at all impressed or intimidated by her intensity.

"We can't turn my bedroom into a recording studio." Jimmy shakes his head. "I don't have that kind of equipment."

Micaela scoffs. "You know we can use the campus studio, right? They legitimately have a recording studio."

"I know, but—"

"No buts. Tomorrow."

"Works for me," David adds.

Behind him, someone clears their throat, and Xander sidesteps him, keys in hand. "Don't you have plans tomorrow night, Cae?"

"Cae"? She has a nickname?

This time, Micaela's the one to blush. "During the day while you're at work. We're not getting together till late."

Oh.

They're going on a date tomorrow night.

I think I might throw up.

Prue catches my attention with a covert smirk. "So next weekend," she says in a hushed voice, and I relax, thankful for the distraction. "You, me, Cynthia, Dahlia…anybody else coming for our sleepover?"

I snort. "I don't know any other girls, Prue."

"Did someone say 'sleepover'?"

I turn, alarmed by Micaela's interjection. "Uh, yeah. Something small next weekend."

"Nice." She tries to play it cool, but Micaela is an open book. "It always sounds like you're having so much fun when you two get together. I wish I had girl friends to hang out with."

My eyes drift to Xander, but he's focused on Micaela, brow furrowed, jaw slack.

"Do you want to join us?"

Her face lights up at the invitation. "That'd be amazing! I'd love to." She glances at Xander and Jimmy, then back to me. "I'm excited to get to know you, Billie."

It's hard to tell how genuine she is. My go-to is to believe she's lying. Or at least improving the truth. Because I have no idea why she'd want to hang out with the ex of the guy she's going on a date with tomorrow night. If I were her, I wouldn't want anything to do with me.

I settle on: "Great."

She grins again, and I force myself to return it.

255

Twenty-Nine

THE FLOOR CREAKS UNDERFOOT AS I STALK ONE DIRECTION, then cut back the other way. I cannot stop pacing.

"Billie, you're going to wear a hole in the carpet."

I send Prue a glare as she sits cross-legged on my bed. Beside her, Cynthia is surrounded by textbooks and notes— she agreed to attend the sleepover if she could study. Prue was pissed.

"Calm down." She pushes off the bed and stands beside me. "This will be okay."

I stop. "No, this is a bad idea."

"You got yourself into this situation."

"I didn't have another option."

Prue lays her hands on my shoulders. "You didn't have to invite her."

"Anything else would've been rude."

And I shouldn't be rude to Xander's new girlfriend. Not that they're official, but they have a second date planned for tomorrow night.

"Hey!"

We turn to see Dahlia in the doorway. She's wearing jeans and a light jacket, a drawstring bag slung over one shoulder. The grin on her face slips, and I step away from Prue.

The last thing I need is for her to decide my platonic best friend isn't platonic just because Prue's bi. God, she'll think there's something between me and Jimmy next. Fat chance.

"Lia." I press a kiss to her lips, but her response is overzealous. I have to pry myself away. "I'm surprised you're not in pajamas."

She gives a one-shouldered shrug and wraps an arm around my waist. "I figured I'd wear yours," she murmurs in my ear.

"Let's get snacks!" Prue announces, stepping around us to head downstairs.

I follow.

The kitchen is dark and empty. Prue and I specifically chose a night both Xander and Jimmy have an evening shift at Draft Horse so they wouldn't be around—that was especially important after Micaela decided to tag along.

Prue tears open a bag of Funyuns. "You guys have the best food."

I snort and snatch a piece. "Do you eat food at your own place? Because you're always stealing mine."

Dahlia wraps her arms around my waist from behind and rests her chin on my shoulder. "You're so warm."

I try to shrug her off, but she doesn't budge. Instead, I offer her a Funyun.

She places a couple kisses along my neck and nudges her cold fingers under my shirt.

Prue doesn't hesitate before gagging.

I pat Dahlia's hand before slipping out of her grasp. "This isn't couple time," I remind her in a quiet voice.

The doorbell rings.

That must be Micaela.

On the other side of the front door, Micaela holds out a box of goodies—chocolate, Sour Patch Kids, some rom coms, and a bottle of white wine—with a grin.

After all these months, she hasn't picked up on the fact that I don't drink. Irritation tugs at my stomach. Why have neither Jimmy nor Xander told her?

"I brought provisions," she announces as the door closes. "I brought my corkscrew in case you don't have one."

"Oh."

I focus on the bottle. It can't have a high ABV—it's a California Moscato. But this is supposed to be an alcohol-free sleepover.

"Uh, thanks." I nod toward the kitchen, where Prue and Dahlia munch on Funyuns. "We're getting snacks."

I carry the box to the kitchen and lay it on the counter, avoiding eye contact with Prue. She notices the wine immediately.

And so does Dahlia.

"Oh, this is a good brand." She snatches it from the box and reads the label. "Only twelve percent alcohol. Shame." Then, she shrugs. "Although, that's high for Moscato."

I raise a hand. "Dahlia, no…"

But she twists the corkscrew into the top. It pops open with remarkable force, and she drinks straight from the bottle. "Bubbly."

Micaela frowns. She must realize she won't get any of that bottle. Not if Dahlia has anything to say about it.

"Come on," I say in a small voice. "Let's go upstairs."

Prue walks with me, Dahlia behind us, and Micaela

bringing up the rear, box in her arms.

"You're not going to say anything?" Prue whispers.

I keep my voice low as well. "What am I supposed to say? This isn't the first time I've been around alcohol since quitting. I can handle it."

"Yeah, but your girlfriend should be respectful of your choices."

We reach the top of the stairs and file into my bedroom, where Cynthia is engrossed in her homework. I doubt she noticed when we left the room—except to enjoy the silence.

"Shouldn't I also respect her choices?" We sit on the edge of the mattress, Prue with the bag of Funyuns in her hands.

Dahlia plops down on the carpet by my feet. A third of the bottle's gone.

This time, Prue doesn't bother keeping her words quiet. "Not if her choices are damaging to you."

Micaela awkwardly sets the box by the door and pulls out a pack of Twizzlers. She joins Dahlia on the floor, facing the rest of us. "So what's the plan?" Her voice is upbeat, eager. She's trying too hard.

Before I can speak, Dahlia takes another swig of wine and hunches forward, a smirk on her face. "I heard you and Xander went on a date. How'd it go?"

Micaela blushes. "We didn't do anything spectacular—grabbed a late dinner and walked around downtown, talking—but he's so sweet."

"It's nice to see him find someone like you," Dahlia says. Another drink of wine, and she runs her free hand up my leg. "You two are perfect together."

I didn't think Micaela's blush could intensify. It can.

"No, not perfect." But she beams at the thought. "Maybe

we can be. He walked me home afterward and kissed me goodnight, and he's so romantic. I was walking on air."

Prue nudges me with the Funyuns, but I can't eat. "Aren't you graduating in May?" she asks. "How 'perfect' can you two be when you'll move in, what, three and a half months? Unless you're staying in town."

Micaela fiddles with the silver and blue beads around her neck. "I wasn't planning to. I want to move to Seattle—it's the birthplace of grunge. But you know, if things pan out, I wouldn't mind putting that on hold for a year." Her fingers stop at the cross and hold it tight enough her skin fades white.

"That's awfully fast," Prue says.

Dahlia shakes her head emphatically. "Not fast—romantic!"

"Actually…" Micaela shifts so she's sitting up more, abandoning the rosary. "I was hoping you ladies could help me…"

"Yeah?" Prue stuffs another Funyun in her mouth. She's probably eaten half the bag by now.

"Well, we've been on the one date, but I've liked him since I met him in June. But he's always been distant. It took forever for him to ask me out, and I know he knew I liked him." She heaves a sigh. "I don't mind him waiting so long. I want him to be sure this is what he wants, not because I have a crush on him."

Prue's unamused. "So what's the problem?"

Micaela releases a nervous laugh. "You two have known him for a while, right? Billie? Prudence?"

"Since day one of freshmen orientation," Prue says.

"Has he always been so closed off? The date went fine—

great, even—but we spent the whole time talking about me. Any time I asked him about his life, his family, his goals, he turned the tables and brought the conversation back to me." A strand of shimmering brown hair falls in her eyes, but she focuses her attention on me and Prue. "I've dealt with guys who do that to get in a girl's pants, but that's not what it was. He genuinely didn't want to discuss his life. Was his childhood that bad?"

The mattress squeaks as Prue shifts uncomfortably. "I'm not qualified to answer that. We've never had an intimate relationship."

I snort.

Unless you count them sleeping together freshman year. As Prue tells it, the encounter wasn't particularly intimate. She propositioned him, he said sure, and they had sex. She was the first person he slept with at Bradford. Rumor has it, he didn't last long.

"What about you, Billie?" Micaela turns worried eyes on me. "Do you have any insight?"

I have no idea what to say.

"I'm at a loss." Her voice trembles. "And I've tried talking to Jimmy about this because he knows Xander better than anyone, but any time I bring it up, he gets annoyed. I don't think he likes us dating."

I try to sound nonchalant. "I don't think Jimmy likes anyone dating Xander. It encroaches on best friend time— between classes and work, they don't hang out as much as they used to."

Micaela frowns. "They work together."

"Xander's front-of-house and Jimmy's back-of-house. They rarely see each other while working. Besides, Xander is serious about his job."

"Okay, but that doesn't help. Seriously, what do you think, Billie? Am I wasting my time here?"

But Dahlia interjects before I can speak: "Of course not! You two are great together."

The bottle's an inch away from empty. I doubt she'd get tipsy from a bottle of twelve-percent wine, but at this pace, it's possible.

"I like to think that," Micaela says, blushing again, "but like Prudence said, I graduate in May. If this doesn't go anywhere, I'm leaving for Seattle. I won't stay in St. Clare another year if this isn't serious."

I roll my eyes. "You can't expect him to become attached that quickly."

She offers me a sad smile. "I'm not looking for magic or reaching for the Moon. I need something concrete. Someone stable. Someone I don't have to piece back together. I have big goals, and I need someone who can work with me."

"I don't know what to tell you, Micaela. He's not broken—you don't have to piece him together—but he's not whole either. He's just Xander."

"Okay." Micaela lays her hand firmly on her knee. "I know you two dated. It must've been weird dating one of your best friends, but you dated. Can you tell me anything useful for this situation?"

My breath catches. "What do you mean 'it must've been weird'?"

"Xander explained everything. A two-week relationship. Nothing serious. Amicable parting. It ended because you realized you were platonic, right?"

She says it matter-of-factly. Like her words aren't a

sucker-punch to the gut.

"What?"

There was nothing amicable about our breakup, and those two weeks weren't awkward or weird or "platonic." Nothing about my relationship with Xander has ever been platonic.

But he told her our relationship wasn't serious.

I can't focus.

He lied to her.

Or he lied to me.

I blink to stop the tears. But they don't stop.

And Micaela's too focused on her own problems to notice.

"So," she continues, "do you have any suggestions to get him to open up?"

"You'd have to *get* Xander."

She freezes. "What?"

"And you don't."

Micaela opens her mouth, but nothing comes out.

I shift forward, my hands wrapped firmly around the mattress edge. "I know you like him. You've liked him since I met you, but in all that time, you haven't gotten to know him. Part of that's because he closes himself off—he has some unresolved issues with his parents—but if he opened up, you wouldn't understand him."

Dahlia shifts on the floor, but I ignore her.

"If things got serious, would you expect him to go to Seattle with you? You're fooling yourself if you think that would work. Xander's ambitious and smart, and he does not settle. Moving there because that's your dream would be settling."

"There are plenty of things he could do in Seattle."

"He spent all of his childhood neglected. His family moved around so much he never learned how to make friends. His father cares more about his business than his son—and sees that son as a means to an end. Xander doesn't want 'plenty of things'—he wants to make his own choices. It's incredibly presumptuous to think he would abandon the family he found here for someone he's gone on one date with."

I'm cold where Dahlia no longer leans against me.

Micaela hugs her abdomen. "It's not crazy to assume we would make those decisions together in a serious relationship."

I scoff. "But it's not going to get serious."

She bites her lip. "Why not?"

"You aren't a challenge."

She lifts a hand, but I cut her off.

"Xander needs someone to keep him in check. Someone who helps him grow. Someone who makes him a better person. You can't do that."

No one says anything.

But Micaela studies me in awe. "You're in love with him."

I gape at her. "No, I'm—"

Dahlia rises from the floor, eyes narrow. "After all I've done, it's still about him." Her body quakes.

"What do you mean?" Despite my previous resolve, my voice quivers.

"He never cared about you," she snaps. "You heard what she said. 'Nothing serious.' It was only sex. But everything I've done—everything—I did for you. Can't you see that?"

"Wait—"

She lifts the bottle of wine. It's empty now. "God, I need a fucking drink stronger than this." She stomps from the room, her footsteps jarring in my ears.

"Dahlia!"

I stumble after her.

"Dahlia, what are you talking about? What did you do?"

Thirty

She's in the kitchen when I reach the bottom.

"Dahlia…" I grip the door frame.

But she doesn't turn. Doesn't look at me. Doesn't register I spoke.

Instead, she yanks open the freezer, lips in a narrow line, and scoffs at the contents. She rifles through cupboard after cupboard, shelf after shelf to no avail. "Where the fuck is the alcohol?"

"We don't have any."

"Oh, come on." She approaches, nostrils flaring. "They have a stash somewhere—no matter how much you think they care about you. They barely talk to you. They don't treat you like a friend. You're constantly in the way. A burden. Why the hell do you live here?"

"Dahlia, what did you do?"

"I protected you. He would've hurt you, and I protected you."

"What do you mean?" My words aren't even a whisper.

She grips my shoulder, tight enough it hurts but only just. "Do you really think that would've lasted? He dictated everything—the drinking, the exercise, who you spent time

266

with. How is that a healthy relationship?"

"Xander didn't dictate my behavior. I listened to my therapist."

"He would've left you. He was never good enough for you. No one is." Her hand squeezes—affection. "And you went along with it. You didn't question anything. He was going to hurt you. No one else was looking out for you."

I recoil, shake her off. "You can't be serious."

"I'm very serious about us."

"I knew...I knew you didn't want me to date him. I knew that. But I didn't realize." My hand finds the door frame again. My legs quiver. "You spent months telling me I could do better, encouraged me to date other people—and when I refused, you were so excited. He was helping me, but you couldn't let me be happy. Everything you did, everything you said was meant to drive a wedge between us. You did that on purpose."

She follows me, step for step. "I was protecting you."

"Stop. Stop talking. I don't want to hear it." I close my eyes, but nothing goes away. "You got inside my head. I want to help you, to be a good influence for once in my life. But that doesn't mean anything because you're the one trying to control me. Not Xander."

Her hand touches my waist. "Billie, that was always going to fail. The longer it went on, the more it would hurt you."

"You don't know that."

"I was protecting you. Like I protected you from Jay." She's close enough she presses against me. "You deserve so much better."

My words catch, and I have to try again. "You told him

I manipulate men, that I lead them on. That was you."

"Someone has to protect you."

"Stop saying that."

Dahlia leans her forehead against mine. Holds me close. Her breathing is erratic. Labored. Her heart beats hard against her chest. So hard it pounds in mine too. "I am not going to lose you."

My cheeks are wet with tears.

I don't know why I'm crying. I shouldn't be surprised. I think part of me always understood what she was doing, but I hoped I was wrong.

She kisses me. Her lips are hard, then wet. Her hands clamp around my hips, holding me to her. Her tongue pushes inside my mouth, touching every part, every inch, and I am overwhelmed.

A hand yanks at my waistband, dragging the pajama pants aside.

I break away. "What are you doing?"

"I'm not going to lose you. You mean too much to me."

"No." I force her away. We need distance. "You don't want what's best for me. You don't care about me. You only care about how I make you feel, who I am in relation to you."

She steps closer.

I hold up my hand. "I'm done. We're done." I cannot stop crying. "You need to leave."

But the tears don't stop.

When she's gone, I can't stand anymore. My legs give out, and I slide to the floor. I don't know what to do other than cry.

Someone sits beside me.

I can't see. My glasses are coated in salty tears. The world is blurry.

But I know the smell when he holds me to his chest. He's still wearing the leather jacket.

Xander.

"Hey, you're okay." He presses a kiss to the top of my head. "You're okay, Dixon. You're okay."

I struggle to stop the shaking. I can barely get my words out. "What are you doing here? Why aren't you at work?"

"Don't think about me. Don't think about Dahlia. Focus on your breathing." His hand finds mine, and he threads our fingers together.

I ground myself to those fingers.

When I steady my breathing, the shaking fades too. But the tears refuse to stop.

Xander's warm lips find my temple. An attempt to reassure me.

"Why're you here? Why do you still pretend you care?"

His fingers clench around mine. "What do you mean, Dixon?" His voice is a whisper. His nose nuzzles my ear. "Of course I care."

"Why did you tell Micaela we had a fling? That the reason it didn't work was because it wasn't serious?" I pull away to look at him. "Were you lying to her or were you lying to me?"

"I had one date with her—that's hardly the time to explain our entire history. And you know how much I cared about you. I still do." He squeezes me closer. "You were the one who didn't want to pursue the relationship."

But I will not be dissuaded.

"You shouldn't have lied. Am I supposed to pretend none

269

of that mattered? That it didn't happen?"

"Of course not."

"I cannot pretend. Despite what I was going through, those were the best two and a half weeks of my life. I will not forget it just because you decided it wasn't worth remembering."

"I'm not asking you to." His words are drawn out and quiet. He cups my cheek, his mesmerizing eyes pleading me to believe him. "And I never said it wasn't worth remembering."

All at once, his lips are on mine.

The kiss, wet with tears, has a slow beginning. During the two years we've allowed our lips to meet, few of our intimate moments have been slow. But he holds me, one hand at my cheek, the other still entangled with mine, and kisses away my worries.

His warmth courses through me. From his tender lips, it trickles down and pools into my stomach. Then, it begins the systematic bombardment against my core. His kiss is gentle, but he claims me, devours me from within, until his heat finally settles as a fever between my legs.

I can no longer maintain a slow kiss.

Discounting that distressing drunken make-out he probably doesn't remember, I've longed for him for almost a year. Now that he's here, holding me in his arms, I waste no time.

I open my mouth to him and crawl onto his lap, flattening myself against his chest until clothes are the only thing between us. He sucks in my lip, fingers threading through my frizzy locks, and his tongue invades my mouth. Beneath me, his cock pulses, eager to join the fray.

The moan that slips out is proof of my impending defeat.

Without effort or malice, he renders me defenseless. I am at his mercy, and I am eager to surrender.

Then, it's over.

And I can breathe and think again.

He presses his forehead to mine, holding me tight. "I remember everything." He's panting. "And I don't intend to forget. The memory of you, of us, is burned onto my brain for eternity."

"Xander." I barely manage to speak. "What are you doing? You just started seeing Micaela."

For a second, he blinks at me, brow furrowed with confusion. "We've been on one date. We're not in a relationship."

His erection strains against its confines, and I am heady with desire, but this would be a mistake.

"She's in my bedroom." I swallow, gathering the words. "Micaela is upstairs in my bedroom, and she cares about you. Don't throw that away because I'm crying. You don't owe me anything."

He exhales slowly.

Someone clears their throat.

I look up, but my vision's obscured.

"Actually," Micaela says in an uneasy voice, "I'm not upstairs."

Prue and Cynthia stand not far behind her. Apparently, there is something interesting enough to tear Cynthia away from her textbooks.

I grip the counter to clamber off of Xander's lap, but my legs are faint. From the kiss or the crying, I don't know.

Micaela withdraws her keys from her pocket. "I should go."

No one stops her. Xander doesn't move.

The front door closes behind her.

Prue steps closer and wraps an arm around my shoulders. "Come on, Billie, let's go upstairs. Watch a movie or something. You can relax."

"That sounds nice," I manage.

Cynthia trails behind us.

Leaving Xander alone on the kitchen floor.

Prue sits me on the edge of the mattress, her arm holding me to her. "Lemme clean your glasses. You've got a spray, right?"

Cynthia closes the door, then locates the tiny bottle atop my dresser, and I hand the glasses to Prue.

"Well, this has been an eventful night." Prue sprays the cleaner on and wipes the lenses dry. "It's not even ten o'clock."

I snort. "'Eventful' is the nice way of saying it."

She nudges me. "Yeah, well, how would you like me to say it?"

When she hands the glasses back, I fold them up in my fist. I'd rather be blind.

"We went downstairs when it got quiet." Prue's voice is hushed. "What happened?"

"Dahlia and I broke up." The tears have stopped, but my eyes and throat ache from holding it in. "We've been heading in that direction since our first kiss, but I don't know…"

Prue squeezes my knee encouragingly. "You believed in her."

"Too much." I force a laugh, but it sounds hollow. "More than she deserves."

"She's not all bad—and I know you know that. You

looked past all her faults and still care."

I wipe away the remnants of my tears—rub away the ache behind my eyes—and collapse onto the mattress, clutching the glasses to my chest. "And Xander…"

But I don't know what to say.

"You were sitting on his lap."

Footsteps shuffle around the room. Must be Cynthia.

"He was comforting me." I sniffle. "We were fighting, and then, we were kissing, and it was…"

"A really good kiss?" Prue suggests.

"Well," Cynthia says from the far side of the room, "three of five cars are gone now."

I tick them off in my head. Dahlia left. Micaela left. Obviously, Prue's car is here, and Jimmy walked to Draft Horse because it's a nice night.

Xander must've left.

"No," I murmur, "it was…an amazing kiss."

Where did he go?

I pry my fingers away from the glasses. I don't want to break them.

"So what now?" Prue asks.

I choke on my laughter. Because what options do I have? My relationship with Dahlia is over. I ruined any chance for Xander and Micaela. And I ruined any chance for me and Xander a year ago.

"I have no idea."

Thirty-One

"YOU'VE PUT IN A LOT OF HOURS." FELIX INCHES CLOSER TO Dahlia's pensive, half-finished face on a thirty-six-by-forty-eight-inch canvas. "This is...vastly different than what you showed me six weeks ago, Billie."

Standing a few feet behind him, I hope I haven't taken this in the wrong direction. "I'm not done with that one."

And I don't know if I'll finish it. I might need a replacement model.

Felix turns to the painting of Prudence, a secretive smile on her bright face—her natural state of being. Both images are closeups of their faces and torsos, ending just below the waist. The composition fades at the edges, to create the illusion of continuation.

"I'm impressed." He retreats. "You took my critique to heart."

I survey the incomplete painting of Dahlia and run a hand through my mass of curls. "You were right. I learned a lot when I studied Alberto Giacometti and the others, but I had no idea how to apply it. What's the point of a painting study if you can't use it to improve your original art?"

"I see the influence now. Your lines are strong and

intentional, and they give these characters a structure they wouldn't otherwise have. But it's not overpowering." Felix pauses to examine the painting of Prue. "You have three more paintings to complete by finals—and you need to finish this one." He nods toward Dahlia's image. "Do you have your models picked out?"

Here, I hesitate.

There are plenty of people I could ask, but I don't know who would agree. Sitting for hours while someone scrutinizes your entire body has to be awkward. After all, I'm not the one being reduced to lines and curves and paint on an enormous canvas that'll be displayed for all of campus and St. Clare to see and critique at the end of semester.

"My friend Jimmy said he'd do it. But I need two more. Maybe one could be a self-portrait?"

But I haven't done a self-portrait since high school. My skill level wasn't up to the task, and I hated all of them.

His lips press into a thin line in concentration. "Using a mirror or a photograph?"

"A mirror would be more organic." I step forward to assess the crook of Dahlia's arm, where my brush strokes fade unnaturally. We haven't spoken since our breakup.

"Yes, using a mirror allows more freedom for you to control your composition. When doing portraits, you need to be your own director, so working from photographs can be helpful, but it's limiting."

"Yeah." I appraise the criss-crossing lines along her arm and waist. "But everyone else will think I look funny because of the mirror image."

Behind me, Felix laughs. "Most viewers won't notice." He lays a hand on my shoulder. "You've made phenomenal improvement, Billie. For the first time, you're actually painting."

Without another word, he squeezes and moves on, and I study Dahlia's unfinished face.

◆

"Oh, Billie!" Elise steps up beside me. "You have your hair down. It looks nice."

I have the wipe the frown off my face before turning. "Thanks. What can I do for you, Elise?"

She examines the gallery as the door closes behind our only visitors during the last hour. "I wanted to touch base with you. We need to discuss your future."

That's never a good sign.

"Of course."

Elise inclines her head toward her glass-enclosed office. "Let's chat."

We're not supposed to leave the floor empty, but the odds of having another guest before we close in the next five minutes are low. I follow her.

"Have a seat." She gestures to the open chair and reclines in her own.

I sit and clasp my hands. "How can I help?"

Elise's soft smile holds no comfort or warmth. "I have an announcement. Normally, we'd gather all our employees and discuss this as a group, but I had to let Amelia go."

My jaw gapes. "You fired her?"

I saw her last week during the First Friday Gallery Hop.

She grimaces. "Not exactly. And that's what we need to discuss."

276

"Am I getting fired?"

She holds her hand aloft to silence me. "No, Billie, I'm not firing you. In fact, I specifically wanted to ask if you could stay on while we prepare to close."

Oh.

I lean back, uncertain. "The gallery's closing?"

Elise pinches the bridge of her nose. "Yes, we are. Unfortunately, the gallery is no longer fiscally viable. Greg hoped that the Lilly Parkinson exhibit in March would help, but Ms. Parkinson had an emergency and is unable to do the exhibit."

"So what are we going to do?"

"We've decided to move the Emerging Artists exhibit forward by three weeks and keep it open until we close mid-April. We reached out to several attending artists. Most of them can accommodate the change, but some will add their pieces at the originally planned date."

For a moment, I can only stare. "When's our last day?"

"The fifteenth of April, a Friday." Elise flashes me an uncomfortable smile. "Will you be able to help us?"

My mind races. "Of course I'll help, but Elise, I need to find a new job right away. I cannot afford to wait until the gallery closes."

"If you need to leave before then, I understand." She glances out her glass office walls. "It's time to close up."

"Right."

◆

The art building is always empty late at night. That's when I enjoy it the most. I prefer the silence. Unfortunately, painting portraits means I have to spend my time in the studio with someone else.

"When you painted Prudence, how long did it take?"

Even when that someone else is my oldest friend, I miss working alone. In the last six months, Jimmy and I haven't occupied the same comfortable silence we used to enjoy on a regular basis.

I squint at the canvas. I finished the first layer—it's always the fastest—but there's a long way to go.

"With Prue, we did two sessions." I squeeze out a portion of flow improver to thin the cad yellow. I need to redraw my lines before starting the second layer. "Each session was two to three hours plus some breaks."

Jimmy shifts in his seat before fixing his position—the stool was his decision—and I measure out the lines again.

"Felix says I'm a fast painter if that makes you feel better." I flash him a smile around the easel.

"He's your professor?"

"Yeah."

With him in position, it's easy to lay down the lines of his form. I outline again the large folds in the curtain draped behind him, the broad shoulders, and the messy brown hair, already in a different place than the previous layer.

"How many layers? You said you do it in layers, right?"

My eyes meet his around the side of the easel. "Depends on how much I fuck up." Bright yellow fogs up my water cup as I rinse the brush. "Four to eight."

"How do you screw it up?"

I shrug. "A million different ways. There's so many things to take into account—contrast, composition, color palette, plus accuracy to the subject matter."

As I wipe the wet brush on a stack of paper towels, he nods.

"Why the sudden interest?" I ask.

His brow furrows. "You know, I don't think I've seen your paintings this year. The last ones were what you shipped from France, and that was…a long time ago."

I return to the painting, but I have to wait for the line work to dry before charging into the next layer. "You wanna take a break? There's a snack machine downstairs."

He stumbles off the stool, excited to move around. We head out once I have my wallet and lanyard from the supply cart.

Downstairs, we stop at the snack machine, and he peruses the merchandise while I insert a bill for a bag of chips. "There's Bugles on the bottom right," I say as I retrieve my food, and with a victorious laugh, he inserts his own money.

I tear open the bag while I wait, and he types in the code for his selection. I close my eyes, trying to relax while he pulls out his snack, the hinge squeaking as the door falls back into place.

"I don't know why you're here."

My eyes flash open. I know that voice.

Down the hall, Dahlia stalks inside the building, brandishing her ID. Before the door locks behind her, Brent marches after her, eyebrows knitted together. "You asked me to come," he calls after her.

"That doesn't mean I want you here."

They disappear inside the ceramics studio before coming anywhere near us.

I clutch the foil chip bag in their wake. She didn't react to seeing me.

Jimmy stands up, sporting a furrowed brow of his own. "You okay?"

I push away from the wall. "Let's go back to the studio."

It's not like he approved of our relationship. No one did.

He follows me upstairs, trailing behind, and I pause at the top so he can catch up. He falls into step with me, munching on his Bugles. Walking together like this is familiar and relaxed, but there's a barrier between us.

In the studio, we sit on the edge of my makeshift stage and finish our snack. Even with my music, the silence between us is heavy.

When I finish, I flatten my bag and fold it in quarters, anxiously trying to determine my next move.

I don't know what to say to him anymore. All our conversations are strained and awkward. He's holding something back.

The bag crinkles in my hands as I twist it between my fingers. He eats at a leisurely pace, and I don't want to push him toward the stool if he's not ready.

"Well," he says after eating the last bite, "I guess we should—"

"What happened to us?"

Jimmy stops. "What do you mean?"

My grip on the bag tightens. "We used to be best friends. We talked about everything. Now, we can't talk about anything."

He crumples his empty bag in his fist.

"I know the drama with me and Xander screwed things up. I know it's hard to be friends with both of us when we couldn't look at each other for months. But I never thought you and I wouldn't be friends anymore."

"We're still friends, Billie." He runs a hand through his messy hair. "I've been going through some stuff lately, and this is difficult. It's not that I don't want to talk to you, I promise."

I knew something was going on, but what could possibly be happening that he can't discuss with me?

"I don't know how," he says in a quiet voice.

"You don't have to tell me everything, you know." I rise from the stage and offer my hand for his crumpled bag. "We can discuss other things, can't we?"

He hands me the trash but doesn't meet my eyes.

"Yeah, I guess," he says when I sit beside him again. "I just…you know how terrible I am with secrets. It's easier not to talk to you."

"How long have you kept this from me?"

"Over a year." He releases a long sigh. "In some form or another."

Whatever the hell that means.

"But you're not keeping it from Xander?"

He opens his mouth but immediately closes it. Of course Xander knows.

"I know I'm not the greatest friend and we rarely see eye to eye, but our friendship is one of the things I value most." I curl my hands up under my chin. "I miss you. I shouldn't miss you this much when we live together, but I miss you."

He doesn't look at me. "I miss you too. I'm sorry, but I'm not ready."

"You know I'm here when you are." The last thing I want to do is pressure him.

"I know, and I'm glad for that."

Thirty-Two

"WHAT'RE YOU WATCHING NOW?" PRUE PLOPS DOWN BESIDE me, a box on her lap and a grin on her face. "Is this *Gilmore Girls*?"

"I may have binged the first season in my spare time." I quirk a shoulder. "Breaking up with your girlfriend has some perks."

Prue casts her gaze around the house, searching. "Where are the guys? Both cars are in the driveway."

"Jimmy's taking a shower. He just got off his shift."

"And Xander?"

"He walked to work."

He hasn't said a word to me since our make-out session on the kitchen floor twelve days ago. He regrets his rash behavior.

Prue turns her attention to the box on her lap. "Can we paint our toenails?" I send her a glare, but she rebuts it with nothing more than a smile. "We're supposed to hang out. You're not allowed to mope around and watch this stupid show."

I purse my lips. "It's not stupid. I rather like this Jess character."

She snorts. "Of course you do."

"What does that mean?"

She snatches the remote from the coffee table and pauses it on his irritated face. "He's a smug but lonely, intelligent guy who wears a leather jacket and crushes on the nerdy main character—plus, he's brutally hot. Why wouldn't you like him?"

I flush at the implication. "I don't like him because he reminds me of Xander."

"I don't believe that for a second." She tears open the box to sort through her many bottles of nail polish. "Now, time to do something fun."

My mouth quirks to the side. "Painting our nails is fun?"

"Yes."

"What else are we going to do? Play dress-up? Braid our hair? Have a sexy pillow fight?"

She snorts.

"Where's Cynthia?"

Prudence rolls her eyes. "Who cares? She only hangs out with us when I drag her here. All she wants to do is study."

The stairs creak, and Jimmy, hair wet, appears at the bottom and heads into the kitchen. A moment later, he returns with a drink and a stick of string cheese.

"Hey, Jimmy," Prue calls. "We're having a girls' night. Wanna join?"

He raises an eyebrow. "I feel like I'm supposed to be insulted, but I'm mostly curious."

I snort. "Yeah, Jimmy, do you want to paint your toenails with us?"

He shrugs. "Sure, why not?"

"Okay, put on some music," Prue demands. "Something

peppy."

Jimmy sits on the armchair while she rifles through her box, pulling out over a dozen different polish colors, and I switch the television to a music app and play a P!nk station.

"Okay, what colors do you want?"

I peruse the options as the first song—"U + Ur Hand"—plays and take a silvery blue. "This one's fine."

Jimmy finishes his cheese and grabs black. "Okay," he says as he lifts one foot onto the coffee table, "is there a specific way I'm supposed to do this?"

I can't help laughing at his serious tone. Prudence helps him with the big toe before handing the brush over, and he continues with determined eyes. I haven't taken off my socks yet.

Beside me, Prue picks out a lime green and dark violet and alternates between the two. "Okay, Billie, your birthday is a month away. We need a plan. What do you want to do?"

I freeze. "What?"

She flashes me a grin. "We have to celebrate somehow."

I tear off my socks, place my feet on the edge of the table like them, and shake the little bottle. "I don't need to celebrate my birthday. It's not a big deal."

Jimmy bites his lip, struggling to keep the polish off his skin. "I know you don't care about birthdays, but we want to celebrate."

"Yes!" Prue pauses for her nails to dry—she's an expert. "Let's do something. Bowling was fun last year, but we can do better."

I shake my head. "Guys, we don't have to do anything special. Who'd come?"

"Me," she says immediately. "We might be able to drag

Cynthia away from her textbooks."

"You know I'm there, and Dave could come. You know he's moving to New York when he graduates?" Jimmy pauses before adding, "Xander could come if you want him there."

I hold the bottle close to my chest. "I doubt he'd want to."

My words are met with silence.

After an unsettlingly quiet moment, Jimmy asks in a hushed voice, "Why do you say that?"

I set the bottle on the coffee table and pull my knees up. "We haven't spoken in two weeks. I ruined whatever chance he and Micaela had at a legitimate relationship."

Prue caps her bottles and blows lightly on her toes. "You know that's bullshit, right?"

I turn on her.

But it's Jimmy who responds. "He never should've asked her out in the first place. We had a fight about it—and you—the night you guys had your sleepover. Kylie sent him home."

That's why Xander showed up out of nowhere.

Wait.

Xander and Jimmy had a fight?

They bicker like an old married couple, but they don't fight. What could have happened that Xander was sent home? When he's upset, focusing on work is what he does best.

Prue crouches forward. "Micaela's sweet and all, but you were right. They aren't a good match. I doubt it would've gotten serious."

Jimmy squints as he focuses on polishing his toenails.

"I shouldn't have said those things. I was mean."

"You were passionate." Prue's tone leaves no room for arguing. "Because Xander is something you're passionate about. There's no shame in that."

"That doesn't matter if he stopped talking to me."

Jimmy sighs. "Come on, Billie, you know Xander. He keeps everything to himself—pretends nothing touches him. That doesn't mean he won't come to your birthday party."

I lay my head on my knee. "No, he regrets kissing me. It was stupid. And when we were finally friends again."

Prue lays an encouraging hand on my wrist. "You two haven't just been friends again. It's more than that, and you know it."

I sit up, shaking my head. "Saying that completely trivializes my relationship with Dahlia. I know it was fucked up, but I wanted that to work."

"Dahlia trivialized your relationship on her own by manipulating you and blatantly sabotaging any other potential romance. Do you want me to paint your nails for you?" She gestures to the abandoned polish on the coffee table near my feet.

Grateful, I nod.

She shakes the bottle, the little ball bearing clanking against the glass. "I understand why you feel that way," she says, untwisting the lid, "but Xander probably assumes you don't want to talk to him. You were the one who left the room crying, not him." She makes the first stroke on my big toe.

"I won't know until we talk. And considering we have a great history of avoiding important topics in favor of being stupid and angsty, I don't know when that'll be."

Instead of pushing the matter, Prue clears her throat.

"Okay, we got sidetracked. What are we doing for your birthday? We won't throw you a huge party with alcohol, so what're we doing?"

I close my eyes, processing this conversation. "I don't know, Prue. I don't care. You decide."

She pauses, her hand wrapped around my right foot to hold it in place. "Really?"

"Sure."

"I get to plan everything?"

The excitement in her voice is overpowering, but I have no regrets. She'll come up with something far more entertaining than I could.

"Feel free to go a little crazy."

◆

Prue gives me a hug goodnight before she leaves, and I pad across the tile floor, stretching my toes as I walk. Jimmy went to bed once his polish dried. He couldn't stop yawning.

The kitchen light is still on. I should get one last drink before bed.

I open the fridge door and stoop to glimpse the contents. Nothing in here sounds appetizing—not that I'm particularly hungry—and there's one bottle of water left. Should I take the last one? Do we have more somewhere? I prefer bottled if I'm taking it to bed.

A long sigh escapes my lips, but I grab it and let the door close. In my hands, the bottle is cool, but I hesitate.

"Go ahead and drink it."

I jump, spinning to find the source, the bottle tight between my fingers.

Xander stands in the doorway, sweaty, his black hair mussed to one side, wearing his work clothes.

"What the fuck is wrong with you?"

My reaction doesn't faze him. "I bought another twenty-four pack."

"Don't go sneaking up on people." My heart's racing.

He doesn't speak, but he approaches and grabs a can of soda from the fridge. A hint of nostalgia tugs at my stomach when he pops the tab on the Dr. Pepper. He doesn't drink it often anymore.

The fridge closes louder than expected, and he faces me with a shrug. "Not my fault you didn't hear the door. Or my footsteps. You're in your own little world, aren't you, Dixon?"

He's close now, and I falter at the scent of alcohol on his clothes. Vodka. That's definitely vodka.

But that's not what I focus on.

Heat radiates off his body. And more than anything, I want to close the distance between us. The last time we were in this room, he kissed me. I'd give anything for him to kiss me like that again.

"You alright?"

I open my water bottle and take a sip, trying to force more space between us.

But he doesn't retract or show any sign of understanding. His eyes follow my movement with a stoic tranquility.

"I'm fine," I manage. "You've been working a lot."

He averts his gaze. "Yeah, I've been…I needed to focus on something solid." His jaw tightens with newfound resolve, and he looks to me again. "You haven't been here much either."

"Painting." I take another sip, then twist the lid on and set the bottle on the counter. "Next week's spring break, and I'm behind on my project."

"You'll have lots of time to work on it over break, right?"

"I will, but…"

But it requires someone there with me. I finished both my portraits of Prue and Jimmy. The Dahlia portrait will remain unfinished until I find a replacement. I have the first layer of my self-portrait. And that leaves me in search of one more model.

"But?"

"Do you think you could help me?"

He cocks an eyebrow.

This time, I'm the one to step nearer, my chest grazing his. His mouth falls open as I level him with an intense gaze, but his attention is quickly captured by my lips.

Everything I was about to say disappears.

At his side, his hand twitches, and he taps two forefingers against his thigh.

This is suddenly uncomfortable.

I'm not sure what should happen now. All I know is I want him to kiss me—and that look, the stare, the dilated pupils says he wants to kiss me too.

He leans in.

My eyes flutter shut. "Can I paint you?"

The kiss never comes.

After a moment, I open my eyes.

His breath brushes my face, but he stares uncertainly. "Wait, what?"

"Can I…" I try again, shifting to get more comfortable. "My project this semester is a series of portraits. Can I paint you?"

"Oh." Xander recoils, a frown spreading across his face. "Um, is that a good idea?"

Probably not.

But I can't stop thinking about it. About him. I haven't drawn him in a year, and I miss my favorite subject matter.

Instead of answering, I launch into an explanation of the process: "My portraits of Prue and Jimmy have taken ten hours each. I have access to the studio twenty-four-seven, so we can do it any time you're available. I don't have much work over spring break. My schedule's pretty open."

His eyes bulge. "We can do it any time I'm available?"

The way he says that makes me blush. "Yeah."

His gaze holds mine for a long minute. "Okay, Dixon, let's do it."

Thirty-Three

THE STUDIO IS EMPTY AND DARK.

Despite having never been here, Xander stalks into the room with absolute purpose and comes to a stop at my station. He glances over his shoulder before returning his attention to the stack of paintings against the wall. "I'd recognize your style anywhere." The top painting—the only one visible—is Jimmy's portrait.

I roll my eyes. "It also helps that your best friend's face is staring at you."

He releases a strangled chuckle. "Doesn't hurt."

I set my phone and wallet on the supply cart and get things ready. I have to fill up my water cup and pick a pigment for the initial line drawing.

"So how does this work?"

After shedding his leather jacket by my finished paintings, Xander steps onto the stage with little preamble, studying the armchair and backdrop. His fingers glide along the chair's back as he peruses the area, then he stops and waits.

I return to my palette. "You can sit or stand or any position you like, and as long as you stay still, I paint you."

His fingers tap an uneven beat atop the headrest. "Do I decide the pose? Or are you going to position me, Dixon?"

My gaze shifts to him sharply. "What do you mean?"

He shrugs one shoulder. "Are you going to direct me?"

I swallow. "Do you need me to?" My words are a whisper. "I haven't done this before."

He must realize what his words mean. And what they do to me. Nothing he says is simple or harmless, but he looks at me with those intense eyes, and I am speechless.

A beat passes.

Too long.

Finally, I cross the distance to the stage. "You'll be more comfortable if you sit."

He plops down on the chair without a second's hesitation, then awaits my next direction.

I step close enough to touch him and I nudge his thigh outward. His body is malleable and willing under my touch, but I bite my lip, trying not to let my hands linger.

I clear my throat. "Um, look at me when I'm painting."

"Anything else?"

I stumble off the stage and scurry to the canvas. "If you get uncomfortable, let me know. We'll take a break."

He nods, and I return to the easel, where the prepped canvas is waiting.

My lack of sleep this semester is catching up to me. By the time the clock hits midnight, I'm rubbing my eyes and pinching the bridge of my nose as I rinse my brush. I'm done with the second layer, but I don't want to stop yet.

Honestly, I'd like to get this painting over as quickly as possible—without detriment to the quality of the work.

This is more awkward than painting Jimmy.

"You need a break?"

I nearly drop the paintbrush. Sometimes, it's hard to remember the model is an actual person.

Xander assesses me with a stern eye. "You look tired."

"I'm alright. We should keep going."

But he stands without waiting. "Nah, take a break. There were water fountains in the hallway, right?"

"Yeah."

I follow him into the hallway, leaving the studio door open, and he drinks from the taller fountain before allowing me a turn. The water is cool and refreshing, and the hum of the building's heater sets a relaxing atmosphere.

Xander reclines against the wall next to me. "When do I get to see it?"

I wipe my mouth, considering. "The painting? When I'm done."

"Can I see something else you've made lately?"

I hesitate but lead back to the studio. He follows close behind.

The studio door slides shut behind us, and without hesitation or asking, Xander walks right up to my stack of paintings from this school year and flips through the canvases. The ones on top are the portraits—Jimmy, Prue, a couple layers of my self-portrait, but he pauses on Dahlia's half-finished face.

I stop behind him. "Once I have these five done, my project's complete."

His focus is solid. He studies every brush stroke, every line, every inch of the thick fabric.

"What do you think?"

"These are...wow." But he focuses on Dahlia. "I mean, I knew you were better, but these are so different from your drawings. Yet completely the same." He lets the paintings lean against the wall again. "Like you."

The final words catch my attention, but he stays facing the wall, and I don't ask.

I don't know what he's talking about. I don't think I've changed, but maybe I'm unable to recognize it. Maybe I'm not meant to see the differences. Maybe they're bad differences. How can I know?

Xander, quiet, sits on the edge of the stage, legs spread, relaxed. "You haven't finished the portrait of Dahlia yet."

I drop into the open space beside him. "It's been, what, two weeks? I haven't wanted to see her, and she hasn't said anything."

"But you're still going to paint her?"

"I don't know. I might need to find a new model, but I don't know who to ask. I've run out of friends."

"It wouldn't be hard to convince someone once they see your work," he says in a hushed voice. "Or are going to suck it up and ask her? You can't stay away from her."

I don't want to hear it, but it's true. Once again, he holds me accountable.

"Dahlia and I are over." But I have to force conviction into the words. "There is nothing she could say or do to change my mind. Finishing that painting wouldn't change anything."

Xander hunches over, elbows on his knees, hands clasped. "I know you believe that, but it's not the first time you've said it. She's your Kryptonite."

I scoff. "She intentionally undermined my self-esteem

and mental health so I wouldn't date you."

"No offense, but I don't know how you didn't figure that out when it happened. She preyed on your naiveté and insecurity."

"I'm not blind now."

He shoots me a look of disbelief. "How long before you're sucked in again?"

"It's spring break. She's graduating in two months."

"And I don't want to spend the next two months watching you hurt yourself all over again."

I grit my teeth and scoot closer to the edge. "Can we stop talking about Dahlia? Please."

Xander's hand clasps around my wrist before I can stand. "I'm sorry."

"Okay."

He sighs. "For everything."

"What do you mean?"

"Like you said, it's spring break. It's been a year."

My eyes clamp shut. "My mother's wedding anniversary was two days ago."

"I've been thinking about it a lot." He releases me. "And I figured I should apologize. I never wanted to pile more stuff on top of what you were dealing with, and then, I did exactly that. My timing was shit."

I force a shrug. "You got tired of waiting for me. I understand."

"I did. But that's the thing—you're worth waiting for."

With a shaky breath, I hug my legs to my chest. "I'm sorry about Micaela."

"Huh?"

"She…you two were starting to date."

He barks with laughter. "You do remember I kissed you, right? You have nothing to apologize for."

"She's so nice, though. And you deserve to be happy more than anyone. I'm sorry I screwed that up again."

"With two months till she graduates and leaves St. Clare, there's no way that would've gotten serious."

"I still feel guilty."

"Well, stop."

My eyes flash open.

"We weren't in a relationship. You didn't break us up. And my motives for asking her out weren't the most noble. Jimmy was pissed." I raise an eyebrow, and he shifts uncomfortably. "I was trying to find a better way to distract myself."

"From what?"

"You have to ask?"

I have to be sure.

"I've spent the last year trying to get over you, and I have failed every step of the way." He pauses a beat. "While I'm at it, I should apologize for my birthday. I don't know what happened that night, but I was an asshole the next morning—and you still tried to take care of me." A soft, humorless chuckle escapes his lips. "I don't deserve you."

I push up from the stage and stumble toward the easel. The infant painting is waiting for the next layer. I need to redraw the lines. How am I supposed to do that when I can't look at him?

"We should...we should get back to work."

"Yeah."

When I muster the courage to look again, paintbrush in hand, Xander's glued to my stack of paintings.

"Can you get into position?" I ask in an anxious voice.

He nods but doesn't move. "You should put these in your gallery or something. Maybe during the Gallery Hop?"

I try not to laugh. "My gallery is closing three days after my birthday. I'll never have an exhibit there. I'm spending my spring break applying for jobs—aside from when I'm here, of course."

A frown tugs at his lips. "That…"

"Sucks? I know."

He rises for closer inspection again. "You deserve an exhibit. Everything you make is beautiful."

I quiver, unsteady from the compliment. "Everything I make is ugly and messy and fucked up."

He flashes me a smile. "That's what makes them so beautiful."

I swallow, trying to temper the heat rising to my cheeks. "Thanks."

"No matter what's happening, you refuse to give up, and you've thrived because of it."

I drop the brush and cross the space between us. "You shouldn't give up either, Xander. You're smart and ambitious enough not to need a business partner. Don't hold yourself back because one hasn't materialized. You need to fight for your dreams." I give him a gentle punch on the shoulder, trying to maintain a lighthearted attitude. "No one else will."

His eyes flit to my mouth, mesmerized, and he rises and slides his hands in his pockets. "Why do you have to say things like that?"

"Like what?"

He shifts away. "It's impossible to get over you. And I need to be over you. But there you are…"

How can I respond to that? He can't possibly be under the impression I got over him. It's not feasible.

But like always, words fail me. I rise on my tiptoes and press a kiss to his lips. My fingers clutch his shoulder, the fabric gathering in my grasp, but he doesn't respond or reciprocate.

I retreat. "Uh, sorry. I'll grab another drink."

God, that was a mistake. He didn't kiss me back.

"Dixon."

I don't look. What's the point?

A hand wraps around my wrist, and I stumble as he yanks me backward.

There's no time to protest before his fingers bury in my curls and his mouth crashes to mine. I moan against his lips, eager to taste him, but he draws away before my enthusiasm takes control. "Don't be sorry."

The words rush out of his mouth, his voice ragged, and he covers my lips with his.

Thirty-Four

WEAK-KNEED, I STUMBLE, BUT XANDER FOLLOWS. I CLUTCH his shoulders, fingers tearing at the blue cotton, but even with his hands hugging my hips, we trip backward until I hit the wall.

He breaks away, eliciting a long whimper from my lips, but he doesn't disappoint.

Relief floods my body when his mouth switches to my throat, and I gasp as he bites down. Our last kiss ended in less than pleasant circumstances, and I refuse to allow something similar tonight. It doesn't matter we're in public or that it's midnight or that this is fast and rough and sordid. All that matters is he needs me as much as I need him. The burgeoning erection is proof of that.

I waste no time in stripping him to his underwear, and he is happy to return the favor. While I trace the black ink dragon on his side, he tears off my bra, ignoring the clasp in favor of brute force.

His lips capture mine again, but I have no patience for distractions.

My hands trail down his taut abdomen to the hem of his boxers and slide underneath.

He breaks away with a gasp. "Wait, here?"

I know I should, but I don't care about his hesitation. The past year of separation has been torture, and more than anything, I need him inside me. I need him to fill me, to claim my body, to consume me.

Besides, his eagerness to remove all but my soaked underwear renders that hesitation meaningless.

"There aren't cameras in here."

When I shove the boxers down, he steps out of them without protest.

I bite my lip and shut my eyes when his freed cock nudges my hip, and his fingers graze my inconveniently underwear-covered ass. A moan of satisfaction escapes my lips as he pushes the underwear out of the way and tosses it to the floor with the rest of our clothes.

But he pauses. "I don't have a condom."

I roll against him, and his cock throbs at the pressure. "I don't have STDs."

A bark of laughter grazes my neck, and a smirk dances across his face. "Neither do I." When he juts out his hips, his erection slaps against my stomach. "But I'd wager you're not interested in a pregnancy scare."

My fingers twist into his dark halo of hair and yank him into another kiss.

I need him to stop talking, to stop thinking, to stop anything that isn't burying his cock inside me and fucking me against this grungy studio wall. Because if he continues, he might decide it's too high a risk. Even a logical and well-meaning rejection would be the death of me.

He returns the kiss with equal fervor but untangles himself from my tight grip. "Doesn't mean I'll leave you wanting, though," he whispers, husky, in my ear, and I close my eyes, whimpering in anticipation as he drops to his knees.

Searing kisses trail over my breasts, my abdomen, my heat, and I fist his hair as he spreads my folds. Hot breath brushes my clit, then the tip of his tongue, and a gasp escapes my mouth. This wasn't what I had in mind, but he lifts my legs one by one over his shoulders and buries his face in my core.

Tears prick my eyes, and I knead my breast in sync with his spastic rhythm. My muscles quiver, tense from bracing against the wall, but his hands grip my ass and drag me closer.

For the longest time, I forgot what it was like to miss his touch, but our kiss the other week changed everything. Memories no longer carry the same weight. Denial no longer placates me. And self-gratification does not satisfy as easily or as quickly as Xander's talented tongue.

I buck against him, unable to control myself, but he doesn't pause. Not until my moans reach peak volume and my limbs tremble from the orgasm.

When he retreats, I cling to the wall, panting, unable to stand without his assistance, and I grasp his shoulder as he rises from the floor, a proud grin on his perfect, smug face. It takes a long minute to catch my breath before I can speak: "I'm on birth control. If that makes a difference."

His body stiffens. "You're serious?"

I rest my forehead against his shoulder and nod.

"I've never…" He nudges me with his chin. "I've never had sex without a condom."

"I trust you."

He presses a kiss to my temple, and I twist to capture his mouth, hoping I've won him over. A possessive growl rumbles in his chest when my fingers close around his thick cock, and he bites down on my lip as he thrusts into my hand. He's been holding back in favor of pleasuring me—or he finds my admission of trust particularly arousing.

Without warning, he lifts me into the air and pins my back to the concrete as he ravages my mouth. My legs hook around his waist reflexively, and his erection grazes my core.

But I can't handle the anticipation.

Fingers clenched tight, I guide him to his destination and shake my hand free just before he plunges inside.

I break the kiss with a hoarse sob, and he mumbles my name into my hair, lips kissing and sucking at my neck. My arms lock into place at his shoulders. I don't want to ever let him go. He'll slip from reach again, and I cannot handle the separation. I don't want another day without his smile, his arms, his laughter, without him nearby.

"God, I fucking missed you," he murmurs against my neck.

Words have never been my strong suit. He knows that, but he also deserves an explanation, an admission of my feelings. He needs to understand how special, how important this moment is—how important he is. He needs to know my affection never waned. He needs to know I missed him too.

But all I can do is show him.

I yank him into another kiss by the hair and tighten my grip around his hips. His rhythm is strong and steady—but tantalizingly slow—and I pant in tune with his beat. "Harder. Please."

He obliges without question or restraint, cupping my ass and shifting my hips for a deeper angle. His next thrust is rough, tearing into me with insurmountable pleasure. My fingernails scrape his back. My moan echoes through the studio, and he smothers my imminent ecstasy with his lips.

Everything slows down when I come, though Xander doesn't pause.

His lips move to my neck, and I relax in his arms, eyes shut as he devours my flesh, as he pummels into me. But he doesn't approve of my calm—he slips a hand between our bodies to thumb my clit, and I whimper at the overstimulation.

Alien Ant Farm echoes in the room.

It takes a moment to place it. My phone. My ringtone. It's on the other side of the studio. Who's calling me?

His speed increases, his fingers stroking in rhythm, and my ache builds again. Without his lips on mine, my moans grow shameless, hoarse, unstoppable, until I fall apart in his arms for the third time.

Who cares about the phone when he can do this?

My sounds subside, but he pounds into me a moment more, and after he comes, he can no longer support me. He holds me against the wall, his sweaty forehead against mine. When he pulls out, I land on unsteady feet.

I don't know when my phone stopped ringing.

Come seeps from my entrance in his absence, and gradually, I untangle my underwear from the inside-out jeans to wipe myself clean. I tug on my shirt and jeans before seeking the phone. I don't have time to worry about my undergarments.

No one calls me this late. Must be important.

I snatch the phone off the supply cart.

The call was Imogene. We haven't talked in a while. Between Dahlia and Xander and this project, I was too distracted to call her.

I drop to the edge of the stage, uncomfortable without panties, and call her back.

"What the hell took so long?" No greeting tonight.

"Mo, what's going on?" Why's she so flustered?

"Mom's in the hospital. She went into labor."

I freeze. "Wait, already? Doesn't she have a month left?"

"Two and a half weeks." Imogene scoffs. "But not anymore. Mom and Rob are in the delivery ward, and I'm stuck in the waiting room. Nothing exciting is happening yet. These things take forever."

"Oh."

"When can you come home to meet the baby?"

I tug at my jeans again. Having wearable undies is a plus for condoms. "I don't know."

"It's your spring break."

"And it's half over. Besides, I'm working and painting. I need to use this extra time to find a new job. I can't disappear for a few days." Plus the money issue. I can't afford to fly across the country on a whim.

She heaves a sigh. "I know. I just wish you were here. You are coming home for my graduation, right? You promised."

"Of course I'll be there. I wouldn't miss it."

In the background, something hard bangs against something else. "I'll send you a picture, alright?"

"Of the baby?"

"Yeah."

"Text me updates too."

When she's gone, I clutch the phone to my chest, trying to process…well, everything.

"What was that?"

I glance over.

Xander's fully dressed, Vans and all, his hair mussed from exertion and sweat. He hovers on the far side of the studio. His face is white.

"My mom went into labor."

He offers an awkward smile and steps to the side. "It's early?" Closer to the door.

"Not really. Not preemie anyway." When I look down, I'm in my socks. My Converse are tangled on the floor near Xander.

"Well, that's good." He's even closer to the door. "Not a preemie's good." His words are clipped and terse.

"Yeah."

His fingers grasp the handle. "Uh, we can finish the painting later, right? It's like one a.m. now, and I have a morning shift."

My throat hurts. "Yeah, of course."

Because a morning shift at Draft Horse means he works at eleven. Needing to sleep isn't the reason he slips into the hallway.

My fingers are numb, but I focus my blurry eyes on the phone in my hands. He was also my ride.

Prue answers right away. "What're you doing up?" She sounds tired.

I run a hand through my afro, trying to quell the nausea in my stomach. "Can you pick me up? I kind of got stranded at the art building."

"What happened?"

305

"I'll, um, tell you when you get here, okay?"

She exhales slowly, but she's more awake now. "I'll be there in fifteen minutes."

"Thanks."

That gives me plenty of time to clean up. My paints are still uncovered, my brushes are dirty, my water cup is a dingy green—and Xander's leather jacket sits on the edge of my makeshift stage.

I blink back the tears.

He was in so much of a hurry to get out of here he left his favorite jacket. That's how much he didn't want to be here. How much he didn't want to be with me.

Thirty-Five

ELISE DROPS A LEGAL BOX IN FRONT OF ME WITH AN IRRI-
tated grumble. "Put everything from that cabinet in there.
Same order. Greg and I will go through it all when he gets
into town."

My thumb skims across the files in the drawer. "We won't
need these in the next couple weeks?"

She sends a final glance toward the filing cabinet before
returning to her desk. "No, it's fine." She plops into her
chair with a frazzled sigh and runs a hand through her long
brown hair.

If anyone is taking the gallery closure hard, it's Elise. I
almost feel sorry for her.

But come on, she knew this was coming.

And I should've too.

The gallery is empty most of the time. Most of our sales
occur during shows, and that's not often. When you make
commission, you need the art to sell in the first place. The
system doesn't work if no one in St. Clare is buying art.

This job was supposed to provide me with the opportunity to explore the art world and find my place in it. All I've
learned is I'm joining a profession that doesn't make much

money. Goody.

"How's the job hunt going?"

My box is half full now. "Oh, you know, going."

Elise doesn't bother to look at me. "If you need a recommendation, all you have to do is ask."

I'm not sure how helpful a recommendation from a closed art gallery would be when I can't find any other art jobs in town.

"Thanks."

"You know," she says, "if I'd been smart five years ago, I would've told Greg not to bother opening an art gallery in this small of a town. He insisted we'd do well because there's no competition—not realizing the reason there's no competition in a small town is because there are very few art collectors."

I focus on my work. I'm not sure I'm supposed to respond.

"If you want to make it in this business, Billie, I highly recommend moving to a bigger city. Even Burlington would offer you more options."

"You're probably right."

We fall into silence, but it doesn't last.

A moment later, my pocket vibrates and rings. It's Imogene.

"Can I take this?"

Elise considers me.

"My mom's in labor."

She nods me out of her office.

The gallery is dark and quiet. Elise asked me to stay after hours today to pack a few boxes, and I was more than happy to agree. I haven't seen Xander since last night, and I'd like to postpone that awkwardness.

I was a mess when Prue picked me up. She kept telling me it wasn't that bad, but I do not believe her.

"Hey." I slump against the wall. "How's everything going?"

Imogene breezes right past pleasantries—understandably. "Seven pounds, nine ounces. Born twenty minutes ago."

"Does he have a name?"

"Niño." She releases a sigh. "Real original."

"Doesn't that mean 'boy'?"

"Yep. I'd let you talk to Mom, but she's recovering from pushing a seven-and-a-half-pound baby out of her vag. I'd wager she's tired."

I snort.

"Rob said she's going to take a nap after they finish up. Something about a placenta and sewing things. Suffice to say, I'm not interested in having a baby for the foreseeable future."

I laugh again. "You say that now, but you always loved children."

"Sure, once I find a guy who's adult enough to have potential as a father." She scoffs. "I've yet to encounter a single one."

I blink away any thoughts of last night—of the fact that I'm not sure I've encountered any either. "Have you seen the baby yet? Is he cute?"

"Rob showed me a picture." A soft chuckle echoes through the earpiece. "It's fuck-ugly, but Mom's doula assured me that's normal. Something about being pushed out of the birth canal. I dunno."

"Send me a picture when you can."

309

"Sure." She pauses a beat. "You should've seen Rob. He's going to be a great dad. He was so excited over this ugly little blue thing, and I just—I don't know."

My eyes flit around the dark gallery, then toward Elise's office. "That's good, though. Because something tells me Mom isn't going to cope well. Her age and all."

"Yeah."

"I need to get back to work, Mo."

"You're at the gallery? I thought it closed at five."

"Working on a few after-hours things. Text me a picture, okay?"

"Right."

When she hangs up, I clutch the phone to my side.

Last night, there was a moment. Before she called about Mom going into labor, there was a moment I thought Xander and I could have another chance. That maybe we'd have a shot at something serious.

But even with everything else—the gallery closing, Mom giving birth, plus the regular—all I can think about is the intense regret on his face as he backed out the studio door.

◆

The ride home is short, but a large part of me wishes it were longer.

I lock up my bike by the porch per usual and pull out my keys. Both cars are in the driveway, but that doesn't mean the door's unlocked.

But the knob turns without effort, and I slide my keys into my pocket as I slip off my shoes and hoody. I hang it on the only unoccupied hook, right next to Xander's leather jacket, where I left it upon my return from the painting studio.

There are voices in the kitchen, and I take a deep breath before heading in that direction. I need water, and I haven't seen Xander since he stranded me at the art building last night.

The guys are chatting in the kitchen. Jimmy's making a quick meal while Xander, dressed in his Draft Horse uniform, clutches the counter. He stiffens at my arrival.

I smile—Jimmy is the only one to reciprocate—and fill a glass with ice water.

But when I turn around, they're both watching me. "What?"

Jimmy glances expectantly at Xander, then turns to the stove, and I give Xander my full attention.

He swishes a sip of water around his mouth, mulling over his words—or trying not to think about last night. I don't know.

When he doesn't speak, I step toward the door, and Jimmy says, "Just come out and say it."

Finally, Xander swallows and sets the cup on the counter. "This won't come as a surprise." He won't look at me. "I figured I should give you two fair warning so you can make plans. Our lease is up in two months, and I started searching through apartments around town."

I freeze.

"Where've you been looking?" Jimmy asks. He's been expecting this.

Xander answers, but the anxious beat his finger drums against the cupboard holds my gaze. My hands clench into fists, and I strain to listen to the words, but the sound is

311

muddled and far away.

"You're leaving."

The words barely come out, but he turns to me, and his fingers stop moving.

"Yeah, I am." And he turns back to Jimmy without any sign of emotion. "I always planned to live on my own after we graduate. Might as well start now."

Is this because of last night?

"Anyway," he says, nonplussed, "I have to finish getting ready for work. See you later."

He doesn't wait for a response before heading upstairs.

I hold the counter for support, trying to focus on anything other than the conversation.

"You alright?" Jimmy asks uncertainly.

I force my legs to move. "I—I need to go."

Upstairs, Xander's bedroom door is ajar, and light spills into the hallway. I don't bother knocking. "Xander?"

He looks up from grabbing his keys and wallet, quickly masking his surprise. "Yeah?"

"You're just going to leave?"

He slips his wallet into his side pocket. "This year has been difficult enough for both of us." He snatches his phone off his dresser and marches past me. The door shuts in my face.

"But—but last night…"

He stops, his back to me, and pockets his phone. "We both know last night was a mistake, and frankly, it'd be a lot better for both of us if we prevent any further mistakes."

"A mistake? You can't—"

"This is for the best."

My hand grips the door frame, and I am silent as he heads downstairs.

I need to be somewhere else.

◆

"Dad?" I call as soon as I arrive. "Dad, you here?" I close the door behind me and search for light.

"In the kitchen," he yells in the distance, and he meets me halfway, wiping his hands with a cloth. "I'm almost finished making dinner—and you're early." His face falls once he sees me. "Is everything alright, Mina?"

I follow him into the kitchen.

The hot smell of chili powder and cumin sweeps through the room, and the pot on the stove simmers. I forgot he planned to make chili—my grandmother's recipe. Sure enough, there's a pot of spaghetti on a second burner.

When I lean against the island, he presses a hand to my shoulder. "Mina?"

I don't know what to say.

But he pulls me into a hug and places a kiss atop my head. "Whatever's going on, it'll be alright."

I wrap my hands around his arm and relax. "I know, Dad. But it doesn't feel like it, and I don't know if there's anything I can do to fix it."

"What happened?"

My fingers tighten, but he spins me round to face him. His hazel eyes say nothing about my smile is convincing.

"Mina, what happened?"

I take a deep breath and release it as a shaky sigh. "He's leaving."

He waits for me to elaborate.

"Xander…he's moving out when our lease is up."

Dad squeezes my shoulder. "Didn't you expect that? This has been an uncomfortable year for you two. Him spending Christmas with us didn't change that."

I nod despite myself. "But if he moves out, will we ever talk again? Jimmy separates the time he spends with each of us. We'll never have class together again. Now, even if it's awkward and uncomfortable, I get to see him and know he's doing okay."

Dad raises an eyebrow. "Is he doing okay?"

My forehead scrunches together, and I look down at my clasped hands. "Probably not."

"And how are you, Mina?"

My gaze shifts upward, and I cock my head.

"It's almost six." He glances over my shoulder. "Have you taken your pill?"

I withdraw my phone from my pocket. It's 5:56, and my alarm will go off in four minutes. And no, I didn't take my pill.

Before giving myself time to consider, I unlock my phone and make the call.

Jimmy answers on the second ring: "Hey, Billie. What's going on?"

"Can you do me an enormous favor?"

He chuckles. "What does that entail?"

"I need you to bring me something."

"Where are you?"

"My dad's."

For a moment, the line is silent. "I don't think that's a good idea, Billie. I mean, I'm in my pajamas, and—"

314

I roll my eyes. It's a little early for pajamas. "I biked over here. I'm not biking back unless I have to. Can you bring me my Zoloft?"

"Oh shit." Something in the background clatters, but he continues as if nothing happened. "Yeah, where is it?"

When I finish the call, Dad is draining the steaming spaghetti.

"You should have more." Dad nudges the serving bowl toward me.

Unfortunately, I have no appetite. I put a small portion on my plate, and my plate is still half full twenty minutes later.

But I grab a little more just to make him happy.

"Have you narrowed down your birthday plans?" Dad takes a bite. "I know it's a couple weeks away, but I'd like to do something."

I try to muster some form of excitement. "Prue and Jimmy are planning something for the following weekend. They refuse to tell me what it is."

Mostly, I'm happy they're getting along. Prue's been mad at him since we got home from Paris. While part of me understands—I was incredibly hurt when I realized how much he pulled away—I want everyone to be friends.

"Then your actual birthday is free? We should have dinner."

"That sounds great, Dad."

The doorbell rings.

"I'll get it." I head for the foyer to open the door and pull Jimmy into a hug the moment he's in view. "Thank you," I mumble into his neck. "You're a lifesaver. Come in."

I tug him inside and accept the proffered bottle, but he hovers by the door, shifting nervously.

"You want some chili?" I close the door behind him.

Hesitantly, he hangs his jacket on the nearby hook. "I'm not hungry, and you know, I don't want to impose."

I scoff. "You know it's not a problem. Come on."

I lead the way to the dining room, taking a blue pill from the bottle. When I return to my seat, I swallow it with some water.

Behind me, Jimmy awkwardly stands in the doorway.

"Seriously, have a seat. I'll grab a plate."

While I rise from my chair, he shuffles forward and takes the seat beside me, and I get an extra plate and fork from the kitchen.

When I return, the tension is palpable.

My dad quietly eats his chili and spaghetti, but Jimmy, on the opposite side, hunches down and fumbles with his phone.

I leave the plate and fork in front of him. "Am I missing something?"

Jimmy shifts in his seat. "What?"

I send him a sharp look and take my seat. "You're nervous. What's going on?"

His eyes dart over to my dad before meeting mine. He's flushed. "Billie, I don't know what you're talking about."

"Stop lying to me."

For a moment, Jimmy stutters, struggling to form words. "I need to leave. I'll see you at home later." He scoots the chair out and stumbles as he stands.

Across the table, Dad sips his water. "Like you left after you slept with my daughter?"

I hold up my hands to separate them. "What are you talking about, Dad? We absolutely never..."

Oh.

Jimmy tries to hide his beet-red face.

"When did you sleep with Mo?"

Thirty-Six

Jimmy tugs at his collar. "I've been trying to figure out how to tell you for the past year."

"You slept with her a year ago?"

His mouth falls open. "No, no, no."

Dad rises from the table to clear the dishes—including the plate I've barely touched—and disappears into the kitchen without a word. He's angry. Dad doesn't get angry.

"Then what?" I try to relax. "Sit down."

Jimmy slides into the seat again and lays his head in his hand. "Over the summer, while she was here with your dad."

"You taught her how to drive."

He nods.

"And she paid you in sex?"

He blanches at the words. "It wasn't like that. She wouldn't…and I wouldn't—"

But I release a short laugh. "Jimmy, calm down. It's okay. I mean, I figured you had a thing for her after you got all pissy about her boyfriend. This is more than I anticipated, but it's okay."

His mouth gapes. "How is this okay? I've been keeping

318

secrets and lying to you. That's not what friends do."

"Look, I don't have the best track record for honesty in this relationship. I can't judge you for keeping it secret."

But he tilts his head, unconvinced. "You should hate me. I took advantage of your little sister."

I try to hide my amusement, but it makes my snort louder. "I may be late to the party, but even I know there's no world in which you took advantage of Imogene."

He drops his glasses onto the table to rub his eyes.

"Wait a minute. Mo didn't turn eighteen until September."

If possible, his face turns redder. "Technically, the age of consent in Vermont is sixteen."

My eyebrows arch upward. "You looked it up?"

He pinches the bridge of his nose. "She did. She knew I didn't feel comfortable, and she wanted to—" he pauses to exhale a shaky puff of air "—convince me."

I should've expected that. My dear little sister is nothing but ambitious when it comes to the men in her life. If she wants something, she'll do anything in her power to get it. But I'll admit, I never expected her to want awkward, geeky Jimmy—the same guy who's still too scared to look at me.

"Here's the part that bugs me…" I tap my fingers on the tabletop. "You've liked her this whole time, right? While you were dating Tiff?"

He sends me a stern glare. "That's the part that bugs you? Like how you liked Xander the entire time you dated Dahlia?"

"Fair enough."

"Besides, it's not like I acted on these feelings. She didn't…want to talk to me over winter break." He clears his throat. "And a year ago, when she kissed me on New Year's Eve, she had a boyfriend. The whole time we were playing video games together, the whole time she was flirting with me, she was dating Ethan."

"How in the world do you remember his name?"

She's had so many "boyfriends" over the years I stopped committing them to memory before graduating high school.

Jimmy's ears tinge pink. "I remember all their names."

"How long have you liked her? I mean, how stupid am I for not noticing?"

He chuckles. "Really stupid."

"Years?"

He nods.

"How many?"

"Since freshman year, high school."

My mouth gapes. "That's seven years, Jimmy. Why didn't you say something?"

"You're my best friend, and she's your little sister. What could I have possibly said?"

"Did you never consider I would've loved the idea? Sure, awkward if you break up, but have you met her boyfriends? The guys I've met—which, granted, isn't many—have been real assholes. It would be nice seeing her with someone who cares about her. And you do."

"Billie, you're talking like this is a possibility." He shakes his head. "She has a boyfriend. She isn't talking to me. And she's going to UVA in the fall? Virginia's like six hundred miles away."

"It's closer than she is now. That didn't stop you from sleeping together."

"Right, she should spend her freshman year in a long-distance relationship with a dork."

I snicker. "A dork who writes her love songs."

"She should be having fun. Not spending time on Skype with me."

"You two Skyped?"

"Not like that." But his face turns a fierce red. "I mean, there was one time she, I don't know, forgot we were on Skype..."

I snort. "When did that happen?"

"Freshman year. During your, uh, post-Zane hermit days." He hesitates. "It wasn't anything—"

"Are you placating me about a Skype strip tease when you've slept with her?"

His blush deepens. I wasn't sure that was possible. "It wasn't a strip tease."

"So she happened to forget she was on camera and, what, took off her clothes for no reason?"

"She was changing into pajamas. Which is totally normal at bedtime. I saw glimpses."

"Did you get hard?"

"Oh my God, Billie. This is why I didn't tell you. Having Xander tease me is enough—especially when he did so with you curled up on his lap. My embarrassment is more amusing when you're oblivious."

My face falls. "You seriously thought I'd hate you?"

He runs a hand through his messy hair. "I was scared you would. It wouldn't be unreasonable with how everything ended."

"But why didn't you tell me you liked her before anything happened?"

"She's pretty and popular, and she's had a different boyfriend each week since she started high school. In what world would I have a chance?"

"You know she had the biggest crush on you when we were kids, right?"

"What?" His voice is sharp—risen an octave.

"She followed us around for years because she wanted to spend time with you. She had enough on her plate with Mom, but she wanted an excuse to be with you." For a moment, I study him. "She never stopped liking you."

He drops his head to the table. "Now, I'm even more of an asshole."

"Tell me what happened."

"Where should I start?"

"Usually, the beginning is the best starting point."

He lays his head atop his arms, but he's tense. "Do you remember in ninth grade when we were talking about first kisses? Right before your parents separated."

"Mindy Costello and Philip Park had sex, and everyone was talking about it."

"Right. And we talked about how neither of us had our first kiss, and Imogene's dance practice was canceled that day, so she came with you. She was playing around on my tablet."

"Is this going somewhere?"

"Then, you went to the bathroom."

I raise an eyebrow.

"And she took off her headphones and asked me if I wanted to give it a try. I didn't realize what she meant until she kissed me. It was over before I realized what was happening. When you came back, she returned to the tablet like nothing happened."

"She was twelve."

He forces an uncomfortable smile. "She was also dating Thom MacCaulay from the freshman football team, and they were already messing around."

"But you haven't been able to stop thinking about her since?"

"Don't make it sound so cheesy."

I snort. "You've written her easily a couple dozen love songs. Trust me, the cheese factor is already high."

He shoots me a quick glare. "She lost her virginity the summer after our senior year. A month before we left for Bradford."

"At fifteen?"

"Your mom had a new job, so we were hanging out at your house for once. She was curled up on the kitchen floor with a pint of Ben and Jerry's when I got there. I sat with her, and she cried and hugged me for half an hour and asked if I thought she was a slut." A shaky sigh slips from his mouth. "I could never think that."

My eyes flutter shut, trying to take it in.

He bites his lip. "Everything changed after that. We talked every day when I came to Bradford. About you mostly. There were a lot of conversations about her boyfriends, though it was the last thing I wanted to think about. But you know, that's what friends do."

"You're a good friend."

"Our relationship was platonic, and with the long distance, I never expected anything. So I tried to move on."

"Cynthia Allen."

"Yeah."

"Until?"

"New Year's Eve last year." His eyes clench shut. "You and Xander ran off and spent the night together, and she was worried. Did you have a fight with your mom that night? That's what Imogene said."

"A big one."

"We went to my room to talk. She told me about asking your mom to help with the therapy, and she made me promise not to say anything. And at midnight, she surprised me with a kiss, and um, we made out for a few minutes. She's a good kisser."

"And then, you panicked?"

He releases a cross between a laugh and a sigh. "And then, I panicked. She went back to the party, and I locked myself in my room. And after a night of not sleeping, I called Xander, and he came to calm me down."

"She spent the next week flirting with you before we had to leave."

"Yet again, she had a boyfriend."

"She didn't have a boyfriend at my mother's wedding."

"Something might have happened if things between you and Xander hadn't exploded that night. I think we might have…"

I scoff. "Sorry to cockblock you."

He glares. "I'm not blaming you."

"It wasn't a serious apology."

"Besides, I would've chickened out. By the time we had sex, she was frustrated."

"Tell me about the summer."

Jimmy shrugs. "A lot happened. Your dad was teaching summer classes, and I got my job, but it wasn't very many hours. I just got my truck, so she asked me to teach her how to drive. We were hanging out more, and I know it was summer, but I'm not a hundred percent sure her clothing counted as clothing."

"Well, I'm glad I missed the summer of your raging hard-on."

He sends me a brief glare. "She literally had to lock us in my bedroom, take off her clothes, and tell me she wanted to have sex for me to get the picture."

"Wow."

"It was so embarrassing. I had no idea what to do, and she kind of took charge. She's way too hot…oh, God, this is awkward."

I snort. "Premature ejaculation?"

"Why is this not super awkward for you?"

"I'm not going to say it's okay, but honestly?" My lips flatten into an unamused smirk. "Jimmy, you've heard me have an orgasm. Multiple times. I can manage to listen to how you lost your virginity, even if it was with Mo."

"She showed me how to get her off afterward."

"On second thought…"

"And when everything was done, she got dressed and said goodbye. 'That was fun.' Like it didn't mean anything."

My mouth drops open. "Ouch."

"Later, she suggested we continue having sex. Keep it our little secret. I don't know why I agreed. I didn't want it to be just sex. But she smiled, and I…caved."

"Well, she didn't want it to be just sex either. She pretended to be sick for the last ten days she was here."

"I know. When you got home, I panicked. I can't compartmentalize like that. It was easier to cut it off cold turkey than to be friends when all I want is to kiss her."

I frown. "Trust me, I understand."

"Also…" He rubs his face, hand shaking. "I'm a complete hypocrite, and you have every right to hate me. I gave you so much shit about not dating Xander last year, and three months later, I did the same thing to your sister."

"Well, you're not the only one pulling a Billie move."

He tilts his head.

"Xander and I had sex last night."

His eyes bulge.

"We went to the studio so he could sit for a portrait, and we were talking, and then, we weren't talking."

"You had sex in the painting studio?"

"Yeah."

"Don't they have cameras?"

"Not in the studios."

"Where'd you get the condom?"

I flush.

"You didn't use a condom?"

"We didn't have one. Anyway, I'm on birth control."

"What if someone walked in?"

I roll my eyes. "Condoms don't protect against that. Besides, no one's there at midnight on spring break."

"The janitor?"

"I don't know."

"That explains the hickey."

My hand jumps to my neck. I was too distraught this morning to pay attention. Now, I know why Elise gave me weird looks all day. "I'm not saying it was smart, but it happened, and we didn't get caught, so it's fine."

Jimmy's face falls. "But today he announced he's moving out."

"You should've seen the way he looked at me. Like I'd tricked him into it or something. He rushed out the second he got dressed, said he had a morning shift. He didn't work till five tonight."

He grimaces. "I'm sorry."

"For one tiny moment, I thought things could be different. I want a relationship. A serious relationship. But his face was only regret. There isn't going to be a 'this time.'"

"Hey, you don't know—"

"Please don't try to placate me. He has every right to not be interested. What we had last year was fucked up. I was basically using sex as a coping mechanism."

"I don't think he minded too much."

"Well, he definitely minded the part where I was too scared to commit to a relationship. I want him to be happy. If moving out is what makes him happy, it's the right thing to do."

But Jimmy purses his lips. "That's bullshit. You should fight for the things you love."

"At what point do you give up? I've done enough damage."

"No offense, but you have never fought for him. You watched him flirt and sleep around. You never told him you liked him. You couldn't admit it to yourself because you thought emotions were some fatal flaw. And when everything came to a head, you watched him walk away. You didn't argue. You didn't try to change his mind. You just watched."

"What could I do now? You can't force someone to date you."

"How do you know he doesn't want to?"

"He looked at me like I tricked him. I messed up his chances with Micaela. No matter how hard I try, I fuck everything up."

"Oh, come on. From what I heard, he kissed you, not the other way around." Jimmy taps his fingers hard against the tabletop. "If you want to be with him, then for once, you need to say that. He won't know if you never tell him."

"You know the same holds true for you and Mo, right?" I flash him a smirk. "If you don't tell her you want her to bear your children, she'll keep assuming you don't."

Jimmy flushes. "Don't say something so ridiculous."

"At the very least," I add, more seriously, "you should apologize for how things ended."

"I know."

I clamp my eyes shut, focusing on his advice, but all I see is Xander's face before he went to work. Devoid of emotions.

Thirty-Seven

I PUSH DOWN THE ANXIOUS BALL IN MY STOMACH AND FOCUS on mixing paints. The mechanics of the process are the only thing keeping me from engaging in conversation.

Not that Dahlia's trying hard.

Her nose is pointed and delicate, and her heart-shaped face is framed by her long, honey-brown hair. But her eyes are dark and shadowed, hard to decipher. Impossible.

She's beautiful, but not due to any particular makeup maneuver she applied or how she styled her hair. She's beautiful in a Daisy Buchanan sort of way—mesmerizing but sad, cynical, self-destructive. Not sure how well I can portray that.

"How much longer will this take?" She struggles to maintain her pose. "Not that this is hard or anything, but I do have a senior project due at the beginning of May."

"I know." I rinse my brush and scoop up some violet. "I should be done in an hour, and we can come back later for a few touch-ups."

"That works."

The palette is mostly blues, violets, browns, and oranges—complementary colors to highlight her own

329

complementary features and disposition. In the style of Giacometti, most of the painting now is an array of lines, sorting, organizing, and illustrating her form: the protruding brown eyes, the high cheekbones, the shallow cleft in her chin, and the straight line of her mouth. She doesn't smile.

At night, the studio is conveniently silent, but the quiet does nothing for Dahlia's mood or the aura I want to convey. I pause to play some music on my phone—something soft, melodic—before returning to the painting.

"Thanks for doing this," I say, loud over the music. "I wasn't sure whether you'd agree to come back."

For a second, Dahlia stiffens. It takes a moment to realize she's trying not to laugh. "Of course I'm here. What I can't figure out is why you didn't pick a new model."

I strive to concentrate. "I admit, I wanted to see you again before you leave St. Clare for good."

Dahlia's jaw tightens. "That's the only reason?"

I spend a minute mixing the cobalt, manganese, and yellow azo to make a low-intensity blue to separate her from the dark background. The gloss medium and flow improver smooth the paint, and a hint of retarder keeps it wet long enough to meld with the composition.

"Yes," I finally say.

"I don't believe that."

Dahlia's voice is so quiet it's unnerving, and I strain to hear over the music. I almost pause the song midway through the Foo Fighters, but the music provides me with the comfort of anonymity.

"You miss me."

I purse my lips. "I'm working."

She's not necessarily wrong. Of course I miss her, but

that wasn't my motivation for meeting her here.

More than anything, I needed to prove to myself I could do this. Xander doesn't think I can spend time with her without getting sucked in, and I want—need—to prove him wrong.

I need to know I can do this.

"I know you miss me." She lifts her head, determined. "You wouldn't move on that fast."

Despite my best efforts, I cannot look her in the eye. "I already did. Get back into position. I want to finish this tonight, remember?"

Dahlia jolts upright. "You did what?"

"We need to finish this painting."

For a moment, she studies my face. "No, if you two had gotten together, I would know."

I wet my lips. "I'm serious, Dahlia. The painting. I have something to do when we're done here."

At last, she relaxes into her position, pleased. "Sure, let's do this."

And I press paintbrush to canvas again.

◆

The Jittery Bug is busy—and short-staffed—but she isn't here yet. I get in line behind an older woman with a recent perm and wait.

It takes five minutes to reach the register, and the line trails all the way to the door.

The guy behind the counter grins. "What can I get you today?" His name tag says 'Jeremy.'

"A chai latte please."

He keys it into the register. "It's double shot day. Do you want to add a shot of espresso at no extra charge?"

I don't need the stimulant. "Uh, no, thanks." But I pause on the worn notice dangling from the counter.

Is this 'Now Hiring' sign as old as it looks?

He reads off my order and fee, then gives me a number and takes my debit card. "Shouldn't be more than five minutes."

Once I escape the crowd, I see her.

Micaela's sitting in a booth on the far side of the coffee shop, her hands cupping a bottle of water. Did I miss her?

A forced smile spreads across her face when I sit down. "Hey, Billie. How are you?"

"I'm okay. How have you been?" I didn't expect her to be nice.

She shrugs. "Decent. I was surprised when you texted me. I didn't know you had my number."

I may have stolen it from Jimmy's phone when he wasn't paying attention.

"Yeah, well, I wanted to touch base with you."

"About?"

I lean forward, elbows on the tabletop. "I wanted to apologize for the sleepover. For what happened with Xander. Things got out of control, and I have no excuse for my actions."

Micaela shakes her head. "Billie, you don't have anything to apologize for."

"Of course I do."

She frowns. "I'm not happy, but Xander was right. We weren't in a relationship. We had one date."

"I know how you feel about him. I've always known."

"You and everyone else." She takes a sip of her drink, but her movements are slow, mechanical. "I care about him a lot, but you were right. I don't know how compatible we really are. Besides, he has feelings for you. He already apologized."

"No, that's not right."

I'm not sure how this conversation was supposed to go, but this is not it.

Micaela smiles—and it seems genuine. "He lied about how serious your relationship was. You two obviously love each other. I'm not going to get between that."

I have no words.

"I'll get over him, I promise." But her lone reassurance is a shrug. "Plus, I'm moving to Seattle in two months. My living situation's set up. I have no regrets about this."

"Oh."

Micaela reaches a hand across the table to squeeze my tense fist. "But you two deserve another chance. Talk to him." Without another word, she rises and carries her water bottle out of the cafe.

A server drops off my latte and snags my number from the tabletop.

Now, I don't know what to do.

Thirty-Eight

THE LONG HAND ON THE GRANDFATHER CLOCK MOVES TO twelve, but the chime at the front door signals someone has arrived. I turn toward the doors with a bright smile—this may be our last day and we may close in one minute, but I'm a professional.

Prudence is the one standing there. "How long until you're done?" She waves me closer. "Got my car waiting."

Once I'm beside her, I stretch to yank the chain on the open sign, and the light flickers off for the last time. "I have to close up."

"Should I wait in the car?"

"Yeah, gimme ten minutes."

Prue pulls her key from her pocket, and I wave her goodbye and lock the door behind her.

A moment later, I knock on Elise's door and peek my head inside. The office is in disarray. "Hey, Elise, is there anything I can help you with before I close up?"

She glances up but returns to the paperwork. "Don't worry about it, Billie. Greg will be here this weekend, and we'll take care of everything. The artists from the exhibit pick up their work next week, and we have to have everything out by the end of the month." Her small smile, unfortunately, is of little comfort to either of us. "But you, you're done."

"Right."

Now, I really need to find a new job. Despite hours of applying online and in person, I didn't have any luck over spring break.

"Thank you for all your help, Billie. I appreciate your hard work."

When I slip out of the gallery a few minutes later, Prue is waiting in the driver's seat of her Honda Pilot. A grin spreads across her face when I climb into the SUV beside her. "How's the birthday girl?"

I roll my eyes. "My birthday was two days ago."

She shifts the car into gear. "Yeah, but this whole weekend is your celebration. And Jimmy and I put something fun together."

Despite mild irritation, I buckle my seatbelt, and she drives toward the house. "Are you going to tell me where we're going yet? It's the day of. I shouldn't be left in the dark."

Prue snickers. "Everyone's left in the dark, not just you—and that's how it should be. It's a surprise for a reason."

"It's also the reason I had no idea what to pack for the weekend."

"You packed a bikini, right?"

I scoff. "Prue, it's April. It's cold."

"Well, grab one before we leave. The guys are packing Xander's car."

We've barely talked since he announced his move, and

our communications haven't been long or meaningful. I wasn't sure he'd come.

My fingers tap an uncomfortable rhythm on my knee. "Why can't you tell me?"

"I'm not ruining the surprise, no matter how annoyed you are." She smirks as she parks along the road in front of my house. "Besides, we're in a hurry."

Like she said, Xander, Jimmy, and David are loading up the trunk of the faded red Camaro. Cynthia awkwardly waits on the front steps, her textbook in hand, as the guys move back and forth between the house and car.

I unbuckle my seatbelt. "I don't know how this will work, Prue, but I'm sure it'll be a disaster."

But she meets my hesitation with a surety I cannot fathom. "This weekend is going to be the best weekend you've had in months. I will make sure of it."

Outside the car, Prue pops the trunk, and we head for the house. Her and Cynthia's bags are inside the SUV, but I need to grab mine—and pack a bikini. Where the hell are we going that I'll need a swimsuit?

Jimmy grins when we approach. "Are you excited? This is going to be so much fun."

I don't know how to respond.

Beside him, Xander looks more irritated than anything else. He probably didn't like giving up his weekend night shifts. I imagine that's when he makes the best tips.

David comes out of the house, a small bag slung over his shoulder, and pulls me into a one-sided hug. "Happy birthday, Billie."

"Thanks, I guess."

Prue tugs on my wrist. "Come on. Let's finish packing."

In my bedroom, Prue sifts through the contents of my duffel bag while I stand on the sidelines, waiting for her approval. She pushes things around, lips pursed, ruining my perfect organization.

"No bikini," she says when she withdraws. "What happened to the one we bought in France?"

I cross the room to my dresser with a laugh. The bikini, which Prue insisted I purchase against my better judgment, is nestled in the back of my underwear drawer. I tug the two-piece free and toss it toward her, and she stuffs it in the bag. "What the hell are we doing while we're there?"

She zips the bag shut and tosses it over her shoulder. "Don't you worry about a thing." Then, she pauses, examining the room. "We missing anything? It's time to go."

I pull open my underwear drawer again to retrieve my pills and dangle the bottle in front of her nose. "This is kind of important, don't you think?" I shove it into the bag's side pocket and lead the way.

At the bottom of the stairs, I freeze. She's standing in my living room, facing the opposite direction, honey-brown hair down to her waist.

Who the hell let Dahlia into our living room?

She turns at the noise, and excitement lights up her face. "I need to talk to you."

"Go ahead," I tell Prue.

"I'll finish packing the car." She steps around me and continues toward the front door, a scowl on her face.

Dahlia crosses the room to meet me, but I don't move.

There's only one reason Dahlia would come here, and it's not happening. I don't know what she thought that painting session meant, but it definitely wasn't that I want to get back together.

"What can I do for you, Lia?"

She preens at the nickname.

Bad idea.

"I'm sorry I missed your birthday." She steps close enough to take my hand.

"It doesn't matter." I tear away from her grasp. "We're not dating anymore. And I have friends to celebrate with."

She sends an inquisitive glance toward the front door. "Is that why you're all packing the cars? Where are you going?"

"That's none of your business."

Not that I could tell her if I wanted to.

But Dahlia shrugs it off as no big deal. "We need to talk."

"We have nothing to talk about. I'm in a hurry."

She shakes her head. "I'm not leaving here until we talk."

I grit my teeth. "And I'm not staying here to talk to you."

"Fine. Tell me where you're going."

I scoff. "You're not invited. We're leaving, and you need to get out of my house."

When I reach the door, Xander, Jimmy, and David are inside the Camaro, and hands tight around the steering wheel, Xander peels out of the driveway. I'm not the only one irritated by Dahlia's sudden arrival.

"Out." I nod her over the threshold so I can lock the door behind her.

She complies hesitantly but waits for me on the porch. "I'm going with you."

"No, you're not." I pull the key out of the deadbolt, and the door doesn't budge. "We're going away for the weekend. You'd leave without a change of clothes?"

"For you, of course."

I send her a scathing look before heading for Prue's SUV.

Cynthia has relocated to the back seat, though her textbook is still out, and Prue closes the hatchback after dumping my bag inside and takes the driver seat.

But Dahlia hasn't given up yet.

I level her with a glower. "When I get back, maybe we can talk. But unless you tail us for the next two days, we're not having this conversation."

She follows me down the steps. "Fine."

◆

"Where are we going?"

Prue sends me a glare. "It's a surprise," she says over the pop music. Her eyes dart to her side mirror, and she turns down the volume. "Billie, is there a reason Dahlia's two cars behind us? She's been following for the last half hour."

I bend forward to catch a glimpse in the passenger-side mirror. There's her black Accord, two cars back, like Prue said. "Dammit."

"You didn't know?"

I scoff and recline against the headrest. "Of course I didn't know. I didn't expect her to do it."

Prue leans forward to fiddle with the dials—a fog is rising up the windshield and side windows. "You invited her? That puts a damper on our plans."

"No, not technically."

"What does that mean?"

"She wants to talk." I drag my finger in a loop through the condensation. "I imagine she wants to get back together or something equally stupid. I said unless she tailed us, we wouldn't talk this weekend."

Prue rolls her eyes. "You should know better."

"Or Dahlia shouldn't take what was obviously sarcasm as an invitation."

"You want me to lose her?"

I inspect the highway. "I don't want to die." There are too many cars around us.

Prue snorts. "I'm a good driver."

"That doesn't mean other people are too."

For a moment, she doesn't say anything, instead focusing on the road. "How pissed do you think Xander will be when she pulls in behind us?"

I frown. "Where are we going?"

"Nowhere."

Her response is utterly predictable, but my irritation has another source. "Xander has no reason to be pissed about Dahlia's presence. He made it abundantly clear he's done. Moving out solidifies how he feels about me."

Prue sighs. "Billie, you don't know that."

"How can I when he can't make up his mind? Dahlia and I broke up, so he kissed me. Then, we don't talk. When we do talk, we have sex. But the second that's over, he decides to move out." I run a hand through my tight curls. "What am I supposed to think?"

"Yes, he has some shit to sort out, but he's going to be pissed. Did you see his face?"

I scoff. "If he's seriously jealous she came to the house uninvited, he needs to get over himself. I'm done."

Before she can say anything else, I lean forward and turn up the music—loud enough I can't hear myself think.

Thirty-Nine

THE DESTINATION, AS IT TURNS OUT, IS A CABIN. ONE OF those fancy log cabins—thankfully without all the dead animals. Prue wouldn't have put up with that.

She parks next to Xander's red Camaro. "You're going to love this."

I frown. Not too sure about that.

We climb out of the car as Dahlia takes the remaining parking spot. Prue doesn't pay her any mind as she leads me by the hand inside the cabin.

The room is wide and open—a kitchen and living space, a few closed doors, a balcony with a nice view of Vermont's trees, leafing out, and a staircase leading down to a basement, where I assume the bedrooms are.

Prue grins as she drags me around. "Jimmy and I picked this cabin out specifically."

She shows off the living area first, though it isn't anything special—two couches, a fireplace, a coffee table, and some tree-inspired decorations—and drags me downstairs.

"These are the bedrooms," she announces, gesturing around the small living space.

"There are four doors."

Well, plus a bathroom, a tiny laundry room, and a door leading outside. Three of the rooms have the overhead light on. It's a walkout basement.

"Four bedrooms down here and two upstairs. There's plenty of space for everyone."

Not Dahlia.

But she wasn't part of the plan.

"Let's look outside…"

Yet again, she drags me out onto the back patio, where a hot tub is whirring under a cover. So that's why I needed a bikini in mid-April. Above us, the main level leads out onto a balcony.

Prue smirks. "See, this is going to be fun."

We wander around the patio toward the front of the house again, and I examine the area.

"Where is everyone?"

"Putting all their things away?" She nudges me forward. "Let's get you settled."

I follow her up a steep staircase to the driveway. The back of her silver Pilot is popped open, and we carry our bags inside.

Cynthia is inside now, sitting on at the dining table with her textbook and notes spread out. Studying already. Did she put her things away?

Prue heads for the stairs, but she stops when I follow her. "Oh, I'm in the basement, but this is your room." She drops her bag at the top of the stairs and opens the nearest door, not far from the kitchen and dining area. "This is the master bedroom, so naturally, it's yours."

I consider the enormous room. The king-sized bed doesn't take up much space, and the rest is filled with a small closet and dresser with vanity mirror, two wingback chairs, access to a private balcony, and an elegant chandelier. A door leads to what I assume is my master bathroom.

"Wow."

Prue giggles. "This place is great, isn't it?"

"This is a lot. How could you afford this?"

But she shrugs it off. "We all pitched in. It's your birthday, and you know, we figured you'd much rather go somewhere with some peace and quiet than do something big and exciting. Much better than Xander's birthday, right?"

I pull her into my arms. "Thank you."

"No problem." Prue wraps me in a tight hug. "I should put my stuff downstairs. Have a look around and get settled in. We'll talk about food in a bit."

I glance toward the living space and whisper, "What should we do about Dahlia?"

"That's up to you, birthday girl. If you want her to stay, she has her pick of three different couches. I'd understand." She moves toward the door. "I'm not sure Xander would, though," she adds before closing the door behind her.

Alone, I heave my duffel bag onto the bed. I didn't bring enough stuff to fill this room. What the hell am I supposed to do with all this space?

The dresser drawers are empty, so I slip my clothes inside and move to the vanity to pull my hair up in a loose bun, out of my face. Something tells me Prue will want to jump in the hot tub tonight. It's prepped and ready. And I don't want chlorine in my hair.

When all but a few toiletries are put away, I flop down on the bed. I have no idea how this weekend will go, but it can't be good.

I love the idea. The cabin. Prue and Jimmy were so thoughtful to choose something I'd like—and I'm equally impressed they collaborated so well.

But with Dahlia here, I'm at a loss.

I should tell her to fuck off and go away. But she won't leave without a fight, and I admit, even if she did, I'd feel guilty. Add in Xander's irritation, and I have no idea what to expect this weekend.

Not that I was expecting things to go swimmingly before, but I'm allowed to dream.

With a tiny huff, I force myself up. If we're not going anywhere—and I suspect we're holing ourselves away for the weekend—I'm changing into something comfy.

I kick off my jeans and grab my pajama shorts from the dresser, but now I have to pee.

Oh well. I haven't seen the bathroom yet, and I have toiletries to put away.

I tuck the bag under my arm and march into the bathroom.

Much like the bedroom, it's huge. A double sink with plenty of vanity space, a toilet tucked into a corner with a hint of privacy, a door opposite me, a shower stall, and a jetted tub. What's the point of having both a hot tub outside and a jetted tub inside?

This bedroom and bathroom could house a family of four.

I cross to the sinks to drop off my toiletries and pause to examine my reflection. "You can do this. I know you can do this," I murmur to myself.

The door opens.

The other door. I thought that was a closet.

Instead, I spot Xander through the mirror and twist around. "What're you doing here?"

He pauses in the doorway, head tilted. "I thought this was my bathroom. This is my bathroom." A quick search of the room reveals my open door. "Is that your room?"

I nod. "And that's yours?"

"Yep."

I inhale sharply. "And everyone else is in the basement, right?"

"Yeah."

"We're alone up here." I groan. "Of course we are."

That's why Jimmy and Prue were so chummy. They put us here on purpose. Only two on the floor. Sharing the same bathroom. They're setting us up.

When I refocus on Xander, it takes a moment to realize what he's staring at.

I'm in my underwear.

I clear my throat, and he looks up.

"Uh, sorry. I'll, um, leave you to it." He backs out of the room and shuts the door behind him.

I stalk across the room to twist the deadbolt into place.

When I emerge from my bedroom, everyone else is in the kitchen. Prue and David are putting away a box of food the guys brought in the Camaro, and Cynthia continues to study.

Jimmy rises from the table to join me. "What do you think of the place?"

"It's nice." But I lower my voice as Dahlia comes in through the front door. "I didn't realize I'd be sharing with Xander. The bathroom."

But Jimmy shifts his weight from one foot to the other as Dahlia crosses the dining and kitchen area toward us. "I didn't realize she'd be here."

"It wasn't—"

"There you are!" Dahlia doesn't stop until she's close enough her arm brushes mine. "I was looking for you." She can't stop smiling.

"Uh, yeah. I've been setting things up in my room." I point over my shoulder toward my cracked door.

Her eyes wander in that direction. "Oh. You could give me a private tour later…"

Wow.

Did she really…?

I try to repress the grimace—it's probably safest not to openly scorn her—but I fail. "Probably not."

But that doesn't faze her: "We have a lot to talk about, Billie."

"I don't know when I'll find the time."

Dahlia presses closer, and her fingers grip my waist as the door behind me opens. "I'm sure we can make time," she says into my ear.

Jimmy stumbles backward.

I lay my hand on her shoulder to separate us, but she doesn't retreat until Xander forces his way between us.

"You're in the way," he grumbles.

But one look at Dahlia after he reaches the fridge, and I swallow hard. If that smile is any indication, I won't get rid of her easily.

This is going to be some weekend.

Forty

"I FORGOT HOW CUTE THIS IS." HER FINGERS TIGHTEN THE cord around my back and tie it in a bow. "You know who won't be able to keep his eyes off you?"

When I catch my reflection, the white crocheted triangle pieces barely cover my breasts, and without the fringe skirt, the bottoms wouldn't cover much either. "Dahlia."

Prue shoots me a disapproving glare through the mirror. "I was talking about Xander."

"Why are you doing this, Prue?"

"We're celebrating your birthday, remember? Don't forget your towel."

Without another word—and without giving me time to respond—she heads for the door, and I clutch the towel to my chest as we walk out. Thankfully, no one's in the dining area but Cynthia, cleaning up her homework. She insisted on studying while we ate dinner.

"You going to join us?" I ask.

Cynthia closes her textbook and piles everything into a stack. "For a little bit."

Outside, in the dark, Prue tears off the hot tub lid and dips a hand in to check the temperature, even though it's clearly shown on the display. "This is perfect." She climbs in, but I hesitate.

"When do you think they cleaned this last?"

She settles on the opposite side with an irritated huff. "They cleaned it before we got here. Put down your towel and get in."

I drop my towel on a nearby chair, climb the steps, and slip into the water. There are a few seats along the sides, and I take the one next to Prue. Cynthia comes out a moment later, now in a pink one-piece, and joins us.

"Stop stressing," Prue says quietly. "There's room enough for six people."

"There are seven of us," I remind her.

"One of whom wasn't invited."

The water is hot and bubbling, and I slide deep enough the water reaches my collarbone. This bikini is too small—at least, too small for my comfort level. The tub is relaxing, though.

The sliding glass door opens, and Jimmy emerges from the basement in a pair of swimming trunks—and David and Xander follow him through the doorway.

Is there any way to be less conspicuous?

The guys drop some towels on the chairs and climb in without much more than a greeting.

Xander gets in last, his jaw set firmly into a scowl, and sits beside the stairs, the only exit.

"You like the place, right?" Jimmy offers me a bright smile.

I can't help smiling back. "Of course I do. This cabin is beautiful."

"And secluded," Prue adds.

I send her a brief scowl. "We're going to have a talk about this later," I whisper.

She doesn't flinch. "Secluded for my extremely introverted friend."

On the other side of the hot tub, Xander reclines, one arm resting along the top edge of the tub. If he weren't so intent on avoiding eye contact, he might look relaxed. The water covers all but the head of his dragon tattoo.

The final person to arrive is Dahlia.

She's still dressed in her jeans and fitted shirt. She didn't bring anything else. But she doesn't blink before saying, "Mind if I join you?"

"You don't have a swimsuit," Prue reminds her.

"No matter."

Dahlia yanks off her shirt, then undoes the button and zipper of her jeans. Her underwear is the same black lacy lingerie from when we did the photo shoot at her apartment.

There aren't any more seats in the tub, but she slides into the water and forces herself between me and Jimmy. "This is cozy," she murmurs, close to my ear. Her hip brushes mine.

I lean forward to catch Jimmy and Prue's attention. "Since you two are in charge, what's the plan for food? Did you bring enough to last the whole weekend?"

I get the distinct impression we're not going anywhere now that we've arrived. There was a tiny town we passed through on the way here, ten minutes down the highway if we need a grocery store.

Jimmy brushes away my concern. "We brought plenty, relax. Hot dogs, buns, and stuff for smores. There's a fire pit."

"What about the vegetarian?"

"Don't worry about me." Prue elbows my ribs. "We thought of everything."

"Do we have plans for the weekend?"

Fingers, vaguely colder than the water, graze my bare thigh and tug on the bikini's fringe.

On the opposite side of the tub, David flashes me a grin. "You wouldn't believe how many games they brought."

I swallow. "Like what?"

Dahlia's fingers—they don't belong to anyone else—slip closer to my hem and snap the elastic.

I yelp, scooting closer to Prue, who keeps talking despite the disruption.

"...Cards Against Humanity, Disturbed Friends, Exploding Kittens—the norm." That doesn't stop her from shooting a sharp glare in Dahlia's direction.

And she's not the only one.

Xander hasn't been happy since the moment we arrived at the cabin, and there's no sign of improvement.

"That sounds fun," I say, trying to relax again.

Dahlia, though, smirks. "More fun if I get the vodka in my car..."

Before I can protest, she stands and clambers out, pushing past Xander, who grimaces at the momentary contact.

"Dahlia!" I call after her, rising partway out of the water.

She wraps a towel around her body—one she definitely didn't bring out—and trots inside the house.

I release a long groan.

Prue lays her hand on my shoulder. "I'll take care of it. You're not supposed to worry about a thing, remember?"

I settle into my seat, and Prue climbs out. As she grabs a

towel, she waves her hand at Cynthia. "Come help."

Cynthia rolls her eyes, but complies, and soon, the two of them, wrapped in towels, follow Dahlia inside the house.

When they're gone, Jimmy watches me anxiously. "You know, I never got your explanation for why you invited her at the last minute. You two aren't getting back together, are you?"

As expected, Xander's pretending not to listen. Not to care.

I sigh. "She hijacked the conversation and decided she was coming. She wants to talk, and I told her I didn't have time."

"What do you think she wants to talk about?" he asks, lowering his voice.

But across from us, David snorts. "I doubt 'talking' is her actual goal."

A scowl tugs at my lips. "I don't care what her goal is. I didn't come to a cabin in the middle of nowhere to get laid."

David shrugs. "That's what I'd want for my birthday."

I grimace. "Your sex life is the last thing I want to think about, David."

Beside me, Jimmy entertains himself with my discomfort. "She still thinks of you as our RA," he says before turning back to me. "We're not eighteen anymore. A lot more mature."

My gaze gravitates toward Xander. "Some of us more than others."

"Plus, we've all had sex now, so—"

"I didn't realize you could so easily write off screwing my sister as a rite of passage."

"What?" His face pales. "No, I didn't mean that."

But I laugh. "I'm never going to let you live that down."

Xander shifts in his seat. "I didn't realize you told her."

"Technically, he's chicken." My lips twist into a devious smirk. "My dad…"

He inhales sharply. "Not someone I recommend crossing."

That makes me pause.

"Why do you say that? Dad doesn't get angry about anything."

Well, except Jimmy breaking Mo's heart. And he was pissed about me dating Zane freshman year. He probably wasn't too keen on Xander after our "breakup" either.

"You know," Jimmy says, rising from his seat, "all that talk about food earlier made me hungry. I'm gonna grab a snack. Anybody want anything?"

I shake my head and so does Xander, but David gets out of the tub too. "You know, I think I'll tag along."

"You sure you don't want any food?" Jimmy wraps a towel around his waist. "Or a drink? I'll bring you some water."

But when they disappear inside the house, I have to force myself to relax again. They left me and Xander alone.

"Just because you never see your dad get mad," he says in a quiet voice, "doesn't mean he never gets mad."

I strain to hear him over the jets. "I know that."

He turns toward the dark sky, and I follow suit.

There aren't any lights, and the roads toward town are on the opposite side of the house. We really are alone out here.

Me and Xander alone.

Goddammit, they left us alone on purpose.

I rise from the tub and move toward the stairs. I'm not

giving in to their ploy. But Xander sits right next to the exit, and I hesitate to get close to him. Especially when his eyes dart toward my movement.

Now that I'm uncovered, he blatantly ogles me.

I stumble to a stop. "What're you looking at?"

"Nothing." Xander shifts nervously to stare off into the darkness, a hint of red on his cheeks. "Why? What're you looking at?"

I'd laugh if I weren't so uncomfortable. "Nothing."

He glances in my direction, and again, his eyes catch on my dripping wet body. "You going somewhere?"

"Yeah, um, I'm getting overheated."

"Right." His gaze trails down, then back up, and a shiver surges down my spine. "You look hot."

His words are simple and matter-of-fact, but I flush.

Xander stiffens, averting his eyes again. "You know, temperature-wise."

I inch toward the exit, ready to escape, but pause, one knee on the open seat beside him. "Of course. You didn't mean I look attractive."

He turns at my irritation, but he's stunned by my breasts at eye level. "Definitely not that." His words are breathless.

With a huff, I step onto the stairs and carefully start my descent. The last thing I need is to slip and fall on my ass on this concrete.

"Dixon?"

I turn, gripping the edge of the tub for support, my feet on the final step, and freeze. Xander's turned toward me, bending over the edge, and we're face to face—closer than I anticipated.

"Yeah?"

He clears his throat. "I didn't mean you weren't pretty. I never expected you to wear something like that."

I give a one-shouldered shrug. "Prue thought it'd make me feel confident."

"Does it work?"

"I haven't figured it out yet." This is the first time I've worn it since we returned from France.

"Trust me, you should. You look good."

I smirk. "Do I now?"

His fingers grip tighter to the tub, and he shifts forward, licking his lips. "You do…"

The sliding door swooshes open but doesn't close.

I stand up, twisting to find Dahlia, the towel draped around her neck, still in her underwear. She stands on the threshold, her hand holding the sliding door open.

"What's going on?" Her voice is dangerously quiet.

I cross the patio to grab the final towel. "Nothing's going on." I run the towel over my amber skin.

"Not that it's any of your business," Xander snaps.

My nostrils flare. He's back to being pissy in an instant. I wrap the towel around myself and move toward the door. "I'm going to bed."

But Dahlia holds out her arm to stop me. "Can we have our talk now? It's barely ten."

I try to pass her, but she blocks my path again. "No, I'm going to do yoga and go to sleep. We're not having this discussion."

"Oh, come on, Billie." Her hand grips my waist over the towel. "I don't mind doing a little yoga with you. Let's talk."

I scoff and shove her out of the way. "I said no," I snap before climbing the stairs.

Prue, Jimmy, David, and Cynthia are sitting around the dining table with a deck of cards. They all look over as I stomp into the room.

"How's it going?" Hope shines from Jimmy's eyes.

I stop beside them. "I thought this weekend was supposed to be about me?" I snap.

"It is," he says.

"No, this is about you two—" I point between him and Prue "—thinking you know what's best. You want to get us back together, and it's not going to work."

David snickers.

Prue shoots an unimpressed glance in my direction. "If we were, why wouldn't it work?"

"He's moving out. He made up his mind."

But Jimmy tilts his head. "I dunno. Xander's not so stubborn he wouldn't consider an alternative if presented with one."

I scoff. "Maybe I don't want to give him an alternative. Maybe I'm tired of him flip-flopping and don't want to deal with his bullshit anymore. Maybe I'm done."

Behind me, the staircase creaks.

I tear away from the table. "Whatever. I'm going to bed."

When I reach my door, Xander is halfway up the stairs, a scowl on his face.

How much of that did he hear?

Forty-One

"WHERE ARE WE EXACTLY?" THIS AREA OF THE WOODS IS primarily maples, birches, and elms with a few conifers intermixed, and I stop between a full-grown white pine and a young elm tree. "There are trees everywhere." And they block the view of almost everything else along the hillside.

Prue pauses beside me. "Plus the lake."

"Right."

"You hungry yet?" She glances behind us. "David said he'd build a bonfire, so we're gonna roast hot dogs and stuff."

I shrug. "I am hungry."

The leaves crunch underfoot as she turns toward the cabin. "You didn't eat enough at lunch."

"It's hard to have an appetite with Dahlia in my face. She won't stop."

Prue casts a glare in my direction. "Tell her to leave. You don't even want her here."

I pause beside an elm, my palm on the bark. "Yeah, but I don't want to upset her either. She wouldn't handle it well."

"So what? We can kick her out."

Wind rustles through the trees.

"I know that."

"But?"

"I don't want to hurt her, Prue. Sure, I don't want to be with her, but that doesn't mean I should kick her out and tell her I never want to see her again. I don't want to be mean."

Prue leans against the tree. "The longer you let her control the situation, the harder it will be when you do tell her. She's taking advantage of you being a pushover."

I heave a sigh.

It's true. Dahlia wouldn't stop hanging all over me while we played games in our pajamas this morning. Prue and I had to go on a walk so I could get away without isolating myself in my bedroom.

Not that everything else has been great either.

Xander snapped at me when I asked him to pass the spicy mustard while making sandwiches this afternoon. I don't know if that's because of Dahlia or the fact that we almost kissed last night—or both—but I do know it was uncalled for.

"You should tell her to leave." Prue's voice is hushed. "Before she moves into your bedroom. You know she will."

"And that would ruin your plans, right?"

Prue chuckles. "I'm not admitting to anything."

I roll my eyes. "I'll take that as a yes." I push away from the tree and move toward the house, up on the ridge. "Come on. Let's go back."

◆

It's getting dark when we arrive, and like she said, the guys have a fire going.

They moved seven chairs over, and the three guys surround the pit, David stoking the coals with a long stick. Dahlia, enveloped in a thick blanket, is curled up on one of the chairs, fiddling with her phone. Cynthia, I assume, is studying again. She's nowhere to be seen.

Prue nudges me toward the seat beside Xander before heading inside.

When she returns, she's carrying a stack of empty cups and a couple bottles of soda, and she takes the chair between David and Jimmy.

The remaining seat, should Cynthia decide to join us, is between me and Dahlia.

"Have fun exploring?" David's smile carries a tinge of excitement. This morning, I discovered he was an Eagle Scout. "Did you make it to the lake?"

I raise my hands to warm them, front and back. "Nah, we didn't walk that far. It's pretty out here, though."

Xander rises from his chair and stalks toward the cabin without a word.

"A little cold, though," Prue adds, and I rise to reach around the fire when she extends a cup of Sprite. "Anybody bring out more blankets?"

Dahlia gathers up her blanket, switches chairs, and offers me part of hers. "I don't mind sharing."

"No, I'm not cold." I sip the soda and set the cup next to my chair, careful not to bump it.

She purses her lips and pulls the blanket to her chest.

Not that I was being honest. After a long walk through the forest, I'm cold—especially now that the sun has set. But there's no way I'm sharing a blanket with Dahlia.

In the distance behind me, the sliding door opens and

closes, and Xander returns with food and roasting sticks. He drops them on his chair and organizes the supplies.

His movement creates a breeze across my back, and despite my best efforts, I shiver. I try to hide it by moving closer to the fire, but Xander stops, and something warm drapes over my shoulders.

I reach for it, surprised, and frown at the heavy, shiny material.

Xander has never let anyone wear his leather jacket, but I won't complain. I hide my pleasure in the collar as I slip my arms inside the sleeves. "Thanks."

He grunts in return.

The scent leaves me heady, and I relax into the warmth. Spicy and sharp. Something that smells like lighter fluid—motor oil. And though it's been months since he quit, a hint of cigarette smoke.

"You want some food, Billie?"

I turn toward the voice. Jimmy.

"Uh, sure. I can cook it."

Caught up in my own little world there. Not a good sign.

I rise to grab a roasting stick and two hot dogs to skewer. There's also a plastic bin with some sliced veggies for kabobs—good, Prue has something to eat.

"Jeez, you look hungry." Dahlia, suddenly beside me, takes a stick. Her blanket sits, abandoned, on her chair.

I avert my gaze. "It's two hot dogs."

She pinches me with her free hand. "You don't need to eat more."

Telling someone with an eating problem they shouldn't eat more is completely counter-productive. She should know that better than anyone.

I try to step around to return to my seat, but she blocks me in, her hand on the nearest chair. "I need to get past." My food is ready to cook.

Dahlia studies me for a moment, and a smirk tugs at the corner of her lips. "Do you really?"

"Yes."

I move again, but she places her hand on my waist and presses her body against mine. Her other hand drops her roasting stick on the empty chair and cups my cheek.

I have no escape route.

Except to jump into the fire.

Or over it.

She's going to kiss me.

"Are you fucking kidding me?"

Dahlia shrinks away, eyes narrowing at Xander, and I stumble backward. My fingers catch the top of the chair to prevent falling. One glance says I'm not as close to the fire as I thought.

"If you two are going to fuck, go somewhere else," Xander snaps. He turns away and extends his stick over the hot coals.

I clutch my roasting stick to my chest.

Despite an obvious desire to remain inconspicuous, everyone is watching. Prue winces and returns her attention to cooking her veggies.

I scowl at Dahlia. "We're not."

I hate to admit it, but Xander has a point. If I wanted to get back together with her, which I don't, in front of all my friends is hardly an appropriate time and place to make out. But that doesn't faze her in the least.

"We still need to have that talk," she reminds me in a

quiet voice.

Behind me, Xander snorts.

Dahlia's lips twitch. "You don't have to pay attention."

"It's hard to miss." He scowls. "You haven't stopped throwing yourself at her since you got here."

"That doesn't mean you need to look."

I push the nearest chair out of the way and scramble toward my own. This cannot be fucking happening.

Xander rolls his eyes. "Don't play innocent. You want me to pay attention. You want everyone to pay attention. You thrive off people's vulnerabilities."

Dahlia sneers. "You're awfully full of yourself. I don't care what you think."

"I never said you care. You're so insecure in your nonexistent relationship that you need to make sure I know you're still in the picture. You need everyone to think you're in charge. But you're not."

My fingers grip the top edge of my cup, and I take a sip. I'm on the edge of my seat.

"In charge of what?" Dahlia scoffs. "I was never the one telling Billie what to do."

He snorts. "The amount of denial you're in is fucking ridiculous. No one wants you here. You weren't fucking invited. You don't get to ruin her birthday weekend because you don't have friends anymore."

Dahlia's nostrils flare.

"What the hell is wrong with you two?" I abandon my roasting stick on the chair as I stand.

Everyone turns to me.

"This is not a fucking contest, and you're both selfish assholes. I realize you two have hated each other for the last

361

year, but there is no reason to hash this out here."

Xander crosses his arms over his chest. "That's bullshit. I cannot believe you're getting back together with her."

"What the hell are you talking about?"

"Why else would you let her stay here? You're making a nice show about keeping your distance, but if you didn't want her, you would've told her to leave."

My hand grips the cup, so tense my knuckles are white. "You have no idea what you're talking about."

"You were about to go at it right here. That sends a pretty fucking obvious message."

I grit my teeth and chuck the cup at his face, Sprite splashing everywhere in the process. "You complete moron."

The plastic clatters to the ground.

The fire hisses from the spray.

Soda drips down Xander's shirt.

"Dahlia Finnick isn't the person I want to get back together with."

He blinks and wipes the soda from his face, his eyes surveying me.

To my right, there's movement, but I don't turn.

But when a minute of silence passes, Xander simply steps away from the fire and says, "I'm going to clean up."

He disappears in the cabin.

I seek out Prue on the other side of the fire pit. "This is a disaster."

Prue shakes her head. "It'll be okay."

Dahlia has disappeared. Where'd she go?

"No." I force away the frustration, but calming down won't happen here. "I'm sorry. I'm gonna go to bed."

Forty-Two

WHEN THE DOOR CLICKS SHUT, I TWIST THE DEADBOLT INTO the locked position. I need the privacy.

So far, this weekend has not been what I hoped. Considering we're heading home tomorrow, I don't know how to salvage this.

I recline on the king-sized bed and stare at the extravagant chandelier, but it is not relaxing. I need to change for bed and do my yoga.

My stomach growls.

And maybe grab some food since I didn't eat my hot dogs.

With a huff, I rise and slip Xander's leather jacket onto the bed. I change into my favorite t-shirt and pajama shorts, but while I'm hungry, I'm not ready to leave the safety of my room.

I don't want to run into anyone.

Instead, I lie back and inhale the heady scent of Xander. The Charmander shirt stopped smelling like him nearly a year ago, but this jacket is different. Special.

I won't get away with keeping this. It's his signature look. The jacket envelops me again, and I slide my arms inside, relishing the smoothness, the warmth, the complete Xander experience.

A knock sounds on the door.

I bolt up from the bed and move to the door. I suppose I should give Xander his jacket, especially if he's going back outside after cleaning the soda.

I undo the deadbolt and open the door. "Yeah, yeah, yeah, you can have your—"

It's Dahlia.

My fingers grasp the doorknob, and I hold my ground. "We don't have anything to discuss."

She glances at the jacket, then my face. "We have a lot to discuss, Billie. That's the whole reason I came here. To talk."

I purse my lips, but she's right. "Fine."

"Can I come in?"

"No." I step out and shut the door behind me. "We're talking out here."

Dahlia hesitates but, after a moment, relents. "I'm sure you know what I want to talk to you about—"

"You want to get back together. That was obvious the moment you showed up at my house, Lia."

"Right." She releases an anxious chuckle. "I do, but I understand it isn't that simple. I lost your trust, and for a relationship to work, we need to trust each other."

I shake my head. "I don't see any way for my trust to be restored."

"I also wanted to apologize."

That part is surprising.

"I've never been good at being honest with you. We both have a lot of trust issues, and I know I didn't help, but you have to understand how important you are to me." Dahlia runs a hand through her sleek hair, her fingers quivering. "I love you. I've loved you since we first became friends, and I'd never do anything to jeopardize that."

"But you already have. We broke up."

"I never did anything to hurt you. I want to take care of you. I want to make you happy." She reaches for me, and I allow her to clasp her fingers around mine. "I'm ready to talk to you—about my mom and Darius, about Brent, about my anorexia and my therapy, about everything. I'm ready."

I temper my smile so she won't get any ideas. "I'm glad you started therapy, and I hope it helps you."

"Please give me another chance." She squeezes my hand. "I want to prove I can be better. That I'd do anything for you."

A scoff escapes my lips, and I silently berate myself. I wasn't supposed to show emotion. I need to have a sturdy front to get my point across. "But that's the thing, Dahlia— you already proved you'd do anything for me." I shift to get better, firmer footing. "No matter how crazy or controlling or vindictive, you're willing to get your hands dirty."

"That's not what I meant—"

"For how long?" I tug away, and she doesn't resist. "If we got back together, how would it be different? You might be more honest in the beginning, but I cannot trust you to keep that up."

Dahlia's lip quivers. "You're not giving me a chance."

"No, that's the problem—and what you can't wrap your head around. I've given you too many chances." My hand clutches the doorknob behind me, ready to retreat into the bedroom once this is over. "Look, I appreciate your honesty and the gesture, but there's nothing in the world that could get us back together."

She stumbles away. "You don't mean that. You're lying."

"I can't keep letting you suck me in. You need to leave."

For a moment, she stares.

"I'm sure Prue and David and Xander wouldn't mind escorting you."

Tears prick the corners of her eyes before she takes another step backward. Without a word, she reaches into her pocket, her hands snagging on jingling keys, and turns toward the door.

I breathe a sigh of relief when it closes behind her, but I force my legs to move. I feel sick, and I need a drink. I'm not getting a snack now. Lost my appetite.

"Well, that only took a year longer than it should have."

I stop.

Xander stands in his doorway, nothing but a towel wrapped around his waist. Water glistens on his bare chest. Apparently, he needed a full shower to wash off my soda.

"What?"

He moves toward the fridge, leaving his door open. But while I'm frozen on the spot, he fills a glass from the cupboard and heads for his bedroom. "You heard me."

The door shuts behind him.

I grit my teeth.

But what can I say? He's gone.

I return to my room without a glass of water. The door slams shut behind me, but I can't stop.

Despite insisting he would move on, that asshole has flip-flopped between wanting to fuck me and wanting nothing to do with me for the last year.

I stop pacing with a scoff.

That's not moving on. That's not even close.

Ugh. I'm still wearing his stupid fucking jacket.

I push into the dark bathroom and rap my knuckles against Xander's bedroom door, harder than necessary. Under the crack, light and faint music sneak through, and I tap my foot against the tile floor, impatient.

When it opens, I have to blink away the glare.

"What do you want, Dixon?" He's a bit drier, but the towel hugs his hips in a way that would be overwhelmingly attractive if he were remotely likable.

"You." I shove past and, once in the middle of the room, spin to face him. "You are a complete asshole."

Unimpressed, he crosses to the queen-sized bed and rifles through the contents of his backpack, which dangles from the corner of the footboard. He doesn't even acknowledge my accusation.

"We broke up," I snap, pacing back and forth. "Over a year ago. You're not allowed to be a jealous ass every time I consider dating someone."

He pulls up with a fresh pair of boxers—Deadpool, his favorite—and adjusts the towel at his waist. Is he going to get dressed right in front of me?

"Xander!"

He shoots a glower over his shoulder.

"You're not paying attention. I'm trying to—"

"You're pissed," he says with a noncommittal shrug. "I get the picture."

I stomp my foot on the hardwood, but he doesn't flinch. "No, you don't get the fucking picture. You're not listening."

He turns, the boxers clamped in his fist, and arches an eyebrow. "Would you like me to sit for your rant?" He doesn't wait for a response before plopping down on the edge of the bed and gesturing for me to continue.

Asshole.

My foot taps an unsteady beat against the floor. His snarky stunt ruined my train of thought.

"Dixon, perhaps you should calm down." His obnoxiously steady voice finagles its way under my skin—like every other inch of this impossible man-child.

I grit my teeth. "Perhaps you should stop acting like you know better than me. You're not smarter than me. Your experiences don't give you any special edge when it comes to my life. And just because you're cocksure and headstrong doesn't mean you're braver than me."

Xander leans back on his hands, and the loose towel jostles with the movement. It was already slung excruciatingly low—enough to show off his hips and a narrow trail of thick dark hair.

"You're not. You are absolutely not braver than me. You're a coward."

He makes no protest. No denial. No surprised gasp—not even in jest.

Instead, his lips flatten into a thin line.

"If you were brave, you wouldn't attack me in front of our friends, using your anger and jealousy to ridicule me. You wouldn't make stupid assumptions about me and Dahlia instead of dealing with your insecurities. You wouldn't beg me not to sleep with a guy under the refuge of alcohol—and you certainly wouldn't use that lack of sobriety to grope me in your bedroom."

This time, his mouth quirks to the side. His brow furrows.

He doesn't remember that.

"You wouldn't—" My voice falters. "You wouldn't only want me while you're drunk. You're not brave. You're a scared little boy who's never had anyone love him."

He crosses one leg over the other, ankle to knee, and the towel shifts, revealing an increasingly large section of thigh. But still, he doesn't speak.

I start my spastic march again and flex my fingers, trying to gather my thoughts. "You can ignore me. You can act like my opinion doesn't matter. Hell, you can hate me if that makes it easier. But hopping back and forth between loathing me and pretending you still have feelings for me is bullshit, and I'm fucking tired of it."

At last, he taps a finger against his bare knee. "Are you done yet?" Somehow, he remains eerily calm.

"No."

He holds out his hand, signaling for me to proceed.

The towel was haphazardly thrown on because it moves far too easily. At that small gesture, the fabric slides back. I should not be able to see this much skin.

"You sound done."

My mouth twists up into a snarl. "Stop being an asshole. You'll know when I'm done."

But when I fall silent, he nods me toward the bed. "Sit down."

Against my better judgment—and only because his unnaturally tranquil demeanor unsettles me—I comply. I lay my head in my hands, closing my eyes, trying to calm the unsteady beat of my overworked heart. "I'm glad you're moving out. Finally, I won't have to deal with your bullshit."

"You want me gone?"

I blink and slowly turn to survey the sudden change from emotionless quiet to his newfound quivering uncertainty.

"I never lied." He doesn't look at me, but his hands clasp atop his lap, the Deadpool boxers abandoned among the sheets. "And my feelings for you were never make belief. I'm sorry if walking out after we had sex upset you, but you've given me no indication that was the wrong decision."

I scoff.

"As long as you can't commit to a relationship, I can't keep putting myself in this position." He releases a shaky breath and toys with a fraying edge of the towel. "Don't get me wrong, I'll miss spending time with you, but I don't have another solution. Every moment we spend together, I fall deeper."

"Deeper into what?"

"You're not wrong, Dixon..."

I tilt my head, eyebrows drawn together at his subject-hopping.

"I'm not nearly as brave as I like to think. When you returned from study abroad, I looked for easy ways to distract myself. So I didn't have to feel anymore. I let Dahlia get the better of me, though I knew she wanted to piss me off." He blinks and blinks again. "But there is something you're wrong about."

"Oh?"

"I always want you. Not only while drunk. I'm just a colossal idiot." He shoots a glance my way but quickly averts his eyes. "But if you really want to be rid of me, I won't argue. It's probably for the best. Moving out is the only guarantee I might get over you."

I swallow. My throat's dry. "Deeper into what?" All

anger's dissipated.

An uncertain smirk tugs at his lips. "Deeper into you."

"Xander, do you really need me to spell it out for you?"

A shrug. "Considering how things ended last time, yeah, I do."

I pinch the bridge of my nose and nudge my glasses up into my afro. "Sometimes, I'm a coward too." His bed is easily as comfortable as mine when I lie down, body quivering, eyes misty. "I didn't mean it. I don't want you to move out. You're one of my best friends. I lost you once—I don't want to do it a second time."

The mattress creaks. "I thought you don't care if I hate you." His voice is closer than before.

"Of course I care." I pull the jacket tighter around me, cling to it for courage. "I love you. Even if you don't want me anymore, even if you leave, I love you."

Fingers trace the edge of my lips, trail up to slide the glasses from atop my head, and I tremble under his touch. The hard plastic clatters against the nearby nightstand. Before I can open my eyes, he silences any hesitation with a delicate kiss, his hand cupping my cheek. "Dixon, I've wanted you from the second you threw me out of your dorm room two days into our first semester. Nothing changed that."

My laughter is breathless, and my eyes open to his smiling face above me. "I never got over you. You know that, right? When I was with Dahlia, I didn't…"

"I know."

Warm arms wrap around me, one slipping under my neck, the other encircling my waist, and pull me into his embrace. My eyes flutter shut as I curl onto the bed, facing him. Xander bridges the gap so we're nose to nose, brow to brow, and finally, mouth to mouth.

"If you keep stealing all my clothes," he says when he pulls back, tugging at the jacket, "I'll run out of things to wear."

One glance down reveals the towel long ago stopped covering him properly. "What a shame that would be." His partial erection peeks from under the lavender cloth.

"I might lose my job." He tries to look somber as his fingers skim my side, leather bunching under his touch. "Or I might get better tips."

I roll my eyes. "If we're going to do this, you need to stop being so conceited."

He lays a kiss atop my nose. "Oh, the lady has terms? Do tell."

"You can't flirt with other girls."

"I don't."

I send him a sharp glare.

"I never flirted with someone else while we were together."

"Not even for a better tip?"

"Not seriously." Deft fingers trail down the curve of my hip, to the bottom of my pajama shorts, then back up. "Besides, if we're going to do this, you need to have a little faith. I can keep my work and personal lives separate."

My fingers thread through his hair, and he presses another kiss to the corner of my mouth. "So you have terms too."

His laughter drives away my last reservations. "You bet I do."

"What's first?"

His fingers inch up my spine, the t-shirt clumping together as he massages each nub of vertebrae through the cotton, and I shiver when he unwittingly reveals my flesh to the elements. Soft, eager lips capture mine, and I melt into his embrace.

Last time, our kisses were a necessity—passionate, greedy, desperate—and my hunger increased with every seductive sensation. I needed him. I needed the reminder of how his skin sears mine, how his cock throbs inside me, how easily he overwhelms me with ecstasy. Because that's exactly what happened. He fucked me, and I was keen and malleable in his calloused grip.

Now, he kisses me simply for the pleasure of kissing me.

"What's always first." His hand at last slips under the t-shirt. The skin-to-skin contact pries a moan from my mouth. "You need to take care of yourself, Dixon. And listen to your therapist."

"I do." I drag his mouth to mine, caressing his cheek, and he sucks my lip between his teeth.

He hums into the kiss, skeptical. "Most of the time."

His erection convulses against my thigh. I'm not sure what the point of the towel is anymore. It only adds to the distance between us—and I want to eliminate that distance.

My fingers graze down his side, crossing the inky dragon tattoo, and stop at his waist. The lavender towel barely clings to him, and a tiny flick of the wrist frees him from its grasp. I inch closer, my hand on his hip, and burrow my face in the crook of his neck, breathing in his heady scent. It's decidedly stronger here than on the leather.

"Any other requirements?" I murmur into his ear.

"No more secrets." His lips trace my hairline. His hand,

under the shirt, supports the curve of my lower back. "If we do this, we're a team. You need to tell me when you're having a bad day or I can't help."

I withdraw to look him in the eye. "It works both ways. You can't keep everything to yourself either—even the things you don't want anyone to know. We're a team, or this means nothing."

He pulls me into another lip-lock to signal his acquiescence.

A moment later, I rest my forehead on his, panting from the potent kisses. "Xander, I want to be close to you."

Eyes alight with understanding, he works his fingers from under my shirt and begins the reverent removal of my clothing. He pulls me atop his waist and peels off the leather jacket one arm at a time, his passion-darkened eyes roving my form. I raise trembling arms next, and he eases the t-shirt over my head, breasts quivering upon release.

The spark in my stomach ignites with arousal when he captures my nipple, sucking lightly, and I hum my approval.

His hands settle on my hips, clutching the remaining barrier. "Dixon—" his voice is deep, husky "—I need you in this a hundred percent."

"Hmm?"

He sucks my nipple hard, teeth scraping the pliable flesh, and I blink my eyes open. "You know I'm all for sex, but that can't be the basis of our relationship. I still have the same wants, the same requirements as a year ago. I need you in this a hundred percent. Complete commitment."

I lie atop him, chest to chest, and cover his lips with mine. "I was scared before—scared everything would change, that we'd never be friends again, scared I'd destroy you when I imploded. I don't want to lose you again, and I don't intend to."

In one swift movement, he rolls me onto my back and hovers above, my legs hiked up to his waist. "Good." His fingers locate the hem of my shorts, then the underwear, and he tugs the final obstacle over my ass. I gasp—his hands graze past my core—and release a pleased moan when he drops the clothing to the floor.

We are, at last, skin to skin.

He cradles me in his arms, and I squirm as he sweeps tender kisses across my collar. Unsteady fingers ghost over my body, touching the newly exposed flesh. I entangle my hands in his thick hair, glide my lips along his temple, hook my legs around his bare hips. His erection presses against my heat—and he jerks at the sudden contact.

A sharp cry escapes my lips as his cock nudges my entrance.

His tongue swirls around my nipple, hand cupping the breast, and he pulses, dipping inside. "You still on the pill? This okay?" His hips seem to move of their own volition, rolling and jerking in suspense, and I moan at the cursory penetration.

"I don't see a condom miraculously appearing."

Although, I'd wager Prue and Jimmy brought some in case we needed one.

"We can stop if that's better," he adds, but I writhe in his arms.

"I need to be close to you. Come inside me."

I don't know when my need for him reached this level, but I can't hold back anymore. Thankfully, I don't have to. The second he thrusts inside, I rock in tune with his slow and steady rhythm.

He overwhelms me with his lips, sedates me with hungry kisses, and I am pliant in his embrace. I soak up the moment, memorize his patient mouth, his unyielding hands, his taut muscles. He strains to keep the pace leisurely, even as he throbs, and I cling to him, moaning and sighing as he plunges into me.

"You know," I murmur into his neck, "there's a point where going slow gets pretty difficult."

He hums with laughter. "Think you can handle it?"

A long sob escapes my lips when he angles my hips up and delves deep. I latch onto the cotton sheets, and he matches his pace with my deafening cries—faster, harder, dissonant—crashing into me as I come.

But he doesn't stop. His thrusts are jerky now, and I hold on, riding out my bliss.

"Say it again." His words are jumbled, uncertain.

"Huh?"

He wrenches me closer, and I moan, arching my back.

"Say it again," he grunts with his next jerk, but the pleasure he provokes makes it hard to focus. I'm going to come again.

I struggle to decipher his meaning, but he leans close enough for me to see his face and sends me a meaningful look—and I yank him into a momentary kiss.

When he resumes his frantic rhythm, he's too far away.

"Xander, I love you."

He drags me up into a kiss, and I wrap my arms around his neck to keep from falling. He adjusts to support us, his lips insatiable, and continues driving inside me.

When he finishes, I'm dazed and wet from his come,

but his intense blue eyes hold me steady. He runs a hand through his mussed hair and flashes me a dazzling smile. "I love you too."

I collapse onto the bed as he uses the shirt to clean up. I cannot sit up without support, but I need to go to the bathroom before I fall asleep. I need to protect my hair with a headwrap.

When he's done, he lies beside me, close enough I can see the satisfaction on his face. "You still scared?"

"Right now, I'm too tired to be scared of anything."

Xander rolls his eyes.

"Of course I'm scared." I press my mouth to his and run a hand through his tousled locks. "But some things are worth the risk."

Forty-Three

"You want anything before you head out?"

I spin round, away from the paintings on the wall, to flash Jeremy a smile and zip up my hoody. "Not tonight. I'm, you know, waiting for Xander to finish his shift."

Jeremy returns to the register.

The Jittery Bug isn't nearly as busy as it was last Friday, but most college students are done with classes now. Plus, last Friday was St. Clare's May Gallery Hop.

And today?

Well, today was Bradford College's graduation day. Hard to compete with that.

Yet, the next person at the register is a young woman with long honey-brown hair and high cheekbones.

Dahlia should be ready to leave town—she graduated today, and St. Clare is hardly big enough to warrant staying—but she's wearing pajamas. Jeremy hands her an empty to-go cup for the self-serve station.

Right next to me.

She doesn't make eye contact as she passes. She fills her cup with black coffee and tops it with a lid. Her gaze does, however, drift upward, where a series of five portraits line the brick wall, far out of reach. Hard not to look when you're the subject of one painting.

I got my first exhibit. Even if it's only in a coffee shop.

I may have gotten that exhibit because I landed a job at said coffee shop, but you have to start somewhere, right?

"You've been staring at these every day for the past week."

I twist around and pull Xander into a hug. "What took you so long? I've been waiting forever."

He chuckles. "Your shift ended five minutes ago. Considering I gave away my tables because we're in a hurry, you have nothing to complain about." He watches the self-serve station, where she's surveying the paintings, to-go cup in hand.

Dahlia slides on her lid and heads out.

"Glad it's graduation day?" Xander's voice is a whisper.

But I shake my head. "I don't think she has anywhere else to go."

An irritated scowl tugs at his lips. "She staying in town?"

"I don't know."

When she disappears, I return to the paintings and hold his arms tight.

He nuzzles my temple. "You can keep staring, but I don't think it'll get old."

"No, it won't."

"But your sister will be pissed if you miss her graduation, and since I'm your chauffeur, she'll be pissed at me too."

I roll my eyes. "You're not my chauffeur. That's been long established."

"What?" He fakes a gasp. "Are you actually going to use the B-word?"

379

"Exactly." I take his hand and drag him to the door. "Where'd you park your car, butthead? We need to get home and shower."

He catches up with a grin. "Shower, huh?"

My snort is covered by the chime as I push open the door. "We don't have time for shower sex, Xander. But I don't want to spend the next twenty hours in a car with you smelling like beer."

Surprisingly, his Camaro is two parking spots down. He must've moved closer.

His fingers clamp around my hand, and I stumble as he yanks me backward into his arms. The kiss that follows is firm and demanding, and I melt into his embrace.

Because this—kissing him in the middle of a downtown sidewalk in broad daylight—doesn't get old either.

I wrap my free arm around him and nip at his bottom lip. A soft sigh escapes my mouth when he returns the favor, but I swallow down the desire and anticipation building in my chest and slowly untangle myself.

Xander refuses to release me. He holds me to his chest, his forehead against mine. "Dixon, there's always time for shower sex. We just have to make it."

Laughter bubbles from my lips, and I tug toward his car. "We have to reach the shower in the first place."

He presses one last kiss to my mouth, then allows me to lead the way.

◆

Struggling to repress his laughter, Jimmy keys his desired time into the microwave as I enter the kitchen. "You know, you wouldn't be running late if you two would stop having sex for more than two seconds."

I roll my eyes. "Buy some earplugs."

"Your bedroom is the one that needs soundproofing," he adds. "When are you heading out?"

Behind us, the front door opens and closes.

"He's loading the car now." I push a few strands of damp curls out of my face. "You sure you won't come with us?"

"That's not a good idea, Billie. I…can't go. Imogene doesn't want me there." Jimmy glances at the microwave, but there's twenty-five seconds on the timer. "Besides, I'm working all weekend."

"Imogene would be thrilled if you came to her graduation, and you know it."

But he turns away. "It doesn't matter. I'm barbacking tonight."

The microwave beeps, and he withdraws the mug of stale coffee.

"Fine." I wrap my hand around the fridge handle, but I'm not ready to let this go. "We'll miss you. She'll miss you."

He gives a one-shouldered shrug. "Actually, I was wondering…"

"Yeah?"

He sets the mug on the counter and disappears through the kitchen doorway.

Confused, I snag a couple bottles of water from the fridge. It's a twenty-hour drive to Springfield. The fridge door slams shut when I slip away.

"Can you give this to Imogene?"

When I turn, Jimmy holds a sealed envelope toward me.

"What is it?"

"A card. Congratulations and all that." He shifts on his feet, waiting, but he hesitates when I reach for it. "Careful, it's…"

My fingers close around the envelope—the contents are hard and thick. "Fragile." It's a CD. "I'll get it to her in one piece."

"And say hi to my parents for me."

"Of course."

Finally, he moves around me and grabs his coffee. "Now, get going. I want to enjoy my weekend alone for once. I almost regret—"

"What?" I purse my lips. "Joining forces with Prue in an evil plot to get us back together?"

He scoffs. "Hardly evil. You like the plan."

"I like the plan when it's mine, not yours."

The front door slams shut, and I turn as Xander joins us.

"Besides," I add as he wraps an arm around my waist, "when you plot against me, you leave yourself wide open."

Xander tugs me into an affectionate kiss. "Everything's in the car. Unless you forgot something. You've got your pills?"

"Of course."

When I turn back, Jimmy's brow knits together. "What do you mean, 'wide open'?"

I lean into Xander, relishing his embrace, and he nips my neck. "For retribution."

Jimmy sends us a scowl. "You know, I wish you were moving out at the end of the month."

Xander chuckles against my skin before lifting his head. "You could move out, you know."

His eyebrows shoot up to his messy hair. "Right, because

you two should definitely officially live together after like three weeks of dating."

Xander shrugs.

"Of course—" Jimmy stirs his coffee with a finger "—it's not like you've spent a night apart during that time. I'll enjoy the silence while you're gone."

"Yes, gone." I turn toward Xander. "We need to leave now. Mo's expecting us much sooner than we'll get there."

He presses a quick kiss to my mouth and offers to carry the water bottles. "Let's go."

"Text me when you get there," Jimmy calls after us. "I don't like listening to your sex, but it'd be nice to know you're alive."

I send him a quick wave as Xander leads me to his Camaro by the hand.

Inside, I examine the envelope curiously. "You know, I wish you had a CD player."

"Why?" Xander straps on his seatbelt, steps on the clutch, and starts the engine, but he refuses to drive until I'm wearing mine too.

"Because," I say once we're on the road, "I want to be nosy." I hold the envelope aloft. It's sealed by a small sticker—easily removed and returned. She wouldn't know.

"What's that?"

"Graduation card from Jimmy." I tap my finger against the envelope, and the hard surface returns a hollow sound. "And there's a disk in here."

Xander's busy racing around a Ford Explorer doing ten under the speed limit. "That's for Mo."

"Yeah, but don't you want to be nosy?"

"Nope."

I scowl. "Jerk."

"I saw and heard way too much while she was here over the summer. I have no interest in more."

A grimace spreads across my face. "That's gross."

"You're telling me."

"But this is his music. You know it has to be." I flip the envelope over and over before tucking it into the door pocket. "And it's Jimmy—he wouldn't be crude while writing her love songs."

Xander shifts gears. "I dunno. She'd probably get off on it. She seemed to like—"

"Do not finish that sentence about my little sister."

"Hey—" he flashes me a grin at a stop sign "—I'm not the one who fucked her…or vice versa. She was the one in charge."

I clap my hands. "Okay, done with that conversation." I drag out his box of cassette tapes from under my seat. "This is a long trip, so I need music." I slide the album into the tape deck and wait for the initial chords to play.

Xander chuckles as the opening riffs of "Back in Black" crackle to life.

"What?" I slide the box under the seat with a smile. "This is my favorite AC/DC album."

Forty-Four

DESPITE MY SLEEP-ADDLED BRAIN, I IDENTIFY THE POWELLS' house without doubt. It's the same as it ever was—beautiful, elegant, sleek design—but the house beside it is unrecognizable.

For the first time in ten years, my mother's house has a fresh coat of paint, lovely landscaping, and a bright and cheerful 'For Sale' sign near the road.

"Damn." Xander parks the car at the curb. "I guess it's official."

"I didn't realize it was on the market. Mo's not leaving for college till August."

He frowns. "What happens when it sells? This is a nice area, and if they updated it well, it should sell fast."

I wrap my hand around the handle and open the door. We didn't drive all this way to sit in the car. "She could visit for the summer again."

Xander snorts. "That'd be an interesting experiment on Jimmy."

"All the more reason to convince her."

The lawn is greener, brighter, healthier, as we approach the house, and we pause on the stoop. I'm nervous to knock, to open the door, to see my mother for the first time since her wedding, to meet my new little brother—so much younger than me that it hardly counts.

But Xander doesn't hesitate before pressing the doorbell, and I send him a quick glare that he blatantly ignores.

The door opens a few seconds later, and Rob's anxious face peeks through the gap. "Billie." He nudges the door open the rest of the way to reveal a green bundle in his arms. "Come in. Your mother is sleeping."

I step over the threshold, Xander at my heels, and Rob closes the door.

"Is that the baby?" I hesitantly peek toward the bundle. "Niño?"

Rob pushes the bundle into my arms, and I hold it—him—close so he's stable. "Your brother. Support the head."

The baby, asleep and silent, is nothing but fat rolls and thick black hair. He stretches an arm at the relocation but otherwise doesn't seem to notice. A lot cuter now than in the initial photos.

He has the same golden-brown skin and black hair as his father. If she hadn't given birth to him, I wouldn't think him related to my mother.

"I need to make a bottle," Rob announces in his quiet voice, and he heads for the kitchen.

Leaving me alone with the baby.

"How does it feel?"

Well, and Xander.

I roll my eyes. "Heavy."

He snorts. "I meant holding a baby, not how the baby literally feels."

"Oh."

But he leads me toward the kitchen. "I suppose that works for both, though."

I sit on the stool while Rob pours warm water into a bottle and twists on the top. I guess it's time to wake up. Xander sits beside me, curiosity etched on his face as Rob closes the lid on the formula tin while shaking the bottle.

The baby's forehead scrunches together, and his mouth contorts into a scowl, then a pout, a smile, a frown. His nostrils flare.

"You handle that well, Billie."

My mother, lips pale, studies me from the doorway. She's in pajamas, her blond hair pulled into a bun that's fallen halfway down. There are bags under her eyes. Whoever says motherhood's beautiful is lying.

"Hey, Mom," I murmur, trying not to disturb the baby.

His cry starts as a whimper but transitions quickly. His eyes don't even open.

And Rob takes the swaddled baby from my arms and offers the bottle. "Come here, *mijito*."

Damn. He's timed napping like a science.

Now that I'm free, Mom gives me a quick hug. "I'm glad you came home."

I pat her back, but her kind words don't ease the discomfort. This hasn't been home in a long time, and she's aware of that.

She gives Xander a hug next. "Thanks for coming."

"I wouldn't miss it." He glances toward Rob and the baby before finding me again. "You make cute babies." He sends me a little wink.

A snort comes from the doorway.

Imogene, dressed in a flowing pink crop-top and floral

shorts, pauses on the threshold. Her hair, a shimmering golden blond, is twisted into a simple updo. "Real classy, Xander."

He grins and nods her closer.

She doesn't hesitate before crossing the room to him, and he tugs her into a tight embrace. "You know I get to say I told you so, right?"

I didn't realize they were on hugging terms.

He chuckles as they separate. "Yeah, I know. We can discuss how well you know your sister later."

She knows me a lot better than I know her.

Rob carries the baby, now eating, toward the living room so we can talk, but my mom hovers nearby.

Finally, Imogene steps closer and wraps me in a hug. "I'm glad you're here," she says into my afro, and I tighten my arms around her petite form. "I was getting worried."

"Sorry," I mumble. "We had a late start."

She retracts. "Why didn't you come upstairs and get me?"

Xander laughs. "Somebody was wrangled into holding a baby right away."

Imogene snorts. "Be glad he wasn't awake. He mostly eats and sleeps and poops, so it's not super exciting." She glances toward Mom. "He does smile a little too. Honestly, I'm impressed Rob got you to hold him."

Mom moves around the counter and throws, "You two hungry?" over her shoulder. She sifts through the contents of the fridge. "We have veggies and hummus, string cheese, hard-boiled eggs…?"

Imogene sends me a conspiratorial eye-roll. "She went super healthy with the pregnancy, so we've got plenty of that shit."

"Language," Mom calls from the other side of the counter.

"Hummus would be perfect," Xander says.

Mom brings the food over. "You're staying with us, right?" She drops the hummus tub and a bag of baby carrots in front of us.

Xander pries it open right away and hands me a carrot. "Of course."

But Mo reclines against the counter between us. "You don't have a bed anymore. That's the baby's room."

She already told me when they got the room ready two or three months ago.

"The couch will be perfectly fine," Xander says. "Anything you need to do before graduation tomorrow?"

Imogene shrugs. "Not really. I have my dress and shoes and gown and hat. There's nothing else to it. It'll be boring."

"Aren't you excited?" I tilt my head to the side, studying her.

She doesn't answer.

In the living room, the baby starts to cry, and Mom's eyes dart toward the doorway. "I'll check on them." She disappears without waiting for a response.

Beside me, Mo purses her lips. "What's there to be excited about? I mean, theoretically, I should care about getting my diploma and saying goodbye to my classmates, but I don't know why." She moves around the counter to reach the fridge.

Xander stretches a hand across the space between us and squeezes my knee—signaling me to eat. We haven't had breakfast yet. I suppose I am hungry.

"Are you still dating Donovan?" I snag another carrot.

389

She pauses in the middle of pulling out a bottle of juice. "No."

I cock an eyebrow at the abrupt tone. Apparently, that is not to be discussed.

Xander squeezes my knee again, then stands from the stool. "Bathroom," he murmurs before disappearing.

When he's gone, Imogene takes a cup from the cabinet and pours herself a drink. "I was happy when you said you were bringing him, Billie. Surprised but happy."

Anxious, I glance toward the doorway. "I didn't know if he'd want to. We haven't been dating that long."

She chuckles. "Yeah, but he's been in love with you forever. Did you see that look on his face?" The bottle goes back in the fridge.

My brow furrows. "What look?"

"When you were holding the baby."

"Oh no." I shake my head. "That's not... We're not having any babies."

"Ever?"

I dip a carrot in the hummus, buying more time. "Not yet."

A bright smile spreads across her face. "I missed you, you know. I'm glad you could make it."

"Of course I'm here, Mo." I swallow. "I didn't realize the house was on the market yet. What happens if it sells before you go to UVA?"

She shrugs. "Mom and Rob and the baby go to California."

"What about you? You could come to Vermont. Stay with Dad again—or with me. I work at the coffee shop, but otherwise, I'm all yours."

She winces. "That's not going to happen. I signed up for a summer dance program through a local group. I'm touring for a couple months, so I only need to worry about the last two weeks before class. It'll be fun."

"Oh."

Laughter bubbles from her mouth. "Don't sound so disappointed, Billie. If you wanted me to visit, you would've asked me ages ago."

"Dad didn't think you'd want to."

She cringes.

A sad sigh escapes my lips. "When was the last time you talked to Jimmy?"

Mo turns sharply at the sudden change. "I don't know. It's been a while. Why?"

I try to keep my tone nonchalant. "You two used to talk and Skype all the time. More than you and I talked."

"We've grown apart. Why does it matter?" She scoffs. "I don't need to sit through an hour-long monologue about his current favorite band, and frankly, he's out of practice with the piano."

I stifle a snort.

There are plenty of things she could complain about that wouldn't be so obvious. She always enjoyed discussing—arguing—music with him. And out of practice, his skill on the piano is still above average.

"I always thought you liked hanging out with him."

Besides, she used the "Jimmy's boring" excuse months ago. I didn't buy it before I knew they slept together, and I don't buy it now.

She releases a huff. "He's fine. We don't talk anymore. There's nothing else to it."

"Of course."

Try as I might, I don't know how to broach the subject. If she wanted to tell me what happened last summer, she would have.

I check my person, but the envelope is in the car. It'll have to wait.

Forty-Five

CHARLIE AND THEA POWELL WAIT AT THE END OF THE ROW, and they rise to greet us. They're dressed semi-formal for the ceremony, Charlie in a polo shirt and khakis, his gray hair parted on the side, and Thea in a green summer dress, a shawl draped over her shoulders. The skin by her eyes wrinkles when she smiles.

"Good to see you, Billie," Charlie says when we reach them. "I see Xander came with you."

I accept a hug from Thea, then a shoulder squeeze from Charlie, and Xander shakes their hands.

Behind us, Mom and Rob, holding a fussy Niño, file into the bleachers too, and we take our seats.

Xander flips through the program and elbows my side. "How long do these things take?"

I rub at my ribs and shoot him a glare. "Didn't you attend yours?"

"Nah, no point." He flips to the next page. "My dad was in New York, and my mom forgot. I picked up my diploma the next day."

"Oh." I lay my hand on his knee and lean into him. "We'll be here a while. It's a lot of boring speeches, a really long line, and way too much noise."

393

He kisses the top of my head and threads our fingers together. "You'll love this."

On my other side, Charlie chuckles. "She spent the hour before hers arguing with her mother about whether she needed to walk."

My anxiety over the event probably was funny to an outsider, but it wasn't to me.

"Squeeze my hand when you're nervous," Xander whispers.

"I'm surprised," Thea Powell says loudly. "Jimmy said he'd try to take time off work."

For a moment, I'm impressed Jimmy managed to lie to his mother. He didn't request time off—Kylie would've granted it—and he never planned to attend Mo's graduation.

Charlie laughs nervously. "I'm sure he tried."

Something about his voice says he knows a lot more than his wife. At least I can take solace in the fact that I'm not the last person to learn Jimmy and Imogene slept together.

Out on the floor, Imogene rises, a speck amongst a sea of dark green graduation robes, and waves. She smiles, but I know it's for the cameras.

◆

Afterward, Mo meets us on the green space under the trees, clutching the fake ceremonial diploma. A couple guys try to stop and chat with her as she crosses the grass, but she ignores them.

Mom pulls her to her side, the baby in her other arm, and kisses her cheek. "I'm so proud of you, sweetie."

Imogene twists up her nose, mocking, when her eyes

meet mine over Mom's shoulder.

Afterward, everyone else wants a turn to congratulate her. Thea snaps a picture of each hug.

When it's my turn, I hold on tight. "I'm sorry Dad couldn't make it," I whisper. "You know he wanted to be here."

"I know." She keeps her voice low. "I asked him not to come. I figured he wouldn't want to see Mom and the baby, and it would be weird."

"He didn't say anything." But it explains the way he moped around the past couple weeks.

She shrugs.

"Imogene, Billie, come here," Mom calls. "We need a family picture with the graduate."

I slip my hands into the pockets of my hoody. My fingers brush something hard.

Oh, the envelope.

"Before I forget…"

Mo turns back. "Yeah?"

Imogene takes the envelope with a quivering hand, her mouth quirked to the side in confusion. But she freezes when she sees her name in his cramped handwriting.

"A card," I say.

"From Jimmy." She tears it open, turning away for some semblance of privacy.

She reads the front two or three times, but when she opens the card, the disk slides out. She barely catches it before it falls. Curious, she studies the writing on the disk— two words I can't read from this angle, scribbled in thick permanent marker—then turns her attention to the hand-written note inside the card.

"Family picture," Mom yells again.

Imogene blinks before closing the disk inside the card and clutching it between her fingers. "Come on."

She joins Mom and Rob by a red maple, and I follow close behind. The four of us—five with the baby—smile for the camera.

"Wait a minute." Imogene sprints forward to grab Xander's arm. "You're part of the family now."

He grins at me and allows her to drag him into the frame.

◆

"How does it feel to be a high school graduate now?" Xander's thumb aimlessly rubs my shoulder over the red t-shirt.

Mom and Rob go to bed by ten now—they've spent a significant time sleep-training the baby to get a precise schedule—but Imogene curled up on the couch with us.

"Exactly the same as yesterday." She sighs against the armrest. "This whole day was stupid."

I force a laugh. "Why do you say that?"

"Nothing in particular." But her eyes drift to the envelope on the ottoman.

She hasn't gone upstairs since we returned to the house an hour ago. She's in the lavender sundress she wore under her robes, though she abandoned the heels and jewelry as soon as we arrived.

"Why can't you visit over the summer?" Xander asks, and I lean into his touch, enjoying his warmth.

Imogene scoffs. "I have plans, remember?"

"We liked having you in St. Clare last summer." His

chest rumbles with the words.

I nudge myself between his legs and curl up against him. My fingers slip under the hem of his shirt to warm up with his hot skin.

"I enjoyed being there," Imogene says in a hushed voice. "Most of the time. Maybe I'll visit for Thanksgiving." She clears her throat and snatches her phone off the ottoman, then flips through her pictures. "You know, you can't break up with him now. He's in our family pictures."

She holds the phone out to me, one of the photos from this afternoon displayed on her screen. Mom, holding the baby, and Rob stand in the back with me and Xander on either side of Imogene, dressed in her dark green robes. He looks uncomfortable but happy at the inclusion.

I relax against his warm chest. "Oh no, you trapped me in this relationship by having our picture taken."

Imogene rolls her eyes. "He's family now."

Xander's laughter quakes my body. "I thought you adopted me last summer."

"Yeah, well, somebody had to make you laugh. You should've seen him, Billie. He moped around the house, day and night, the entire time you were in France."

I lay my hand over his on my stomach and thread our fingers together. "No more moping."

He presses a kiss to my temple. "I don't know what I'd mope about." Then, he turns to Mo. "I'm impressed you could pay that much attention. You were pretty preoccupied with your driving lessons."

Imogene scoffs and turns away. "I'm going to bed." She grabs the card off the ottoman and rises from the couch. "See you in the morning."

"Night, Mo."

When she disappears, I twist around to face him. "You're incorrigible." But I struggle not to laugh. "She thinks I don't know."

His lips capture mine, but the embrace is short-lived. "She's in denial. It's pretty obvious you know." His hand stretches to slip beneath the red t-shirt and squeeze my breast.

"Why won't she tell me?"

His fingers tug at my nipple, and I gasp at the pressure. "Because she doesn't want to admit she got her feelings hurt." His voice is rough and shallow.

I pull him into another kiss, and he holds me tight and releases an anticipatory moan when I nibble his lower lip. I force my tongue inside, and my hand sneaks between us. His erection strains against my hip and responds fervently under pressure.

He leans back. "You know, if she'll be in St. Clare for Thanksgiving, we can force them to live in the same house and share the same bathroom."

I snicker. "And throw in an ex for good measure?"

"Eh, it might work better without the ex."

I press another kiss to his lips. "Yeah, I'd say so."

"They need to talk." His fingers pinch my nipple, and he trails his lips along my jaw. "Get her to come for Thanksgiving, make sure Jim doesn't go see his folks for the holiday, and we can have a fancy dinner at your dad's. Lock them in a closet."

My laughter bubbles out at his blasé tone.

"Hell, convince her to stay the weekend with us. She can have my room. We're usually in your bed anyway."

"Xander." I draw back. "Why're you so set on this? Maybe they don't…"

"You didn't see how happy they were together." His mouth contorts into a frown. "But when you came home, he got scared and pretended it didn't mean anything, and I wasn't the only one moping anymore. She got her heart broken, and I understand."

I push up on my knees and cup his face. "I love you, you know that?"

"I do."

I cover his lips with mine, and he holds me to his chest, squeezing a happy sigh from my mouth. His fingers grope my ass over the jeans.

"Now," he says, nudging my nose with his, "we need to change for bed, and I want to undress you before Rob and the baby get up at two a.m."

I toy with the tuft of chest hair at his collar. "And why would I let you do that?"

His face breaks into a grin. "Because I want you to."

I bite my lip, trying—and failing—to hide the smile. "You make a very convincing argument."

Acknowledgments

Writing books is hard and lonely, and this book wouldn't exist without many supporters. My husband is the kindest person I know, and none of this would be possible without him. Thank you to my family for always encouraging and believing in me. I am forever grateful for my friends Samantha, Marissa, and Shane for beta reading and insisting this book isn't as shitty as I thought it was. Thank you to Michelle for helping mold this into something readable with your outstanding editing skills. Thank you to Sarah for designing one of the most kickass covers I've ever seen. Thank you to Rayona for dedicating so much time in her busy schedule. Thank you to all my proofreaders, beta readers, and ARC readers for your time, effort, and helpful suggestions. And thank you to anyone who supports me with your kindness and goodwill.

D. L. Pitchford

A Note on the Author

D. L. Pitchford is a wife and mother of two,
living in Springfield, Missouri. She graduated
from Drury University with a Bachelor's in
English, Writing, and Fine Arts in 2013.

Learn more at:
www.DLPitchford.com

A Note on Reviews

If you enjoyed this book, please consider leaving a review on Amazon or Goodreads. Reviews are like food for new and aspiring authors. This is not an instance where you shouldn't feed the wildlife. Please feed the starving artists with your reviews.